ACKNOWLEDGEMENTS

During the years, and I mean many long and tedious years, of writing and rewriting my first novel and then the years working toward getting it published, I was often asked by many friends and acquaintances who had sparked my interest in writing and, more importantly, to persevere in completing the project once it was underway. Certain individuals always came to mind each time I was asked, they were the real people, the people who cared about others, the people I was fortunate enough to interact with as I was growing up. They influenced me most.

My high school English teacher, Joan Northey, Downsview,

My university professor, Walter "Spike" Romanow, Windsor,

My law school professor, Edward J. Ratushny, Windsor,

My father and mother, Mel and Dorothy, Home,

My grandfather, "Bompie", My Second Home,

My sweetheart, Cathy, Home.

NOVELS BY
FLETCHER DOUGLAS

RIDE A CROOKED ROAD – Spring 2004

OTHER EDGE OF JUSTICE – Fall 2004

Five high schools in the city are devastated by disability and death by a bad ship-ment of Ecstasy that hits the streets one weekend. Shortly after the funerals of the victims, the local street dealers that preyed upon the students of those schools are murdered, one after the other, and then their suppliers, further up the food chain, start to lose their lives all in the same way. It's not long before the media and the police are calling the unsolved killings, the Oyster Shucking Murders.

In memory of a friend,

LYNN KELLY O'DELL

"Love can appear as quietly as a carriage ride in Central Park or as loudly as getting hit by a train, either way, once it happens, your life is changed forever!"

. . . Douglas M. Flett, 1978

RIDE A

CROOKED ROAD

CHAPTER ONE

Four men in camouflage army fatigues, laden with heavy backpacks and weapons, had walked silently for the past three hours along dirt paths in the sweltering heat of the tropical rainforest, deeper and deeper into the Chapare. Carlos Ramos and his bodyguards had started their mission in Medellin and had driven their gray Land Rover north, on the only paved road into that region of Colombia, until they had run out of pavement. They had then continued into the dense jungle on gravel roads that had eventually become narrow trails. When the trails had ended, they had parked and hidden their four-wheel drive vehicle in the thick underbrush.

Ramos marveled at the beauty of the emerald-green rainforest that enveloped all of the mountains and valleys in that part of the country. The blanket of thick foliage was much more than just beautiful; it did an extraordinary job of concealing the Medellin Cartel's illicit drug activities that were taking place in numerous locations throughout the jungles of the northern region. Ramos laughed to himself as he thought about the area through which he was walking because it produced about one-third of the annual cocaine supply that was snorted up noses throughout the world. Despite the joint efforts of the Colombian and American governments to stop production of the *white gold*, most of the cocaine produced in the Chapare and Magdalena Valleys of Colombia ended up on the streets of North America.

Ramos, a second-level lieutenant, was a thirty-five year old, native Colombian who had grown up an orphan and street urchin in the slums of Antioquia, in the northern part of the large, sprawling city of Medellin. Over the years, he had amassed more money than he would ever need in his lifetime and he had become deeply entrenched in the good life of restaurants, bars and young women. The only exercise that he got during the cartel's boom years was of the horizontal kind. His five foot, nine inch frame didn't carry his one hundred and ninety pounds very well. By the time two AK-47-carrying men waved his group through the well-guarded perimeter of their destination, he was gasping for air and holding his paunch with one hand.

Ramos had never before had occasion to visit the cartel's oldest and most successful cocaine processing facility, the Alejandro Factory, which was hidden deep in the mountainous jungles of the northern Chapare. He had met Cesar Alejandro only once, two years earlier in Bogota, when he had personally delivered money that was owed to him and additional funds to keep the factory operating at full capacity so that the cartels production quotas would be met. They had partied together for a week or so and had become good friends.

Ramos' trip into the wild interior was not one of his usual tasks. He was involved in much more deadly matters, such as disposing of the many *sapos* or informants who took money from the government and passed on information that could harm the cartel. He also arranged the numerous assassinations or disappearances of judges, politicians, newspapermen, policemen and members of competing gangs, as each one was ordered by *Patron*, the boss of all bosses, Pablo Rivas, and he made sure that they were carried out with precision. He also ran an Assassination School from a large, underground cavern in the mountains just east of Medellin, where he trained young and eager recruits how to make bombs and kill people.

Ramos had made the trip into the northern mountains only because his boss had made a special request of him to do so. Pablo Rivas had wanted Ramos to personally deliver production money and a large bonus that was long overdue to their old friend and compatriot, Cesar Alejandro, and thank him personally for always meeting the onerous production schedules and quotas required by the cartel.

***

By the time Ramos arrived at his destination, he was totally out of breath and exhausted. He was feeling so rough that he took a moment to thank God that his journey was over.

"Ah, Carlos! *Que mas, cabellero*?" Alejandro called out as Rivas and his men entered the factory area and the two men embraced each other warmly.

"Cesar! *Buenos dias*! It has been too long a time to see you, *amigo*!" Ramos thought that his friend had aged during the past couple of years because there were many more noticeable creases in his weather-beaten face and his hair had changed color. What was once a dark beard was almost totally gray. Alejandro was four inches taller than Ramos, thinner and in much better physical condition. Even though he was fifty-six, he was a striking figure dressed in military fatigues and combat boots with a silver Colt 45 on his belt. His appearance alone made it very clear to everyone in the camp that he was in charge.

"It's a good time to visit, *amigo*, because my factory is ramping up to full capacity. It's going to be a good year. The quality of the coca leaves is the best I have seen for two or three years. The first of six coca harvests has just begun and loads of *oro verde* have been arriving here for the past ten days. The jungle trails are filled with mules carrying thousands of bales of *green gold* to factories like this one all through this part of Colombia."

"Some of those plants are over two meters in length! Where the hell does it all come from?" Ramos asked showing interest in his friend's passion.

"Back when I started with the cartel, we brought the coca leaves in from Peru or Bolivia and had to transport the thousands of bales we needed back to Colombia and then up here to the factories. Now our farmers actually grow more than they do in those other countries. The government recently reported that there are over four hundred thousand hectares of coca planted in our mountains."

"There are huge stacks of plants all around the factory and more and more have arrived since I got here. How much do you go through?"

"As much as the farmers can bring us, it's a continual process. The coca leaves are best when they're grown on the eastern slopes of the valley at two to six thousand feet above sea level. The problem is that one hectare only produces two hundred kilos of leaves and from that amount, we get less than two kilos of cocaine, so we go through thousands of bales."

"I had no idea your operation here was so big and well organized," Ramos commented.

"There are six laboratories that can process coca leaves twenty-four hours a day. There are dormitories and cooking facilities back in the jungle to house and feed a hundred and twenty workers at one time. I have eighty-two natives working now and I'll be at full capacity in a couple of weeks. There are also two airstrips, with a Cessna at each one, half a mile from here, so I can immediately ship the finished product to wherever Pablo wants it to go."

"Where the hell do all the drums of chemicals come from? It looks like there are hundreds of them stored around here."

"Hundreds? I probably have close to four thousand steel drums stored and hidden in the jungle around the compound. Believe it or not, all the chemicals that end up here at the factory come from Shell and Exxon right out of the United States and Europe. The Americanos would be shocked if they knew how easy they are to obtain."

"I brought you lots of cash to pay the farmers. Pablo sends his best wishes to you and a large bonus, in American dollars, for doing a good job here," Ramos said as the two men walked into an area where many of Alejandro's men were working at various tasks.

As he walked, Ramos counted nearly forty dark-complexioned natives working under the cover of the thick foliage on the outer edges of a small clearing that was the center of the cocaine processing factory. The complex looked makeshift, but it was well laid out. The laboratories, equipment and chemicals were invisible from the sky above as they were hidden under the cover of camouflaged netting-systems that blended right into the dense, green jungle surroundings.

Cesar Alejandro, who had been processing cocaine for more than half of his life, had become a folk hero to the drug lords and cocaine traffickers of Colombia because his factory was the most successful ever put into production. It had produced more cocaine and had operated longer than any other location that had been set up by the cartel in the northern mountainous regions. It had been an amazing accomplishment to have survived for so long during the recent violent times when the Colombian Military and the American DEA, or Drug Enforcement Agency, were paying snitches for information and jointly combing the mountains on search and destroy missions almost daily. During his association with the Medellin Cartel, Alejandro had earned enough money to retire anywhere in the world and live in the lap of luxury, but greed and easy money, lots of easy money, kept him in the jungle.

"I have been promised this money for a long time," Alejandro answered as he took hold of the knapsack that Ramos offered him.

"How much does Pablo send me?"

"There's six hundred grand, *amigo*! Three hundred for you to pay the farmers and Pablo said that he had promised you, personally, a quarter of a million American, is that right?"

Alejandro nodded agreement. "That amount was promised to me so long ago it's almost time for another payment. Every time I am owed money, it takes forever to get paid to me."

"The good news is that there's an extra fifty thousand American for you because it has taken so long to get here. You know as well as I do about the problems we're having, not only getting the cocaine out of the country, but also getting it safely to the North American and European markets. We're in a full-blown state of war with the police, the military and the Americans. We lose shipment after shipment. Even if shipments get through, we have a helluva time getting the money back here to Colombia. I don't think this is a good time for me to pass on your request for more money to Pablo. He's not a happy *hombre* these days."

"*Si!* The extra fifty thousand is better than nothing. Tell Pablo, from the look of the leaves, this will be a bumper harvest. I should be able to produce about twenty-five per cent more of the white powder than with the last crop," Alejandro explained.

"That will make him happy because he is working on a new plan to send very large quantities into the northern part of the United States and Canada in the coming months. I think he's just about ready to start the shipments."

Ramos looked at the rundown, wooden sheds and wondered how the factory could produce so much cocaine. Half of the natives working around the clearing were knee-deep in a thick, white glue, mashing green coca leaves into coca paste with their feet. The men in the tanks were a ghostly shade of gray as the fumes and vapors from the toxic chemicals reacted with their skin. Their feet and calves were blistered and peeling from the extreme acidity of the mixture and they were in constant pain. The dangerous blend also gave off a nauseating odor that the workers had become accustomed to, but Ramos had to stay well back because it irritated and burned his nostrils. The fact that the peasant workers were extremely well paid, by Colombian standards, had more than a soothing effect on their discomfort.

Ramos stood back and listened to Alejandro bark orders at the natives who were adding *puna* wood to the fires and feeding the troughs with coca leaves. The green leaves went into a mixture of sulphuric acid, hydrochloric acid, acetone, ether and various other chemicals that transformed them into a white paste. The fires that had to be kept burning continually were fed with *puna* wood which yields very little smoke so that the location of the factory site cannot be detected from afar. The mixture that the workers were standing in was extremely volatile and if it was mishandled, it could cause an explosion that would destroy the lab and kill everyone nearby. Ramos watched from a distance as Alejandro bent over one of the tanks.

"What are you doing now?" Ramos asked as he stepped a little closer to his friend and the dangerous mixture. *Too close!* He thought, as his nostrils began to burn.

"I'm testing the consistency of the coca paste. It looks to be nearly ready. I just drop a small piece of this Clorox bleach into it and see what happens."

"What's supposed to happen?" Ramos, now curious, said as he moved closer to the tank and the fumes tore at his nostrils and lungs even though a hand covered his face.

"See that yellow, oily film forming on the surface. That means this batch is of a very high quality. It's ready to be moved into the sun to be dried into that fine white powder you like so much. Then it can be bagged for its long journey."

As the men walked out into the clearing in the middle of the factory, they talked about the good times they had together in Bogota at the time of their last meeting. Ramos looked at the clear sky and the rainforest and thought that it was one of the most beautiful days in the jungle that he could remember. Rays of bright sunlight beamed through the openings in the thick, green, natural ceiling that concealed the factory, while bird and animal sounds resonated through the trees and out into the clearing.

The peacefulness and serenity of the dense jungle was slowly disrupted by a very strange, almost inaudible, sound. A sound most of the natives had never heard before. The thick foliage, tall trees and steep mountainous cliffs around the factory site seemed to stifle the new sound so the men couldn't tell exactly what it was or from what direction it was coming.

"What the hell's that faint humming sound?" A concerned Alejandro asked Ramos.

Listening intently, the two men walked further out toward the center of the clearing with their eyes and ears glued to the treetops. They were both quite concerned that the noise was coming from the sky, but they couldn't be sure because it was very soft and muffled.

"Jesus Christ!" Ramos yelled in terror. "*Vamoose!* Follow me quickly!"

He and Alejandro bolted toward the jungle cover. The faint noise that they had heard was now very distinctive. Three dark, camouflage-green, military EH-101 Attack Helicopters that were bristling with mounted machine guns and rocket launchers and full of soldiers came out of nowhere from behind a nearby rocky cliff into full view of everyone in the factory. The helicopters were suddenly hovering over the complex and the sound that was so faint only moments ago, now filled the clearing with a deafening roar. As soon as the pilots and soldiers realized that they had found the Alejandro Factory, the gunships fanned out to the sides of the clearing and machine guns and rockets razed the whole area and the jungle all around it.

"Head for the trail! We can disappear into the jungle!" Alejandro screamed over the noise of the copters and the firefight as the two men ran for their lives.

As they tore for the safety of the jungle, Alejandro and Ramos weaved through the bullets and explosions that seemed to be all around them. The natives scattered in all directions as they too headed for the dense undergrowth. Two workers to the left of Alejandro and Ramos were hit by machine gun fire almost immediately. They were thrown forward by the impact of the bullets and rolled into a bloody heap. Then without warning, a rocket exploded at the edge of the clearing just to the right of the two men who were tucked low to the ground. Three more workers were blown into the air and body parts flew in all directions. The machine guns and rockets continued to ravage the jungle undergrowth all around the clearing.

Alejandro and Ramos raced under the cover of the trees and camouflage netting, past the coca paste tanks and turned toward the narrow path that went into the jungle. At that moment, a rocket from one of the helicopters landed a direct hit into the middle of the barrels and tanks of chemicals fifteen feet away from the two men. The thundering blast from the devastating explosion of the extremely volatile chemicals was the last sound that the two friends ever heard.

Alejandro and Ramos would never know the fate of the most productive cocaine factory that had ever been established in Colombia. Hours later, when the three military helicopters gently raised themselves out of the clearing and floated down the Chapare Valley toward Medellin, the painted sunset was just stretching itself across the western sky. The soldiers had left behind eighteen dead bodies piled on the burning remains of the Alejandro Factory. The dead bodies of the many workers, Alejandro, Ramos and the what was left of the factory, after the explosion of the large caches of chemicals, would be a smoldering pile of ashes by morning.

As soon as the soldiers arrived back at their barracks, on the edge of the sprawling city, the whole platoon was commended for a job well done by both their superiors and the American advisors. It wouldn't be long before they would be back at work, in their helicopters, on other search and destroy missions against the Medellin Cartel and Pablo Rivas.

CHAPTER TWO

I t was Friday evening, just after seven-thirty, as Joe McConnell passed through the revolving, glass door at the main entrance of the Crowne Plaza. The unique hotel was attached to Toronto's largest downtown convention facility adjacent to the CN Tower, the world's tallest free-standing structure, and the SkyDome, the home of the twice World Champion Blue Jays. As he entered the spacious hotel foyer that was filled with people coming and going, he heard his name called over the dull roar of the crowd. Joe turned toward the voice and recognized two well-dressed men standing at the bar in the Trellis Lounge.

The sprawling, dimly lit room located in the northeast corner of the complex was an open-concept solarium with plush furnishings set-up in private, conversation areas that encroached out onto the edge of the lobby. It was full of real trees, plants and other shrubbery with comfortable couches, chairs and tables scattered throughout the greenery. The voice that Joe heard belonged to either Stan Stillman or Hugh Lillico who were having cocktails before going up to the reception in the ballroom on the second level. They were two of Joe's better clients who owned a chain of forty art and picture frame outlets that stretched across Ontario. Joe had invited them, as well as many other friends and clients, to a reception in honor of Benton W. Sanderson, one of his law firm's founding and senior partners, who had recently been appointed to the Supreme Court of Ontario.

"Same as usual?" Stan, a rotund, gray-haired man of about forty, asked.

"Yeah, thanks," Joe answered as he shook hands with both men.

"What celebrities will be attending the party tonight?" Hugh asked.

"I think anyone in Toronto of any importance in the legal profession and court system will be here as well as the Lieutenant Governor and a few other federal, provincial and local politicians. Benton is well respected in the legal community."

Joe's Johnny Red, on lots of ice with a little water, arrived and he took a long drink.

"What's going on after the party?" Stan asked.

"If I don't get tied up with Benton and the other partners, I can meet you guys for a drink. How 'bout Little Anthony's at Richmond and York? Stan's been there before." Joe drained his glass and slapped Hugh on the shoulder. "Thanks for the drink, I'll see you guys upstairs."

Joe wound his way through the many guests that were milling around in the spacious and elegant hotel lobby that was lavishly decorated with earth-tone marble floors and walls, unique antiques, statues and paintings. He stepped into an elevator and went to the second floor convention level where the main ballroom was located. The reception had started an hour earlier, but Joe was late because of a mid-afternoon legal crisis with one of his clients.

Joe checked his coat in the hall and as he entered the ballroom, he stopped for a moment to get his bearings. The red, gold and black room was half the size of a football field and had countless ornate chandeliers illuminated above the crowd of people who had gathered in small, casual discussion groups throughout. There were no windows in the large room except for a few skylights scattered across the far side of the ceiling. Wet-bars and tables of food had been set-up at various locations for easy access by the guests. In the center of the room, a bubbling fountain surrounded by all kinds of hors d'oeuvres rounded out the décor.

Joe was pleased that the province's most important judges, lawyers and politicians were in attendance. The Lieutenant Governor was there, as well as many of the firm's clients, to bid

Benton W. Sanderson a last farewell to the profession. Many of the men in the room had brought their wives or girlfriends to the reception. Those who were courageous had brought both.

As Joe made his way through the large, noisy crowd toward the newly appointed Justice and his wife, Anna, to formally congratulate them, his eyes were drawn to and became fixated on a beautiful woman. She was a dark-complexioned, brunette who was with a group not far from Benton's gathering. At that exact moment, her head turned slightly and their eyes locked and they smiled at each other ever so slightly. During that initial moment of eye contact, both felt a strange stirring that neither one could quite understand. Her smile became more of a grin, as Joe, whose gaze had never left her, bumped into some unsuspecting guest. He couldn't take his eyes off her. She was stunning. She appeared to be about five foot six, maybe a hundred and fifteen pounds, around thirty years of age, and was tastefully dressed in a dark green, leather jacket and pants with a light green blouse showing through. Joe didn't recognize her and was wondering who she was when Benton interrupted his fixation.

"Joe, this is Mr. Justice Scott. Wally and I have been great friends for years and now we'll have an opportunity to work together. This is his wife, Mary, and of course, you know Anna and Mrs. McCabe. This is one of the rising stars at Sanderson, Sturgess, Joe McConnell."

Benton, always the quintessential lawyer, had been Joe's mentor over the years and they had truly enjoyed working together and being in each other's company. Viola McCabe, a very attractive and well-dressed woman in her mid-fifties, had been Benton's main secretary and legal assistant since he had started practicing law nearly thirty years before.

"It's wonderful to see that so many of your friends showed up to give you this farewell," Joe said with a smile and acknowledged the introductions.

As he continued to visit, Joe glanced toward the brunette once more and found her looking directly at him. He thought to himself, *Who is she? Should I know her?*

"Joe, before I forget, would you meet me in my office at eight o'clock Monday morning. I'm dropping by to pick up my personal things and there is a matter I want to discuss with you before I leave." Benton transferred his glance from Joe to the others. "It seems so strange that after all these years, Monday morning will be the last time that I'll ever go into that office."

"Don't worry, it won't be long before you're so busy on the bench that you'll never think of your old office again," replied Mr. Justice Scott.

"Congratulations once again, Your Lordship, and the same to you Mrs. Sanderson," Joe said, shaking hands with the two Justices and nodding to the ladies. "I'll see you bright and early Monday morning," he confirmed and excused himself from the group.

It was time for Joe to make the rounds and acknowledge the presence of some of his clients who he had personally invited to the soiree. First, he needed another drink, so he began to make his way through the guests toward one of the six portable bars that had been placed around the perimeter of the room. As he left, he looked directly at the brunette and their eyes met once more. Joe returned her smile but had to turn away to acknowledge a client that had grabbed him by the arm.

The image of the brunette was imprinted in Joe's memory. Questions were flashing through his mind, *Is she a lawyer? Is she a client of the firm?* As soon as the bartender handed him a scotch and water, with lots of ice, he slowly looked toward her. Again, she was looking in his direction and their eyes made contact. She was in a group of four but appeared to be standing with a good-looking guy about her own age. Joe was past the point of caring if she had a date or not as she seemed to exude some kind of magnetic force that pulled him to her.

As he moved in her direction, he stopped to talk to various people and shook hands with a number of the firm's clients. Periodically, as he worked the room, he would glance at her and their eyes would meet time and time again.

The booze flowed freely and the large crowd became progressively noisier. Joe mingled with judges, clients and friends and had another drink and some hors d'oeuvres as he schmoozed his way toward the brunette. At long last, he found himself talking to two clients who were standing right next to her group.

It was the first time that he had looked at her up close. Her skin was clear and smooth with very little makeup and her complexion made her look as if she had a permanent tan. She had gentle, dark brown eyes and full, perfectly formed lips. She had beautiful white teeth that flashed when she smiled and spoke. She looked directly at Joe once again. He took advantage of the opportunity and excused himself from his clients and stepped toward her.

"Hi, my name's Joe McConnell. You look familiar. Have we met before?"

"No, I don't think so," she answered with a slight accent and a smile that showed that she knew a line when she heard one. "My friends call me Trizzi. I'm here with Don," she nodded to her left, "who was invited by his lawyer." Her companion extended his hand to acknowledge that Joe had joined their group.

"Joe McConnell. I'm a lawyer with Sanderson, Sturgess."

"Don . . . , John O'Donnell does all my legal work."
Joe didn't quite catch Don's last name because of the way it rolled off his lips or because of the dull roar of the loud, booze-fueled conversations around them.

O'Donnell was in the Corporate-Securities section which suggested that Don was some kind of a businessman. He was the same build as Joe, around six feet tall and about a hundred and ninety pounds. He had a friendly smile and a personable way about him.

"This is David Atman and Mark Fallaise," Don said as the men acknowledged him.

"Nice to meet you," Joe answered and he shook their hands and then turned to Trizzi.

"Trizzi, are you and Don both from Toronto?"

"No, Don is from Mississauga and I'm from Montreal. I've been in Toronto on business for a few days and he was nice enough to invite me to this gathering."

As soon as Joe heard that she was from Montreal, he recognized her accent to be at least partly French Canadian, but there was still something very different and strange about it.

"Are you staying in Mississauga or here in the city?" Joe asked with a smile.

"I'm staying at the Hilton." She smiled and continued, "Don and his wife asked me to stay with them but I wanted to be downtown rather than deal with the traffic."

"You already know what I do. What do you do in Montreal?"

"I'm with a real estate investment company that deals in industrial properties. My company owns thirty buildings in the Greater Toronto Area, so I have to visit here regularly."

"Keeping them rented must keep you busy. Would you like another glass of wine?"

"Sure, I'm ready for another one."

Joe loved her accent. The other men in her group were engaged in a serious discussion about the pros and cons of moving money to offshore banking jurisdictions and were virtually ignoring Joe and Trizzi. That suited Joe just fine.

"Do you want to stay here until I get back or would you like to join me?"

"I'll go with you. These guys are just talking business so they won't miss me," she said with one of those beautiful smiles. "Don, I'll be back in awhile."

Joe allowed Trizzi to walk ahead of him and the crowd seemed to open up for her as she moved slowly and gracefully toward the bar just to the right of the ballroom's main door.

"What kind of wine were you drinking?"

"A dry, French red." She then continued, "I'm just going to slip out to the ladies room in the main hall while you're getting the drinks. I'll be right back."

As Trizzi walked toward the exit door, Joe noticed a number of men's heads turn in her direction and their glances followed her until she was out of sight. He was smitten.

While Joe waited at the bar, he reflected on his past relationships with women. He had married Susan, a flight attendant with Air Canada, when he was in his second year of law school. They had been married for nine years and had three boys, Jeff, Chad and Brett, who were all living with his ex-wife and her new husband, also a lawyer, in a comfortable home in the west end of the city. Joe had been separated and finally divorced for over three years and although he had dated lots of women, including Benton's only daughter, Donna, none of the relationships had become serious. This dark-complexioned beauty seemed to be stirring up some strange feelings in his mind and body, feelings that he had never experienced before.

Trizzi was wearing a large diamond between two smaller sapphires on the ring finger of her left hand, but it didn't really look like an engagement or wedding ring. He wondered, *Is she engaged? Is she married?* Joe was afraid to even think about it. He picked up the drinks and turned just in time to see her enter the room. He got a really weird feeling when he saw her coming. *Christ!* he thought, *I know that I fall in love easily, but this is ridiculous!*

"Cheers! Here's to new friends and the start of a wonderful evening!" Joe proposed.

"To new friends!" She clinked his glass and their eyes locked as they took long sips.

"How long are you staying in Toronto?" Joe asked as he unconsciously stirred the ice in his glass of scotch with his index finger; a bad habit that he was trying to break.

"I would have gone back to Montreal this evening but Don invited me to this party."

Joe took a deep breath and asked, "Is there someone waiting for you in Montreal?"

"There is a guy expecting me to come home," she answered with that smile and purposely let her reply linger as his heart skipped a beat. "I share the main level apartment of an old mansion in Mount Royal with a really great guy." She laughed, "My brother, I'm not married!"

"Boyfriend?"

Trizzi didn't want to go there. She periodically dated a guy she worked with but it was a relationship that had originally started out of loneliness and had continued more for business reasons rather than love. It had served her well and had made her an extraordinary amount of money over the years.

"Not really. I date a couple of guys, but there's no one special. What about you?"

"Divorced for almost three years after nearly nine years of matrimonial bliss. I'm not seeing anyone special either. I've got three boys who live with my ex and her new husband."

"How old are your children?"

"Eight, seven and five. I get the kids every second weekend, but I get along well with my ex and her new husband so I can pretty well see them anytime it's convenient for everyone."

"Practicing law and helping to raise three kids must keep you busy."

"It does, but you gotta do what you gotta do. Before we go back and join your friends, do you and Don have any plans for later this evening?"

"No, he'll likely just go home to Mississauga and I was going to get a good night's sleep and head out to the airport early in the morning."

"I've really enjoyed meeting you and I think that we should spend some more time together. Why don't we slip out of here in awhile and have a late dinner? I'll take you to one of my favorite restaurants and I promise I won't keep you out too late."

"I'm not very hungry but I'd really like to spend some more time with you too."

"We can just share some appetizers or something and have a couple of drinks."

"Sounds great! I'll let Don know what I'm doing so he can make his own plans."

"Do you want another glass of wine before we join them?"

"Sure!"

Joe got the drinks, and once again, Trizzi led him through the crowd back to where her friends were embroiled in a discussion about international banking and methods to combat the low value of the Canadian dollar.

"I invited a few good clients of mine here tonight and, because I met you, I haven't even acknowledged them. I had better make the rounds but I'll be back in fifteen or twenty minutes and then we'll get out of here."

"That's fine, just don't forget to come back."

"There's absolutely no chance of that happening!" He smiled.

As Joe talked to a number of his clients, he periodically looked toward Trizzi who seemed to be enjoying herself. Their eyes would lock periodically through the faces in the crowd and they would acknowledge each other with smiles. By the time Joe joined Trizzi and Don near the main door, the other two men had left.

"Don. Trizzi and I are going out for a bite to eat. Would you like to join us?"

"I appreciate the invitation, but I don't need anymore to drink. I'd hate to get arrested."

"You shouldn't be driving now," Trizzi responded. "If we're ready to leave, let's go."

They all left the ballroom together, picked up their coats and went down the hall toward the elevators. As one opened, all three stepped inside. Trizzi pushed the button for the main floor and Don pushed the button for the underground garage.

"That was a nice evening," Don said, as he kissed Trizzi on both the cheeks as the elevator stopped and then Joe and Trizzi stepped out into the hotel lobby as the door opened.

"Thanks for inviting me to the reception. I'll talk to you soon."

"It was nice meeting you, Don. The next time you come by the office to see O'Donnell, you guys give me a call and we'll get together for lunch or cocktails."

As the door to the elevator closed, Trizzi took Joe by the arm as they walked through the busy lobby toward the Trellis Lounge and the main door of the hotel.

"I'm really sorry Don didn't join us. I'm kind of nervous being all alone with you."

"I'll bet!" She answered with a laugh and held his arm tighter. They were both still laughing as they went through the revolving door and out onto Front Street West. As they hit the street, Joe's curiosity got the better of him.

"By the way, what does Don do for a living out in Mississauga?"

"He's a charter pilot and I think he also buys and sells used airplanes," Trizzi explained. "Where are you taking me now?"

"A client of mine just opened a new restaurant right near your hotel. You'll enjoy meeting Bobby Antoniou, but he'll probably try to steal you away from me."

"There's definitely no chance of that happening." She squeezed his arm tighter.

Trizzi was having a nice time and was also glad that Don had gone home. The walk to Little Anthony's took about ten minutes and they found the cool night air very refreshing after spending the evening in the stuffy reception. While they walked, they talked about the restaurants they liked in Montreal and Toronto and strangely enough, had a number in common that they both really enjoyed.

They entered the main door of Little Anthony's and went through the French doors toward the long bar where four men who looked like stockbrokers or mining promoters were gathered. Bobby was dressed as a maitre d' in a dark suit with a tuxedo style shirt and bow tie. He turned toward Joe and Trizzi with his hands held out in his usual friendly greeting. He was quite a nice-looking, forty-five year old, physically fit Greek, slightly shorter than Joe, with a full head of black hair and one of those sexy accents that all of his female customers enjoyed.

"Welcome! I'm sorry that I missed the reception but it's Paul Ankcorn and Philip Yeandle's birthdays today," he said with his usual accent. "They're down at the back Peter Merry, Ross Beatty, Bob Van de Mark, Glenn Wilkie and a whole bunch of other guys."

"I know Paul and Philip and all the boys. Bobby, this is Trizzi, my new best friend. Don't say anything to embarrass her, or me, until you get to know her better!"

"Don't be crazy! I'll be really nice!" He kissed her on both cheeks and on one cheek twice, as was his custom. Bobby always bragged that the extra kiss was a special Greek way of saying hello to pretty ladies. His accent and mannerisms charmed Trizzi.

"Trizzi, this is Mike Pickens, Jim Fairbairn and Dan Farrell," Joe said as he introduced his date to the other men that were standing at the bar.

"It's nice to meet everyone," Trizzi said with that beautiful smile. "Bobby, how late can we get something to eat?"

"For you two lovebirds, time doesn't matter! Take a romantic table by the windows. Margit, please get them a bottle of wine on me. By the way, some guys named Stillman and Lillico were in and they told me to tell you that they were going to Red's to meet someone."

"Hi, Joe! What's your pleasure?" Margit, an attractive, thirty-plus, blonde gal asked.

"Margit, this is Trizzi." The girls shook hands. "If Bobby's buying, how about a Chateauneuf-du-Pape?" Margit nodded. "We're going to take that table over by the window."

"I'll bring it right over with a couple of menus and I'll even turn the lights down a little."

As Joe and Trizzi walked toward the table that was well away from the noise of the birthday party at the far end of the room, Joe acknowledged the celebration.

"Happy Birthday, Paul and Philip. It looks like you guys started early."

"Thanks Joe," Paul answered and waved, "you only turn forty once."

"This is a great place," Trizzi commented as she and Joe settled in at their secluded table.

The newly opened restaurant sat about a hundred and fifty people in the lower bar and raised dining area. The long bar of dark walnut and the raised eating area were separated by a wall of internal windows. It was quite pleasant and even a bit romantic when the lights were low.

"What do you feel like?" Trizzi asked.

"Do you like fresh seafood? The grilled calamari here is absolutely fantastic," Joe suggested, "and it comes laid out on a small salad of some kind."

"I love all kinds of seafood!"

"Why don't we both have an appetizer? The portions are quite generous."

"Sounds great to me, that's all I really need to eat this late."

Everyone was having a great time. The Ankcorn and Yeandle party was going full blast at the far end of the dining room and the group was still chatting at the long bar. Joe and Trizzi were sipping their wine and were lost in conversation in the darkness near the windows. They felt very comfortable with each other. The conversation flowed smoothly, but Joe noticed some reluctance on Trizzi's part to talk very openly about her personal life, her family and her work in Montreal. She spoke very generally and would not reveal many specific details. Whenever Joe started asking questions about her, she would turn them around to him.

"So what exactly do you do when you're not lawyering?"

"What do I do for fun? I jog the odd morning and work out two or three times a week. I take Karate lessons a couple of times a month just for the exercise. In the winter, I try to get away on a couple of ski-ing vacations and I play in a non-contact hockey league once a week."

"I spend a lot of time skiing in the Laurentians. What do you do in the summertime?"

"I golf and sail. I've got a forty-seven Jeanneau sloop that I keep down at the waterfront."

"I love sailing too, but I don't do it very often. I've always wanted to learn to play golf, but never got around to it. You sound like you work hard and play hard."

"I keep busy. I'm also a member of a gun club and shoot every couple of months. I used to go into competitions, but I haven't done that for a few years."

"I learned how to handle guns too. This is really weird. We seem to have a lot of the same interests," she laughed. "Do you think it means something?"

"I hope so!" Joe answered with a smile as he gently squeezed her hand.

They talked and laughed through the food and a second bottle of wine and didn't even notice the time until Paul and Philip and their birthday gang passed by on their way to the door. It was nearly twelve thirty and neither Joe nor Trizzi had any idea where the time had gone. They were both wide-awake and thoroughly enjoying each other's company.

The Hilton was only a hundred yards west from Anthony's. Joe and Trizzi walked slowly along Richmond, laughing and holding hands, through the reception parking area and into the lobby. The couple soon found themselves all alone in an elevator.

"I'm sorry, I can't wait any longer," Joe said with a serious look on his face.

He moved close to her and took her beautiful face in both hands and kissed her gently. Their lips met perfectly, as if they had known one another forever. The moment turned into a minute and they didn't stop kissing until the door began to open on Trizzi's floor. The long, slow kiss had left them both light-headed as they wandered down the hall. Trizzi was the first to speak as they stopped at the door of her room and she fumbled for her key-card.

"Do you want to come in for a nightcap? I know there's some of my favorite Grand Marnier in the little bar in my room."

"Sure, that sounds great. I love that stuff too."

Trizzi turned and laughed and grabbed Joe by the lapels of his coat and kissed him again, "This is an invitation in for a drink, not for the night, so you behave yourself!"

"I'll be good, I promise," he smiled.

It was a standard room decorated in various shades of green. The drapes, wallpaper, pictures and bedspreads were all perfectly coordinated. They threw their coats onto one of the double beds and Joe took off his suit jacket. Trizzi turned on the radio that was already set to CHUM-FM and Joe recognized the voice of Roger Ashby, who was just announcing *A romantic song for folks who like to snuggle*. She opened the mini-bar and pulled out two small bottles of Grand Marnier.

"Will you grab me the two glasses over on the table?" She asked. Joe poured the sweet liqueur from the small bottles into the glasses and after they clicked them together, they took a sip. As they stood close together, each still holding their glass, they looked deeply into each other's eyes and kissed again. Joe and Trizzi had very strange feelings toward each other even though they had just met. After the long kiss, they moved toward the bed next to the one with the coats. They both leaned back on one elbow and sipped their drinks and just looked at each other.

Trizzi spoke first. "I knew that I would be in trouble if I kissed you."

"You're not in any trouble. I promise that I won't do anything you don't want me to do."

"That's what I mean! I'm in serious trouble!" She giggled.

They continued to talk, laugh, sip their drinks and kiss. Joe still sensed that Trizzi was reluctant to be very open about her personal life, but he thought she must have her reasons. When the glasses were empty, they moved together on the bed and kissed again and again, more tenderly and more deeply. They wanted each other at that moment more than anything else in the world and they both knew it. Their bodies ached for more, but they both stopped at the same time, before they went too far. Neither one wanted to do anything to spoil their first evening together. They were starting to care for each other and there was absolutely nothing they could do about it.

"Do you really have to go back to Montreal tomorrow?"

"I should've gone back earlier today. I do have some commitments this weekend."

"Cancel them! Stay over 'til Sunday and I'll take you sightseeing tomorrow. We can spend the day together and go out for a nice dinner tomorrow night."

I'd really like to, but I don't think I can."

"The way that I'm beginning to feel about you means you really do have to stay. I can't let you just slip away from me so soon. We're just getting to know each other."

"I know, I feel the same way, but I really can't stay. Let me think about it and maybe I'll make some phone calls in the morning."

Trizzi had absolutely no reason to go back to Montreal, but she knew, deep down, that she shouldn't stay over. She was afraid of the strange feelings she was experiencing. She was terrified of falling in love. She just couldn't let that happen. There was no way that she could allow Joe to become involved in her complicated and dangerous life. She kept telling herself that over and over again, but her heart wasn't listening.

"You can give up your hotel room in the morning and stay at my condo down on the waterfront. You can even have your own bedroom and I promise that I'll behave myself."

"It's not you I'm worried about!" She laughed.

Joe kissed her again, a long warm kiss. "Please, think about staying. I don't want you to go home. We may never have this moment again if we miss it now."

"I promise I'll think about staying and I'll let you know in the morning. I also promise that I'll call you, one way or the other, and if it turns out that I do have to leave, maybe you can drive me out to the airport if you have time."

It was just after two o'clock when Joe wrote his home number on the back of one of his business cards and left it on the dresser. Trizzi was standing beside him holding his jacket when he finished and she helped him on with it.

"I really want you to think seriously about staying. I have a strange feeling about us, it's a feeling that I've never had before and I like it."

"I promise that I'll call you first thing in the morning."

As Joe put on his overcoat, Trizzi moved close to him and put her arms around him in under his coat and jacket. She leaned against him and kissed him again. She held him tightly and he held her. He kissed her one last time and went out the door. Joe got a hollow, empty feeling as walked down the hall to the elevators. He had never before had such strong feelings for a woman that he had just met. He couldn't just let her disappear. He wouldn't.

***

As soon as Joe got into the Beck Cab, in front of the Hilton, his mind started to play tricks on him. *I don't even know her last name! Why didn't she mention it? Maybe she didn't give it to me on purpose?* All he could do at that moment was wait until morning to see if she called. If any kind of a relationship was going to develop between them, it was entirely in Trizzi's hands. As the taxi neared his condo at Harbour Square, a knot formed in the pit of his stomach as he wondered if he would ever see her again.

CHAPTER THREE

Just after one o'clock in the morning, a blood-curdling scream sliced through the night silence and echoed down the rows of old and dilapidated houses in the dark and deserted streets of El Pablado, one of the poorer sections of Medellin. The rundown neighborhood sprawled over the rolling hills on the outer edge of a city that had ballooned to almost two million people in recent years as peasants moved from the rural areas to look for work.

A white Lincoln Town Car and a black Chevy Suburban, both of recent vintage, were parked ominously, in a dark, narrow street in front of a bungalow that, even at night, appeared to be well-kept and newly painted. The upscale state of the house clearly indicated that the owner had more money than most of his neighbors. Four men were stationed near the cars watching the street and nearby houses. Two of the men were holding *changones*, but the sawed-off hunting rifles could hardly be seen in the darkness. The others carried homemade machine- pistols. The *sicarios* were there to make sure that the neighbors stayed in their homes and didn't interfere in the cartel business that was taking place that night in the dimly lit house. The residents who lived nearby heard the agonizing screams, but knew that they would end up dead if they got involved in any way. They all remained in the darkness of their homes.

"Stuff 'em in his fuckin' mouth," Pablo Rivas yelled in his Colombian street-dialect to Hernan, the scar-faced killer, who was quite excited about being able to use his favorite knife.

The terrible brute of a man had just cut the genitals off of the nude and beaten *sapo* who was being held flat on his back on the dirty floor by two other *sicarios*. As the *mafioso* did as he was ordered, he smeared even more blood onto the bloated face of the writhing victim. The tortured and bleeding *sapo*, who had worked at the Alejandro Factory for years, had been named as an informant. After some brutal persuasion, he had confessed to Rivas that he had given certain information to General Humberto Torres, the head of Colombia's anti-drug police, that had resulted in the loss of the cartels oldest and highest producing cocaine factory in the Chapare Valley. The *sapo* had also caused the deaths of two of the cartel's best men, Carlos Ramos and Cesar Alejandro, and the loss of millions of dollars worth of cocaine, chemicals and equipment. The name of the sapo that had caused this terrible blow to the cartel had been given directly to Pablo Rivas by a cartel associate, a paid mole who worked directly under General Torres as a member of his office staff.

At the sight of the genital mutilation, the sapo's wife and fifteen year old daughter, who were being held by their hair in two chairs nearby by other henchmen, both let out gut-wrenching screams. The screams echoed and ricocheted through the deserted streets and filthy alleyways of the neighborhood for all to hear. Rivas turned violently and hammered the wife on the side of her head with his Glock 40, semi-automatic pistol, just to shut her up. A large gash opened on the side of her jaw and blood spattered in all directions. In the same motion, he gave the young girl a horrendous backhand across the side of her face. The terrified women were silenced by the force of the blows and stared in horror as they watched their loved one being slowly murdered.

"I want everyone in Medellin to know what happens to *sapos* if they turn against the cartel and Pablo Rivas! This son-of-a-bitch cost me millions of dollars, my best factory and two of my best men! Hernan, you know what to do to this bastard!"

The words were no more than out of Rivas' mouth when the man with the deep scar swung a machete as hard as he could at the left leg of the informant and the blow landed just above his ankle. His foot immediately separated from his leg and lay by itself nearby as more dark-red blood oozed onto the spattered and dirty floor. Without losing momentum, the killer brought the large blade down once more with terrible force on the other shin of the writhing victim with the same results. The victim's face was wrenched in excruciating pain as he made a useless attempt to roll away from his attacker. He tried to scream. Only hoarse moans emerged from his throat. As his head heaved back and forth in agony, his genitals slowly fell out of his mouth and onto the floor beside him. His gurgled attempt to scream was almost inaudible as his life-blood began to flow into dark pools of *sangrenegra* all around him.

Rivas continued in a terrible rage. "Hold the bastards' head up so he can see what happens to traitors and their fuckin' families!"

The dying man's bloody eyes were bugged wide-open as he watched Rivas take the dripping red and silver machete from the man with the scar. Rivas instantly swung it around in a large arc, lopping off the wife's head and nearly hitting the arm of the man that was holding her by the hair. Blood spattered on the walls, on the daughter, everywhere, as the woman's body slumped to her left from the force of the blow and fell to the floor with a thud. The young girl jumped up from her chair as she screamed in horror, but the sound was muffled by yet another fist to her face that nearly rendered her unconscious. The *sicario* holding her from behind was the only thing that prevented her from falling down on the floor beside her mother's still body.

Rivas, still shaking violently, screamed, "I want everyone in Colombia to know what happens to *sapos* if they cooperate with the government and the Americanos against the cartel!"

He looked down at the man with no feet who was lying in the gathering pools of blood, and even though he was almost dead, Rivas knew that he could still comprehend what was happening. He turned quickly and very roughly ripped the dress and underwear off the fifteen-year-old daughter who was still being held by the hair by one of her captors. Rivas looked down at the informant once again.

"Before you die you bastard, I want you to know that we're all going to rape your little girl until she's nearly dead and then I'm gonna kill her myself!"

Still on the verge of losing control, Rivas swung the blood-stained machete as hard as he could, twice more, in rapid succession. Each blow cut off one of the traitor's arms near the elbows. It then became quite obvious to everyone in the room that the man on the floor would die at any moment. Rivas' rage seemed to subside slightly and then, more in control, he handed the dripping machete back to the man with the scar and leaned over the bloody trunk of the *sapo* lying in the pool of thick, almost black, blood.

"I, Pablo Rivas, vow to have my *sicarios* kill all *sapos*, their wives, their children, their parents, their brothers and sisters. All informants will be taught a lesson today!"

A burst of five quick shots from the Glock turned the informant's face into mush and fortunately, put an end to his suffering.

The young girl made an attempt to scream, but she wasn't able to muster enough breath to make any noise at all.

"What about the girl?" The scarred killer asked as Rivas turned and looked at the terror in her bloody face as her thin, naked, shaking body was forced back down onto the chair. She was sobbing and shaking uncontrollably. "Can we take her with us for some fun?"

"No more fun. It's time to *vamoose*. She must be found here with her family as a message to those *sapos* who think they can turn against the cartel and get away with it."

He raised his Glock once again and pumped two rounds into the bruised and beaten face of the young girl. The force of the bullets hitting her head, threw her small body and the chair over backwards, onto the blood-spattered, wooden floor. The girl's body didn't move or even twitch as it lay there, right next to the headless body of her mother. The girl had died instantly.

As the leader of the Medellin Cartel and his group of *sicarios* left the blood-soaked room, the scar-faced killer passed by the detached head of the informant's wife and without even missing a step, kicked at it as if it were a soccer ball. The woman's head lifted off the floor and landed in an old and worn easy chair that sat in one corner of the room.

The gang of *los mafiosos* and the boss of all bosses, *Patron* or *El Doctor*, as he preferred to be called, got into the two cars that were parked out in front of the house and leisurely drove away into the darkness. The men were all very quiet as the vehicles moved slowly through the narrow streets. In the Suburban, it was Pablo Rivas who first spoke.

"You must get your enemy where it hurts most . . . the wife and the fuckin' children!"

News of the murders of the informant and his family spread like wildfire through the Colombian underworld. If anyone linked to the Medellin Cartel had been thinking about providing the DEA, police or military with information about cartel dealings, they had second thoughts. In time, however, the sapos would forget the warning and more information about the cartel and its business would be given to the authorities in exchange for money or leniency in the courts. Then more seizures would take place and more arrests would be made. Those events would trigger more killings of *sapos* and their families. The police even knew who was responsible for the murders but had no direct proof because witnesses never came forward.

Four days after the torture and murder of the family in El Pablado, General Humberto Torres and his young driver stopped in the official, gray Mercedes Benz for a red light at one of the busiest intersections in downtown Medellin. He had been to an extended luncheon with local representatives of the DEA to discuss the increased violence and terrorism in the city that was a direct result of the cocaine trade and what could be done to stop all the killings. A very relaxed General Torres was in the backseat of the car, on the telephone talking to his assistant, when two men on an old, fumes-spewing motorcycle pulled up beside the official car and stopped. The passenger on the bike looked right at General Torres through the dark, tinted window of the rear door, smiled a broad smile, and immediately pulled an Uzi machine pistol out of his jacket. The sicario sprayed the inside of the car with dozens of bullets, killing both the General and his driver instantly. The motorcycle then, as the light turned green, just as quickly as it had arrived, disappeared into the busy afternoon traffic. Once again, there were no witnesses.

CHAPTER FOUR

Joe had slept later than usual. It was almost eight o'clock. He was always an early riser and never used an alarm, but last night he had tossed and turned most of the night with Trizzi on his mind. He was totally shocked at the feelings that he had for her. His first thought as he awoke was, *Is she going to call me this morning or just disappear?*

He lay in bed for a few minutes and then rambled into the ensuite for a leak. As he stood in front of the toilet, he looked at himself in the smoked mirror that surrounded the double Jacuzzi. He looked and felt more tired than usual so he immediately stepped into the shower stall in the corner to see if he could wake up. It wasn't long before the drowsiness left him. After the shower, he had a quick shave, brushed his teeth and combed his hair.

Joe walked back through his bedroom, out into the hall past the guestroom and down the stairs onto the main level of the condo. He had lived in the same building on the thirtieth floor at Harbour Square, right next to the Westin Harbour Castle Hotel complex, just a ten-minute walk from his office. He continued on through the dining room area and into the kitchen to the fridge. Cold orange juice always helped the morning after the party. He put enough coffee in the Braun for four cups, or two large mugs, and started the machine and then wandered down to the small foyer and the main door where he found the morning Globe and Mail.

Back in the living room, Joe sat in his favorite light brown, leather recliner with the newspaper on his lap. The large windows and patio door that overlooked the harbour islands and Lake Ontario were behind him. As he opened the newspaper, a vision of Trizzi flooded into his mind, *Is she really going to call me?*

Joe was updating himself as to how spring training was going for the Blue Jays in the *Grapefruit League* in Florida when his telephone rang. He didn't want to seem too anxious, so he waited for the third ring and as he lifted the receiver, he prayed that it would be her.

"Hello!" He said with his fingers crossed.

"Hi, how are you this lovely morning?"

"Great! I'm sitting here reading the paper hoping that you would call. Please tell me you made your telephone calls to Montreal and you can stay here for another day?"

"I hate to tell you," she answered with a bit of a lull on the line as Joe's heart sank, "but I can! I don't have to go back to Montreal until tomorrow night."

Trizzi's heart had somehow taken over her common sense. Something that she couldn't control or understand was keeping her in Toronto against her better judgment.

"Fabulous! Are you going to spend the night here? There's really no point in keeping that room because you're not going to spend any time there anyway. As I mentioned to you last night, I've got a guest bedroom and a private bathroom that's all yours if you want it."

"Yeah, right!" She laughed. "Do you think I'll be safe?"

"You'll be fine. I promise. When do you want me to pick you up?"

"I've already had a bath and I just have to get dressed, so why don't you pick me up in half an hour. I'll be in the lobby by nine-thirty. See you then."

Joe took the steps up to his bedroom two at a time and quickly made his bed and got dressed. There were no plans yet as to what they were going to do for the day, so he just threw on his blue jeans, a denim shirt and slip-on casual shoes. He did a quick run through the condo and picked up anything that was out of place. He made sure that the dirty dishes, usually piled in the kitchen sink, were in the dishwasher. He grabbed a jacket and headed for his car.

It was a beautiful spring day without a cloud in the sky. Joe went north on Bay Street for about five minutes and turned west on Richmond toward the Hilton, just a few blocks away. He pulled into the reception area parking right on time and walked directly into the lobby. Trizzi had checked out and was on her way to the main door carrying her purse, a small suitcase and a hang-up bag folded over one arm. She was dressed in black pants and a rust-colored blazer over a black, silk blouse, all of which showed through the opening in her off-white, spring coat.

"Trizzi! You look great!" Joe remarked, as he took her luggage and moved close to her and they kissed each other very gently.

"Thanks. I hope we're doing the right thing."

Her heart told her that she had made the right decision, but she knew deep down that she had made a terrible mistake. She really shouldn't get too close to him. Her personal life and work didn't leave room for a serious relationship with someone outside of her world.

"We are. Come on, I'm parked just outside."

Joe let her go into the revolving door first and followed. He popped his trunk from his key ring as they walked toward the car and put the baggage in and closed it. He then opened the passenger door for Trizzi and went around to the driver's side.

"Did you have any trouble arranging to stay over?"

"No, everything worked out. Even the flight home tomorrow night had a seat."

She didn't have to make any phone calls. She had trouble making up her mind. She was afraid to stay. She was afraid of falling in love. Her work related long-term relationship was far from perfect. She had wanted to break it off for sometime but it was really more for business than pleasure and she was physically afraid of the guy. He was a dangerous man.

During the ride to Joe's condo, they talked about having brunch somewhere and doing some sightseeing. Although Trizzi had been to Toronto a number of times, she had never acted like a tourist before. She was looking forward to a relaxing day.

They walked into Joe's condo foyer and up the few steps onto the bright, main level where the morning sun always flooded into the room. Trizzi went directly to the twenty-eight feet of glass and sliding doors and looked out over a dark blue Lake Ontario and the Toronto harbour islands. Joe set her luggage down by the steps that went upstairs and followed her as she walked gracefully across the spacious room.

"What a great view! Is that a ferry crossing the harbour?"

"Yeah, they run all year round. In winter they're mainly used by the full-time residents of the islands but in summer, throngs of Torontonians and tourists use the parks, beaches and marinas over there, especially on weekends."

"How long have you lived here?" Trizzi asked turning away from the view.

"Just over three years. Come on, I'll show you the rest of the place."

Trizzi followed Joe as he picked up her bags and went upstairs. He turned right at the guest bedroom and put her bags, coat and blazer, on the bed.

"Your very own room as I promised," Joe smiled. "Come and see the great city view!" Joe said, as he led her to the master bedroom and the large window that faced north. "You've probably been to the SkyDome and the CN Tower and there's the Royal York Hotel. That's the Hilton where you stayed in the background."

"I've never been to the top of the CN Tower now that you mention it."

"Later today, we'll go up to the top for a cocktail. There's a revolving restaurant and bar that overlooks the whole city. Maybe we'll have lunch there."

"I don't care what we do. I'm just glad that I was able to stay here with you."

"I am too. If you don't care what we do, come here."

He pulled her close to him and put that smiling face between his hands and looked into her dark, flashing eyes. He could tell that she was happy. He kissed her slowly and intimately for a long time and their arms went around each other. Joe laid her down across his bed and lay beside her and their bodies were pressed together. His right thigh found a place to rest between her legs and they pushed against each other. Joe lay partly on top of her as they continued to kiss and explore each other's faces. She could feel his hardness against her. She kissed him deeply and moaned as she moved. Trizzi spoke first.

"I can't believe how comfortable I feel. It's as though I've known you forever."

"I feel the same way. I wanted you the minute I saw you at the reception last night."

"What are we doing? I'm afraid that if we just jump into bed, we may lose something. The special feelings we have for each other might just fade away." She said and kissed him.

"I don't know what the hell's going on but we both know how we feel about each other. I'm just crazy about you. There's no way we're going to get through the day without making love. Why don't we just decide that this is the right time?"

"I want what you want. I just want you to know that I have never had the feelings that I have for you about anyone else in my life. I was awake all night missing you, wanting you, and we'd only just met. It's totally crazy!" She said and kissed him once more.

Joe and Trizzi felt the passion growing from within but neither wanted to rush things. They wanted to move slowly and savor every moment. They were relaxed and comfortable and wanted their first encounter to be a moment in their lives that they would never forget.

"If we're going to make love, why don't you hang up your clothes in the other room and I'll get a couple of small glasses and some Grand Marnier. We could make it our drink."
Trizzi kissed him again and got up and went to the guest bedroom.

Joe brought a part bottle of the liqueur and two small glasses up from the dining room and set them on a bedside table. He also took a condom out of the top drawer. He pulled the drapes closed and threw his clothes on a chair near the bed. As he turned, Trizzi came through the bedroom door in her bra and panties. As they kissed, their undergarments fell to the floor. The two lovers continued to kiss as they slipped in under the covers.

"There's one thing I have to know before we make love," Joe whispered. "I don't know your last name. I wouldn't have been able to find you if you hadn't called me this morning."

"I think it's more romantic if I don't tell you right now. You'll find out soon enough."

She didn't know what to do. She shouldn't even be there. She was scared, but she pulled him against her naked body and kissed him and before either one of them knew it, they were closer to each other than either one had ever been with anyone else.

It was twelve-thirty when Joe reached for his watch. Making love with Trizzi had been even more wonderful than he could have possibly imagined. It was as if they had been lovers forever. They were falling quickly, into a deep chasm, and there was absolutely nothing that either one of them could do about it. It was just happening.

"After we have a drink, I'm going to take you for lunch to the CN Tower."

"I'd be just as happy if we stayed in bed all afternoon," she smiled.

"Here's to *our* drink." They clinked glasses. "We can stay in bed all day tomorrow, but today is a beautiful day and we should do something. This is the first day that we have ever had together and I want you to remember it as being something special."

"I'll never forget it now," she said as she rolled on top of him, kissed him and let some of the warm Grand Marnier slide from her mouth into his. Lunch would have to wait.

Trizzi enjoyed the glass elevator ride up the side of the tower and they sat against the windows on the extreme outer edge of the revolving dining room. She could see the whole city and even Rochester and other parts of New York State to the south across the lake. During lunch, Joe did most of the talking. They started off with Bloody Mary's, they both liked them spicy, and ended up splitting a chicken clubhouse with a chilled bottle of Macon-Lugny Saint-Pierre Chardonnay. After lunch, they walked back to the waterfront.

As soon as they took off their jackets in the condo, Joe kissed Trizzi, picked her up and carried her upstairs. She kept kissing his neck and giggling, so it was quite obvious to Joe that whatever was on his mind was fine with her. The lovemaking was something that they had only dreamed about. They couldn't keep their hands or mouths off of each other. It was even more wonderful than the morning encounter. Hours later, Joe went to the kitchen for ice water.

"I decided that I'm going to take you to Bymark for dinner. It's the hottest restaurant in the city just up on Wellington. I ate there last week and the food was fabulous."

"What kind of a place is it? Do I have to dress up?"

"Wear what you had on today. The place is really neat because the restaurant is underground and the glassed-in lounge is above it in a small park. The owner has had another restaurant for years, up at Yonge and Eglinton, called North 44 that's also excellent.

They cabbed it to Bymark, only five minutes away. The long bar had only two vacant stools so Joe and Trizzi took them, and near-by, a number of retro-looking seating areas were full of people. The view from the bar through smoked-glass windows, floor to ceiling, overlooked a small park full of bronze cows that were resting in a small grass field nestled among three office towers. As soon as Joe ordered vodka martinis with olives, he slipped downstairs to con-firm his reservation and tell the hostess that they were in the lounge when their table was ready.

Joe's name was called just as they finished their martinis and they made their way downstairs to the restaurant. As soon as they got seated, in an alcove at the rear of the large room, Joe ordered a bottle of Crystal because it was a special night for the lovers. They started with grilled calamari appetizers, and for dinner, Joe had the rack of lamb and Trizzi had the poached salmon. Both were perfect. Neither one had laughed so much in a long time. They finished dinner with Grand Marniers and then hit the street.

They kissed and held each other in the elevator to the thirtieth floor and as soon as they got inside the condo, the clothes began to fall every-where as they made their way to Joe's favorite, leather chair. They made love for a long time in the livingroom, in the chair, on the couch, on the floor and when the lovemaking was over, they made their way up to the bedroom and went right to sleep in each other's arms.

***

Joe was first up in the morning and slipped quietly out of the bedroom. He put on the coffee and leafed through the Sunday edition of the Globe in the quietness of the living room. An hour later, he slipped back to bed and Trizzi, half-awake, greeted him with a hug.

"I had fun last night. I haven't enjoyed myself that much for a long, long time."

"Me too, I'm kind of sorry the evening had to end."

"Can we just stay in bed all day? I don't want to go anywhere except to the bathroom."

She threw the covers back and got out of bed. Joe couldn't believe how beautiful her figure was even in the dullness of the room. He could see every nook and cranny of her gorgeous body as the light from the lower level engulfed her.

"Do you feel like a coffee and Bailey's?"

"Sounds great! I'll be right back."

Joe was pouring a shot of the light-brown liquid into each mug as Trizzi came back into the room and slid under the covers. He handed her one and they settled back to talk.

"We can have a bite to eat out near the airport before you leave tonight."

"That sounds fine, but I really do want to stay right here with you for the whole day."

Joe found her accent really sexy and leaned over and kissed her.

"What time will your brother be expecting you?"

"I'll call him later and tell him what time to pick me up at the airport."

"You haven't said much about your folks. Do they live in Montreal too?"

"We can talk about me later. Put my cup on the table for me and let's just relax."

He put the coffee mugs aside and they slid deeper under the covers and got lost in the moment. They lost all track of time.

By mid-afternoon, the two lovers were in the swirling water of the Jacuzzi drinking Chateauneuf-du-Pape from one glass. They kissed and fondled in the warm bubbly water until the wine was gone and then dried each other's wet bodies and got back into bed. The Jacuzzi had given them new life and they kissed, fondled, licked and sucked themselves into many enjoyable and sensual positions and eventually made love one last time. They lay on the bed in the darkness of the room, intertwined and looking into each other's eyes when Trizzi spoke.

"I know it's a strange thing to say because we just met, but I've fallen in love with you! I can't bear the thought of leaving even though I know I have to go home to Montreal."

Joe leaned closer to her and kissed her again, "I think I've loved you from the first moment I saw you through that crowd. I can't believe this is all happening so quickly."

"I've never, in all my life, felt such strong feelings for someone. My whole body aches to be near you." She kissed him gently and tears formed in her eyes and ran down her cheeks.

"I feel the same way. It's hard to believe."

They wrapped themselves around each other tighter and kissed again. When their lips finally parted, they just looked into each other's eyes. Joe wondered where their relationship was going to go. Trizzi knew deep down that it could go nowhere.

"We have to slow down. This whole thing scares me to death."

"I know, but I want you to promise that you'll think about me every day."

"I will, I promise. Please kiss me."

They snuggled deep under the covers and held each other. They kissed in a slow, tender and loving way as the lust of the initial encounters had subsided and they just enjoyed the closeness because they knew that she would have to leave soon.

By five o'clock, they had showered together and got dressed. Trizzi had on the same outfit as when Joe had first seen her at the reception and she looked like a businesswoman again. Joe called Air Canada to confirm that her flight would be leaving on time. They weren't hungry, so they headed straight for Lester B. Pearson International Airport. Trizzi held Joe's one hand in both of hers on her lap as they drove west on the Gardner Expressway, the Queen Elizabeth Way and then north on Highway 427 to the airport. Joe was the first to speak.

"You never did tell me your last name or anything about your family. You also forgot to call your brother to pick you up at the airport."

"I'll call him before the plane leaves. He knows I'm coming home tonight. There's not much to tell you about my family. My father was born in Bogota and my mother was French Canadian. They met when my mother was an exchange, nursing student and we continued to live there until my brother and I were teenagers. Then we moved to Quebec. My father used my mother's maiden name, *Bouchard*, because it was easier to do business in Quebec with a French name. My parents died in a plane crash in Colombia six years ago and I have one brother."

She didn't give him one vital piece of information. She failed to tell him that she and her brother had always used her father's surname and had never gone by the name *Bouchard*.

"I'm sorry about your parents. What does your brother do in Montreal?"

"He works for an international import and export company."

"I hate to say it, but here we are," Joe said as he pulled up to the curb in the departure area of Terminal One. "You go and get your ticket and I'll park the car and join you."

"Joe, I don't want you to come in with me. You'll just get me upset saying goodbye because I really don't want to leave. I had a wonderful time," she said and kissed him as tears formed in her eyes and started to run down her cheeks.

"You haven't even given me your phone number so I can call you!"

"I've got your office and home numbers. I'll surprise you. Things have happened so quickly this weekend, I think that we both have to take a moment and think about it all. I think that I've fallen in love with you. The way I feel is a totally new experience for me."

"I know that I'm in love with you too and I want to be able to call you."

"Leave it for a week and see if this is all real. I'll call you and surprise you or I may get home and never think about you again." She kissed him. "I'm coming back in about three weeks and we'll get together then. It'll be too hard on me if I talk to you everyday."

"I can't wait that long. I could fly or drive to Montreal, it's not that far."

"I'll phone you, but let's take some time and think about what happened this weekend. You may never think of me again after I leave."

"I'll be thinking about you all the time, so don't be afraid to call day or night. Don't ever forget that I really do love you with all my heart!"

"I love you too. Don't get out of the car!"

She kissed him one last time and her eyes filled with tears again. As she opened the car door, Joe popped the trunk. She took her luggage, closed the lid, and walked toward the automatic doors. She looked back at Joe only once as she went into the terminal and disappeared into the crowd. He saw tears streaming down her face.

As Joe drove home in the light traffic, he thought about Trizzi and the fantastic weekend. He was absolutely sure he was in love with her. He already had a knot deep in his stomach missing her. After making love with her, it was as is he had never made love before. All of the other relationships in his past had been erased from his memory. He had never experienced the emotions that were going through his mind and body at that moment.

He knew that she really cared for him but couldn't understand why she had been so aloof about her family, business and personal life back in Montreal. They were subjects that she just didn't want to discuss and had avoided. The thought that she was married crossed Joe's mind, as did the possibility that he might not ever hear from her again. He pulled into his parking garage as that final thought tore him apart and the knot in the pit of his stomach tightened.

Joe walked into his condo shortly after seven o'clock and thought that Trizzi's plane would be just taking off. He hit the buttons on his telephone for his messages and there was only one. It was her beautiful voice, *Thanks for the most wonderful weekend of my life. No matter what happens, I want you to remember that I will always love you!*

CHAPTER FIVE

"*Hoy estoy*" *de mal humor!* The Alejandro Factory was the last straw! There's no money left to fight this bloody war and something has to be done about it . . . Now!" Pablo Rivas yelled into the telephone. "And Diego, I mean right now! Time is running out!"

Diego Castrillo knew that he was in serious trouble with *El Doctor.*

"I'm putting the finishing touches on a plan to ship large shipments into the northern part of the United States or Canada. I'm almost ready to do a test flight into the Province of Quebec in eastern Canada."

"Do something about our cash flow! We're running out of money. Diego, you and I have been friends for a long time, but if you can't find a way to solve these bloody problems soon, I'll havta get someone who can. *Comprendo, amigo?*"

"I understand, Pablo. I have a foolproof plan to solve our problems and I will have it in place very soon. The new route will provide you with millions of dollars each month," Castrillo answered, "it'll be just like the old days."

"I don't give *burro shit* about the old days. We must solve these cash flow problems today. I'm going to meet with you in the next couple of weeks and I want you to be able to tell me that my cash problems are no more!" Pablo snarled and the phone went dead.

Diego Castrillo, the worldwide sales manager for the cartel, knew that he had to ship more cocaine or his job, and maybe even his life, was at risk. He had to generate more cash for cartel coffers and he had to do it quickly. Over the years, only two other men had held his position as the second most important and powerful man in the cartel. Rivas had murdered both of them in fits of rage. One of the men had said the wrong thing while flying to the Magdalena River Valley and Rivas had physically thrown him out of a helicopter. The other man had been beaten with the butt end of a rifle and then Rivas had run over him a number of times with his Range Rover. Castrillo and Rivas had been good friends since they were nine-year-old orphans on the streets in Medellin, but he knew only too well that the same fate could befall him at anytime.

Pablo Rivas and his followers had surrendered to the government as part of an amnesty agreement and were put in a prison that had been specially built for them. They had escaped from the jail just in time. An informant had warned them that the military was going to storm the prison and kill everyone involved with the cartel. The government had found out that Rivas had not given up his drug empire and was in full control of the prison. He and his favorites often went to soccer games or out on the town barhopping and even brought young women back to the facility. Cartel business had continued from behind bars during the period of incarceration and the flow of cocaine to North America had never missed a beat.

Ever since the embarrassment of the escape of Rivas and his henchmen, the pressure that the authorities were putting on the cartel had been more extreme than ever before. The cartel's ability to do business was seriously hampered because the Colombians and Americans were finally working together in a last-ditch effort to hunt down and kill Pablo Rivas and destroy the largest and most successful drug cartel in the world. The government had put a multi-million dollar reward on Rivas' head in a country where the average wage was only a few thousand dollars a year. The large reward coerced more and more cartel associates into cooperating with the authorities to provide information about Rivas, his whereabouts, the locations of his safehouses and the cartel's production facilities in hopes of becoming very rich. Even though the sapos knew what could happen to them and their families, information continued to flow to the government. The cartel's laboratories were being found and destroyed on a regular basis and many of the cartel's associates were being arrested, jailed and killed.

Castrillo had moved cocaine out of the country in almost every way imaginable to maintain the supply of money that was needed to wage a full-blown war against the government and the Americans. Thousands of kilos had been sent both by air and boat to Panama but once it got there, it was often lost to the military regime in power that pretended to be a partner in the war against cocaine distribution. Castrillo knew that after the white powder was confiscated, that government proceeded to distribute it on its own behalf and the money found its way into the pockets of the politicians and generals. The cartel sent hundreds of shipments into the unpopulated keys of southern Florida, and other parts of the everglades, only to have many lost to the DEA that patrolled the area. Planeloads and boatloads were sent to the Bahamas through Norman's Cay and other islands and then on to the United States, but the shipments were often lost in seizures by the DEA in joint efforts with the island authorities. One of the safest and easiest routes to North America was through Puerto Rico, an island country that had become the drug capital of the Caribbean, but it was a very expensive place for the Colombians to do business. A number of flights had also been sent directly north from Colombia to the United States and Canada, however many of those planes had been intercepted by the authorities and had resulted in the loss of the pilots, planes and payloads.

Castrillo and the Medellin Cartel understood that times had changed and new, innovative solutions to the shipment problems had to be found. He had to make sure that the cocaine not only got delivered to the markets in the north but that the money got back to the cartel coffers. Castrillo had studied all of the cartel's past successes and failures and put together the best of all that information into a new plan. He had to find a way to confuse the Americans and Canadians along the miles of virtually undefended border between the two countries.

While he was studying the cartel's past methods of distribution,

Castrillo realized that many of the trips into eastern Canada had been the most successful. He made a decision to arrange for a test flight that would take a planeload of cocaine north from the Caribbean and inland along the mutual border of Canada and the United States and then north into the Province of Quebec, close to Montreal, where the major Canadian distributors are located. Castrillo had to find a solution to the cartel's financial problems before it was too late for the cartel, and more importantly, too late for him.

CHAPTER SIX

I t was just before eight o'clock in the morning as Joe made his way
up to the seventy- second floor of First Canadian Place, the tallest
building in the city, from his office a floor below, for the meeting
that Benton Sanderson had requested at Friday's reception. Benton, a
founding partner of Sanderson, Sturgess, had taken Joe under his wing
when he had joined the firm as a law student nearly ten years earlier.
The men had clearly liked each other from the beginning and Benton
had often got Joe involved in his complex commercial transactions
when he needed the help of a junior lawyer. He always treated Joe like
the son that he never had. Joe was happy about Benton's appointment
to the bench, but he would really miss working with him.

At the end of the long hall, Joe could hear Viola McCabe,
Benton's legal assistant and private secretary of many years, already
packing up her own personal things in her small office just outside
her boss' door. She was a few years younger than Benton and very
attractive with a personality that matched her looks. She was always
pleasant, always well dressed and had been divorced for at least
twenty years. Joe had always wondered if she and Benton might be
more than just friends because there really seemed to be something
very special between them.

"Good morning, Mrs. McCabe."

"Good morning, Joe! Mr. Sanderson called from his car. He's
on the Don Valley Parkway stuck in a traffic jam and asked me to
tell you that he'll be along shortly." Mrs. McCabe offered, "Would
you like a coffee while you're waiting?"

"Sure, black as usual! Have you any idea what he wants to see
me about?"

She and Joe had always gotten along well during the time that he had been associated with the firm. Over the years, Joe had often worked closely with Benton and Viola, who he always called *Mrs. McCabe*. They had been able to have lots of laughs even during the high pressure and hectic times they shared which helped alleviate the stress associated with working on complicated commercial transactions that had important closing deadlines.

"He didn't say, but he asked me to come in early too. This will be his last couple of hours in the office as he has quite a few personal things to pack up. He's been in great spirits since his appointment and I think he's looking forward to his new career," Mrs. McCabe explained as they walked into Benton's spacious office and she motioned him toward one of the two enormous, leather chairs. "I know that all of his files have already been turned over to you young lions so that's not it. I'll be back in a minute with your coffee."

Mrs. McCabe left the office and Joe sat alone in the silence of the early morning and gazed out over the city. At that time of the morning, there were very few bodies on the three floors utilized by the law firm as most of the seventy-six lawyers didn't arrive until eight-thirty or so. Benton's large and beautifully decorated office was situated in the southwest corner of the building that was located in the heart of the megacity's financial district. The two walls of the office in the corner were floor-to-ceiling glass that overlooked Lake Ontario and the Toronto waterfront. To the west, Joe could easily see the cities of Mississauga, Oakville, Burlington and Hamilton.

Joe was comfortably seated in one of the green leather, highback chairs that were located in front of a very beautiful and well finished, antique, oak desk. There was a more casual sitting area with a couch, a loveseat, another easychair, a couple of end tables and a round coffee table in the dead corner of the room opposite the windows. The works of art that adorned the walls were very unique and tied the various colors used in the decor together to give a warm and friendly atmosphere. Viola's exquisite taste certainly had some influence on the office.

"How are the boys?" Mrs. McCabe asked as she came back into

the office with the coffee that Joe had ordered. "They must be really getting big."

"They seem to be doing just fine. I have them every second weekend and Susan is usually very cooperative if I want to see them any other time. I actually think that I see more of them now than I did when we were living together."

"I'm sure that often happens," Mrs. McCabe said as she walked back toward the office door. "If you want a refill, just give me a shout. I'll be at my desk."

Joe heard Viola speak to Benton, with a bit of humour in her voice, as she got to the hall.

"Good morning, Your Lordship!"

The new judge had arrived and she was being cute.

"Good morning, Viola! Is Joe here yet? Ah, there you are!"

"Morning, Benton! What was the problem with the traffic this morning?" Joe asked.

"Sorry I'm late. There's some damn construction on the Parkway and things got backed up a bit more than usual," Benton explained as he put down three or four empty cardboard boxes that he had brought with him to pack his personal things in and he continued talking as he put his old, leather briefcase to one side of his desk. "I'm sure that I didn't inconvenience you too much by asking you to meet me early today. Aren't you always the first one at the office anyway?"

"Yeah, I'm usually in early. I can really get a lot accomplished when there's no one else around to bother me and the phones aren't ringing."

"You're probably wondering why I wanted to see you," he said, as Mrs. McCabe placed a cup of coffee in front of him. "Thanks, Viola. Don't let anyone disturb us for the next twenty minutes or so and hold all my calls." She left the office and quietly closed the door behind her. "Joe, as you are no doubt aware, my appointment to the bench took effect immediately and I'm no longer a partner in this firm. I'll be out of here in a couple of hours and even now I'm not one of your bosses. I wanted to find the time to sit down and have a talk with you before I left for good, not as your boss or associate, but as your friend and supporter."

Benton slightly turned his swivel chair and stared out over Lake Ontario with a pensive look on his face. He seemed to be putting his thoughts together. Joe had no idea what to expect.

"Will it be much of a problem transferring your files to other lawyers?" Joe asked.

"No, Jim took care of everything. I've sent you a number of my clients because you have worked with them before. Your secretaries probably have the files by now, but that's not why I wanted to see you. Since you joined us, as you probably know, you've always been my fair-haired boy. I've always been proud of you in terms of the quality of your work and the number of clients that you've attract-ed to this firm, but lately, I've been worried about you."

Joe didn't say anything. He just sat there and listened.
Benton continued. "During the last couple of years, I've noticed quite a change in your attitude toward the law. You seem to have lost the edge. I know how hard you've worked in the past because your numbers always blew away the other young lawyers and even some of the older ones. To get to the point, you seem to be a bit of a fuck-up lately. You don't have the old spark or interest that you once had and I think that your attitude has affected the quality of your work. I've been keeping an eye on you since the sale of Frank Paton's docking facilities about a year ago. If I hadn't caught that mistake you made, it would have cost this firm a lot of money and a good client. You don't seem to be working nearly as hard as you used to and I get the impression that you're not enjoying practicing law like you once did."

"I hear what you're saying and . . ."

"Let me finish now that I've started. Rumour has it that you've bought and sold most of the City of Toronto. I know that you come into work early everyday, but I've noticed that you often leave early to deal with your personal business matters and that time away from the office is beginning to show. I'm not the only one that has noticed and is concerned about you. Jim Sturgess and a couple of the other partners have seen this change in you too and they asked me to have a talk with you before I left. What the hell is the matter with you anyway?"

Joe was kind of taken aback and really didn't know how to respond to his friend.

"I hate to admit it, but I know exactly what you're talking about. During the last couple of years, I have had some reservations about practicing law for the rest of my life and often feel that I'm tired of the continual grind. I find myself thinking about taking a break or even quitting. I wasn't aware that my feelings were affecting my work here at the firm."

"The reason I'm talking to you about this situation is because you're on the short list to be admitted as a full partner at the mid-November partnership meeting. Between now and that meeting, before you have to make a decision that will not only affect your future, but the future of this firm, you had better get your bloody head straightened out and get back on track. As I mentioned, others have noticed the change in your attitude and your work habits too. You're not the hard-working, happy-go-lucky guy that you used to be."

"All of you are probably right. I haven't enjoyed the constant pressure of practicing law for some time and I have been thinking about talking to the partners about taking a sabbatical. Maybe a change of pace for awhile, or a rest, is all I need to get straightened out."

"I can't pinpoint anything specific about you other than a lack of interest. Are there too many personal deals? Are you having financial problems? Are you drinking too much?"

"I certainly did get caught up in the inflationary real estate market here in the city and have been spending a lot of time dealing with those projects, but I'm far from being in financial trouble. In fact, if I take a sabbatical, I won't have to worry about money. As far as drinking too much, it seems to be a vice that most of us lawyers develop. If we're not out with clients, then we have a drink with friends and associates to relax. Then one becomes two."

"How you perform is no longer my concern. I just happen to like you and I know that if you wanted to, you could be one helluva lawyer. Before you accept a full partnership in this firm, you must know that you want it. You have to do some real soul searching between now and the November meeting. Jim will want to know that you are ready to give the firm a one hundred per cent, long-term commitment before he makes the offer, so be sure to stay in touch with him, talk to him, let him know what's bothering you."

"I do appreciate you talking to me because I have been trying to sort out my feelings about the law for some time. One minute I'd pack it in and do something totally different, and the next, I would finalize some litigation file or commercial deal that was really rewarding, and I'd love the feeling. I also think about the eight years in school and another eight here building a good practice and a decent reputation both with our clients and the legal community."

Benton leaned forward with his elbows on his desk. "I'm afraid that I can't help you with your decision. There is one thing that I can tell you. Since Jim and I started this firm, over thirty years ago, you have been one of the brightest and most successful young lawyers that has come through our ranks not counting your performance of the last year or so."

"You've always supported me which I really do appreciate. It's obvious that my doubts about the law and my role in it have created some sort of noticeable change in my attitude and performance. I thought that the problem was my own and not apparent to the rest of you."

"You've got a few months to get your head together and show Jim and the others where your interests lie. By the time the partnership meeting comes around, you will have to know what direction you want your life to take, at least, as far as the law and Sanderson, Sturgess is concerned. Are you going to be in a position to make a long-term commitment to the firm or are you going to leave the law altogether and go on to bigger and better things?"

"Thanks for taking the time to talk to me because it has brought this whole matter to a head. I certainly have to make some important decisions in the near future."

"I hope that you'll consider all of the alternatives that are available to you carefully, because with the right attitude, there's no telling how successful you can be here at Sanderson, Sturgess. Enough has been said about that!" Benton said as he ended the discussion, obviously feeling that he had made his point.

"Are you ready for the move to the new office?" Joe asked.

"I'm ready but I'm really going to miss seeing everyone around here."

"You're going to have a new office and new associates and you'll probably be so busy you won't even think about us. It's nice to hear that Mrs. McCabe is going with you."

Benton knew that, over time, Joe had probably become aware of the loving glances that had passed between the two long-time associates.

"She's been keeping me organized for so long, I really don't know what I would do without her," Benton said with a warm smile and then stood up and moved around his desk as his eyes seemed to moisten, "Joe, it has been a pleasure working with you over the years."

"If you need a hand moving your personal things to your new office, don't be afraid to call me. Thanks again for taking this time to talk to me." Joe said as he shook hands with his friend and then leaned forward and embraced him. "I'm gonna miss having you around here!" He continued as tears formed in the corners of his eyes too.

Joe then walked toward the office door, opened it, and went out into the hall.

"Mrs. McCabe, take good care of Benton over there on Queen Street and don't let him work too hard," Joe said as he walked by her office.

CHAPTER SEVEN

It was a crisp and clear, starlit night as the King-Air 200 cruised smoothly along in a westerly direction at an altitude of eight thousand feet above the Canadian and United States border that separated the Province of Quebec and the State of Maine. The long trip north from Norman's Cay, in the Bahamas, had been quiet and without incident. The two Colombian pilots were looking forward to dropping off their payload and heading back home.

"Fausto, be sure to keep drifting back and forth across the border and with a little luck we won't be detected, but if we are, we may be able to confuse both the Canadian and American radar centers as to where we're actually going." Carlos Centeno, the acting Captain on the flight from the islands, spoke to his co-pilot in Spanish.

The actual dialect of his words had been altered by his harsh life growing up as an orphan in the streets of Medellin. He had learned to do anything that had to be done to survive. Carlos was a ladies man with a medium build, about five ten, with a full head of black hair and was just over thirty years of age. He and his co-pilot, Fausto Ortega, had worked for the Medellin Cartel since they were teenagers, slowly working their way up through the ranks to positions of importance and riches beyond their wildest dreams.

"How long do we continue to fly without lights and in radio silence?" Fausto asked with a little concern in his voice, as this was his first flight into northern United States and Canada.

He had heard about the lengthy jail terms that drug traffickers receive in the United States so he didn't particularly want to get caught south of the border when their destination was actually in Canada. He had made many other runs into the Caribbean and

Panama to deliver cocaine and pick-up other goods such as stereos, VCR's and televisions that were smuggled back into Colombia and sold on the black market by the cartel. He had also flown many loads of the *white powder* into the Florida Keys and Mexico. He was slightly shorter than Carlos, with a dark mustache, and had a large scar across his forehead and into his hairline that was a souvenir from a plane crash in the dense jungle of the Magdalena Valley. His associates had loaded a Cessna so full of cocaine that it hadn't been able to clear the trees at the end of a dirt runway.

"The radio stays off and we don't put the lights on until we get near the airport at Sorel in Quebec. The rendezvous time there is scheduled for two o'clock in the morning and we should be right on time," Carlos answered. "Did you see the paint job on the tail of this plane? You can hardly read the numbers and that red leaf or whatever the hell it's suppose to be doesn't even look like a Canadian Flag."

"Those assholes in the Bahamas don't know what the hell they're doing. We're lucky they filled the plane with enough fuel for us to get here. When the bloody starboard engine sputtered out over the ocean, or wherever the hell we were, I thought that it was all over."

"I've flown to Canada about six times but I always landed on the east coast. This is the first time in United States airspace and then north into Quebec," the Captain explained. "It looks like we may have flown through the U.S. radar installations in Maine without being detected and usually the Canadians are asleep at the switch anyway."

"Did you always carry 1000 kilos on other trips?" Fausto asked as he had always flown smaller loads down in the Caribbean. "This must be worth a small fortune up here."

"Always more on other trips because planes like this one that are used for the long hauls north have lots of carrying capacity. I carried two thousand kilos on one trip and dropped it safely and headed back home. This load is smaller than usual because this is some kind of a test run. It's the first time that they've had me fly a load this far west into Quebec. I think they're trying to find a new route to the northern markets because of all the shipments that they've lost in Panama, Mexico and Florida. The *white gold* onboard is probably worth about twenty million American to the cartel after expenses and the street value in North America is six or seven times that amount."

"I heard that they lost a couple of plane loads on the east coast of Canada in the last year or so. Is that why we're flying further inland on this trip?" Fausto asked as he poured a hot coffee from a thermos bottle into a cup. "Do you want coffee?"

"Yeah," he said to the offer. "They've been working on some sort of new plan to fly larger loads further inland to be closer to more major markets," Carlos explained as he reached for the cup of coffee and took a sip. "Jesus Christ!" He yelled as the plane bounced and the hot coffee spilled down his chin and all over his chest.

Out of nowhere, two ghost-like jet fighters had blurred past the King-Air and the turbulence caused by the close encounters caused the aircraft to bounce and lurch from side to side. The whole plane rattled and shook and all kinds of things crashed to the cockpit floor.

"What the hell was that?" Fausto yelled in terror.

"It looked like two fuckin' American F-16's traveling about five times our speed. They went by so fast they hardly even had a chance to take a look at us. We'd better head north right now and get across the St. Lawrence River into Canadian airspace as quickly as we can. With a little luck, the Americans won't be able to follow us there."

"Where the hell did they come from?"

"We flew over Maine. They're likely from Loring Air Force Base. We were probably picked up by the Bangor radar installation, and because we were in radio silence, they likely sent those guys up to see what or who we were. That's the river below us, so we'll soon be over Canada. I don't think we'll see them again."

The lone radar controller on duty that night in Bangor had attempted to contact the unidentified plane a number of times without any response, so he had no alternative but to contact the closest U.S. airforce base, Loring, to have them check things out.

"I hope we don't have much further to go. After that long flight, the gages are showing low fuel," Fausto commented.

"We'll be in Sorel in about twenty minutes."

"Are we gonna be flying into Quebec from now on if this delivery's successful?"

"Before we left, I met with Diego Castrillo and he wasn't sure whether Sorel would be a regular drop-site. He wanted to test the flight route along the border to see if it was viable. He seemed to think that such a flight path would confuse both countries into thinking that the other had the plane covered. The cartel has sure lost a lot of shipments lately. Two main gangs control drugs in Quebec, the Hells Angels and the Rock Machine, but there are other smaller players such as the West End Gang. The cartel has it's own representatives here who market directly to those distributors who constantly seem to be at war with each other for a larger share of the user market in Canada."

The flight through Canadian airspace was uneventful until the two pilots, at about the same moment, saw the rows of lights flash on and off at the airport on the outskirts of Sorel.

"There's the airport!" Fausto said looking into the distance. "They'll flash every two minutes until we're well into our decent. In the last moments of our landing pattern, they will turn them on and leave them on so we can see the runway."

The Colombians were right on schedule. As the King-Air made the final bank in its landing pattern and headed toward the runway, Centeno switched on all of the plane's landing lights. At that moment, the runway lights came on and stayed on, showing the pilots exactly where they had to land. The pilots straightened out the plane for the final approach and just as their heading was set, the two F-16's blurred past once again, dangerously close to the cockpit, and the plane bounced around in the sky.

"Those bastards must've got permission to enter Canada's airspace so that means that the Canadians know we're here," Carlos yelled excitedly as both of the pilots immediately started to wonder just how fast they could get unloaded, refueled and back into the air.

"What the hell happens now?" Fausto asked nervously.

A flash of brilliance went through Centeno's mind. "How the

hell do I know? But we can't let anyone land behind us. There's no way that the F-16's can land here but the Canadians could be on their way in smaller planes to intercept us. As soon as we touch down and the landing gear stabilizes, we'll drop all flaps full and hit the breaks as hard as we can so this thing will stop halfway down the runway."

"How long will it take us to get unloaded, refueled and outta here?"

"Not long, I hope. I'm sure those guys on the ground heard the jets so they're gonna want to get outta here quickly. Get ready. Let's stop this damn thing as soon as we hit the runway!"

As the plane slid to an abrupt stop halfway down the runway, two dark colored vans that had been stolen earlier in the week in Montreal suddenly came out of the night and stopped quickly near the rear door of the King-Air. Centeno opened the door of the plane and was met by what seemed to be an army. There were three men and what appeared to be a woman with submachine guns and at least six Hells Angels that were decked out in all their glory, including long, scruffy beards and all kinds of tattoos. The very attractive woman, with an Uzi, who was dressed in black leather, seemed to be in charge and gave all the orders in French and the bikers moved very quickly. Fifteen minutes later, all one thousand kilos of the white gold had been transferred to the two vans.

The silence was broken by a terrible scream from one of the bearded bikers.

"*Il y deux maudites helicoptere sur la piste sud de l'aeroport! Foutons le camp!*" He yelled as the sound of blades sliced through the air at the far end of the airport.

Moments later, the two vans were roaring across the field in the darkness without any lights on and the woman with the Uzi and all the bikers that had been around the plane had disappeared. Centeno and Ortega were left inside the storage area of the plane all alone. Sixty seconds later, two Canadian Armed Forces helicopters hovered over the King-Air 200 and their spotlights lit up the plane and surrounding area like it was mid-afternoon.

A voice came over a loudspeaker, "This is the Royal Canadian Mounted Police! All occupants of the plane! Immediately drop your weapons and move to the ground slowly and place your hands on the back of your heads!"

The two Colombians had no choice but to follow the instructions of the RCMP. There had been no time to refuel the plane for the trip back down south and the fuel truck had left with the vans. The two pilots had been left there all alone to fend for themselves. The shipment of cocaine was halfway to Montreal by the time the two helicopters landed. The two men were immediately arrested and the King-Air was seized on behalf of the Government of Canada.

Carlos Centeno had often heard about Canada's federal police force, the Royal Canadian Mounted Police, their strange uniforms and their motto that, *The Mounties Always Get Their Man!* Back in Colombia, the RCMP's motto had been turned into a bit of a gay joke, in that it was always repeated with a lisp, which suggested that the Mounties were a bunch of sissies. He shook his head as he and Ortega were handcuffed and led to one of the cruisers that had arrived at the airfield. Somehow the joke about the Mounties didn't seem as funny at that moment as it had when Centeno had first heard it back in Colombia.

CHAPTER EIGHT

Joe was a mess during the days that followed the weekend that he had spent with Trizzi. He had fallen head over heels in love with her and couldn't wait to hear her voice again. The telephone call that she had promised to make never came. He found himself waiting for the phone to ring. He had tried to find her telephone number by calling Montreal information and searching the name *Bouchard* but had no success. He couldn't sleep or concentrate at the office. It was just pure luck that his workload was light that week.

The passing of time didn't help. He took longer lunches and even got into the booze, something that he rarely did under normal circumstances. He called the office only to find out if Trizzi had called and when he found out that she hadn't, he often extended his lunches and only went back for messages late in the day. On Friday, he left the office at noon and told his legal assistant that he wouldn't be back. He was a total disaster.

Joe had lunch and cocktails at Kit Kat, one of Al Carbone's two restaurants in the Entertainment District, with another lawyer and a couple of stock brokers. Al and John Carbone were both there and periodically joined the group for a glass of wine and some conversation. By mid-afternoon, Joe thought about calling John O'Donnell, his associate who acted for Trizzi's friend, so that he could call his client to get her phone number for him but decided against it. He was already in trouble at the firm for his recent work ethics so he decided not to get O'Donnell involved in his personal life. He stayed at Kit Kat until after five and then he and his drinking buddies took a cab to Little Anthony's for just one more drink. He had a lot more than one and stayed out way too late.

***

The next morning, Joe found himself on the couch in his living room where he must have lay down and passed out the night before. He was flat on his back with his head tilted toward the cushions to protect his eyes from the bright morning sun when the phone on the end table beside his head exploded with a loud ring that startled him out of his semi-comatose state. The sound resonated through his whole aching body as his hand fumbled for the telephone receiver as quickly as possible so the noise would stop.

"Hello?" He said into the phone in a voice that was not his own.

"Is Joe McConnell there?"

"Yeah, this is Joe, who's this?" He said in a slightly more distinguishable tone.

"You sound awful! What the hell happened?"

It was Bryan Moyle, a buddy from Lindsay, a small town north of the city.

"I left the office at noon yesterday and met some guys and I guess I got totally pissed. I don't remember coming home. I have absolutely no idea how I got here or at what time."

"What were you celebrating?"

"Nothing, I just had a bad week and got involved with a bunch of guys at noon yesterday that wanted to drink. I think we closed Anthony's."

"You sound like hell."

"What have you been up to lately? How are things with the group home?"

"I moved from the city to this small town to look after all these little bastards, I've got sixteen of them, and now the damn government has changed the rules again about how much funding is available. My cash flow sucks and they're talking about more cutbacks. Now the assholes want me to do a whole bunch of renovations and upgrades at the farm."

"If it's not the government screwing things up then it's someone else. Even the legal profession's a disaster. The liability fees are going through the roof because of all the claims and the schools keep graduating more and more lawyers every year. Lots of them seem to end up unemployed. What the hell can you do?"

"You sound as pissed off with practicing law as I do with the Ontario government but I guess we have to just carry on. I called to see if you were coming to Lindsay today because all the guys are meeting at the Grand Hotel for lunch. It'll probably be the last one this spring because everyone will be golfing and boating soon."

"I don't have any plans this weekend and I don't have my kids. I should drive up there to see my grandfather, he's getting pretty old. If I get rid of this hangover and feel better when I get up and get moving, I'll probably drive up for the night. See you later."

Joe was awake after the phone call but continued to lay there very still in an attempt to ward off the waves of nausea that flowed through his body every half minute or so. The morning sunlight that poured into the room through the glass wall was so bright and intense that it penetrated right through his eyelids and caused him severe pain in both temples. It had been his weekend for the kids, but his ex-wife was going to visit her folks for a Saturday night birthday party and had made arrangements with Joe to take them with her.

As soon as his eyes got use to the brightness, he raised his head slightly to look around and was quite surprised to find that he was fully dressed. His shoes were still on, his tie was still tied and his three-piece suit was hardly wrinkled. His mind was so foggy that he didn't know what to think, but as a lawyer, it was his learned opinion that, *This hangover is the worst bloody hangover that I have ever inflicted upon myself!* Joe decided that he had to get Trizzi off his mind before he did some serious damage to himself.

It was noon when Joe pulled his STS into the traffic on the Gardner Expressway. The sunroof was wide open and the feel of the cool spring air that rushed through the car seemed to help his hangover. The route to Lindsay, the heart of the City of Kawartha Lakes, would take Joe about forty miles east of the city on Highway 401 to the Highway 35/115 exit and then north for about half an hour.

The fresh air certainly helped settle his stomach and he felt much better as he passed through the City of Oshawa and went by the Canadian head office for General Motors, but he couldn't get Trizzi out of his mind. Questions spun around in his head, *Why hasn't she called me? Does she really care for me as much as she let on?* The only explanation that he could come up with, in his own mind, was that she hadn't told him the truth about her situation back in Montreal. He knew that she had his business card and home phone number so he decided that the best thing to do was to leave it in her hands. He shook his head from side to side in a feeble attempt to quit thinking about her as he took the exit north into the rolling countryside.

The half-hour trip from Highway 401 to Lindsay took Joe through gently rolling farmlands that were mainly used for raising cattle and growing feed for them. The extension of the main highway that Joe was traveling on went right into downtown Lindsay.

Joe turned left onto Kent Street West, the very wide main street with angle parking along both sides, just after one-thirty. The town is located on the banks of the Scugog River in the middle of the Kawartha Lakes that are part of the Trent Canal System, which runs through southern Ontario. It had taken over a hundred years for the town to grow to about eighteen thousand people. Lindsay is a nice, little retirement community and Mayor Art Truax and the Town Fathers intended to keep it that way.

As Joe passed the first building on the right on the main street, he reminisced about his family's ties to that small community. The Royal Hotel had been one of the mainstays in the commerce of the busy town in the late eighteen hundreds and it had been owned by Joe's great-grandfather. Tommy McConnell had the distinction of bringing the first *flush toilet* to Lindsay back in the old days after seeing one on a trip to New York City and he had it installed in the hotel. The town council decided that it was totally unsanitary and made him remove it from the premises. It probably flushed right into the main street. More recently, the building had been restored into a number of specialty shops.

Joe continued up the main drag past all the usual buildings and stores that can be found in any small town in rural Ontario. All the national banks were represented, a number of mens and ladies clothing stores, hardware stores, drugstores, shoe stores, a movie theatre and at least a dozen pubs and restaurants. Just past one of his favorite eateries, the Olympia, Joe angle parked in front of the one hundred and fifty-year-old Town Hall across the street from the Grand Hotel.

Joe was feeling much better and took the front steps of the hotel two at a time. The Grand Hotel was a white-brick, three story building with black trim that dated back into the eighteen sixties, and over the years, the owners, Phil and Pat Nieukirk, had maintained the original structure to the delight of the Historical Society.

The area of the lounge where the guys usually sat held about twenty people and it was almost full. Tommy, a local insurance adjuster, who was about five foot nine and overweight, fair complexioned and wore glasses, had quite obviously had a few beers because he was giving one of his sermons on the meaning of life. Mike, an accountant, about the same size as Tommy with jet-black hair and a matching beard, was sitting beside him listening intently. He had to listen. Tommy was his best client. Across from them was Percy Simmer or *Doc*, everyone's favorite Optometrist, who was about the same shape but a little taller. Beside him was Bryan, the guy that had called Joe earlier in the day. He was about six foot three with a mustache and weighed in at about two hundred and sixty pounds. He had the group home for wayward kids. Howie, another slightly overweight guy about the same height as Bryan, was right next to him. He was a local roofing contractor.

Joe acknowledged Mike Bosley and Ed Lyons, local real estate developers, and the car dealers that were represented, Anthony Polito, John Lindsay, Terry Obie and Hugh Manley. Phil, the owner of the hotel, seated next to Claire "Moose" Brown, also said hello and they were chatting with Dr. Bill Percival, everyone's dentist. Bill Konkle, a local restaurateur, Paul Dowdall, another Optometrist, and Greg and Geoff Hickson, local entrepreneurs, were there too.

On the six tables that had been joined together were the remnants of four extra large pizzas, three trays of Buffalo wings and a number of pitchers of beer, the contents of which had found their way into the many glasses that were scattered around. Joe spotted an empty chair at the nearest end of the table next to Doc and sat down.

"Nice of you to drop by and see us once in awhile," Doc commented.

"You know that it's really tough to leave all those pretty girls and come up here to see you loons. Now that baseball is starting, maybe you'll all come down and visit me more often."

"Pizza?" Tommy asked as he handed Joe a slice on a plate and poured him some beer.

The first mouthfuls of beer actually tasted great as Joe sucked back about half a glass and then asked generally, "Have I missed anything exciting in town the last few weeks?"

"The only excitement you missed was seeing that brown Oldsmobile over on Redwing early yesterday morning," Doc cracked and broke up everyone at the table.

In a small town, one of the highlights was to catch one of your friends at some gals place where he wasn't suppose to be and then of course mention it to him as often as possible. On that day, the target was *Moose* Brown, everyone's favorite liquor sales representative.

From down at the far end of the table, Claire responded, "You guys can laugh but you're probably gonna see my car there a lot more often because I'm gonna marry that gal!"

Someone else would be the victim at the next luncheon. The laughter died down and the various groups started different conversations around the table once again.

Bryan spoke to Joe. "You look a lot better than you sounded on the phone."

"I felt terrible when you woke me up this morning but now I think I'm gonna live."

Howard O'Dell, the roofer, and Joe had known each other since they were kids. They had met shortly after Joe had arrived in the Lindsay area from Philadelphia because he had grown up in a rural village near where Joe's family lived on the lake. Howie had a lot of interesting jobs over the years. He had joined the Canadian Navy in his late teens and when he was discharged, had become an under taker. *Mr. Nash*, one of his customers who had been cremated years earlier and had never been picked up by his family, was a permanent fixture on Howie's mantle. He later ran a casket manufacturing company and proved once again, that his sense of humour was totally warped. His son's toy box was a bright red child's casket. Another time, he and Claire Brown showed up at a winter toboggan party with a two-seater casket nailed to snow skis.

Howie also directed his next question to Joe, "Have you been to the Toronto Motorcycle Show yet? It's at the Toronto Convention Centre near the Crowne Plaza Hotel all week."

"I was at a reception there about a week ago and saw it advertised but I hadn't really thought about going. Why? Are you thinking about going to it?"

"I think that we should all get motorcycles for the summer and have some fun," Doc interjected and looked at everyone around the table.

Doc, or Dr. Percy Simmer, wasn't a medical doctor, he was an Optometrist, but for some reason his profession used that title. He had been separated from his wife for a year or so and had two sons who lived with his ex close to where he lived. At five foot ten, he was somewhat overweight and ate and drank far too much. He had way too much fun.

Tom Yates, the insurance adjuster, who already owned a large, cruising Honda Aspencade and was sitting next to Howie, added, "That's a great idea."

Tommy was also in a volatile marriage with two kids, a boy and a girl, and he loved his motorcycle, but always had trouble finding someone to join him on day rides or trips.

Mike Jones, everyone's accountant, was also married and he and his wife had three kids, two boys and a girl. He had a Honda Gold Wing that was similar to Tommy's but slightly smaller and a couple of years older. He rode his bike back and forth to the office on nice days.

"If all you guys get bikes, we'll have an excuse to get together and have some fun," Mike answered, as he grabbed the last piece of pizza left on the tables.

"I was thinking about going down to the city tomorrow for the show. Does anyone want to come with me?" Howie asked.

"If it's a nice day, Mike and I will ride our bikes down and meet you there," Tommy replied and Mike nodded agreement. "If it turns out to be a lousy day, we'll drive."

Doc continued, "Maybe I'll see if my oldest son wants to go and we'll join you. Why don't we all take our boys?"

"If you're taking your sons with you, I'll call Susan and see if I can pick up my guys for the day and I'll go back to the city early tomorrow and meet you downtown," Joe added.

"Are you going to come to Toronto, Bryan?" Tommy asked looking toward the big guy with the mustache for an answer.

"You guys are all out of your fuckin' minds. They don't make a motorcycle big enough for me and besides, they're too damn dangerous, especially for guys who drink too much."

"Why don't you all call me before ten o'clock in the morning and confirm whether or not you're coming and we can decide on a place to meet," Howie said.

Joe answered, "That sounds great! It looks like all the food and booze is gone so I'm outta here. I have to go down to the lake and visit my grandfather."

Joe said his good-byes and walked out of the bar into the brilliant sunshine. The ten mile drive north to Pleasant Point only took Joe about fifteen minutes. He turned off the Bobcaygeon highway and traveled toward the lake. As he went over the crest of *Greer's Hill*, a steep incline that had been named after Theodore Greer, a long dead farmer who Joe had worked for as a kid, he caught a glimpse of the dark-blue waters of Sturgeon Lake through the trees.

Joe turned left at the T-intersection about two hundred feet before the lake and headed south past his Uncle Frank and Aunt Wilma's beautiful, lakefront home. They usually had Joe's grandfather over for dinner on Saturday nights so Joe had thrown a couple of bottles of

Chianti into his car because he knew that he would be welcome too.

Joe's grandfather, Norm McConnell, had retired from Canada Post in Saskatchewan over twenty years ago and had moved to the Lindsay area to be near his two sons. Before his retirement, Frank was Toronto Area Sales Manager for Labatt's Brewery for many years and retired to his summer home on Sturgeon Lake. Mel, Joe's father, had been transferred from western Canada to Philadelphia with Union Carbide before Joe was born, and when Joe was a teenager, he was transferred back to Ontario to run the Lindsay operation. Norm lived with Joe's parents who vacationed each winter in Florida and spent summers at the lake.

Norm or *Bompie*, the nickname that Joe had given him as a small child, happened to be looking out of the diningroom window as the STS pulled into the parking area in the backyard. The old fella was close to ninety but he was still able to take care of himself. Bompie, as he was well known to everyone in the neighbourhood, was five foot ten and solidly built. His head was topped with white, thinning hair that was never out of place. He still walked everyday and often rode his bicycle up and down the country road. As Joe approached the large wooden deck at the back door with his overnight bag in hand, Bompie opened the door and stepped out to meet him.

"How are ya' doin' boy? It's about time you got up here for a visit."

"How've you been?" Joe asked as they went inside. "And how are Frank and Wilma?"

"Frank's been playing hockey in some Old Timers Tournament in Fenelon Falls all day. He's a damn fool to be doing that at his age. All he does for a week after each game is complain about how much his back aches. They said that they'd be home around five o'clock to have a barbecue. I'm sure that they'll want you there too."

"Well, stupidity must run in the family. A few years ago, you had that heart attack while you were skipping rope indoors because the weather was too bad for you to go outside for your usual walk or bicycle ride. I'm sure your doctor thinks that you're nuts too."

Bompie and Joe sat in the front livingroom and visited for a couple of hours looking out over the lake through the large picture window. They talked about Joe's younger sister, Donna, and her family, his younger brother, David, the artist, and his folks, Mel and Dorothy, who were still in Florida. Bompie had just recently got back from spending about six weeks with them in their winter home just north of Orlando.

Joe took a few minutes to call Susan at her parents back in the city and was quite happy when arrangements were made to pick up his three boys the next day. He also called Howie to confirm the motorcycle show in Toronto and they decided on a place and time for the group to meet. Frank and Wilma were later than usual so the two buddies poured themselves another drink and settled in to watch what looked like was going to be another beautiful sunset across the lake to the west. There wasn't a cloud in the sky and the sun was a huge, bright-red ball of fire as it started to disappear behind the treed horizon. The phone rang and Joe answered it.

"Hello!"

"Joe, how the hell are ya'? Get right down here for a drink!" Frank yelled into the phone.

Joe got his drinking habits honestly. His family had been in the hotel business for about fifty years and Frank who worked for a major beer company most of his working life, always said, *I drink for a living.*

"I'm fine. We'll be down there shortly."

"I got a bloody hat-trick this afternoon and it's time to celebrate! We only won the Consolation Playoffs but it was a great game."

Bompie and Joe, with the two bottles of Italian wine, walked down the lakefront path to Frank and Wilma's home and had a great dinner of grilled steak, chicken, baked potatoes, salad and of course, a number of cocktails and lots of wine. After dinner, the neighbours from across the street dropped in for a visit and the conversation and drinks went well into the night. Joe and his grandfather walked back to his parent's place under a gorgeous, starlit sky about midnight and got ready to crash. Joe was more than ready for bed.

The smell of maple syrup permeated Joe's nostrils as Bompie removed the Canadian bacon from the smoking frying pan, "How'd you sleep?"

"Great, I left the window open all night and the cool air made me sleep like a log."

"You still have your eggs over-easy?"

"That'll be fine. I'll make the toast," Joe said as he put some bread into the toaster.

It was early enough in the morning that Joe and his grandfather could have a leisurely breakfast and another visit. He caught up on the family news and what had been going on in the Lindsay area. They really enjoyed each other's company and Joe always felt guilty for not spending more time with him.

It was close to eleven o'clock when Joe left Pleasant Point for the city. He had told Susan that he would pick the kids up around twelve-thirty and he didn't want to be late. He had made arrangements to meet Howie and the others at East Side Mario's, a family restaurant and bar next to the Convention Centre, between one and one-thirty.

CHAPTER NINE

D iego Castrillo had been sitting patiently for hours waiting for his boss, Pablo Rivas. His short and stocky frame was stretched out in an easy chair in the sparsely furnished livingroom of a cartel safehouse that had been constructed high on a mountainside overlooking Medellin. Over the years the cartel had built many such houses that were very humble in appearance and most often in residential neighbourhoods on the edge of the city close to jungle escape routes. The walls were double thick so they would stop bullets and as soon as construction was completed, the workers were immediately killed, so no one would ever find out where they were located.

The over-populated city lay in a deep valley, high up in the Andes, and was surrounded by jungle-covered mountains. As Castrillo squirmed in his chair, he studied the large sprawling city that lay below through a picture window in the front wall and he tugged impatiently at the ends of his thick, black mustache. He spoke to one of his bodyguards, Leon Gonzales, who was seated nearby.

"The last time I was in Los Angeles, I drove along Mulhulland Drive in the hills above the city and that same blue-gray haze that is always hovering over Medellin also covers L.A. The pollution problems that we have are just as bad in parts of the United States," Diego mused.

"Why would Los Angeles have these problems, isn't it located right on the ocean?" Leon asked and then added, "Medellin is right at the bottom of this deep valley with mountains all around it. The pollution has no where to go."

The tropical winds cannot penetrate the wall of mountains to disperse the thick smog that hangs over the city. Cars and trucks, both old and new, have no anti-pollution devices and the high-octane fumes spew out of the exhaust systems and linger in a dark cloud over the city.

"In L.A., the prevailing winds come off the ocean and hold the pollution between the coast and the mountains which creates a constant smog situation just like we have here," Diego answered. "What the hell is keeping Pablo? Ever since we escaped from that damn prison, the escalated manhunt has made it almost impossible for him to move around the country."

"He'll be here soon," Leon offered, "he's just being much more careful than he used to be. The reward offered for him now is over five million Yankee dollars. That's a lot of money!"

"I know I'm in serious trouble because of all the recent losses that we've had even though they aren't totally my fault. Just three months ago up in Caqueta, the government forces found and destroyed Tranquilandria. We lost ten fully equipped labs and forty-six of the hundred and sixty men working there were either killed or arrested. They confiscated five of our airplanes and destroyed four airstrips. We lost eight thousand drums of chemicals that were worth a small fortune and they destroyed fourteen tons of cocaine. Look what happened to Carlos Ramos and Cesar Alejandro and his factory up in the Chapare! Then there was that lost plane up in Quebec in Canada! We're being attacked on all fronts."

Colombia and the United States had just entered into new agreements to try and stop the flow of cocaine to North America. Although there were no American troops in Colombia, there were a substantial number of advisors working with the government and military to help smash the cartels. The Colombian military and DEA were involved in almost daily search and destroy missions and their successes had just recently started to put a dent in the amount of coca that was being grown and the amount of *white powder* that was finding its way to the streets of the United States and Canada. The street shortage indicator was higher prices for users.

The authorities had also attacked the drug problem at its source, but with little success. The peasant farmers had been forced, or monetarily enticed, to grow legal crops such as coffee, black pepper, macadamia nuts, coconuts or ginger, but they made a lot more money growing coca. Most farmers grew *oro verde* or *green gold* because the Colombian climate yielded up to six crops a year instead of only one for coffee and other legal produce. The cartels pay much more money for coca, than the government pays *Juan Valdez* for his coffee.

"Why did Pablo surrender to the authorities and then escape from the prison that had been built specially for him and the members of the cartel that surrendered with him?" Leon asked because he had never heard the whole story. "Pablo's escape certainly created problems."

"A couple of years ago, agreements were signed between Colombia and the United States that would force Colombia to deport any arrested cartel members back to the U.S. to stand trial," Diego explained. "This made it much more attractive for fugitives to surrender to the local authorities because cartel members could then negotiate not to be extradited to the U.S. where the penalties and prison sentences are much more severe than here in Colombia."

"What was the deal that Pablo negotiated with the government?" Leon continued.

"At that time, the cartel was under siege and Pablo felt that it was only a matter of time before he would be arrested, so he negotiated a surrender. The terms of his deal required a special prison to be built to incarcerate him and any of his associates who were willing to give themselves up and the cartel was to immediately cease operations. It didn't take the government long to figure out that Pablo not only ran the new prison, but continued to do cartel business from the facility. The flow of cocaine to North America never missed a heartbeat."

"Why did Pablo and the rest of you escape from the prison?" Leon went on.

Diego poured himself another *vaso de vino tinto* and continued, "We actually ran the prison, but after serving about a year, Pablo received information from a paid informant that the military was going to raid the facility. The cartel members who were incarcerated feared for their lives, so we escaped just as the army was closing in on the prison. The escape renewed the war between the cartel and the government and touched off an increased number of bombings and political murders. This renewed war has made it more difficult to ship cocaine north and the cartel's cash flow has seriously deteriorated. I'm absolutely sure that's why Pablo is coming here. He wants to know what plans I have to solve these problems."

Just as Diego finished speaking, he heard a number of footsteps on the back stairs. As he turned, Pablo Rivas entered the room in the midst of four heavily armed bodyguards.

Pablo spoke first, "I want to be alone with Diego."

He moved his arm in a manner that had the effect of clearing the room of Leon and the other four men who had arrived with him. Three went back down the stairs and the other two went out onto the balcony and closed the patio doors. Pablo approached Diego and the old friends embraced. They then sat down at the large glass and stainless steel table that was located at one side of the large room. It was covered with papers and maps of Colombia, Central America, the Caribbean, the U.S. and Canada.

"It's good to see you Pablo, you look well," Diego said thinking that Pablo had gained some weight and had a lot more gray at the temples than he had remembered.

"Diego, *no trates de eng fiarme!* No more bullshit, you know why I'm here! What the hell was that fiasco in Canada? Our cash flow is almost non-existent and I want to know what you're doing about it?" Pablo's face turned a bright red as if he was really trying to control a terrible temper that was on the verge of erupting.

"As I told you when we last talked, I have a new plan and that flight to Canada was part of it. I found out that it's too dangerous to fly along the Canada-U.S. border without a proper flight plan filed with the authorities."

"It cost a fuckin' plane and two good pilots to find that out?" Pablo snapped. "At least Bracho and the Cartel Montreal took care of the money and we didn't lose it too!"

Diego Castrillo wanted to defuse the situation so he continued. "I have a new plan to ship large shipments of cocaine over a new route into the United States through Canada that will be operational within two months. It will solve the two problems we have; sending large shipments directly to major distributors and immediately getting the money back to the cartel."

"I know it's been difficult since our escape from prison. The government and the DEA have been carrying out this new offensive against us, but it's your job to deal with these problems," Pablo said in an almost understanding way and then turned serious. "If you can't solve them and improve our cash flow very soon, I'll have to get someone who can. Tell me about this new plan of yours."

As Diego shuffled through the papers and maps on the table, Pablo looked out through the patio doors into the valley. There wasn't a breath of breeze that afternoon and the downtown business center was hardly visible through the thick, blue haze.

"*Tengo algo que decirte.* I will tell you everything. I know we lost a King-Air 200 in Canada, but I have now solved the detection problem along the Canada-U.S. border. I had Luis Bracho, from the Cartel Montreal, meet with the pilots who were arrested in Quebec to find out what had happened during their flight north, and more particularly, what had happened while they were flying along the border. As soon as I received that information, I came up with a way to solve the detection problem. I also have some good news. The Canadian government is deporting Centeno and Ortega back to Colombia as we speak."

Pablo was becoming impatient and snapped, "What about this new fuckin' plan?"

"Cessnas, each piloted by a cartel pilot, will fly cocaine directly from our factories, in the Chapare and Magdalena Valleys, across the

Caribbean to the small island of St. Kitts out on the edge of the Atlantic. Once the small planes arrive with their cargo, they will be unloaded with the knowledge of certain airport officials and workers who will be well paid by us. The cocaine will then be transferred to a larger plane that will have a pilot and co-pilot, for the trip into northern United States through part of eastern Canada. It will take six plane loads to fill the larger plane that will be waiting at St. Kitts International Airport."

"That sounds interesting so far," Pablo commented, "where does the plane go from there and why will it be undetected?"

"Well," Diego continued, "the larger plane, with fuel capacity for a non-stop flight, will leave St. Kitts and fly north along what we all call *The New York Express*. The route is just outside the United States' electronic fence of radar systems that has been installed all along the east coast mainland. There's no chance that the plane will be detected by any authorities until it flies inland on the last leg of its journey."

"Why won't there be trouble for us once the plane enters U.S. or Canadian airspace?" Pablo asked as the plan began to unfold.

Diego continued. "The larger plane will fly north at about twenty thousand feet, which is much lower than commercial airlines, until it approaches the most southerly tip of the eastern Canadian Province of Nova Scotia. At that time, still well out over the Atlantic, the plane will drop to a very low altitude to get under any Canadian or American radar that may be operating in that area and continue to fly toward the coast."

"So the plane will land in Canada?"

"Not so!" Diego went on. "As the plane from St. Kitts approaches Nova Scotia, it will take up a flying pattern just above another plane that will be scheduled to take off at that precise time from a nearby airport. The captain of that plane will have already filed a flight plan with both authorities taking it from Nova Scotia, over the eastern U.S. states, and into northern New York State. The two planes will *piggyback* so that only one plane will show up on the Canadian and American radar screens. Then they will continue to fly in that pattern until that second plane can drop under the radar and land at a small out of the way airport in Maine. Our plane, with the full load of cocaine, will then continue on to its destination."

"And where is that destination?" Pablo asked becoming more interested.

"I haven't exactly decided yet but I do know of a small airport that might be ideal for a drop site that is located about thirty miles north of Albany in New York State. We used it once before a long time ago. It has a three thousand foot, gravel runway that can handle the size of the plane we will be using for the direct flights from the Caribbean."

"I really do like the sound of your plan," Pablo said in a complimentary manner, "because the New York State destination is close to a number of major U.S. and Canadian drug markets."

"That's right," Diego went on, "only our largest distributors that have the cash to purchase large amounts of cocaine at the time of delivery will be invited to the party. They can pick up their product, pay for it and make their own arrangements to transport it back to their cities. Our plane will then return back to Nova Scotia, the same way that it came, with a proper return flight plan filed with the authorities, and then slip back out into the Atlantic and back to the Caribbean with the money."

"That's very interesting. What size shipments are you going to send north," Pablo asked.

"I'm planning to start with shipments of three thousand kilos."

"When did you say you'd be ready to start the new shipments?" Pablo asked with real interest as he multiplied the number of kilos per flight by the American dollar market price.

"I need about two months to work out some minor details and put the finishing touches on the plan."

CHAPTER TEN

All the guys met at close to the agreed upon time and they all had their oldest boys with them for the afternoon except for Joe, he brought all three of his kids. After a couple of beers and some nibblies for the kids, the group of twelve headed next door to the Convention Centre and The Toronto Motorcycle Show.

The small kids and the *big kids* really enjoyed themselves. They saw all kinds of interesting motorcycles and even though Tommy and Mike had large, cruising Hondas, the rest of the gang couldn't get past the Harley-Davidson show area. There were some great models on display, both with wheels and in bathing suits.

"I think that I'd look good on that tall, blonde model draped in the Harley-Davidson banner," Howie commented. "I really like her lines but I'm sure she's out of my price range. I also like the lines on that *FXRS Low Rider Convertible*."

"I'm not interested in the bike unless she comes with it!" Joe interjected.

"Well, I think that this is the bike for us," Doc said excitedly from his position on the seat, "I think we should order them right now!"

"Let's look around at the other manufacturers displays a bit more and talk it over. The show special is good until next weekend," Howie answered.

The group wandered around the show for a couple of hours and when everyone had enough, they left and took all the boys to a restaurant called the Organ Grinder for dinner. It was located about four blocks east of the show, on the Esplanade, right near the Hummingbird Centre. The choices of food on the menu catered to kids but there was a small adult section that worked perfect for the guys. There was a huge mechanical organ on a stage on one side of the room and it had actual moving, musical parts that operated at various locations throughout the restaurant. Music blasted out of different areas of the room, depending on what peddle the organist, who was dressed as a clown, stepped on during the performance. The kids enjoyed the entertainment and laughed as loud musical sounds bombarded them from all sides.

After dinner, Joe's buddies all headed back to Lindsay and he delivered his guys back to their mother's home just before the seven o'clock curfew. He must have been on time because Susan invited him in for a short visit and to give all three kids a big hug and a kiss goodnight.

It had been a wonderful day for everyone. Joe had spent some unscheduled time with his boys and they liked the motorcylces. The *big kids* enjoyed the day most of all. Howie, Doc and Joe had decided that they would order new Harleys from the Peterborough dealer because they had spent a lot of time talking to him and he was fairly close to Lindsay. Howie was going to call first thing Monday morning to order them and confirm the special prices that had been quoted if three bikes were ordered at the same time. Credit cards would be used for the required deposits. The size of the Lindsay Motorcycle Gang had grown from two to five.

Joe got home about eight o'clock and immediately checked his messages. Trizzi was constantly in his thoughts and he prayed that the day would come when there would be a call from her. He got into bed early to watch television but ended up falling asleep. He woke up in the middle of the night, as usual, and tossed and turned with Trizzi on his mind. Once again, he decided that he would quit thinking about her and get on with his life.

Angie, one of the firms many receptionists, was on the early shift and she was the first person that Joe spoke to upon his arrival at the office that Monday morning. She was a pretty, Italian girl, about twenty years of age, with a wicked body and she really knew how to dress provocatively. Joe had a feeling that she had a crush on him, but he always kept his distance, no matter how tempting the situation was, because she was an employee of the firm.

"Good morning, Mr. McConnell! How do you like my new outfit?" She blurted out as she stood up from behind her desk.

She had on a tight, low cut blouse with a couple of the top buttons undone showing lots of cleavage and a short skirt that should have been against the law.

Joe looked her up and down, twice, as he continued to walk by and said, "Wow! You look absolutely fantastic! I love my wife! I love my wife!"

"You don't have a wife!" Angie called after him and frowned as he disappeared.

Joe stopped in the kitchenette halfway down the hall and poured himself a mug of black Colombian coffee that Angie had already brewed and continued on to his office. In the peace and quiet, he drank his coffee and read the National Post. He then lost himself in the piles of files, correspondence and telephone calls. He only had one short court appearance at eleven o'clock and two afternoon appointments. Other than that he would be able to work undisturbed for the rest of the day. Joe put in a full shift. After the court appearance, he had lunch right at his desk, got through his appointments and didn't even notice the time until it was nearly seven-thirty in the evening. He was ready for a cocktail.

As Joe passed through the reception area and waiting room at the main entrance of the firm he was leaving, he bumped into his colleague, John O'Donnell, who was welcoming one of his clients, Trizzi's friend *Don*, whatever his name was.

"Joe, I think you met Don at Benton's big bash a few weeks ago," O'Donnell said as Joe approached the two men who had just finished greeting each other.

"Yeah, nice to see you again," Joe said as he and Don shook hands. As soon as Joe saw Don, Trizzi's face and smile came flooding back into his mind and that terrible feeling of emptiness returned to the pit of his stomach.

O'Donnell continued, "It's really tough to get these guys who live in the country to come into the city during regular working hours."

"Once a country boy, always a country boy," Don laughed as he and O'Donnell started to walk toward the offices.

"Don," Joe took a deep breath, "could I speak to you privately for a moment? John, this is nothing to do with business, Don and I have a mutual friend who I'd like to inquire about."

"Sure! John, I know where your office is and I'll be there in a minute."

O'Donnell left them in the foyer and Don turned to Joe, "What can I do for you?"

"You may recall that I spent some time with your friend Trizzi on the night of the reception. Trizzi and I went out for a bite to eat and actually had a wonderful time together. We really seemed to hit it off and when she left Toronto, she said that she'd call me but she hasn't. I was wondering if it would be appropriate for me to contact her in Montreal or is there something that I'm missing about her situation there?"

"Joe," Don answered, "Trizzi is a very complicated woman with a very complicated life. If she hasn't called you, I'm sure that she has her reasons. She probably won't be calling. The best advice I can give you is to forget about her."

Don knew a lot more about Trizzi and her life in Montreal than he let on. He knew the business associate that Trizzi was involved with and had even done business with him in the past and was fully aware of the difficult situation that she was in. He also knew that there was no possibility that she could get involved with an outsider, someone not in her world.

"I was afraid that you were going to give me that kind of advice. If you happen to be talking to her, please tell her that I was asking for her. Thanks for your time."

"No problem, it was nice seeing you again," Don said as he shook Joe's hand once more, turned and headed down the hall toward O'Donnell's office.

As Joe entered the elevator, the feeling of emptiness deep in his stomach started to become a knot. He felt like someone had just punched him in the gut. His head was spinning and he was having trouble breathing. He couldn't believe the affect that Trizzi's memory had on him and the fact that Don had advised him to *forget about her* really did him in. He loved her. There was absolutely nothing he could do about it.

Before he bumped into Don, he had felt really good. He had worked very hard all day long and was really looking forward to having cocktails with a few friends. After the chance meeting with Trizzi's friend, he was feeling sick to his stomach and was down so far emotionally that he decided to go straight home instead. As he tried to fall asleep, he decided that he would in fact take Don's advice and forget about her once and for all. As always, her memory would not leave him and he tossed and turned all night long.

CHAPTER ELEVEN

"You say that your new plan will be operational within two months. I'm tired of all this screwing around! We have to generate some cash! Tell me exactly what you have to do, how it'll be done and how long it'll take to do it," Pablo Rivas ordered.

The terribly hot and humid day caused the air in the safehouse to become very heavy and the two men began to perspire profusely as they talked and sipped vino tinto.

"Firstly," Diego explained, "we have three factories still operating in the north. There are two in the Chapare Valley and one in the Magdalena Valley and they are all less than a hundred miles from the coast. As we speak, the landing strips at all three are being upgraded and as soon as the work is complete, a *Bolivian Special* will be located at each one. The Cessna 206's will be modified with extra gasoline storage containers in the cockpits that will be hooked up to the engines for the extra long trips and they'll still have enough cargo space to carry five hundred kilos each to St. Kitts. The Commander 980 that will then fly north from the island to Canada and the United States will carry three thousand kilos on each trip."

"What do you have to do next?"

"Secondly," Diego went on, "I have to go to St. Kitts to set up a transfer depot and bribe the necessary officials. I'll take the Commander 980 Executive Turbojet that we own and have sitting outside the city to St. Kitts to be used for the trips north because it has the cargo space and the fuel capacity to easily make the trip into northern New York State non-stop."

Pablo Rivas still liked the sound of the plan and nodded in

agreement as Diego continued to talk. In his mind, Pablo was calculating the value of each three thousand kilo shipment that goes north at the current wholesale price of twenty to twenty-five thousand dollars U.S. per kilo.

"How many trips a month can you realistically make out of St. Kitts?"

"Two a month, that's six thousand kilos at say twenty thousand per kilo net profit. I can generate well over one hundred million a month after all expenses."

"*Ver es creer!* Now you're starting to get me excited again. What else has to be done?"

"Thirdly, I still have to decide on which airport to use for deliveries into northern New York State. Do you remember Polyschuk? He's that young Canadian pilot who has sold and delivered a number of planes to us over the last few years. I know that he can be trusted. As a pilot who's been around, I'm sure that he will be able to help us locate a small out of the way airfield up north that will be perfect for our purposes. I'll contact him immediately."

"Who will protect our interests on each trip into New York State?"

"I'll use the Cartel Montreal to handle the transfer of the cocaine to the distributors and make sure that our money gets back on the plane safely for the return flights to St. Kitts. I know that you have a special relationship with Bracho and she can be trusted. Besides, she's just north of New York State and she'll get well paid for her services."

"I must admit, your new plan sounds pretty fuckin' good, but you had better be sure to do your homework! *Basta con un error para que to do se estropee!* Lately, there always seems to be something that goes wrong! There have been way too many screw-ups," Pablo said as he got up, banged his fist on the patio door for his bodyguard and walked toward the back stairway, "Keep me up-to-date, *amigo! Buenos dias.*"

CHAPTER TWELVE

While growing up, Joe and his buddies had dreamed of owning Harley-Davidsons, but they never thought that they would ever have a reason to buy one. Not that an afternoon at the local pub was a great reason, but at least they would all have bikes at the same time and would be able to use them together. Howie had ordered the three motorcycles from the Peterborough dealer and was advised that they would be shipped to the dealership six weeks after the show. As the days became longer and the spring weather began to arrive, the guys grew impatient.

Joe, Howie and Doc had all ordered *FXRS Low Rider Convertibles* that were very low- slung bikes with medium height handlebars, teardrop gas tanks and leather saddlebags. They looked quite sporty compared to the large cruising Hondas. The bikes came with a standard 1340cc engine that would allow them go a lot faster than anyone would ever want to go. Howie and Joe chose the bright Wineberry Sun-Glo color, a deep maroon, and Doc picked the two-tone Aqua Sun-Glo and Silver, a dark blue. They all ended up spending a lot more money than they had originally planned, but in the end, they had bought real motorcycles, Harleys. For years, bikers have always said, *Once you own a Harley-Davidson, it gets in your blood and it becomes a part of your life.* They all thought that they were going to be great toys for the summer.

Tommy and Mike had owned their motorcycles for the past three or four years. Tom's large touring Honda Aspencade had fiberglass saddlebags, roll bars, a wind ferring and a full windshield. Mike's Honda Gold Wing was about one step down from Tommy's and was a couple of years older, but it still looked pretty much the same.

Usually, bikers with Harleys don't hang around with guys who have Japanese bikes, but Joe, Doc and Howie didn't know any better.

By early May, the three new bikers had arranged to get their motorcycle licenses. The guys had borrowed Tommy's Honda to do their tests, so when the Harleys arrived they were all ready to ride them. When the big day arrived, Tommy and Mike, on their own motorcycles, joined the other guys for that special occasion and they all spent the first weekend roaring around *Cottage Country*. The next month or so was just spent touring the countryside gaining the driving experience that they all needed.

Joe kept his Harley in Toronto, at the condo, because his parking space was large enough to park it with his car, but he didn't enjoy riding it around the city. There was too much traffic and far too many streetcar tracks. He only used it if he was heading out into the country north of the metropolitan area. Joe really enjoyed the experience of owning a Harley.

As Joe returned to the office from lunch one afternoon in early June, that cute, little vamp at the reception desk, Angie, who had on a tight white top and black pants that looked like they had been painted on, told him that she had a message for him.

"A really funny guy from Lindsay named Bryan called to invite you to a barbecue at his place on the lake next Saturday afternoon."

"Did he leave a phone number or did he want me to call him back?"

She handed Joe a pink message slip. "By the way, Bryan also invited me to the party and said that I should ride up to Lindsay with you on your motorcycle."

"I'm sure that you would have a great time at a stag with fifteen or twenty guys. Besides, if you and I ever have a date, I'm not going to share you with anyone!"

Angie smiled back at Joe and said quietly, "I want you to know that I'm available anytime you want to have that date and I really mean, *anytime!*"

"I'll keep that in mind," Joe answered with a smile. "I love my wife! I love my wife!"

Angie shook her head and frowned as she watched him disappear down the hall.

Bryan's lakefront home was on Sturgeon Lake, in the vicinity of Joe's parent's place, just a few miles south and closer to Lindsay. Joe had been to a number of Bryan's luncheons in the past and they all took the same form; booze, steaks, caesar salad and euchre games that lasted all afternoon. He usually held two or three of those get-togethers each summer.

Joe grabbed a coffee as he went back to his office to return Bryan's call. He realized that it wasn't his weekend for the kids to visit so there was no reason why he couldn't attend the party, and besides, he could spend a little more time with Bompie and the rest of his family. He had taken his three boys to his parents twice since they had returned from Florida and everyone had enjoyed the weekends together. Joe planned to ride the Harley north on Saturday if the weather cooperated, and if it didn't, he would drive.

The weeks since the Toronto Motorcycle Show had gone by quickly and Joe had kept very busy at the office. He hardly ever thought about Trizzi anymore, only when the telephone rang and each time he checked his messages, both at home and at the office, and in his sleep. Two or three times a day, something would remind him of her, and her smiling face would appear in his mind. Just the thought of her still gave him that feeling of emptiness in the pit of his stomach even though he was trying very hard to forget her.

Joe was also becoming more disillusioned with the practice of law. He wasn't sure if he was just tired of practicing in general or just tired of the large firm setting at Sanderson, Sturgess. He was sick of the long hours, the internal competition to bill more than the other lawyers and the pressures created by deadline after deadline that had to be met on each and every file. He was thinking more and more about taking some extended time off, away from the law, to see if he could get his head together enough to decide what he really wanted to do. He had thought a lot about taking his sailboat to the Caribbean for the next winter to do some island hopping. One day soon, he would have to just sit down and make a decision and run with it.

The weather report for the weekend was clear and sunny so Joe decided to have a fairly quiet Friday evening. He wanted to be in good shape for the motorcycle ride to Lindsay in the morning. After work, he had cocktails at Little Anthony's with a couple of buddies and then ended up going to the Duke of Westminister at First Canadian Place for a few pints and excellent British fare. Joe even refrained from drinking too much even though his buddies didn't. He left the restaurant with a slight glow on just after eleven and because it was such a beautiful evening, he walked down to the waterfront.

Joe checked his messages as soon as he got home each night and Trizzi was always foremost on his mind. As usual, she hadn't called. He then turned on the television as soon as he got to his bedroom and David Letterman was just starting his monologue. He watched and listened as he got ready for bed and then ended up watching the whole program because, one of his favorites, Madonna, was scheduled to be a guest. Letterman couldn't control her that night and the network bleeped out the *F word* at least twenty-five times. She also wouldn't leave the stage to allow the other guests to participate and was on the show for most of the hour. The embarrassed host couldn't do a thing. All he could do was laugh along with her. The fiasco was reminiscent of The *Gong Show* but it appeared that Letterman did actually have fun. Joe was still laughing to himself as he finally fell asleep.

He slept in until close to nine o'clock, which was very rare, and after he got ready for the day, he had some orange juice, cereal and a coffee while he read the newspaper. It wasn't long before he was in the parking garage firing up the Harley. Just after eleven, his bike roared out of the south garage door into the brilliant sunshine.

On that day, Joe decided to travel straight north out of the city and stay off of the Macdonald-Cartier Freeway or Highway 401. Most of the trip would be on two-lane country roads through farm country. Joe always called it the *back way* to Lindsay because he would have to go through small towns every ten miles or so. The traveling time would be a little longer than the eastern route on the 401 but it was much more scenic.

Joe was really beginning to enjoy the feeling of freedom that came with riding the Harley through the countryside, on the open roads, with the roar of the engine in his ears and the wind in his face. The feeling that he was experiencing at that moment reminded him of the report from a *psychological assessment* that he had gone through five years earlier, along with all the other lawyers at Sanderson, Sturgess. The conclusions had reflected his present state of mind. The psychologist had suggested to Joe that he should have been born about a hundred years earlier. The shrink had felt that if Joe had a horse tied up out in front, deep down inside, he would really like to go outside, get on it, and ride off into the sunset on some new adventure. Joe thought, *I can just as easily escape on a Harley!*

Joe turned north off Highway 36 onto the Snug Harbour Road just minutes from his destination. Bryan also owned a small farm of about forty acres on the edge of Lindsay where he ran the *Group Home* for boys aged from about eight to seventeen. The courts or Children's Aid felt that his kids needed something more structured than a Foster Home, but less structured than a Reform School. Bryan actually got attached to some of the kids as they came and went.

He always had from twelve to fifteen kids at once on the farm and was paid a daily rate for each one, which provided him with sufficient funds to maintain a suitable facility, pay a number of professional staff and leave him with an extremely good income. Recently, he was having some financial problems because of government funding cutbacks and losses on a couple of bad real estate deals. He was also separated and had two teenage boys of his own. Bryan had separated from his spouse the same month that Joe had found his *matching luggage* on his porch, five green garbage bags full of clothes, so the two of them had done a number of five-day week-end trips to Ft. Lauderdale together and had a lot of laughs.

Bryan lived with Pat Zimmer at his home on the south shore of the Scugog River where it meets Sturgeon Lake just north of Lindsay. It consisted of an eighteen hundred square foot, single-level, win-terized cottage with a boathouse that had been converted into a sleeping cabin, both of which were cedar sided, with a large dock that jutted out into the water. The large yard was fully surrounded by a ten-foot cedar hedge, except of course, at the waterfront, with a double garage and blacktopped parking area just off the back road. Joe pulled his Harley into the enclosed yard shortly after one o'clock and parked it near four other motorcycles, two Hondas and two Harleys. He could see a dozen guys standing around on the outside deck with drinks in their hands and soon found out that there were eight more partyers inside playing euchre.

As Joe parked his bike next to the others, Bryan turned and yelled at him, "Get rid of those damn motorcycles! The neighbours are gonna think that a motorcycle gang lives here!"

"If a motorcycle gang lived here, the place would probably be in a lot better shape!"

Joe wandered up onto the deck, past the smoking grill, and greeted all the guys who were standing around and sitting outside. He shook a few hands and then went right into the kitchen to get a beer out of the fridge. The O'Reillys, Jim, Pat and Mike, were all at one card table with Bobby Taylor in the forth seat. Next to them, Tommy, Howie, Doc and Claire were right in the middle of a game of euchre. There were piles of money on the table and piles of larger bills on the floor beside them.

"How much are you loons playing for?" Joe asked.

Claire answered, "Twenty bucks a game."

"What about the side bets on the floor?" Joe went on.

"Just a hundred on this game," Tommy replied and laughed.

Joe exchanged a few words with the card players at the other table and then went back outside onto the deck. The lake looked like a mirror except for the ripples caused by a couple of large cruisers as they motored slowly past the cottage.

"I hear that you're all heading down south on a big motorcycle trip," Bryan said.

"What trip are you talking about?"

"Tommy says that you guys are going to travel down the east coast of the United States next month for a couple of weeks."

"Sounds like a fantastic idea to me, but I haven't heard about it yet," Joe replied.

Mike, who was sitting nearby on the deck, added, "We were talking about maybe leaving around the first of July. The dates seem to work for everyone."

"I may have to rearrange some legal stuff at the office but that sounds great. I'm ready for a holiday and I'd love to go on a motorcycle trip."

Bryan interjected, "If all you assholes are going on a trip, I'm gonna buy a bike and go with ya'. The only problem is that I've never been on a big motorcycle before."

"Do you want to take mine for a spin?" Joe offered.

"Sure, if you show me how to start it," Bryan said as he swallowed the last of his drink and headed toward the parking area and the motorcycles with Joe right behind him.

Bryan had often driven small motorcycles that he had around his farm for the kids to use, so with a few minutes of instruction, he was ready. At his size, all he needed were a few tattoos and a beard. He pulled out of the enclosed yard and disappeared behind the hedge with a loud roar from the exhaust and Joe went back to the deck to finish his beer.

By that time, Tommy and the other guys who had been playing cards in the house had finished their game and joined the crowd on the deck.

"Joe, how the hell are ya'? And how's the Harley runnin'?" Tommy asked in a pumped up voice that seemed to suggest he had won all the money.

"Great!" Joe said answering both questions. "What's this about a motorcycle trip down through the eastern part of the United States?"

"Mike, Doc and I can take a couple of weeks off toward the end of June and the first part of July and Howie thinks that he can get away then too, how about you?" Tommy asked.

"There's no reason why I can't but I'll have to check my schedule back at the office. There's no way that I won't be going with you guys."

Doc added, "I'm always ready for a holiday so I'll be going with your for sure."

Joe heard Bryan and the Harley come back into the yard and turned toward the noise. He walked up to meet him just to be sure that Bryan put the bike on the stand properly so it wouldn't fall over. Bryan's hair was straight back and his eyes were watering. He must have really let the Harley loose on the paved Pleasant Point Road.

"Does that mother ever go! What power!" Bryan said on his way to the porch as he wiped the tears from his eyes. "I'm gonna order one just like it on Monday."

Tommy piped up, "There's a nice looking motorcycle in stock at the Harley-Davidson store in Peterborough. I was in there looking around the other day. You'll like it. I think it was made just for you. It's called a *FLSTF Fat Boy* and the color is Victory Red Sun-Glo, kind of a bright red. It looks very similar to the bikes these guys bought but it's wider."

"A fuckin' bike called a *Fat Boy*," Bryan answered. "I'll go and look at it on Monday."

The party went on all afternoon and the food was excellent, as usual. The steak was rare and tender and the Caesar salad was full of garlic. Joe even won some money playing euchre and that was almost an event by itself. By the time he decided to leave the party, there were only a few stragglers left. At about four-thirty, after lots to eat and lots to drink, Joe fired up the Harley and rode the mile or so to his parent's home at Pleasant Point.

CHAPTER THIRTEEN

There were only two outstanding matters that had to be finalized by Diego Castrillo before his new plan could be implemented. He had to secure the use of an airport in northern New York State and he had to set up operations on the island of St. Kitts that is located just east of Puerto Rico where the Caribbean Sea meets the Atlantic Ocean. He could personally deal with what had to be done on the island, but the arrangements in New York State were a little more complicated in that they would have to be made by a third party. Castrillo could not risk going to the United States himself because his identity was well known to the DEA.

The Cartel Montreal worked with the largest Colombian cartel, the Medellin Cartel, and bought cocaine and sold it to the biker gangs that handled the distribution to the street dealers and users across Canada. Beatriz Bracho ran her organization like a business with the help of her brother, Luis, and a number of trusted members that had worked with her for years. She was totally against violence because it always attracted the attention of the police. Beatriz Bracho, a thirty-ish, dark-complexioned, attractive, woman of Colombian extraction, stayed in the background and was rarely seen unless there was an important deal she wanted to oversee. She left the day-to-day matters to her brother.

Over the years, there had been many rumours linking her romantically with Pablo Rivas that had never really been confirmed, however, she did seem to have some sort of special relationship with the Medellin Cartel. Castrillo decided that the Cartel Montreal could be of great help to him in executing his new plan. Bracho could contact Polyschuk, set up the flights that would be required out of the Province of Nova Scotia and handle the delivery of the cocaine to the buyers and take care of the money in New York State.

Castrillo spoke into his cellular phone, "It's nice to hear your voice again."

He hadn't spoken to Beatriz since the fiasco at Sorel when she had saved his ass big-time. When the RCMP had arrived, she had kept the Medellin Cartel's money for safekeeping.

"It's nice to hear from you as well," Beatriz said recognizing the voice. She knew that there was always an opportunity to make some real money whenever he called.

"I'll talk to you in a couple of weeks about some work that I want you to do for me up there, but in the meantime, I have a favour to ask."

"No problem, but first I want to tell you that your two friends who were visiting us here in our country are now on their way back home," she advised about the Sorel pilots.

"I'm glad to hear that their holiday is over. Do you remember that friend of ours that deals in airplanes? I would like you to get a message to him that I want to see him as soon as he can make the necessary arrangements."

Polyschuk was a goodlooking entrepreneur, in his early thirties, who had been a pilot since he was a teenager. He bought and sold airplanes for a living. He had visited or knew of every small airport in North America and Castrillo felt that he could trust his judgment to find the perfect drop-site in New York State. Polyschuk had not only sold airplanes to the Medellin Cartel, but had also personally delivered them to Colombia. Even though Polyschuk had always stayed on the outer fringe of the drug business, he and Castrillo had become good friends over the years. He was married with a couple of kids and lived somewhere west of Toronto.

As soon as Polyschuk received the message from Beatriz, he immediately booked a regularly scheduled flight out of Toronto from Pearson International Airport directly to Bogota. He knew that there would be an opportunity to make serious money by helping Castrillo without actually being involved in the trafficking of cocaine. As he was about to clear customs at Eldorado International Airport in Bogota, he placed four American one hundred dollar bills in his passport. The Immigration Officers, who made very little money, were not averse to accepting cash in lieu of the usual immigration stamp in a passport that could later prove that he had been to Colombia. Such stamps attract too much attention back in Canada. He then got onto a regional carrier and flew directly to Rio Negro Airport in Medellin where he was met by one of Castrillo's bodyguards. Polyschuk was led to the backseat of a fairly new, gray Lincoln and his friend was seated there waiting for him. The car whisked them away toward the safehouse.

"How are you my old *amigo*?" Castrillo asked shaking his hand. "It's been a long time."

"Christ! I hate coming to Medellin," Polyschuk blurted out. "If I don't die from the smog, some asshole might shoot me because he thinks I'm a DEA Agent."

"That's the price you pay for looking American! Don't worry, *amigo*, there have been no North American tourists shot or gone missing for a couple of weeks now," Castrillo laughed.

The meeting between the two friends was very cordial and relaxed. They engaged only in small talk while the driver was with them during the trip through the busy city and up the winding roads into the surrounding mountains that were on the edge of the urban area where the safehouse was located. They got down to business once they were alone in the house.

"I have a special job that I want you to take care of for me up north."

Castrillo went on to explain exactly what he needed without going into details about the plan because the fewer people that knew all of the particulars, the better.

"I'm sure I can take care of that for you. I have a couple of small airports in mind right now that might be just exactly what you need."

"You picked up a plane for me from a small airfield just north of Albany about four years ago. Why don't you check it out to see if the location and set-up is suitable," Castrillo continued.

"I actually have that one in mind because I know the guy who owns it. I'll take a look at it first to see if it'll work for you and if it's available. I'll need one-hundred thousand U.S. in cash to set up the six landings and take-offs you want to start with and to make sure that there are no people around on the days that you want to use the airport."

"I can arrange that money for you through Beatriz Bracho in Montreal. What do you want done with your fee?" Castrillo asked.

"I want two-hundred grand U.S. deposited into my Grand Cayman account before I leave here and I also want arrangements made with Beatriz so the money will be available as soon as I get back to Canada," Polyschuk answered.

"No problem. I'll take care of both of those things tomorrow. Now it's time to party," Castrillo said with a broad smile.

Polyschuk had been to hundreds of small airports including many in New York State and he knew exactly how they operated. As a dealer in used planes, he was often close to the drug business because of the huge cash profits that were available selling them to the various players. This was going to be the easiest two hundred grand U.S. that he had ever made because he knew that Jerry Flippen, the owner of the airport that Castrillo had mentioned, was always short of money and would turn a blind eye to almost anything for an envelope full of green stuff. As Polyschuk recalled, the airport would be perfect for Castrillo's purposes. The runway was long enough for the plane that the cartel was going to use and it had a number of old hangers.

Polyschuk spent two days and nights in the safehouse before he received confirmation that his fee had been safely deposited into his Cayman account. It had not been a boring stay because Castrillo had arranged a party in his honour and in attendance were a number of young Colombian beauties, none of whom were out of their teens. Castrillo kept them on call for those days when the pressures of being the worldwide marketing manager of cocaine for the Medellin Cartel were too great. Two of the prettiest girls had made sure that Polyschuk wasn't lonely during his stay. He went back to Canada the same way that he had come and when he presented his passport to Canadian Immigration at the very busy Pearson International, he passed through very easily with hundreds of other travelers from the United States and Canada. There was no evidence that he had ever been to Colombia.

It took Polyschuk a few days to make arrangements to meet with Beatriz Bracho at the Hotel Ibis near the airport in Montreal. He had flown his own twin-engine Beechcraft from Toronto to Dorval International Airport late that afternoon, had an excellent dinner in the hotel dining room and then relaxed in his room until the eight o'clock meeting. Beatriz was going to deliver the hundred grand U.S. that was needed to set things up south of the border. She arrived at the hotel in a low-cut, red mini-dress that was at least one-size too small and matching shoes with spiked heels. After a few pleasantries and a short discussion about business, the money was handed over to him in a brown leather briefcase and Polyschuk slid it under the bed without opening it. He trusted her.

"Well, now that the business part of this meeting is out of the way, I think that we should celebrate Castrillo's new plans that will make us both a lot of money. Do you feel like a glass of champagne? I ordered a bottle of Christal and it should be just about chilled," Polyschuk said as he reached for the bottle that was in the perspiring, silver ice bucket.

"Sure, Don! Why not? I'm all dressed up with no place to go," Beatriz answered with a smile that seemed to be almost forced.

She wasn't as bubbly as usual. She seemed unhappy and was somewhat preoccupied.

"You don't really seem yourself tonight. Are you all right? Is there anything I can do?" Don asked as he handed her a chilled glass of champagne.

He thought that she looked tired and drawn and had lost some weight since he had seen her last about three months before in Toronto.

The one glass of champagne turned into three or four as they chatted. Beatriz drank them very quickly hoping that the bubbly would make her feel better. The wine went right to her head because she hadn't been eating very well during the past weeks and hadn't eaten at all that day. As the champagne hit her, she began to loosen up and became somewhat emotional. For the very first time, in all of the years he had known her, she spoke to Don about her personal life. He had never seen that side of her before. Her eyes filled with tears and they started to run down her cheeks.

"I've fallen in love with someone I can't have and I can't get him out of my mind! It's driving me crazy. I've been sick for weeks. I just don't know what the hell to do."

Don was taken by surprise because this woman was always totally in control of every situation. He had never seen her lose it before. He moved close to her and held her and she continued to cry as she cuddled against his chest and neck. She continued to take short breaths and sob. He kissed her forehead, her cheek and then their lips met for the very first time.

Her eyes were full of tears when she looked up at him, "I know you're married, but I just need someone to hold me."

He kissed her again and held her close to him as they moved toward the bed. Tears were still rolling down her cheeks as they undressed each other slowly and lay down. He couldn't believe how lovely her body was with the dark complexion. The lovemaking was slow and tender and enjoyable for both of them. After they made love, they covered up and just lay there in each other's arms.

Beatriz started to cry once again, "I'm really sorry for taking advantage of our friendship. I just needed someone to put their arms around me and give me a hug."

"What are friends for?" Don said with a bit of a giggle as he squeezed her closer.

The comment made her laugh for the first time that evening.

"By the way, I went to my Toronto lawyer's office at Sanderson, Sturgess and bumped into that lawyer we met at the reception in Toronto, Joe McConnell."

Beatriz burst into tears once again immediately upon hearing his name. She could barely speak. Between sobs she asked, "Did you . . . talk . . . to him?"

"Yeah, he wanted me to tell him how to get in touch with you in Montreal but I put him off. I figured that if you wanted to talk to him or see him, you knew where he was."

"Thank . . . you!" Beatriz managed to say as she continued to cry on Don's shoulder.

After she left the hotel room, Don realized what was causing Trizzi's problems. She had fallen deeply in love with that Toronto lawyer but she knew that he couldn't fit into her life so she was trying her best to forget about him. Don, on the other hand, was more concerned about Pablo Rivas and hoped that he would never find out what had happened between he and Trizzi, especially if the rumours of their relationship were true. He knew that Rivas killed people just for fun. As he fell asleep, with Trizzi's scent everywhere, Don thought that whatever the risk, the experience of making love with her had been well worth it.

The next day, Polyschuk flew out of Dorval and went south over the St. Lawrence, over the Eastern Townships on the south side of the river and across the Canadian border into New York State. He had filed a flight plan with the authorities that would take him to Dunsford Field, just outside of the village of Mechanicville, about half an hour north of Albany. Since he wasn't in any particular hurry and it was a nice sunny day, he took the longer and more scenic route down the full length of Lake Champlain and then flew west toward his destination. As his Beechcraft banked toward the landing strip below, he contacted the airport office for clearance to land. He recognized the voice on the radio as Jerry Flippen.

As Polyschuk pulled his plane up in front of the run-down office and turned his engines off, he could see the silhouette of a large, rotund man inside looking out at him through the window. The guy, in his mid-fifties, was slightly balding with a little gray hair and a paunch from drinking too much American beer. Flippen recognized Polyschuk as soon as he got out of the plane and came out of the office to greet him.

"Christ! Don, it's been years since you dropped by to say hello."

"Things sure haven't changed much around here since I was here last. It still looks like the place is falling down around you."

"Business sucks big-time. The bigger airports with better facilities have stolen most of my regulars and there doesn't seem to be much air traffic come by here anymore."

"It sounds like you could use some business."

"I sure the hell can, I'm ready for almost anything!"

After a short discussion and without providing Flippen with too much information, he agreed to provide an empty hanger for the drug-laden plane that would fly in from the islands and a second hanger for the pick-up vehicles to park in while they waited. He also agreed to allow six landings to take place in exchange for the seventy-five thousand American in cash that Polyschuk had offered and paid to him right at that moment. It was agreed that Flippen would be advised, at the last minute, when the planes would arrive so that only he would be on duty.

The Albany part of Castrillo's plan had been put in place by Polyschuk as he had agreed to do. He had been right, in that it was the easiest money that he had ever made, and he even ended up with an extra twenty-five thousand U.S. for play money. Flippen had been more than happy with the seventy-five grand, that Polyschuk had offered him.

A few days after Polyschuk had left Medellin for Canada, Diego Castrillo and one of his most trusted and capable pilots, Julio Salasar, took off from one of the cartel's hidden airstrips in the highlands just north of the city in a Commander 980 Executive Turbojet. They were headed for the island of St. Kitts. Salasar was a funny looking little guy who had been nicknamed Pinguino because he had a nervous habit of rocking back and forth, from one foot to the other, as he spoke to someone or when someone spoke to him. He had been born in Bogota but moved to Medellin when he was twelve years old and was related to the Bracho family. He had been involved with the cartel for about fifteen of his thirty-two years. They felt a sigh of relief as the Commander left Colombian airspace and headed northeast out over the Caribbean.

"Pinguino, you've worked for Pablo and the cartel for a long-time?"

"Back when I was seventeen and eighteen, I used to fly stereos, television sets and VCR's out of Panama and into Colombia to be sold by the Cartel," Pinguino answered. "I later started flying cocaine to Florida and that's when I started to make real money."

"Why do you keep flying these days, do you really need the money?"

"I have so much money put away I could live like a king back in Colombia, but I can't stay away from this business. I guess it's the easy money and the excitement that brings me back," Pinguino explained. "I've tried to stay at home with my beautiful wife, Delores, and our four little girls, but I keep coming back when I'm called upon."

"We stay in this business far too long. By the way, Beatriz Bracho is handling things up north. Didn't you spend some time with her and her brother the last time you were in Canada?"

"Yeah, I went to New Brunswick to see the pilots when we lost that large shipment a couple of years ago. I went on to Montreal and stayed there for about ten days. We're actually related, cousins, and we played together as children in Bogota."

Castrillo asked, "How did you like in Canada?"

"It was winter and it was freezing, but I had a good time. Beatriz and her brother, Luis, were great. They took me sightseeing and out to dinner a number of times. One interesting thing that we did when I was there was they took me to a gun club or shooting range that was in downtown Montreal, right in the middle of the city. I couldn't believe it but I think it was underground, below all the office buildings. I haven't spoken to her since."

"After I get things arranged in St. Kitts, I have to go back to Medellin and I'm going to leave you in charge of things on the island. As the Cessnas arrive with the six loads of cocaine, the kilos have to be transferred to the Commander on a proper time schedule. The plane has to be ready to be sent north at a very specific time because that plane has to rendezvous with another plane, in the air, at an exact time early in the morning, on the eastcoast of Canada. Just remember that the timing is more than important, it's crucial!" Castrillo explained.

"You can count on me to do whatever has to be done on time," Pinguino answered.

The Commander 980 arrived on the island without any problems and within two days, Castrillo had used his contacts to make the arrangements he needed at St. Kitts International Airport. The required officials had been bribed and a hanger, well down the runway away from all the action, had been rented. Castrillo chartered a private jet to take him back to Colombia to make arrangements for the shipments of cocaine to be sent to the island as scheduled.

Pinguino was looking forward to an extended holiday on the beautiful island paradise so he booked into a large suite at a resort that wasn't too far from the airport, The Jack Tar Hotel. It was the home of the only gambling casino on the island and there was a weekly turnover of vacationing beauties from both North America and Europe, all arriving to have as much fun as they could on their holidays. All Pinguino could think about was broads, gambling and sun. Once he did what he had to do, there would be all kinds of down time just waiting for the plane to return from up north. He thought to himself, *What a tough way to make a living!*

CHAPTER FOURTEEN

The end of June arrived sooner than Joe had anticipated. He was all ready to go on the holiday except for a Construction Lien court hearing for a builder-client that was scheduled for the Monday the guys wanted to leave. He couldn't get out of it so the other bikers agreed to wait until the Tuesday. Joe and Susan had worked out the kid thing but Joe had to agree to take the boys for the weekend before he left on vacation, which he had wanted to do anyway.

Joe's delay wasn't the only problem. Bryan had received a last minute phone call on the Friday before that weekend advising that the Department of Social Services inspectors would arrive at his farm on Monday morning. He had jerked them around once too often and they weren't going to put up with it any longer. After all, he only had a license that could be easily cancelled. Bryan had to be there for their visit.

The escape from the pressures of family and business life was underway and all the guys had agreed not to take their cell phones. It was going to be a real holiday. There wasn't a cloud in the clear, blue sky as Joe weaved his way in and out of the light Tuesday morning traffic going north on the Don Valley Parkway. Joe was dressed in his navy blue, leather jacket, a blue, short-sleeved, sport shirt, blue jeans and tan boots. He felt great and was really ready to get away from everything for a couple of weeks. Unfortunately, Trizzi's image accompanied him and he still got that feeling of emptiness in the pit of his stomach when he thought about her.

Earlier that morning, Joe had packed the Harley with everything that he would need for the trip. The tank bag was full and fastened on top of the gas tank just behind the handlebars. There was a transparent pouch on top of the bag that held a road map folded to the eastern part of the United States that could be easily read while he was riding. Leather saddlebags, full of clothing and other paraphernalia, were hanging from each side of the bike at the back. At the rear of the passenger seat, just behind where Joe was seated, was a rolled up sleeping bag with a pillow inside it held in place by a bungy cord. He was sure that they would be staying in decent hotels and motels along the way, but the large roll would be something for him to lean against when his back got tired and sore.

Joe took the long sloping ramp off the Parkway onto Highway 401 eastbound, and as he hit the entrance to the ramp, the permanent radar-sign that had been installed just before the turn flashed, *TOO FAST*. The pretty blonde in the Mercedes next to him seemed to have control over the speed of the Harley as Joe rode along beside her. He decided to smarten up. He didn't want to get killed on the first day of the trip.

He continued east in the same direction he traveled on his way to Lindsay except when he got to the Lindsay cut-off, he would continue eastward. The traffic became lighter near Oshawa, so he cranked up the throttle on the Harley. Joe had agreed to meet the other guys at the Port Hope Service Centre about on hour east of Toronto.

As Joe rolled into the service center, he saw five motorcycles parked together that were loaded for a long trip. They all had saddlebags that bulged and all but Bryan's *Fat Boy* had a tank bag in place. Bryan didn't need a lot of room for his usual wardrobe of shorts, golf shirts and slip on shoes. As Joe pulled up to the end of the line of bikes and parked, a couple of the guys waved from a table just inside the restaurant window.

"What a great day for a ride in the country!" Joe said as a greeting.

Doc loved to bug Bryan every chance he got and he started as as soon as Joe got there.

"Bryan almost got killed already. He hit a dog on Highway 35 and nearly lost control!"

Everyone started laughing out loud.

"Thank God it was a Cocker Spaniel or I might have fallen off," Bryan added.

"How's the dog?"

"As dead as a door nail!" Howie, the one-time undertaker, said with a laugh.

"Were you able to find out who owned it?" Joe went on.

Tommy explained, "It rolled into the ditch when it got hit so we stopped at the garage at the Mosport corner and told them where it was just in case someone was looking for it."

"What a helluva way to start the trip," Bryan said.

"Where are you guys heading?" The waitress asked as she put a coffee in front of Joe.

"Yeah, where are we going? Have you guys decided yet?" Joe added.

"I called Don Krock in Kingston the other day and told him that we'd stop and see him," Tommy answered, "and then we're going down through the northeastern United States to Cape Cod and on to New York and south to Atlantic City and Washington." "Have a great trip and drive carefully," the waitress said as she went back to work.

Howie said to Joe, "We decided that we'd take Krock out for lunch and that'll take two or three hours if he's still as nuts as he use to be. Then we'll cross the border to Alexandria Bay for the first night. That little town has a lot of great restaurants and bars."

"By the way, how did your hearing go?" Bryan asked.

"It went just fine. The judge lifted the Construction Lien off my client's property and I even got costs," Joe answered. "How was your visit from the Ministry inspectors?"

"The assholes gave me ninety days to spend eighty-five thousand dollars, that I don't have, on building upgrades or they're going to suspend my license. I'm probably screwed!"

"Something will turn up for you Bryan," Doc said hoping to help him relax and forget about all of his problems that he was supposed to be leaving behind for a couple of weeks.

Mike interrupted, "We'd better get the hell going if we're suppose to be in Kingston by noon. Krock'll be pissed if we're late."

"Sounds great to me, I'm ready," Joe said as he swallowed the last of his coffee.

Joe recalled that Alexandria Bay was a small, summer resort town on the south side of the St. Lawrence River in New York State. The town would be full of tourists.

Four bikers fired up their Harleys, two started their Hondas, and they all roared out of the service center onto the Macdonald-Cartier Freeway, or Highway 401, in a pack. The noise as they all left together was so loud it caused people at the gas pumps to turn and watch. Joe was already beginning to feel relaxed. Once again, the roar of the powerful Harley with the wind blowing in his face gave him a wonderful feeling of freedom. He was not going to miss the pressure, deadlines, competition and long hours associated with being at the office.

The *Weekend Warriors* continued to ride east, across southeastern Ontario, often with the north shore of Lake Ontario in sight. The sun was like a ball of fire in the cloudless sky, the lake was a deep blue, the trees among the rock-cuts along the highway were in full bloom, the grass was bright green and the median and shoulder of the highway were unusually clear of garbage and other debris. The bikers were traveling at about seventy-five miles an hour, fifteen over the speed limit, but most of the other traffic was doing the same. Tommy and Mike were in the lead on their Japanese bikes and the others followed. The guys on the Harleys changed positions as someone thought of something funny to try to say, but the motorcycle helmets, which were mandatory by Ontario law, hampered any serious conversation at that speed.

As they rode along, Joe felt like a college kid again, without any cares in the world. They were all out for a few laughs and a good time. *All for one and one for all*, Joe laughed to himself. The sign that flashed by on his right side read *Kingston: Next Three Exits* and he glanced down at his watch. It was almost noon so they would be on time for their lunch date. The rest of the gang followed Tommy off the highway on the Business Section ramp and into a gas station on the edge of town so he could call Krock at his bank from a pay phone.

Tommy came back with the news that Don had made lunch reservations at one of his favorite restaurants, the Bonfire Steak and Seafood House, right downtown. Don had been a bank manager in Lindsay before he got transferred to Kingston and he was an old drinking buddy and good friend. The guys hadn't seen him for two or three years.

Don was sitting alone at a round table for eight in the classy restaurant when the guys arrived. He stood up and shook hands with everyone.

"You silly bastards! You're all too old to be riding motorcycles, somebody's gonna get killed," Don said as he flagged down a waiter to order a round of drinks.

Bryan went on to explain that the only fatality so far had been a little brown, curly haired dog that had run out in front of his bike on Highway 35.

"Are you having as much fun in Kingston as you did in Lindsay?" Joe asked.

Don's wife had been more than happy for the transfer from Lindsay to Kingston to get him away from all the lunatics that he hung around with back there.

"My wife doesn't even like me to mention Lindsay and if she ever found out that I was having lunch with you guys, she'd go crazy!" He laughed.

"Now Don, no bullshit! Do you really enjoy living in Kingston?" Howie interjected. "Have you really turned over a new leaf and settled down?"

"I really do enjoy living in this beautiful town. Its home to Queens University, one of the oldest schools in the country, and the city is just full of history. Canada's first Prime Minister, Sir John A. Macdonald, practiced law in the old part of town over a hundred years ago."

"How about your wife, is she happy here?" Tommy asked.

"She absolutely loves it. The downtown area is full of fabulous shops, bars and restaurants." Don went on. "You guys have been here before haven't you?"

"The only time we were all here was to see the Tall Ships when they were anchored at the downtown docks a few years ago," Bryan answered. "We had a seaplane pick us up at my dock on Sturgeon Lake and fly us here. We flew into the town harbour, over Wolfe Island and Old Fort Kingston, and landed right next to the ships. We had a tour of all the boats, had dinner somewhere down by the docks and then flew home before dark."

"When did all you lunatics get motorcycles?"

The guys related the story to Don as to how they got their bikes and how the trip was planned. They then told him about their plans for the next couple of weeks.

"It sounds like you guys might have some fun. Can I come along?" Don asked jokingly.

"I've got lots of room on my bike if you want to get packed," Tommy replied.

"He'd probably rather ride on a real motorcycle if he's going to come," Howie kidded.

Don's answer was to the waitress. "One more litre of red and then we'd better order."

All the guys ordered a New York Steak, a baked potato and the vegetable of the day because they knew that they wouldn't be eating again until late. During lunch, they chatted about the good times they had all had when Don lived in Lindsay. As a bank manager, he didn't fit the mould. They remembered the euchre games in the lunchroom of Don's bank and the night, after lots to drink, that they almost had him talked into playing cards in the walk-in vault with real money. Fortunately, that didn't happen. They soon finished eating, drank all the wine and wandered out onto the main street of downtown Kingston. They all had on a bit of glow.

After saying their good-byes to Don, the six motorcyclists roared through the crowds of tourists near Marina Park, past the Howard

Johnsons and the Ramada Inn. The outside cafes and patios were full of people and many of them turned to look as the loud bikes went by on the way back to Highway 401. The gang drove east again toward Gananoque and the Ivy Lea Bridge to the United States about half an hour down the road.

The first sign that the group saw just after passing the Gananoque exit read, *Ivy Lea Bridge: Next Right.* Bryan led down the long sloping ramp onto the 1000 Island Parkway and they passed a number of duty free stores before they took the Hill Island exit toward the bridge and the Canadian Immigration booth where they all had to pay a couple of bucks. Just past the booth, the motorcycles climbed onto a large rainbow bridge that spanned the St. Lawrence River.

The view from the crest of the bridge was as clear as a bell and quite spectacular. Joe felt that he could see almost all of the one thousand islands that dotted the huge river below. They continued on Hill Island for about a mile and then all spread out at the American Immigration booths and provided the officers with the required information and documentation to enter the United States. On the same road, they passed by Wellesley Island on the left and then crossed the 1000 Island Bridge that put them directly onto the U.S. mainland. The group was then almost immediately on Highway 81, or the American Legion Memorial Highway, and followed it to the first exit, Highway 12, and then motored east again toward Alexandria Bay which was about ten or twelve miles down the road.

It was close to four-thirty in the afternoon when they traveled down the main street of Alexandria Bay. It was a bustling, little town, full of tourists and traffic. Bryan spotted a neat looking New England style restaurant and bar called Skiff's, to the left, and pulled onto the side street beside it and parked. The rest of them followed and stopped right near him. It was time for another cocktail. The friendly waitress introduced herself to the boys as Bev Dowson.

As the cold beers arrived, Tommy asked, "Bev, could you

recommend a decent place to stay in this town? We just got here and need a place for the night."

"I don't think you guys have a chance of finding anything this late in the day. This is the weekend we have our annual Antique Boat Show and the place is just nuts. My sister and her husband have a small place just up Market Street, the street where you just parked your motorcycles. Do you want me to give her a call just in case there's something left?"

"That would be just super if you could do that!" Doc said and Bev headed to the phone.

Mike, always thinking about his next meal, said to everyone, "Did you see that fancy steakhouse around the corner, it looks great!"

Bev dropped the phone from her ear and said, "My sister has one large room left with two double beds on the main floor. If she puts a couple of cots in it, it's big enough for the six of you if you don't mind staying together. You can have it for ninety dollars for the night."

"We'll take it," Joe answered with everyone nodding agreement. "Can you ask her if there's anywhere safe to park our motorcycles?" Bev went back to the phone. "She says that there's a fenced court-yard at the side of the building, just outside your room's windows, that should be safe for the night."

"Tell her we'll take it for sure and we'll be there within the hour," Bryan said.

The group had two or three beers and talked to Bev and a cou-ple of regulars at the bar. She told them a bit about the town and where they should eat and drink. She also told Bryan that the 1000 Island Liquor Store was down by the town docks at the bottom of James Street, the main street out in front, and that it was within walking distance. Bryan and Howie decided to go and find it. Happy Hour was announced, two drinks for the price of one. As they were nearly finished their second drink, or the free one, the other guys returned with a couple of bags of booze. They thanked Bev for her help, left a generous tip, and went out into Market Street.

***

The River House Inn was a beautiful, old, three-storey, frame building about halfway up the street. The outside of the Inn was painted blue and white, in that popular Cape Cod style, and there was a large porch and patio area with seats, tables and umbrellas. A little courtyard at the side was separated from the sidewalk and road by a three-foot high steel fence with a gate and all the bikes fit into the side-yard easily and were almost out of view from the street.

Their bright room was located just off the patio or porch area. It was a huge room that had a couple of double beds and two additional single cots that had been set up for them. It wasn't the least bit crowded and was absolutely spotless as Bev had promised. The guys really did get lucky. They all brought their belongings in from their bikes and everyone picked a bed. Doc and Joe were the first ones into the room so they grabbed the two single cots so they wouldn't have to sleep with anyone. The other guys got the double beds. It only took a few minutes to organize the room and Doc started pouring drinks.

CHAPTER FIFTEEN

As soon as Diego Castrillo got back to Medellin from St. Kitts, he made his way north to the Chapare Valley. At a clandestine airstrip that had been cut out of the tropical forest, close to one of the cartel's cocaine factories, he stood at the side of a gravel and sand airstrip with his hair blowing furiously. His eyes were squinted shut and a hand partially covered his face to ward off the dust and debris as a *Bolivian Special* inched its way out from under the thick foliage of the rainforest onto the runway. At that moment, at other hidden airstrips in different parts of the valleys, two more Cessna 206's were taxiing down similar runways into positions to take-off on the first of two trips each to St. Kitts. The planes would rendezvous at St. Kitts International Airport with the Commander 980 Turbojet and Pinguino and then return back to the Chapare and Magdalena Valleys for second loads of the *white gold*.

The young, cartel pilot, Edwardo Vasquez, saluted to Castrillo as he pushed the throttle forward and began to move the overloaded plane slowly out into the center of the airstrip. Before starting the engine, Edwardo had made sure that the five hundred kilos of cocaine were spread out evenly in the storage area and back of the cabin so the plane would be properly balanced. He had also double-checked to see that the extra plastic fuel tanks that had been put beside him in the cockpit were full and that they had been hooked up to the engine for the long trip across the Caribbean Sea.

Vasquez pushed hard on the brakes to prevent the plane from moving ahead as he inched the throttle forward. As the old plane built up power and started to rattle, shake and vibrate, he let off on the brakes and it noisily and quickly built up momentum as it screamed down the rough runway and slowly lifted into the air. Castrillo's heart skipped a beat as the wheels of the Cessna touched branches as it cleared the trees. He let out a sigh of relief as the plane banked northeast toward the Caribbean, but knew that he would not relax until his new plan had been successful.

Castrillo had spent a lot of time dealing with the contacts for the Medellin Cartel's largest and most successful distributors in northeastern United States and eastern Canada. All of the players in the major cities wanted a piece of the deal because of the attractive price discounts for cash purchases of larger than usual quantities of cocaine. Castrillo had kept the number of people that were to converge on Dunsford Field to a minimum so the unusual activity around the quiet airport wouldn't attract attention. Some of the distributors had to wait for later shipments to arrive for their orders to be filled. Those who were committed would arrive in small planes, trucks, vans and cars depending upon how far they had to travel to pick up their allotment, pay for it with cash and then make the return trip back to the cities where they did business.

Castrillo knew that if he could generate between fifty and sixty million dollars U.S. per trip, twice a month, it wouldn't be long before he was strongly back in control of the number two position in the cartel. He would also earn a small fortune as more and more deliveries were completed because his bonus plan was substantial. If his new plan were successful, he thought to himself, *The amount of cocaine that will hit the streets of North America will be like the drug world has never seen before.* Each kilo that ended up in the cities would be cut six or seven times and packed into eight ball and gram packages and sold to users to generate a street value well into the billions of dollars.

Four days later, Pinguino watched as the sixth and final load that was due to arrive was being unloaded in the early evening darkness. He stood in the stifling heat and quietness of the hanger that was just off the main runway at St. Kitts International Airport. It was located well away from the main terminal and the hustle and bustle of the crowds of vacationers who were coming and going. The Commander would soon be flying the three thousand kilos north on its way to the noses of North American users. In all the years that Pinguino had worked for the Cartel, this was the largest shipment that he had seen.

As the last kilo was loaded, Pinguino called Castrillo on his cell phone, "Amigo, the last load has been transferred and it looks like the bird is ready to fly."

"Everything seems to be on schedule. Have you had any problems?" Castrillo asked.

"There was a slight complication yesterday. When the pilots fired up the engines to test them, they thought that one was making a strange noise. I didn't know what the hell to do so I flew in a mechanic with turbojet experience from Puerto Rico to take a look at it. He couldn't find anything the matter with the engine when he serviced it and whatever they thought they heard, they don't hear now. So everything is all set."

"If everything's ready, it's a go. I've taken care of everything up north."

"I won't need to talk with you again until they return tomorrow evening. I'll contact you as soon as they get back."

The best cartel pilots were placed in charge of the Commander. They were Filipe Jaramillo, who was nicknamed *Jay*, and Juan Pelez. Both men had been friends of Pinguino since they were teenagers in the streets of Medellin. Jay, the pilot, and Juan, the co-pilot, had years of flying experience. They had fired up the two engines the day before, just for a routine check, and both pilots had thought that there was a strange whining sound in the starboard engine. A jet engine mechanic had been flown in from Puerto Rico and had worked on it for about eight hours without finding any kind of a malfunction. The mechanic had serviced the engine as best he could with the limited facilities at St. Kitts International and when he had finished, further testing indicated that the sound they had heard was gone. The plane had been serviced, refueled, the cargo stowed on board and the pilots were anxious to get underway.

Pinguino asked the pilots some last minute questions just to be sure that they were on side. "You know the exact time in the morning to meet the decoy plane south of Nova Scotia? You know that the contact at Dunsford Field is Beatriz Bracho?"

Pinguino was confidant that they knew exactly what had to be done.

"We'll see you tomorrow night," Jay said as he gave Pinguino a thumbs-up type of handshake and then turned and followed Juan up the stairs that led into the aircraft.

Pinguino's eyes never left the Commander 980 as it gently lifted off the runway on the small tropical island and banked out over the Atlantic Ocean and headed in a northerly direction. He stood and watched the plane as it climbed into the warm, clear night sky until its lights were lost in the stars above. He had nothing to do now but to wait for the return of the plane full of cash so he headed back to the Jack Tar Hotel for more gambling and women. The week that he had spent at the resort had been fantastic. He had met quite a few women from both North America and Europe and had fallen in love a number of times.

As the twenty-minute ride to the resort ended, Pinguino noticed a number of mini-buses unloading passengers at the main entrance. He knew that the group of tourists that had just arrived would include many single women who wanted to do nothing but party. He wandered into the main foyer and past the casino that was in a large room to the left because it was way too early to start gambling. Just ahead of him, at the end of the long hallway that ran from the front door to the rear of the complex, was a large open-air dining room with only a few people still seated. Most of the guests had already eaten and were out in the party area near the outside bar. Pinguino continued down the steps into the crowd of people and heard someone say that two more flights had just arrived from the United States and Canada. The new arrivals were milling around the bar starting their holiday off with that first drink of Island Punch that is always a courtesy of the hotel during the manager's orientation party.

Pinguino, with his trained eye, picked out about ten young women from the crowd that he could tell were traveling alone. He knew that they were looking for fun in the sun and he was going help provide it. He was extremely relaxed and happy that things had gone so well getting the Commander ready for the trip north and he was really in a party mood. There was nothing more for him to do until the Commander returned to St. Kitts the next evening.

CHAPTER SIXTEEN

O nce Doc started pouring drinks in the hotel room at the River House Inn, he wouldn't stop. The guys sat around sucking back cocktails and telling stories until everyone was feeling no pain. Then, as usual, Mike mentioned that it was time for dinner. Just his suggestion made them all start thinking about food and where they would eat that evening.

"There's a nice looking steak and seafood house just around the corner. The one that Mike mentioned earlier," Doc said. "I really feel like some surf and turf."

"All you assholes do is eat!" Bryan answered. "I'm goin' dancin'." He was the biggest guy in the group and always let on that he didn't eat much. Bryan had a habit of getting up early every morning, even back home in Lindsay, and going out on tour. He had been spotted many times frequenting local donut shops for his early morning fix.

"I could eat another steak," Howie agreed.

"McConnell, are you coming to the nightclub down the street?" Bryan asked.

"It's just a kids bar from the sound of the loud music, so I'm gonna pass. I want to have something to eat too. It's going to be a long evening."

The club that Bryan had referred to was just up the street from Skiff's and they had all heard the blaring music and seen the kids hanging around the front door of the place earlier.

Tommy added, "I'm getting pissed! I have to have something to eat soon."

They all freshened up by taking turns using their only bathroom and as each guy was ready for the evening, he went out to the patio with a drink and waited. As Joe got there, Bryan was just sitting down at a patio table, under an umbrella, with a big, heavy-set girl and two friends who were staying at the inn. The background music was soft and romantic.

Bryan used his usual opening line, "Anybody wanna slow dance?"

The largest gal promised that she would have a dance with him later in the evening. As Joe listened, he thought, *A drunken Bryan and the fat girl dancing would be a pretty sight.*

Bryan had the girls and other guests on the patio in stitches as he told his usual stories about the time that he had been a Catholic Priest and how dull things had been when he was in service to the church. He had actually been in the Seminary for a couple of years and had spent some time working with the poor and homeless people on the streets of Chicago.

The guys all ordered another drink from Bev's sister while they waited for Tommy. He was always the last one ready. He was late for everything and always said, *I can't help it because I'm sick!* Unfortunately, he had read an article somewhere that had been written by a respected psychiatrist who expounded the idea that being constantly late was in fact a sickness that could be treated. When he finally joined the group on the patio, all the guys were more than ready to leave for dinner.

They walked back down the quiet street to the corner where Skiff's was located and five of them turned right toward the restaurant they had talked about earlier and Bryan went straight up the street toward PJ's Lounge. The music was still blasting out of the two large speakers that had been positioned just outside and to either side of the main entrance.

"Come on up for drinks after you eat. I'll save you some girls," Bryan yelled as he carefully crossed the busy main street through the slow moving traffic.

The others walked across a paved parking lot on the other side of Skiff's toward a one-storey building that resembled a castle. It was painted light brown with red trim. On the roof was a large, brightly lit sign that read *Cavallario's Steak and Seafood*. The big wooden doors at the entrance opened into a dark foyer with a hostess stand attended to by a twenty-five year old, dark-complexioned, Spanish gal who immediately reminded Joe of Trizzi. The terrible ache suddenly came back and stayed for quite awhile. The interior of the restaurant was nicely done in Greek or Italian reds, blacks and golds, with heavy drapes hanging on the windows and high-back red chairs at all of the bulky, solid oak tables. The beautiful hostess led the guys to a large, round table for six in the middle of the dining room. Joe suggested that the sixth place setting be left because there was the possibility that another party would join them during dinner.

The food was outstanding. Each of the guys, by coincidence, ordered something totally different and they almost tried every entree on the menu, including Surf and Turf, New York Steak, Veal Parmesan, Prime Rib and Rack of Lamb. By the time dinner was over, they had consumed seven bottles of White Horse, which had turned out to be a pretty good California red. The more wine that was consumed, the more laughs the guys seemed to have. Doc had tied his red napkin into a four-cornered hat and wore it throughout dinner. A couple of the others had joined him with napkin-hats of their own with different variations in design.

A gentleman at the next table got a kick out of the performance and leaned over and spoke to Doc, "Is it all right if I copy some of your hat designs for my business? I'm a clothing designer with Halston of New York and I've made many hats and blouses for famous people over the years including Jackie Onassis. A couple of your hat designs might sell."

Doc, of course, laughingly gave his consent. "On the understanding that we get the royalties if any of these styles become the new rage for headwear in the Big Apple!"

"Absolutely! Give me your card and I'll be sure to mail you your royalty cheques as soon as everyone in New York is wearing one!"

They all had a laugh and went back to finishing their meals. As soon as the food and wine was gone, the coffees and liqueurs arrived. At some point, they decided to leave the restaurant and go and look for Bryan since he hadn't shown up during dinner.

As the guys entered PJ's, they could hear Bryan entertaining a group of people. His laugh was very distinctive, especially when he was drunk. He was usually louder than everyone else, even in a busy bar, and he was way too big for anyone to keep under control. When Bryan moved around pissed, he needed a lot of room. The guys all had one more drink with him and met his new friends, then left him there and headed back to the inn. Bryan eventually joined them on the patio back outside their room, but by the time he got there, a drunken Doc had taken a shine to the fat girl that Bryan had met earlier. Bryan had no chance to recover her affections once Doc started to talk dirty to her.

It was close to midnight when everyone but Doc went into the room to crash. He stayed on the patio with his new friend to have one more Couvoisier, a double. The rest of the guys went right to bed and after a few more stories, and a few laughs, they fell asleep one by one.

Joe was awakened by whispering and very quiet laughing and giggling nearby. He couldn't make out what was going on in the darkness but it sounded like Doc had his new, rotund date squeezed onto his single cot with him and they were cuddling. He must have had a least one of her huge breasts out of her blouse because of the sucking sounds. Joe heard the big gal quietly say something about her rent being due and she couldn't afford to pay it. She must have been hinting that she wanted a large tip for whatever it was she was doing or about to do for Doc.

All of a sudden, a wild scream pierced the darkness and there was a loud crash that shook the whole room. The noise probably woke up everyone in the inn. A startled Joe turned on the light beside his cot to see what the hell had happened. As the room lit up, the guys who had been asleep sat bolt upright in their beds with looks of terror on their faces. Joe thought, *What a pretty sight!* Doc, the fat girl and Howie were lying in a tangled pile on the collapsed cot and the gals two huge breasts were hanging out of her blouse. A drunken Howie had stood up on the end of his bed in the darkness and done a swan dive onto Doc's cot and had let out a blood-curdling scream as he was airborne. The big girl had never moved so quickly. She flopped her boobs back into her blouse and went out the door in a flash.

"Howie, you're a fuckin' asshole for ruining my date!" Doc said as he lay back down on the flattened cot and almost immediately started to snore.

The rest of the guys eventually went back to sleep too, after they stopped laughing.

The next morning, Bryan was the first one up as usual and he headed out to see what was going on in the small village. He left the room quietly, at about six-thirty, and he scoped-out the whole downtown area with a coffee and a couple of donuts in hand. About an hour later, when his tour was over, he wandered into the room at the inn and yelled at everyone.

"Get the hell up, it's a beautiful day!"

He then opened the curtains on both of the windows and allowed the brightness of another gorgeous day radiate into the room.

Tommy, with his sheet over his head, bitched, "Why don't you fuck off and come back in about an hour."

Joe decided to take advantage of all the bantering that was going on among the guys so he quietly got up and slipped into the bathroom before anyone else noticed. He wanted to be the first to use the facilities before the place became a disaster area. As soon as Joe was finished, Mike rushed into the small room complaining about the humidity from the shower.

"Would you loons be a little quieter," Tommy said from under his sheet.

Doc, who was by then sitting up on the floor, on top of his crumpled cot, gave Howie a thumbs-up sign as he held a glass of water above Tommy's head. Howie didn't need any more encouragement and slowly dumped the water on the sheet right above Tommy's face.

"You dirty bastards!" Tommy yelled as he jumped up out of bed, with his face and hair all wet and matted to his scalp, just as Mike stepped out of the bathroom.

"Hey, I'm next!" Howie yelled as Tommy slipped in and turned on the shower.

One by one, they finished in the bathroom and got dressed and met out on the patio. Doc's favorite gal was nowhere to be seen. They all left their personal things in the room and wandered down the street to a restaurant that Bryan had found earlier called The Admiral Inn. As they ate themselves through a great breakfast, they planned the rest of their day.

It was decided that they could easily cover the four hundred and fifty miles or so from Alexandria Bay to Cape Cod that day. The map indicated a relatively easy ride by freeway but the whole idea of the trip was to see some of the beautiful countryside, especially the Appalachian Mountains, in the summertime. They all agreed to travel on smaller country roads and to stop in Lake Placid for their first beer of the day. It would take them just over two hours to get to that year-round tourist town in the middle of the Adirondack Mountains.

After breakfast, they went back to the River House Inn and loaded their belongings onto their bikes. Howie had to pay for the damaged cot before they left, but he felt that the laughs had been well worth the price. Doc was still pretending to be pissed that his late night rendezvous with the fat girl had been spoiled. They cruised down to the main street again and roared back onto Highway 12 and went east toward a small town called Ogdensburg. From there they would go inland toward Tupper Lake, Saranac Lake and on to Lake Placid and all that part of the trip would be on country roads that snake through the mountains. Tommy, Bryan and Joe had been to Lake Placid skiing on a couple of occasions during the winter months, but none of the group had ever been there during the summer tourist season.

It was another beautiful day. The sky had only traces of clouds that hardly affected the sunshine that poured down on them as they continued east. The northern part of New York State was as pretty an area as Joe had seen with the rolling hills of the farming communities that would eventually become mountainous green forests and rock cuts that were accessed by winding, scenic roads. The terrain was very similar to northern Ontario where the different shades of the green forests and the various shades of brown and orange rock formations combined to make them feel that they were truly in the wilds. The motorcycles were all running well and the guys were having a bit of fun taking the gentle curves faster than they should have been. They weren't really racing, just testing each other.

CHAPTER SEVENTEEN

"Jay, wake up!" Juan said as he leaned over and shook the pilot who had taken advantage of an opportunity to get some shut-eye as they cruised northward above the Atlantic. "It's about time to change our heading toward Nova Scotia."

"Look at the sun coming up over the horizon," Jay said as he shook off his tiredness and cleared his head. "It looks like the weather's gonna be just great for us."

Jay and Juan had a smooth flight north, well out over the rolling ocean. The night weather had been absolutely perfect and the Commander 980 Turbojet had performed flawlessly. The men continued to talk in Spanish as the plane approached the latitude where the pilot would have to decrease the altitude from their present twenty thousand feet to a thousand feet above the white caps and then bear to the west. They would have to fly underneath the electronic fence of radar systems that were all along the coast as they flew toward land.

Jay took over the controls, "We'll drop down close to the water and set a bearing for Shelburne, Nova Scotia. We're running right on schedule."

"We should be under any Canadian radar that might be operating," Juan commented.

"I'm sure we will be, but even if we're not, it's well known that the Canadian radar employees are not perfect at recognizing unauthorized planes even on a good day. We've sure slipped a lot of cocaine into eastern Canada over the years."

"We'd better keep a look out because we should be able to see the twin-engine Mitsubushi Turbo Prop from Shelburne any minute. It should already be in the air."

"There it is! Right on time!" Jay yelled excitedly.

Jay and Juan could see the most southerly tip of the Province of Nova Scotia to the northwest, and as they approached the other plane, which was also flying at their low altitude, they slowed the speed of the Commander to coincide with its speed. The Mitsubushi had recently taken off from Shelburne Municipal Airport and the two planes were now on the same course heading toward Maine. The Commander increased its altitude and positioned itself directly above the Mitsubushi and it stayed directly below the Commander and maintained the same rate of speed. As the planes continued toward the coast of Maine, they gained altitude together. Since the two planes were flying one above the other, only *one* plane would show up on any radar in the area. The pilot of the Mitsubushi Turbo Prop, pursuant to his already filed flight plan, made a report to the American authorities as *the plane* entered U.S. airspace, as he was required to do. The planes would meet the mainland, at a point somewhere between Bangor and Portland, in an area where there were no major airports and very little air traffic.

"Well, that seemed to work," Jay said to Juan. "The Mitsubushi has already filed a flight plan with both the Americans and the Canadians that will take us over Maine, New Hampshire, Vermont and into New York State just north of Albany to a small airport called Dunsford Field."

"It seems easy enough," Juan commented. "How long does the Mitsubushi stay with us?"

"We'll keep flying *piggyback* until we're well over the mainland. About a hundred miles northeast of Portland, the Mitsubushi will drop below the radar and land at a small out of the way airstrip called Twin Oaks Airport. We'll continue on to New York State on its already filed flight plan. Late this afternoon, we'll pick it up again for the flight back to Shelburne."

The Commander continued to cross the northern part of the United States south of the Canadian border, over state after state, pursuant to the filed flight plan. It touched down at Dunsford Field by mid-morning without incident. The plane taxied down the gravel runway as Jerry Flippen, all alone in his office, watched with interest as it pulled into a large, private hanger, in the midst of a few smaller buildings that were deserted. He didn't want to know what was going on but he wasn't stupid. The pilots noticed about six cars and vans in the nearest building and there were four small planes sitting on the grass nearby.

As the Commander slowly inched its way through the wide doors of the hanger, Jay could see at least six people. Some were large, burly men and all of them had weapons of different descriptions. The smaller one, closest to the plane, was dressed in black leather and held an Uzi. He seemed to be in charge. Jay turned the Turbojet around inside the hanger to point it toward the doorway and the runway and then shut off both engines. Suddenly, there was silence. Jay opened the main door of the plane and lowered the steps toward the hanger floor. The smaller person in the leather was now quite obviously a woman, a very attractive woman, and she met Jay at the bottom of the steps.

"I'm Beatriz Bracho from Montreal. Which one are you?" She asked in Spanish.

"I'm the pilot, Jay, and this is my co-pilot, Juan," he said as Juan stepped down.

"There are buyers here from a number of U.S. and Canadian cities that are going to pay cash for your cargo. The sooner we get this done and get outta here, the better for everyone."

"What do you want us to do?" Jay asked.

"You can unload the *smack* from the plane by handing it out of the rear door to my men. We'll handle the sale and collect the money. As we get things started, I want you to double-check the money count. I'm sure that you'll want to know approximately how much money we put on the plane for the return flight down south."

"Right," Jay answered, "how long do you think this whole thing will take?"

"Hopefully, we'll be outta here in a couple of hours. The distributors will be allowed in here one at a time, the largest purchaser first,

and so on. I have a couple of men with them in the other hanger to
make sure that competitors don't start fighting with each other while
were trying to do business. We don't need that kind of trouble."

"Let's get started then," Jay said as he turned to begin unloading
the cocaine.

"As soon as we're done, a tanker truck will come in here and
refuel the plane."

Bracho turned and gave orders to her men in French. Jay and
Juan started handing wrapped packages out of the plane to them,
each of which, contained twenty kilos of the white powder, and
they were piled on the ground nearby. Bracho already knew the size
of most of the orders and separated some of the larger ones into
separate piles and ordered her second in command, who Jay and
Juan later found out was her brother, Luis, to bring in the first
buyer with his vehicle and his money.

"She's sure one good-looking *chiquita*," Juan commented to Jay
in the hold of the plane. "Is she the one that's supposed to have a
thing with Pablo Rivas?"

"That's the rumour," Jay answered. "She must know him well or
she wouldn't be here. I also heard that she financed all the arrangements here and in Nova Scotia."

The Cartel Montreal had in fact financed the northern part of
the plan. The money was provided to Polyschuk to secure the use
of Dunsford Field and the arrangements for the flight out of
Shelburne were made and paid for by Bracho, but all of that was
not done for nothing. They were going to be extremely well paid.
Bracho and her eight heavily armed men were there to protect her
own interests as well as those of Pablo Rivas.

As the Commander was unloaded and the cash changed hands,
the cocaine was loaded into the other cars, vans and planes. Jay and
Juan worked closely with Bracho's second-in- command, Luis, a
good-looking man in his mid to late twenties, close to six feet tall.
They counted the money as best they could in the short time that
they had before it was stowed away in the Commander. The cash
that was received from each distributor was put into separate

plastic bags with a code as to whose money it was and how many kilos that amount of money had purchased. A second count would be done later in the presence of Diego Castrillo to be sure that no one had short-changed the Colombians. The plastic bags were then taped shut and stuffed into duffel bags that were put into the plane.

"We seem to be right on schedule," Jay said to Luis.

"Everything is going well. We have men keeping an eye on the distributors in the other hanger so turf wars don't flare up. They're also keeping a lookout for the cops."

"I see that the earlier buyers are still here. Why haven't they left?"

"My sister thinks that it's safer for everyone to leave at the same time after the deal is totally completed. There, this is the last duffel bag of money, number thirteen."

"Luis, get those guys moving who are loading that last van," Beatriz interrupted and Luis immediately went across to the other side of the hanger where the men were working. "Jay, I understand that my cousin, Pinquino, is waiting for you in St. Kitts. When he was in Montreal last, he really liked my Beretta," she said throwing it into the last duffel bag and zipping it up. "Please make sure that he gets it when you get back. Tell him it's a gift from me."

"I'll give it to him as soon as we land."

"What do you have to do to get ready to leave here?"

"If all the money's on board, the plane just has to be refueled and we're ready to go. As soon as we take-off, I'll radio the return flight plan back to Shelburne to the American and Canadian authorities using the Mitsubushi information."

While Jay and Juan made the final arrangements to leave, Bracho and her men made sure that the last of the distributors got loaded and waited with the others until everyone was ready. Bracho had received payment of one hundred kilos of cocaine for contacting Polyschuk, for providing him with the one hundred thousand U.S., for arranging for the Mitsubushi Turbo Prop out of Shelburne and for handling the transaction for the Medellin Cartel at Dunsford Field. It was a good payday for the Cartel Montreal, a couple of million American dollars worth of cocaine for an investment of a couple of hundred thousand dollars U.S. She had also purchased another one hundred kilos at a special discount for a total of two hundred kilos that was split into two shipments. One half went into a false bottom of the trunk and under the backseat of a white Cadillac and the other half into the hold of a four-seater Cessna for the trip back to Montreal.

The white Cadillac left first with Luis and three other passengers. Luis would take the long route home to Montreal by traveling northeast toward the Eastern Townships of Quebec where there are many roads into Canada and few checkpoints. Luis remembered a bar on the Canadian and American border just south of Sherbrooke, Quebec that had a line painted across the center of the floor. The north side of the bar was in Canada and the south side was in the United States. The distributors' vehicles left at varying intervals shortly afterwards. It wasn't long before they had all disappeared into the countryside.

After the refueling was done, Jay completed an all systems check in the cockpit before he fired up the two engines of the Commander. Juan made sure that the thirteen bags of American cash were there and stowed carefully in the back of the plane and that the rear door was properly closed and sealed. They were happy that things had gone so smoothly.

As Juan entered the cockpit and settled himself into his seat, he commented, "I hope the fact that there are *thirteen* duffel bags of money is not some kind of a bad omen."

Beatriz Bracho, and three men, got into the Cessna for the short trip back to Montreal and her plane followed the Commander as it taxied out onto the gravel runway. There were also three other small planes in line waiting to take-off. They would all leave right after the Commander 980 was airborne and on its way back to St. Kitts.

CHAPTER EIGHTEEN

The road to Ogdensburg snaked its way through gentle, rolling hills and colorful, treed rock-cuts along the south shore of the St. Lawrence River. The riverfront was dotted with everything from summer cottages to large estates. The New England and Cape Cod influence on the architecture was everywhere. Halfway through the village, the bikers turned inland away from the river and into the country where grass-covered hills replaced the rocky scenery.

As the riders approached Canton, the hills faded into farmlands and one farm after another sprang up in the countryside. There were herds of black and white cattle in all the fields and they passed a small sign that advised that the area was the *Holstein Capital of America*. Canton was beautifully balanced on the winding banks of the Grasse River that meandered through the middle of the small town.

Awhile later, the group cruised into Colton, the home of St. Lawrence University. The large, spread out campus was dotted with stone, vine-covered buildings that were very old and weathered. Rolling hills appeared again east of the town, but were more tree-covered and there were signs everywhere that indicated that the motorcyclists were in the middle of *Maple Syrup Country*. The landscape began to grow as they rode into the foothills of the Appalachians. They crossed the Raquette River and on through the village of Tupper Lake. The bikers encountered their first road construction for the next ten miles and traveled at a slower pace until Saranac Lake, another resort village. The winding roads began a steady incline into the Adirondacks and the fields turned into dense bush.

Ten or twelve miles further along the highway, two of the largest mountains in the area came into view, Mount Van Hoevenberg and

Whiteface Mountain. A small, calm and serene lake became visible as they went over the top of a hill on the way into Lake Placid. The town had been built on the shores of what everyone thought was *Lake Placid*, but the lake is actually called Mirror Lake. The real Lake Placid is in the mountains outside of town.

As they approached the main street, there was a sign that read *Mirror Lake Inn* and *Cottage Cafe* on the left, so Doc made a quick turn into the resort and the guys followed him. They stopped in front of the cafe that had been built jutting out over the water of the lake. The restaurant and bar actually looked like a cottage, nestled among tall pine trees on the rustic shores of a lake that was so calm that it did in fact look like a mirror as it reflected the surrounding forests and mountains. The bar had just opened for business at eleven o'clock.

There was a long, oak bar just inside the main door, with the seating area for the restaurant further back overlooking the water. A tall, blonde girl was working behind the bar and two men were seated at one end, drinking coffee. The guys all sat down on the stools that were equally spaced and attached to the floor right in front.

"Hi, I'm Jennifer. What can I get you guys?"

"I'll have a Bud," Doc answered and the other guys all nodded agreement. The bartender put six cold ones on the bar and started to open them and hand them out.

"Where are you all from?" Jennifer asked.

"We're from Toronto," Tommy answered. "A few of us have skied here in the busy winter season, but none of us have ever been here during the summer."

"Actually, the summer is our busiest time of year. We get all kinds of people here camping, hiking, biking and just relaxing in one of the many resorts in the area."

Jennifer continued to chat while the Canadians sucked back a couple of beers each. As they finished, they wished her well and headed back out to the motorcycles. The laneway of the Cottage Cafe went directly onto the end of the main street of Lake Placid and the group traveled past all the sporting goods stores, clothing stores, restaurants and bars. They passed by the Olympic Centre and the outdoor speed-skating rink, which had no ice on it that time of year, and on to the far end of town to the first gas station that they came across. They decided to top off their tanks and take a few minutes to decide on which direction to go.

Tommy unfolded his road map on his motorcycle seat and made an announcement. "I'd like to go north to Burlington, Vermont and drop in and see a carpet supplier who lives there. I've been dealing with him over the telephone for a number of years."
Tommy's wife was in the carpet business back in Lindsay.

Mike said, "That's all right with me, I've talked to the guy before too."

As Tommy's accountant, he also knew the man Tommy wanted to visit.

"How are ya' going to get across Lake Champlain to hit Highway 89 to Boston?" Joe asked looking at his own map under the plastic window of his tankbag.

"There are a couple of ferries out of Burlington that only take about half an hour or so to cross the lake. It should be really scenic," Tommy answered.

Bryan added, "I wouldn't mind doing that too. A boat ride sounds great."

"I'd like to go south around the bottom of Lake Champlain and stay in the country instead of traveling on those major highways to Burlington. We can cross the lake at Fort Henry and continue cross-country to Lebanon and pick-up Highway 89 there," Joe explained.

Doc said, "I think I'd sooner do that."

"I'll go with these guys through the country too," Howie decided.

Tommy went on, "Why don't we all just meet in Cape Cod, at the Cape Hyannis Hotel, at five or six o'clock unless we happen to meet along the highway later today?"

Someone back in Lindsay had highly recommended that hotel and the guys had planned to stay there while they were in the Cape Cod area.

Everyone agreed to the new traveling plans and at the last minute, just as Tommy and Mike were getting ready to leave, Bryan changed his mind and decided to stay with the guys that were going to take the more southerly, country route. Tommy and Mike said their goodbyes and headed north toward Burlington. Howie came out of the gas station variety store with eight Buds so they all moved their motorcycles away from the gas pumps and over to a nearby picnic table to enjoy another beer before hitting the road. He put the four extra beers in his saddlebags.

They fired up the Harleys and continued along Highway 73, past the two Olympic Ski Jumps at the east end of Lake Placid, and on toward Lebanon on a winding road through very mountainous terrain and dense bush. About ten minutes later, they went through the village of Keene, back onto the highway, and passed by a number of beautiful, small mountain streams, rivers and lakes. They continued on through Elizabethtown and as they approached Westport, they caught their first glimpse of the southern part of a very calm Lake Champlain.

Westport was a small village at the south end of the lake, on the west shore, and seemed to be the center of a summer resort and tourist area. The bikers then headed south along the shore of Bullaga Bay and on through the village of Crown Point which had been established in 1788. Joe was sure that Samuel de Champlain had stopped on its shores so many years before. Four miles south of the village, the bikes climbed a long, arching rainbow-bridge that spanned the lower end of the lake and they all stopped high on the crest. The view was magnificent in all directions. They could see for miles up the middle of the large lake, with New York State to the west and Vermont to the east.

As soon as they motored off the bridge into Vermont, the others followed Howie into a scenic rest area beside the lake and they all stopped for a leak. All of a sudden, the forests and mountains had vanished and the Vermont side of the lake became flat farmland, but the guys could see a new mountain range stretching into the sky far in the distance. Awhile later, they stopped at Pratt's General Store that was way out in the country in the middle of nowhere. It was kind of a strange place in that the doors were wide open but there was no one working in the store. The front desk had a few bills and some change that appeared to have just been left there by other shoppers. Joe thought, *The people in Vermont must be very trusting!* They all had a chocolate bar and left the money on the counter before they left. After leaving Pratt's, they passed through another town called Brandon, and it was there, where the foothills of the mountains of Vermont started to grow toward the heavens.

It wasn't long before the gang rolled into Rutland, the largest town that they had seen since they had left Canada. It appeared to be the banking and commercial center for the whole area. As they left the east end of the town, they stopped at a gas station for a stretch and some gas. Bryan and Doc went into the grocery store for something else to eat and came back to the gas bar with hand-fulls of donuts.

On the road again, the bikers were on a constant incline into more mountains as they continued east on Highway 4 with Doc in the lead. They passed by the Killington and Pico ski areas where the rugged scenery became unbelievable as the beautiful, bright, summer day added another dimension to the highway as it meandered its way through one small, winding valley after another, with mountains, rivers and streams everywhere.

Twenty or thirty minutes out of Rutland, the group came across one of those wooden, covered, country bridges, for which New England is famous, that spanned a stream that ran along the side of the road. Doc made a right turn off the highway and went right through it. The others followed. Just on the other side of the bridge, Doc came to a T-intersection and turned right again and continued a short distance up a narrow gravel road. He then stopped quickly, in front of an old lane of a deserted farm, and parked his motorcycle. The rest of the guys stopped too.

"Why the hell are we stopping?" Bryan asked.

"I'm gonna piss my pants," Doc yelled as he fumbled with his zipper.

Joe and Bryan joined him for a leak.

Howie reached into his saddlebags and pulled out the four Buds that he had stashed earlier and asked, with one of his silly laughs while the other guys were still standing there relieving themselves, "Does anyone want another beer?"

The quiet valley was a perfect place for a rest and so they sat down in the deep, green and yellow grass beside the split-cedar, rail fence that ran along both sides of the overgrown, unused lane. A hundred feet further up the lane was an old, fallen down, farm-house and small barn that had to be over a hundred years old. Behind the ruins was probably the only cleared field in the mountains that had been farmed by settlers a long time ago. It wasn't a big field, about the size of five football fields, end to end, and maybe two or three wide. There were absolutely no other houses or signs of life in the small, secluded valley that was surrounded by steep, rocky and tree covered mountains. The guys had stopped just a few miles west of Woodstock, Vermont.

CHAPTER NINETEEN

The Commander 980's engines purred as it taxied out onto the gravel runway at Dunsford Field. Juan glanced at his watch and it was just after one-thirty in the afternoon. As Jay increased the power in both engines and took the plane toward lift-off, he thought that he heard the same strange noise that he had heard in the starboard engine back in St. Kitts, but as the plane lifted into the air, the sound disappeared. The plane had taken off to the northwest and immediately after it was airborne, it turned to the northeast. As the plane banked, Juan looked back at the runway and caught a glimpse of Bracho's Cessna that had followed them into the air. The three other planes were still on the ground but in the process of taking off for the return flights back to their home turfs, each with their share of the *white gold*.

Jay and Juan were looking forward to a smooth flight back to the Caribbean since the weather was reported to be perfect for the next twenty-four hours. Jay had filed their return flight plan back to Nova Scotia with the authorities as the plane had left the ground. The plan was to fly back the way they had come and pick up the Mitsubushi in Maine, in the area of Twin Oaks Airport, and then *piggyback* to Shelburne. At that point, the Commander would drop down below the radar once again and head directly west out over the Atlantic. Once the plane got outside *the electronic fence of radar systems* on the eastcoast, the turbojet would climb to its cruising altitude, twenty thousand feet, and fly directly south to St. Kitts. The new cargo of about fifty-five million American dollars in thirteen duffel bags was on its way to the coffers of the Medellin Cartel so that it could continue to produce cocaine and finance the ongoing war against the governments of Colombia and the United States.

"I've never seen this much money in one place," Juan said jokingly, "maybe we should just fly straight on to Europe and live in luxury for the rest of our lives."

"It's a nice thought but there would be no place to go where Pablo wouldn't find us. We would soon be dead and so would our families." Jay knew that Juan was just kidding.

"*Amigo*, I think that we both have enough money to live like kings in Colombia right now. Why the hell do we stay in this risky business when we don't need to anymore?"

"I guess it's the easy money that keeps luring us back or maybe the danger and excitement. We should both be at home with our families instead of risking our lives."

"Pablo has always been good to us, neither one of us would ever screw him. Remember when we were kids? We used to steal those fuckin' tombstones from the cemeteries and resell them on the black market. Pablo could always get the best prices."

"It was a lot of fun in those days. Then Pablo got us smuggling radios, stereos and television sets into the country from Panama to be sold on the black market."

"We really made a lot of money, even back in those days, but we're lucky to be here. Remember those shit-boxes that we flew. They were held together with wire!"

Jay went on reminiscing, "There was no stopping Pablo. We became drug traffickers when he found out how much money could be made selling cocaine. He built that first factory in the Magdalena Valley and made us fly the shit into south Florida."

"We're both lucky we didn't get eaten by alligators in the Everglades. Some hombres did! Remember those terrible places we had to land. They were right in the swamp."

Jay and Juan were both very tired, but in a relaxed sort of way, because they knew that they were nearing the final stages of their trip. Once they got back out over the Atlantic, they could take turns getting some sleep. They were looking forward to it.

***

About fifty miles northeast of Dunsford Field, flying at five thousand feet, the calmness of the cockpit was shattered. Red lights began to flash all over the control panel and the sound of loud buzzers and alarms screamed in the pilots ears. The flashing lights on the panel clearly indicated that the trouble was with the starboard engine, the same one that had been serviced by the mechanic from Puerto Rico.

"There's a trail of black smoke behind us," Juan yelled as the plane banked slightly and he glanced back from the side window of the cockpit.

"We have to shut down the starboard engine," Jay said loudly and clearly, still well in control of the situation. "Where's the closest airport?"

Juan, with pages of charts opened on his lap, answered, "There's a small one called Hanover Airport, just north of a town called Lebanon. It looks to be about thirty or forty miles ahead. Can we get there?"

"We should be able to make it on one engine. Shut down the starboard engine and I'll increase the power on the port side to compensate . . . Now! Christ! There's no more power! I can't get anymore power . . . this fuckin' plane's goin' down."

Jay had pushed the throttle for the port engine ahead full and nothing had happened; there had been no additional thrust. More lights began to flash and the noise from more buzzers and alarms filled the cockpit as a small amount of gray smoke began to filter out of the control panel.

The Commander 980 was losing altitude fast and there was nothing that Jay could do about it. Suddenly, red lights started to flash for the port engine and the black smoke in the cockpit got thicker. The plane didn't have enough power to keep it in the air and certainly not enough to fly to Hanover Airport thirty or forty miles away. Both pilots knew that they were going to have to land the Commander in the mountains below.

"We might have enough power to crash land safely if we can find some place to put this thing down in these damn mountains. We can't call in a Mayday with all this money onboard!" Jay said calmly still in control. "Look for a fuckin' place to land!"

Juan coughed as he looked out from the front and side windows of the cockpit, through what was becoming thick, gray smoke and finally saw something that might save them.

"There! Right there!" He shouted excitedly.
He pointed to a small field that had just come into view as the plane passed between two mountain peaks. Juan had spotted what appeared to be the only field in the whole area. It wasn't very big. It was at the far end of the small valley that lay just ahead of them.

"I see it!" Jay yelled back as he wrestled with the controls and blinked his running and burning eyes in the smoke-filled cockpit. "This is our only fuckin' chance, so hang on!"

As Jay struggled to control the listing plane, he and Juan both knew that the small field with the fallen down farm buildings, near the covered bridge, that had just come into view was their only chance. The plane continued to lose altitude. The last thing the Colombians felt was the extreme impact when the Commander hit the ground in that small field in Vermont.

CHAPTER TWENTY

"What the hell is that noise?" Howie asked.

All the guys were stretched out in the deep grass, sipping their beers, and leaning against the old rail fence in the country lane. They heard something very strange and immediately jumped to their feet and looked up into the air without saying anything.

They could hear a faint whining sound and sputtering noise that seemed to ricochet through the small valley and bounce off the mountainous cliffs that surrounded it. It sounded like an airplane was having engine trouble but they couldn't tell where the noise was coming from. It wasn't long before the sound turned into a high-pitched scream. They continued to search the sky but there was nothing to be seen. The noise kept getting louder and louder as it echoed off the walls of the mountains and filled the valley until the sound totally engulfed them.

"Christ! It's a plane!" Bryan yelled as he pointed to the west end of the small valley. "It's on fire and it's gonna crash!"

All eyes were glued to the sky as the twin-engine plane came into view screaming down the canyon about a hundred yards away from them and about two hundred feet in the air. Black smoke was billowing from one engine and the roar was deafening. They all stood frozen in disbelief as the plane tore past them headed toward the ground at about a thirty-degree angle with the closest wing lower than the other one. They watched in horror as it hit the earth at the far end of the small field with a terrible crunching noise. The plane nosed into the ground once and lost the wing that had hit first which left a large hole in its side, and then it became airborne on the bounce, lifting all kinds of grass, sod and dirt into the air along with it. It then hit the ground a second time sending debris flying in all directions. It finally came to rest in a mangled mess at the far end of the field engulfed in a of dust cloud. All the guys had expected an explosion of some kind. It never happened. Thick, black smoke and debris filled the air above the wreckage and all of a sudden the small valley became quiet and peaceful once again.

The four guys just stood there frozen for a few seconds after the plane stopped moving.

"Jesus Christ! We'd better get the hell over there to see if anyone needs help!" Joe broke the silence as he ran toward his Harley.

They all dropped their beer cans in the long grass on the run, fired up the bikes and raced down the gravel road, past the entrance to the covered bridge, toward the crash site. As Joe, Doc and Howie stopped their motorcycles on the side of the road right opposite to what was left of the plane, Bryan's bike flew past them. The three of them jumped the ditch, climbed the fence and ran across the field toward the smoking remains of the Commander. Bryan had found an opening in the fence further down the road and roared across the field and stopped his Harley right next to the wreckage just as the other three arrived on foot.

There was a trail of scattered airplane parts and pieces of metal leading up to where the main part of the plane had stopped. One half of the cockpit was missing and there was large hole in the port side of what was left of the plane. The left wing had been completely torn off and about fifteen or twenty feet of fuselage had gone with it. The interior of the plane was totally exposed. There were no visible flames, just smoke rising into the air from the cockpit and from the one engine that was still attached to the plane. Debris was scattered all over the place and there were pieces of paper strewn everywhere.

"There's the body of a man in the cockpit with half of his head missing," Doc said as he backed away from that part of the wreckage. "I'm sure he's dead!"

They all had to have a look for themselves and sure enough, the blood covered dead man was still buckled into his cockpit seat on the starboard side of the plane.

"There's no doubt he's dead," Howie, the licensed undertaker concluded.

"There's another body over here!" Bryan yelled as he bent down over another cockpit seat that had been thrown about forty feet from the wreckage.

"This poor son-of-a-bitch looks like he's dead too," Howie observed. "There's no pulse and he doesn't seem to be breathing. Look at the way his arms and legs are all bent."
The upper part of the man's body looked like raw meat.

The guys were at the crash site for only three or four minutes during which time they decided that there was nothing they could do for the two pilots. All of a sudden it dawned on them. The paper that was all over the field wasn't just paper, it was money, American money, currency, bills, cash and it was everywhere! There were five or six duffel bags in the grass near the plane and three or four of them had been ripped open during the crash and were almost empty. Their contents were scattered all over the place.

"Look at the fuckin' money!" Doc said. "Why the hell would a small plane, like this one, be carrying bags of money?"
"All these duffel bags seem to be filled with cash! I've never seen so much money in all my life!" Bryan said as he picked up a couple of the open bags and shook them.

"Let's get the hell to a telephone and call the police," Joe suggested. "There's nothing we can do to help these two guys, they're dead."

"What about all this money?" Bryan asked holding up one bag that had been ripped open but still had some money in it and one bag that was still intact.

"We may as well grab a few bucks while we're here. These guys aren't gonna miss it!" Howie said as he held up a couple of handfuls of American hundreds.

"If you fuckin' guys touch any of that money, we'll all be in serious trouble. The money has to be drug related and the police will probably be here any minute," Joe explained.

Doc added, "Leave the damn money. Let's get the hell outta here and call the cops!"

Joe went on to warn Bryan and Howie because they were reluctant to put the money back where they had found it, "Even if this is drug money, you guys will be stealing it if you take it! Have you any idea how long the jail terms are for theft here in the United States? Let's get the hell outta here and call the police. Woodstock is just down the road!"

Joe, Doc, and Howie ran back across the field toward their motorcycles that were parked on the roadside. As they ran, they heard Bryan fire up his Harley that was near the wreckage and head back across the field toward the opening in the fence. As the three guys traveled back through the covered bridge, Bryan pulled in behind them. They turned right on Highway 4 and raced toward the town of Woodstock to report the location of the crash to the authorities.

They were doing close to ninety miles an hour in no time, and as they neared the outskirts of Woodstock, two police cruisers flew past them with sirens howling going in the direction of the crash site. An ambulance with its lights flashing and siren blaring was not far behind. There was no point in the gang rushing any longer, so as the guys slowed their bikes down to the speed limit, Joe pulled his Harley up beside Doc's bike to talk to him.

"I think we should just keep going. There's nothing we can do back there except get tied up for a few hours giving statements to the police," Joe yelled.

"You're probably right. We may as well head straight for Cape Cod," Doc yelled back over the roar of the wind and the engines.

Doc turned back toward Howie and to Bryan, who was riding last, gave a forward wave, and increased the speed of his bike to the usual cruising rate. Not one of them had been able to take their minds off the money that had been scattered all over the field.

It wasn't long before they cruised into Woodstock, a small Vermont town that was in the middle of nowhere. It seemed to be caught up in the tourist industry in some way because there were a substantial number of tour buses stopped in front of an assortment of large older homes throughout the town. A billboard pointed out to the bikers that the little town had been deeply involved with the *Underground Railway* during the Civil War and tourists continued to visit the homes that had hidden the slaves who had escaped to the north so many years before.

An hour later, after they got onto Highway 93, they stopped at a Mobil gas station for a leak and some gas. They all wondered whether or not Mike and Tommy had passed that point yet in their trip to Cape Cod, but knew that it was unlikely that they would bump into them on the highway that afternoon.

"Did you see all that money scattered around the field?" Howie asked again. "I've never seen so much money all in one place."

Bryan added, "Those guys on that plane must have been involved in some kind of huge drug deal. Why else would there be so much cash onboard?"

"The pilot in the cockpit looked like he had a dark complexion from the side of his face that you could still see. He looked South American," Doc recalled

"I only managed to pick up twenty-eight one hundred dollar bills before we got outta there," Howie bragged flashing a handful of money.

"That's just fuckin' perfect!" Joe said. "It's too bad we didn't go back to the crash site to help out. If the police had found that money on you, we'd all be in jail right now."

"There was so much money, I'm sure that they won't miss some of it," Bryan said in Howie's defense. "We should've all taken a fuckin' bag."

"Bryan, you're crazy! Howie *stole* that money! You can end up in jail down here for stealing money," Joe added to let Howie know that he was pissed.

"If we'd gone back, we'd still be there giving statements to the police about what we saw and we probably wouldn't get to Hyannis tonight," Doc commented.

"Let's get the hell back on the road. I can't take it back now. I'll buy dinner tonight."

The Harleys pulled out of the service centre and back onto the freeway. The traffic was moving well and the impressive Boston skyline soon came into view. The rush hour traffic slowed them down through the city as they passed the modern skyscrapers and the large, busy harbour that was filled with commercial ships and pleasure boats. Joe thought that he caught a glimpse of the exact location where the Boston Tea Party had taken place so long ago, but he couldn't really be sure. It was nearly five-thirty by the time Howie led them off Highway 93 at the exit to Highway 3 that went straight to Cape Cod.

The motorcycles began to travel at a much slower pace because of the heavier traffic and congestion as they went over the Sagamore Bridge, a large, steel, rainbow-shaped structure that spanned the Sagamore Canal, which appeared to be the official entrance to Cape Cod. They continued to motor on through Buzzards Bay, Sandwich and Barnstable and on to Hyannis, the playground of the Kennedy family. The traffic was bumper to bumper all the way to the Cape Hyannis Hotel & Resort and it was after six o'clock when the bikers pulled in under the canopy that covered the main entrance.

They soon found out that Tommy and Mike had already arrived and had booked three adjoining rooms on the main floor of the back building at the far end of the inner courtyard. The friendly desk clerk provided two sets of key-cards for each room and gave directions to the parking area at the east end of the complex.

The two wings of the sprawling hotel were joined at the end by a laundry facility with a walk-through to the inner courtyard where the motorcycles could be parked in a private area outside of the three rooms. The guys coasted their bikes through the opening in the building, so the noise of the engines wouldn't bother any of the other guests, and found the two Hondas parked just inside a beautiful garden area. As the group parked their bikes beside the bikes, Mike came out of the patio door of the first room on the left with a drink in his hand.

"What the hell kept you guys? We've been here for hours and the party's almost over."

Howie answered, "You guys should have been with us, you missed all the excitement!"

The four newcomers wandered into Mike and Tommy's room to see what they were doing and to fill them in on the highlight of their afternoon.

"You guys should've seen the plane crash! We were sitting in this field in the mountains just havin' a beer and this small jet came right over our heads, makin' all kinds of noise, and crashed right beside us!" Bryan blurted out, quite obviously still excited.

Doc added, "You should've seen the mess. The plane was in pieces and there were bodies and money everywhere!"

"What the hell are you talking about?" Tommy asked with a puzzled look on his face.

"The one pilot that was still in the wreck was nearly decapitated and the other one landed in the field still strapped in his cockpit seat. Both of them were killed. There was American money scattered all over the crash site!" Joe explained as he got caught up in the excitement.

"You guys are full of shit!" Mike stated.

"What the hell do you think this is?" Howie asked holding up the stolen money.

"I need a bloody drink," Joe announced.

He walked toward the makeshift bar that Tommy and Mike had set up on the dresser next to the television set. He threw Doc a cold beer, poured Bryan a gin and soda and got a scotch and water for Howie and himself.

While Joe acted as bartender and everyone was in Tommy and Mike's room, Bryan decided to unpack his bike and put his stuff in the room that he and Joe were going to share. He untypically made sure that all his personal things were neatly put away in the closet. He rejoined the group a few minutes later.

While they had a few more drinks, the story highlights of the day were more fully explained to the two guys that hadn't been there. They were really sorry that they hadn't gone with the others since their trip to Burlington had been a bust because the guy that they had gone to see was out of town on vacation. They had just stopped somewhere for lunch, taken the ferry across Lake Champlain and then traveled straight through to the Cape Hyannis and had arrived late in the afternoon.

The more Bryan drank, the more excited he became about the plane crash and the American money. He related all aspects of the crash scene to Tommy and Mike in full living color. He expressed real regret that everyone hadn't taken a duffel bag of money when they left the crash site because it was likely drug money. He also reasoned that no one would have seen them take it because they were the only ones at the scene. He also kept harping on the fact that he really needed a score of some kind, like finding a large amount of untraceable money in a field, to sort out all of his financial problems back home.

CHAPTER TWENTY-ONE

In the early afternoon, right after the Commander had taken off from Dunsford Field, Diego Castrillo had received a telephone call from Beatriz Bracho that confirmed all had gone well in New York State and the plane had left on schedule with about fifty-five million American dollars onboard. He had immediately summoned a couple of his young girls to spend the afternoon with him to celebrate and then had continued to relax into the evening. He had felt quite proud of himself for having come up with such a brilliant plan. He knew that he would be well rewarded as soon as the cash started to flow back to the cartel coffers. During the beautiful Colombian evening, Castrillo received another telephone call from Montreal that shattered all of his dreams and put him into a total state of shock.

"*Tel lo dire despues de quete hayas sentado!*" Beatriz blurted out as a warning to Castrillo as he answered his cell. "Are you sitting down? I have some bad news. The Commander has crashed in the mountains of Vermont. It was just on the news here in Canada."

After a long silence, as Castrillo tried to recover from a slight dizzy spell as all the blood rushed from his head, he asked, "Are you sure it was our fuckin' plane?"

"It had to be the Commander. It was in the same area and the broadcast said that the authorities found millions of dollars in cash at the crash site."

"What the hell will happen next? What about the pilots?" Castrillo asked in a daze.

"The news said that one of them was killed and the other one is in critical condition and has been rushed to a hospital in Albany, in

New York State. That's all I know at this point."

There was another long pause as the news from Beatriz started to sink in.

"I can't fuckin' believe it! It's one damn thing after another! See what you can find out about the crash. Get someone to go and see whichever pilot is alive. Right now! Find out what the hell happened and get back to me as soon as you can!"

Castrillo hung up and slumped back into his chair. He slowly dialed Pinguino's number to delay the call to his boss. He knew that Pablo Rivas was going to be more than pissed. He had absolutely no idea how he was going to tell him what had happened.

Prior to receiving Castrillo's call, Pinguino had been pacing back and forth in the stifling heat on the blacktop tarmac outside the rented hanger at St. Kitts International Airport for hours. His flowered, blue and yellow, short-sleeved shirt and white pants were drenched in perspiration as the sun was just setting in the pink western sky. It was another one of those cloudless evenings in the Caribbean and Pinguino knew that the clear night would soon be full of thousands of bright twinkling stars as he looked for the Commander in the northern sky. Jay and Juan were long overdue. Pinguino knew that he would be hearing from Castrillo at any moment because his call to him in Colombia was late.

"What the hell is going on in St. Kitts?" Castrillo asked in a harsh tone.

"I've been here at the airport for the last four hours waiting for the Commander. Why?"

"The fuckin' plane has crashed up north!" He yelled into the phone. "It went down with more than fifty-five million American dollars onboard!"

"What the hell happened? How are Jay and Juan? Are they hurt?"

"Who the fuck cares! The plane went down with fifty-five million dollars onboard and it's all been lost. Pablo is going to kill someone!"

"Settle down! Tell me what the hell happened to the pilots," Pinguino excitedly asked again and immediately wished that he hadn't used that tone of voice with his boss.

"Fifty-five million dollars is spread all over a farmer's field somewhere in the mountains of Vermont and you want me to fuckin' settle down! Someone is going to die!"

Pinguino asked again in a better tone, "*Lo Siento,*" he apologized. "What happened?"

"I just got a call from Montreal. The crash was reported on the evening news. The Commander went down in Vermont about a half an hour after it took off. There was money scattered all over the field where it crashed!"

"Are Jay and Juan all right?"

"One of them was killed and one is still alive, but I don't know which one. The news said that the one that is alive has been taken to a hospital in Albany."

"What happened to all the money?"

"What the hell do you think happened to the money? It either got burned up in the crash or the authorities have it!"

"Remember what I told you yesterday! The starboard engine of the plane sounded funny to Jay and Juan before they left St. Kitts so I flew a turbojet mechanic in from Puerto Rico to service it before it flew north. He worked on it for eight or ten hours, but he couldn't find anything the matter with it," Pinguino explained once again.

"Have the bastard killed! *Qulero que lo hagas!* Now!" Castrillo yelled into phone and hung up.

CHAPTER TWENTY-TWO

The Cape Hyannis Hotel & Resort had about three hundred rooms and a convention centre with all the usual amenities. A restaurant and nightclub overlooked a very colorful pool area, a grass-hut pool bar, the first fairway of a golf course and a two-acre pond filled with cattails. A tower of eight floors and the convention rooms were at the west end. To the east, there were two wings of rooms, each two stories, built slightly bowed toward each other with a beautiful garden full of green trees, multi-colored flowers and plants and a putting green between them. The guys were staying on the main level of the rear building, in the last three rooms, at the far easterly end of the gardens.

After a few cocktails, the rest of the new arrivals unloaded their gear and put it away in their rooms. Doc and Howie took the middle room that had a connecting doorway into the room that Bryan had already claimed. As Joe entered his room, he was shocked that Bryan had put all his things away. It really wasn't like him to be so neat. Bryan decided to have a quick shower while Joe unpacked his belongings for at least a two-night stay.

"Turn the television to a local news channel to see if there's anything about the plane crash," Joe yelled to Howie and Doc through the open door between the rooms.

He heard the channels start to change so he left the rest of his things on the bed and picked up his scotch and water and joined the guys in the other room.

"There isn't any news on right now, just this country station," Howie advised.

As they watched a Shania Twain video, there was a knock on the door from the interior hallway. Joe was standing, so he answered it. "What's happening?" Joe asked Tommy and Mike as they came through the door.

They had both already showered and changed and were ready for the evening.

"We're going up to the restaurant in the hotel for dinner," Mike replied as they went on through the patio door and headed toward the pool and main part of the complex.

"Save us a seat, we'll be along in about fifteen minutes," Doc replied as he got up, went into his bathroom and the shower started almost immediately.

"I'm going see if Bryan's out of our shower yet," Joe said and took his drink.

Bryan was just coming out of the bathroom in the nude. *What a pretty roommate*, Joe thought. He looked like he could wrestle in the WWF. Joe was glad that he didn't have to share a bed with the big guy, not only because of his size, but he also snored. It took Joe about five minutes to have a quick shower and shave and he was putting on his underwear when Howie yelled.

"McConnell, get the hell in here, the news is on!"

The four of them found a place to sit and stayed glued to the television set until the NBC News got to the story about the plane crash in Vermont.

Tom Brokaw advised, "At approximately two o'clock this afternoon, a twin-engine Commander Turbo Jet crashed in a field just west of Woodstock, Vermont, killing the co-pilot and severely injuring the pilot. When Sheriff's Officers arrived at the scene, they found the crash area littered with money. One of our people in the area advised that the authorities also found a number of bags of money at the crash site. There's a good possibility that the incident is drug related. The FBI and the DEA are jointly investigating and further information will be made available as it is released."

"That must have been the pilot on the ground still in his seat. It sounds like he wasn't killed after all," Joe surmised. "Howie, you'd better take a refresher course in undertaking."

Howie commented, "He sure as hell looked dead to me. I couldn't feel his pulse in his neck or his wrist or see any breathing movement in his chest."

"Most of the bodies that you worked on as an undertaker didn't have a pulse, maybe you don't know what one feels like," Joe said with a laugh.

"It'll be interesting to hear the next news report to see what this crash was really all about," Doc added. "It had to be some kind of a big drug deal."

"Enough of that shit," Bryan said as he went to the makeshift bar, "let's party!"

Bryan was in a great mood, more relaxed than he had been since the trip began. He was ready to go out for the evening and have some fun. The others joined Bryan for another drink and Joe went back to his room to get dressed and put the rest of his things away.

"You smell like a hooker!" Bryan remarked as Joe came back through the door and the fragrance of his aftershave permeated the air.

Doc answered Bryan with a laugh, "You loon, you're the only one in the room that would know what kind of perfume hookers wear!"

Joe continued, "Tommy Hilfiger's feelings would be hurt if he heard you talk like that!"

"Are we going to go for dinner or what?" Howie asked with a laugh, "I can't wait to spend some of this money I found."

"Piss on it, let's have another drink," Doc replied. "It's too late to eat. You can buy dinner tomorrow night."

They sat around and traded stories for the next hour or so, and once again, discussed the day's events. Bryan got more and more excited when the discussion centered on the plane crash and all the money that was lying around. He was still adamant that they all should have scooped as much money as they could have got their hands on. He felt that if it was in fact drug money, no one would ever know how much was there because they were the first ones at the crash site. They also discussed plans for the next day. The consensus was that they would spend another full day in Cape Cod and bike out to Provincetown, at the most northerly end of the spit, and leave for Atlantic City the following day. Tommy and Mike came back through the patio door.

"We ate at a table for six and you fuckin' assholes didn't even show up," Mike bitched.

"You eat enough for six anyway! Isn't it time for you to have a shit yet?" Bryan replied.

"I'm gonna go and have a *Bryan Moyle* right now you asshole," Mike said as he left the room through the interior hall door and slammed it on his way out.

"We couldn't get organized," Doc explained to Tommy, "and we listened to the news broadcast about the plane crash. The plane had something to do with drugs and the pilot, the one that was thrown from the plane still in the cockpit seat, is alive."

Bryan commented, "It'll be great to get an update tomorrow."

"What's happening in the lounge?" Joe directed the question to Tommy.

"The place is nearly full. There must be a couple of small conventions in the hotel."

"Are there any gals that might want to slow-dance?" Bryan asked Tommy.

"There's no point in me going dancing," Doc stated as he remembered the fat girl with the big boobs and the broken cot, "if I get a date, Howie'll just try to steal her from me anyway."

Everyone laughed at Doc's comment and Tommy slipped out through the patio door to his room to tell Mike to get a move on. When they returned, all the guys except Bryan went out into the darkness of the gardens and wandered up toward the sound of the music. Bryan stayed behind to lock the patio door in his room and lock the interior door between the two rooms. He then exited through the main door into the inner hallway and made sure that the door was locked behind him before he headed up the hall to join the others in the main part of the hotel.

***

The lounge was packed. A disc jockey in a corner booth kept the music blaring and the dance floor, that had tables and chairs all around it, was full. About two hundred people were packed in shoulder to shoulder. The bikers squeezed their way through the crowd toward a spot at the end of the long bar and ordered a round of drinks. As luck would have it, there were eight gals seated, right nearby, at two tables that had been pulled together.

Doc made Howie promise not to steal his date if he happened to get one that night. They were all feeling no pain, especially Bryan, who walked right over to the table full of girls.

"Anybody want to slow dance?" He asked with a big smile on his face.

At his size, he should have scared the hell out of the girls, but he didn't. He had a taker.

"As long as you don't step on my toes," a cute, little brunette answered.

As she got up from her chair on the far side of the table, the guys noticed that she was quite attractive. The two of them headed for the dance floor. It was hard to believe, but Bryan was actually a great dancer and was extremely light on his feet.

That's all it took to get the party going. Joe and Doc picked a couple of partners from the table and joined Bryan and his date on the floor. Howie, Tommy and Mike sat down with the rest of the girls in the chairs that had been vacated. The girls were on a one-week vacation and hailed from Buffalo. None of the guys held that against them. The girls got a kick out of Bryan because he was totally pissed and he was a big spender. He bought them drinks all evening. At about one o'clock, Tommy and Mike called it a night and left for their room.

Bryan tried to trick a couple of the gals into going back to his room for a nightcap. He was unsuccessful. As he picked up their final tab of the evening, the girls promised that they would be back there the next night. Doc and Howie walked ahead and went out into the dimly lit gardens and wandered down toward the rooms. Joe decided that he had better accompany Bryan as he staggered toward the inner hallway of their wing.

Joe mentioned to Bryan, "You must have spent a fortune on those girls tonight!"

"Fuck it, it's only money. Besides, we're on holidays," he slurred.

"Don't spend all your money before we get to Atlantic City," Joe laughed.

"There's absolutely no chance of that happening!" Bryan mumbled drunkenly, as he continued to wobble down the hall.

Joe was the first one into the room and immediately opened the patio door and the door between the two rooms and wondered why Bryan had locked them before he had left earlier.

"We just banged on Tommy and Mike's door but they wouldn't open it. I guess they're in bed for the night," Howie said as he and Doc came into the room off the patio.

"Let's have a nightcap!" Doc suggested and went straight for the bottle of Courvoisier that was on the dresser next to Bryan's bed. "Somebody grab some glasses from our room."

"I'll have one of those too," Bryan slurred as he flopped into one of the chairs.

"Bring me a cold beer, Howie," Joe called from a horizontal position on his bed.

"You sure as hell spent a lot of money tonight you loon," Howie said to Bryan. "What did you think was gonna happen, you were gonna get lucky?"

"Why didn't you spend some of that money you picked up in the field, you cheap bastard?" Bryan slurred, as he got up and poured himself a water glass full of Courvoisier.

"It's not my fault that you assholes were too drunk to eat," Howie responded.

"You should've picked up a lot more of that fuckin' money and we could have had a great holiday," Bryan said as he took a large gulp of the liqueur and immediately started to heave.

He coughed and was almost sick to his stomach, but managed to choke it down.

"Like I told you before, Bryan, all we needed was one of you ass-holes to steal some of that money and we could've ended up spending our holidays in jail," Joe reiterated.

"Why don't you get fuckin' serious!" Bryan slurred in an obnoxious tone that indicated that he was getting into one of his argumentative moods. "It's absolutely none of your fuckin' business if Howie, me or anyone else picked up money from that plane crash."

"Screw you!" Joe answered showing signs of too much booze too.

"Maybe you'll just have to fuckin' get lost then!" Brian slurred looking directly at Joe and as drunk as he was, he all of a sudden became very serious. "I gotta tell you guys somethin' but ya' have to promise that it'll go no further than this room."

He stood up and wobbled to the patio door, shut and locked it, and pulled the curtain closed. He then closed and locked the door between the two rooms. Bryan was totally bombed and no one really knew what the hell he was doing so Doc kidded him.

"Did you fall in love with that cute little brunette?" Doc kidded.

Howie continued, "You're gonna stay here the rest of the week with your new sweetie and take her back to Buffalo on your motorcycle?"

"Would you guys quit screwing around," Bryan slurred once again in a serious tone. "You have to promise to keep this confidential . . . and I really mean it!"

They all laughingly agreed to be very secretive about whatever it was that he was going to share with them. Bryan got up and staggered to the closet and pulled out what looked like a tank bag that had been hidden under his saddlebags on the floor of the closet and he threw it into the middle of his bed. None of the guys had any idea what he was doing. Bryan immediately unzipped the fairly large bag and dumped its contents onto the bed.

"Jesus Christ!" Doc exclaimed almost dumbfounded.

"What the hell is it?" Joe asked as a terrible thought crossed his mind.

Howie was too shocked to even speak.

In the center of Bryan's bed was a large pile of cash! There were a number of clear, plastic-wrapped packages full of neat piles of

American money and the specific denominations had all been separated into their own taped piles within the plastic. Leave it to
Bryan to have taken one of the larger duffel bags from the crash site.

"Bryan, that's the money from the fuckin' plane! Are you nuts?"
It was Doc as thoughts of stolen money and police, all kinds of
police, ran through his mind.

Bryan, still slurring, explained, "It was right there on the ground
beside my bike, I couldn't just leave it there. How much do you
think there is on the bed?"

As he finished that comment, he spread out the plastic covered
packages of money on the bed and picked up a couple of them. As
Bryan moved the packages, a black handgun became visible from
under the money.

"Bryan, you're out of your fuckin' mind!" Joe finally yelled quite
obviously under the influence as well. "You've stolen that money! It
doesn't belong to you! Not only are you going to be in a lot of trouble, you're going to get all of us involved in this mess too."

"Fuck you!" Bryan yelled defiantly. "It's all unmarked drug
money and no one knows that I took it! We were the only ones
there! Remember! You guys didn't even know I took it!"

"Bryan's right, it's really got nothing to do with you
McConnell," Doc interjected half pissed, "you didn't have anything
to do with taking it so quit worrying!"

"Maybe we all should've taken a bag when we had the chance!"
Howie added.

"You guys are all fuckin' crazy," Joe said, "this money was stolen
and the rest of us were there when it was stolen. We can all end up
in jail!" He looked directly at Bryan. "If you don't agree to return
the money to the authorities tomorrow, I'm outta here. I don't want
to be anywhere near you, that money or all the trouble you're going
get yourself into!"

"We may as well at least count it and see how much there is,"
Doc suggested in an attempt to settle everyone down.

Joe was sitting on the edge of his bed by then, very close to the
money and the gun. The black gun originally looked like a thirty-

eight, but as he picked it up, he quickly recognized it as a nine mil-
limeter, Beretta 92F. Joe immediately emptied the handgun. It was
fully loaded with fifteen shells in the clip and one in the chamber.
Joe put the gun and ammo on the dresser while the others hovered
over the money on Bryan's bed.

"It looks like there are mostly hundreds, some fifties and lots of
twenties and tens," Howie exclaimed.

"Give me a hand sorting it out before we try to count it," Bryan
slurred. "We'll probably need a pen and paper to keep track of it."

Doc reached for the light between the two beds and turned it on
and without anyone realizing it, the whole group started to speak in
very low voices, almost whispers. The numerous packages of different denominations were spread out on the bed, and as the piles of
money grew in the sorting process, all the guys seemed to sober up.

"There must be at least a million dollars here!" Bryan almost
whispered, as the large disorganized pile of money in the middle of
the bed became smaller organized piles.

Joe was still pissed off about the whole thing, but he was pretty
well drunk and got caught up in the excitement of all that money
lying there.

"I'll get some paper and a pen." He said as he opened the drawer in
the bedside table.

"It looks like the denominations are in bundles of one hundred.
This stack of hundreds seems to be ten thousand dollars!" Doc
observed. "There's more than a million dollars here!"

Each of the piles of different denominations was counted carefully and Joe, seated at the patio table, jotted down the figures as
the others gave them to him.

"Christ! There are ten plastic bags of hundreds alone, that's
about four million dollars!" Howie whispered as they all stared at
each other in disbelief.

The excitement continued to grow and began to fill the room.
It took them over half an hour to finish counting the various packages of money.

"You're not gonna fuckin' believe this!" Joe said trying to control his excitement. "The total count is six million and eight hundred thousand American dollars!"

No one said a thing. They just sat there staring at the money. They were converting the amount into Canadian which made the total even more shocking, over ten million dollars.

Howie broke the silence, "Now what?"

"Who wants another drink?" Doc asked as he opened the door to the adjoining room, went in, locked his patio door and then went to the bar and filled the orders.

"Christ! Nearly seven million American! Now what do I do with it?" Bryan asked.

He was not looking for advice. His mind was spinning. He thought that the money would solve all of his financial problems. He obviously wasn't thinking straight or he would have realized that he could just take the money, disappear and forget all his problems.

"Bryan, I think that the only choice you have is to give the money to the authorities before you get yourself and the rest of us in trouble with the law," Joe said.

"You heard the fuckin' news, it's drug money. No one knows that I even have it so why the hell should I give it back!" Bryan responded as his drunken temper flared once again.

"Bryan, trust me! It could be drug money, bank robbery money, lost money or whatever; it's not your money to keep. If you keep it, you're stealing it and you can go to jail!"

"What a bunch of bull shit!" Bryan snarled. "There was money all over the bloody field and there was nobody there but us. We all should've taken a fuckin' bag! There's no way that anyone knows that we were at the crash site or how much money there was!"

Howie stuck his nose in and riled Bryan even more. "Maybe Joe's right. Somebody could miss that much money and you could be in serious trouble!"

"That isn't gonna fuckin' happen," Bryan argued again, "because nobody knows that I have the money except you guys. We were the only ones at the crash site!"

"Bryan, that's not the point," Joe added, "you've never stolen

anything before, why would you start now? You're not a thief! You
have to make the necessary arrangements to give it back to the
authorities before you're charged with some criminal offense and
end up in jail."

"Screw you guys!" Bryan slurred again getting madder by the
minute. "You're all a bunch of assholes. We should've taken all the
fuckin' money we could carry because there's no way that anyone
can link us to the plane crash. We were gone before anyone else
got there!"

"Bryan, you're out of your fuckin' mind!" Joe answered getting
tired of it all.

"Leave him alone until morning. Nothing can be resolved while
we're all pissed. Does anyone want another drink?" Doc said to
change the tone of the discussion.

"I'm not drinking with you assholes, in fact, I don't even like
traveling with ya'!" A drunken Bryan growled in a mood that he
might take a swing at someone.

As he started to pack the money back into the open duffel bag, Joe
put the shell and the clip back into the Beretta, put on the safety,
and threw it into the bag with the money before Bryan zipped it up.
Bryan then took the duffel bag and staggered toward the closet and
made a drunken effort to hide it under his saddlebags and other
belongings. As soon as his money was hidden, he closed the closet
door and went directly into the bathroom.

"I'm going to bed. If you pricks are have'n another drink, go
into the other fuckin' room."

The other guys got up and went through the connecting door into
Howie and Doc's room, turned on the television and poured one
more nightcap. None of them needed another drink but after all the
excitement, they weren't ready to sleep. They had just found places
to sit when the door between the two rooms slammed shut with
a loud thud.

"If that loon locks the bloody door, I'll have to stay here with
you guys tonight."

"He's sure pissed off at all of us," Howie said.

Doc explained, "It's not like Bryan to get mad at everyone when he drinks. I think that he's having trouble dealing with the financial pressures back home."

"He'll probably be all right in the morning," Howie said.

"He's sure adamant that he wants to keep that money but maybe he'll come to his senses when he sobers up," Joe added.

"I'm not so sure there'll ever be any repercussions if he keeps the money. It's a real long shot to think that anyone would link our group to the crash site. Maybe he's right, he should keep it," Doc commented. "Maybe we all should've taken a bag!"

"Is it worth going to jail if for some reason someone does tie him, and even us, to the plane crash?" Joe asked and no one answered him. "We were with him when he stole it. We probably have some sort of legal obligation to report the theft to the authorities and if we don't, we all become parties to the crime. We had better talk him into reconsidering this whole thing in the morning before the rest of us are in trouble too."

The three of them finished their last drink and decided that it was time to go to bed. Joe got up and tried the door into his room and Bryan had left it unlocked. He said goodnight to the other guys and went into his own bathroom. As Joe finished getting ready for bed, Bryan, who was snoring loudly, came to life.

He was still sound asleep, but lifted his head off his pillow, looked right at Joe and said, "You guys are a bunch of fuckin' assholes!"

His head went right back down on his pillow and he continued to snore.

Joe's head was spinning with the events of the day and Bryan's drunken snoring filled the room. He tossed and turned for so long that he wondered if he would ever get to sleep even though it was almost four in the morning. His mind turned to Trizzi as it did every night before he fell asleep. He wondered where she was and what she was doing. He also wondered if she ever thought of him. His thoughts of her beautiful face and great body had some sort of calming effect on him that finally helped him fall into a deep sleep.

CHAPTER TWENTY-THREE

Castrillo had to endure the wrath of Pablo Rivas for the crash of the Commander in Vermont. No matter the explanation, the loss of the plane, the pilots and the money was Castrillo's fault. They had spoken on the telephone on four occasions and Rivas was out for blood. He was really pissed because he had waited months for Castrillo to put his new foolproof plan into effect and the cartel was hungry for cash. The war with the government was taking its toll. The loss of fifty-five million American dollars when it was so close to being in their hands also made Pablo Rivas and the Medellin Cartel the laughing-stock of their competitors.

Castrillo was ordered to contact Beatriz Bracho to have her find out exactly what had happened and report back. She was to find out where the pilot was and get someone to his bedside to speak to him as soon as possible. Castrillo was impatiently waiting for a report.

Beatriz Bracho hadn't waited for orders. She had immediately sent her brother Luis, and another man, Fernando Santiago, from Montreal to Albany, as soon as she had heard about the crash. She knew exactly what Pablo Rivas would want her to do. Her relationship with the *boss of all bosses* was more than just business and she knew that she would have to report directly to him. During her first report to Castrillo, she already knew where the plane had gone down and that one of the pilots, although seriously hurt, was still alive in a hospital in Albany. It was Beatriz's second report to Castrillo a few hours later that was much more informative.

"My brother is in Albany and has found out that Jay is in a guarded room at Albany General Hospital. He is reported to be in and out of consciousness."

Castrillo asked, "Has anyone been able to get in to see him yet?"

"I called Ted Gardner, our New York lawyer, and asked him to get to Albany quickly and meet with Jay, find out exactly what happened and represent him regarding any charges."

"What did he find out?"

"Jay told Gardner that, shortly after take-off, the plane lost one of its engines totally and then lost power in the other one. It started to lose altitude immediately. They couldn't make it to the closest airport so they attempted to crash land in Vermont but they had a hell of a time finding a suitable place to put the plane down in the mountains. Jay had been told that Juan had been killed instantly in the cockpit, but he had been thrown clear of the wreckage and landed in the field still strapped to his cockpit seat. Jay has a lot of broken bones and internal injuries but the doctors think that he'll be out of danger soon," Beatriz continued.

"What the hell happened to all the money that was onboard?" Castrillo asked.

"Jay doesn't remember anything about the crash itself, he must have blacked out, but when he was lying in the field near the wreckage he kept going in and out of consciousness. He vaguely remembers that there was money scattered all over the field because some of the duffel bags had ripped open during the crash. He thinks the authorities have most of the money."

"What the hell did he mean by *most* of the money?"

"He vaguely remembers hearing motorcycles around the plane right after the crash. He thinks he remembers seeing a large, white man, with a mustache, pick up at least one duffel bag of money and put it on a motorcycle. He also thought that there were other people around the plane right after the crash, but he can't be totally sure. He may have just been hallucinating."

"What did Ted Gardner think? Did the police give him any information about who arrived at the crash site first and about how much money was recovered?"

Beatriz continued, "He was told that the airport radar in Albany lost the Commander without any kind of an emergency call, so they routinely reported it to the Sheriff's Office in the nearest town, Woodstock, Vermont, just in case something had happened to it. At about the same time, a resident in the area reported that a plane, in trouble, with a smoking engine, flew over his home. The Sheriff, a Deputy and a couple of ambulance attendants were apparently the first ones to arrive on the scene."

"What the hell's all this shit about motorcycles at the crash site?" Castrillo asked again.

"Ted Gardner was told that the police and ambulance attendants were the first to arrive at the crash site fairly soon after it happened and no one else was there."

"Was he able to obtain information about how much money the authorities recovered?"

"He was told, off the record, that they seized between forty-five and fifty million dollars."

"There was at least fifty-five million on that plane. If there's a possibility that someone got to the crash site before the cops and picked up some of that money before the FBI and the DEA got their hands on it, we have to check it out. If someone actually took five or ten million dollars of our money, I want it back!"

"What do you want me to do?"

"Since your brother is in the area, get him to find out what went on at the crash site and what this fuckin' report about Jay seeing a big, white man with a mustache, on a motorcycle is all about. There was a lot of money on that plane and it sounds like some of it might have gone missing from the crash site . . . get back to me . . . yesterday!" Castrillo said as he hung up.

Beatriz called her brother immediately.

"I just talked to Castrillo and he's really upset," Beatriz said to Luis as he answered his cell phone. "Where are you and Fernando right now?"

"We're still in Albany, what do you want us to do?"

"A large, white man with a mustache may have taken five to ten million dollars from the plane wreck or Jay may be just confused. Castrillo wants us to check it out, so why don't you and Fernando go to the crash site and the nearby town called Woodstock and ask some questions. Apparently, no one other than Jay saw motorcycles near the wreckage."

"We're on our way. I'll get back to you later."

The Columbians, in Fernando's three year old, blue, four-door Continental, went north out of Albany on Highway 87 and took the Glen Falls cut-off east, to Rutland, just west of where the Commander went down. Luis and Fernando decided to make some enquiries at the main gas stations, especially those that sold beer and food, because they thought that bikers would likely stay away from better restaurants. All the people that they met wanted to express their own ideas as to what a plane-full of money was doing in their community and none of them knew anything about bikers riding through town the day before. Just as the two Colombians were leaving the east end of Rutland, they stopped at one more gas station that also sold beer and groceries. Luis talked to the young girl who was working behind the counter in the store while Fernando got gas.

"We're trying to catch up to some friends who are on motorcycles. Have you had any bikers in here in the last day or so?"

"There were three or four guys on motorcycles in here early yesterday afternoon. I think they got gas and a couple of them came in here for some food."

"One of our friends is a big guy with a mustache. Do you remember if he was part of that group or not?"

"Sure, I remember him. He ate a couple of donuts in the store before he even got to the counter to pay for them!"

"Thanks for your help. I'm sure we'll catch up to them soon."

Luis and Fernando continued east from Rutland and traveled on the winding road through the small valleys on the way to the crash site. A few miles before Woodstock, the Colombians saw a police cruiser ahead make a right turn and go through a covered wooden bridge. Fernando followed it to the edge of a small field that contained the scattered wreckage of the Commander. The wire fence that ran along the ditch by the gravel road had been draped in yellow, cellophane police crime-scene tape to warn the crowd of sightseers not to enter the field. The crash site looked like a war-zone with pieces of wreckage everywhere. The cleanup had not yet started but the forensic crews were hard at work. If there had been money lying around the field as was reported, every last bill had been picked up by the authorities.

There was a large crowd of curiosity seekers who were very jovial and talkative. Nothing this exciting had ever happened in their neighbourhood before. Luis and Fernando spoke to many people, but none of them knew anything about a bunch of guys on motor-cycles at the crash site or in the area the day before.

Luis did spoke to an off duty ambulance driver who was standing next to the fence.

` "So the emergency vehicle that was first on the scene came from your detachment?"

"Yeah, but I'm disappointed the crash happened in the middle of my three days off."

"So you missed it all?"

"Yeah, but a guy I work with named Bruce Sim was the first one here. He pulled the dead guy out of the cockpit and ended up tak-ing the pilot to the hospital in Lebanon first and then back to the hospital in Albany because he was so banged up."

"Where is your friend now? Is he still on duty?" Luis asked.

"He's actually working right now. If he's not out on a call, he'll be at our detachment in Woodstock. It's right on the main street as you go through town."

"Great! Your friend's name is Bruce Sim. I'll tell him I was talk-ing to you. Thanks for your help," Luis said as he waved at Fernando to head for the car.

Ten minutes later, they were in Woodstock. It was a fairly small town but they had trouble finding the Ambulance Service on the main street. They drove all the way through town, without any luck, and were just about to stop and ask directions when they spotted a sign, *Woodstock Fire House*, right on the eastern outskirts. It was a single story, red brick building with five bays, three for fire trucks and two for an emergency vehicle and an ambulance. As the Colombians parked their car on the street nearby, they noticed an attendant in front of one of the bays washing an ambulance. Luis, who could speak much better English than Fernando, proceeded alone because he thought that the sight of two South American looking men asking questions about a recently crashed drug plane might make the guy a little nervous or suspicious.

Luis walked up the wet driveway toward the attendant who had his back to him. "Can you tell me if Bruce Sim is around?"

"That's me! The guy said as he turned. "What can I do for ya'?"

Luis replied, "My name is John Bovie. I'm doing a magazine article for the National Inquisitor about the plane crash that happened yesterday just west of town and I've been talking to a few local people. I met one of the guys you work with out at the crash site and he told me that your ambulance was the first one on the scene yesterday."

"Christ! The National Inquisitor doesn't waste any time digging up these strange stories."

"Well, that's what we do. What was it really like at the crash site when you arrived?"

"My partner and I were the first ones there, along with a couple of cops. What a mess! The plane was scattered all over the field and there was money everywhere."

"How many people were in the plane?"

"Just two pilots that both looked dead when we first got there. One was in the cockpit with half of his head missing. The other had been thrown clear of the wreck still seat-belted into his cockpit seat. Just after we got to him, he started to show signs of life."

"Did the survivor tell you anything about their flight plan or all that money?"

"Nah, he only came around a couple of times and was incoherent. I couldn't understand anything that he tried to say because he spoke in some foreign language, maybe Spanish. We rushed him to the nearest hospital in Lebanon, but he was in such bad shape that after they got him stabilized, they sent him directly to the hospital in Albany," Sim explained.

"Were you at the crash site long? Were there any other people there when you arrived?"

"We must have arrived there shortly after it happened because we were the first ones on the scene. No one else was there. A couple of cars arrived just after we did."

"Someone told me that there was a motorcycle gang at the crash scene first?"

"Not when I was there. Just two police cruisers, our ambulance and the two cars that arrived just as we did. Only two more cars had arrived by the time we left."

Luis pressed on, "It's really strange that you didn't see any bikers yesterday when other people did, but thanks for your help."
He shook the ambulance attendant's hand and headed back toward the car in the street and as he got to the curb, Sim called out to him.

"Hey, Mr. Bovie! Come to think of it, when I was about halfway out to the crash site, three or four motorcycles passed me heading this way, toward town."

Luis and Fernando asked a few more questions around Woodstock while they were there and two other people recalled seeing a group of motorcyclists go down the main street in the mid-afternoon the day before. The Colombians looked at their roadmap and decided that the bikers must have continued east toward Lebanon where two major interstate highways intersect. It was going to be a bit of a guess to determine whether they continued east or went south. Luis' best guess was that they went south toward Boston.

Luis dialed through to his sister and reported all the information that had been gathered that day and she in turn passed it on to Castrillo in Colombia. After the full story had been told to him, he had only one response.

"Find those bastards and get my money back . . . then kill them!"

CHAPTER TWENTY-FOUR

The next morning, Joe woke up at about nine-thirty feeling rough. He was dead tired. The first thing he did when his head cleared was look over toward Bryan's bed. It was empty, but that wasn't unusual because Bryan always got up early. Joe lay there for a while and wondered what Bryan's attitude about returning the money would be that morning once he had a chance to think more clearly. Joe thought that Bryan's behavior was totally out of character for him. He finally woke up enough to pull himself out of bed and open the door between the two rooms.

"Get the hell up!" Joe yelled as he pulled open the curtains and the patio door in Doc and Howie's room. "We have a luncheon date at the Kennedy Compound!"

Doc opened his eyes and half sat up in bed, "Are there any cold beers left in the bucket?"

"Comin' up!"

Joe reached into the plastic wastebasket that doubled for a cooler and found that the ice from the night before hadn't melted yet. He opened three Bud Lights and passed one each to Doc and Howie and he took the third. He then turned on CNN and sat down near the patio door.

"Was Bryan able to get to sleep last night or was he too worked up about all that money?" Howie asked as he sat up in his bed and adjusted his pillow on the headboard.

"He snored all bloody night!"

"Where's the loon now?" Doc inquired.

"He's out on tour, the *Fat Boy's* gone from the patio," Joe commented taking a long swig of the cold beer and thinking, *After all, we are on vacation!*

They listened to the newscaster on CNN, but there was no new information about the plane crash in Vermont. They all just relaxed and Joe looked out into the beautiful gardens.

"Bryan sure the hell doesn't want to give that money back," Doc commented.

Howie added looking at Joe, "I thought that he was gonna punch ya' out."

"He probably has a different perspective now that he's not hammered."

"What do you think Bryan should do with the money?" Howie asked.

"I think he should make arrangements to return it to the cops before we all get in some kind of trouble. He could just plead insanity," Joe answered, "but let's wait until he gets back from his early morning jaunt and see if his attitude has changed."

"He can deal with all that shit by himself because I'm sure that he'll get tied up with the cops for a day or two giving a statement," Doc commented. "What are we gonna do today?"

"Tommy and Mike want to bike out to Provincetown at the north end of Cape Cod, have lunch somewhere and then come back through Hyannis," Howie answered.

Joe added, "That sounds like a good idea to me. It'll be a long time before we'll all be back here, so we may as well see as much of the place as we can."

The three of them sat around for the next hour or so and had a couple of beers. They talked about Atlantic City and how much further south they might travel from there. As usual, Tommy and Mike were still in bed. As the time passed, the guys were all quite surprised that Bryan hadn't returned.

Joe wandered into his own room to take a leak and after he finished in the bathroom, opened the curtains and patio door to let in the sunshine and some fresh air. The brilliant day lit up the room and as Joe turned away from the door, he saw a small, white piece of paper on the dresser. He picked it up, read it and headed straight for the closet and opened the sliding doors. He then went to the doorway into Doc and Howie's room.

"Apparently Bryan has decided what he's going to do with the money! He left us a note. It says, *You guys are a bunch of assholes. Gone home.*"

No one had heard Bryan leave. By the time they discovered that he was gone, they figured that he would be halfway back to the Canadian border. As they were trying to decide what to do, Tommy and Mike walked into the room. Once again, they had both missed all the excitement.

Doc told them Bryan's story starting with the bag of money that was dumped on the bed the night before and ending with the note that Joe had just found in Bryan's room. Tommy and Mike were shocked when they heard the amount of money that was in only one bag because the news had said there were a number of bags at the crash site. They were also relieved that Bryan had taken the stolen money and gone home because they didn't want any part of it either. They all decided that there was nothing any of them could do because Bryan had disappeared so they weren't going to let it ruin their day.

"Let's catch the twelve o'clock news before we get ready to leave," Joe suggested.

Tommy, who was closest to the television, turned it to a local Boston channel and a news broadcast was just getting under way.

"A Commander 980 crashed in the area of Woodstock, Vermont yesterday afternoon. The FBI and the DEA have confirmed that the crash is drug related. The plane contained a number of duffel bags of money, some of which was scattered around the crash site. The Colombian pilot is in critical condition in the hospital in Albany. The co-pilot was killed. The FBI reports that the plane had filed a flight plan that would have taken it from a small airport named Dunsford Field, just north of Albany, to Shelburne, Nova Scotia, on the east coast of Canada. The plane's Canadian insignia is believed to be false. The FBI and DEA will provide further details as the investigation continues."

Howie commented, "If there were a number of duffel bags of money on the plane and Bryan's bag contained nearly seven million dollars, it must have been one hell of a drug deal!"

"We'll pick up a newspaper later and see if there's any additional information in it," Tommy said. "I can't believe that Bryan would actually steal that money."

"He has been a bit of a crazy bastard lately, but it's not like him! Let's get the hell moving, I'm starving!" Mike ordered.

"Let's hit the highway to Provincetown and we'll be able to find a place to eat along the way," Tommy announced.

About half an hour later, all the guys were ready and met in the courtyard by the motorcycles and it wasn't long before they were on the road again.

They pulled onto Route 6 and went north toward Orleans and found the village twenty minutes later about a third of the way out on the peninsula. Mike led the bikers into the parking lot of The Orleans Inn, an old, white clapboard, Cape Cod style hotel that had seen better days. What attracted Mike to the place was a sign that advertised an *all-you-can-eat* luncheon buffet for seven bucks. The guys thought, *How bad could it be!* They sat at a table for six next to a large picture window that overlooked a scenic lagoon with the ocean in the background.

The smiling waitress who arrived at the table was as cute as a button, with short, dark hair, slim and extremely well put together. She had unbelievable breasts. For some reason, she had left the top two buttons of her uniform undone and her cleavage caught everyone's attention.

"How're ya' all today?" She said with a friendly smile. "Can I get ya' all somethin' to drink while you're decidin' what ya' want for lunch?"

"We'll have a couple of *jugs* of draft beer. I don't know what made me think of that!" Joe answered and smiled a warm, friendly smile as all the guys chuckled.

Mary, as her nametag revealed, blushed immediately and replied as she gave Joe a dirty look, "We don't have *pitchers* of draft beer here."

It appeared from her reaction that she had heard all the lines before.

"Mary, I'm sorry, I was just being a smart ass. I'll have a Bud Light," Joe said feeling guilty that he was a bit rude and it appeared that she accepted his apology.

The other guys ordered a variety of beers and Mary sauntered off to get them. All of their eyes followed her as she walked across the room.

Mary came back to the table in a few minutes with the beers and Mike immediately ordered the *special* all-you-can-eat buffet. The rest of the gang joined him.

"That was easy!" Mary said. "The plates are at the far end of the buffet table. Help yourselves whenever ya' all are ready."

They headed for the long food-table that was covered with all kinds of appetizing dishes. They filled their plates and as they got back to their table, Doc signaled for more beer.

"I wonder where Bryan actually went? Do you think he really went back home?" Howie was thinking out loud because he still had all of that money on his mind.

"He probably did. He would want to get back to Canada as fast as soon as possible so he could put the money in a safe place if he really intends to keep it," Doc suggested.

"Think about it, if you were going to show up back home with a lot of money, what better excuse than to say that you had been to Atlantic City and got lucky," Tommy commented.

"He likely went home, but with Bryan these days, there's no way of knowing what he was thinking when he got up this morning," Joe added.

The food at the Orleans Inn was a lot better than the state of repair of the building suggested it might be. The guys stuffed themselves because they wouldn't likely eat again until late in the evening. Howie decided to buy lunch for everyone with his newfound wealth and he left Mary a large tip. As he settled the bill, he spoke to her.

"Mary, we're all staying at the Cape Hyannis Hotel. Why don't you bring some girl friends to the lounge tonight for a little dancing?"

"I just might do that, we go there quite often."

The bikers, back on Route 6, continued north on what is called the Cape Cod National Seashore that runs north to the end of the *Scorpion's Tail.* The federal park has about forty miles of Atlantic Ocean beachfront covered with pine greenery and sand dunes that curve back toward the mainland like a scorpion's tail creating Cape Cod Bay. The spit consists of two beaches, one on the bay where all the development of cottages and motels has taken place, and the other on the ocean side where the federal park is located.

Joe had seen enough Cape Cod architecture to last him a lifetime as the bikers rode up over the crest of a small hill that was named by signage, *Pilgrim Heights.* From the top of the rise, Provincetown and Race Point, located at the very tip of the scorpion's tail, came into view. As they approached the busy summer community, there were rows of homes, cottages and resorts on wide, sandy beaches on the bay side and huge, wind-blown, sand dunes on the Atlantic side. The guys passed by a large circular salt pond that had likely been in the same location since the Pilgrims landed back in 1620.

Joe led the bikers through the narrow streets of Provincetown and onto Commercial Street, the main drag, where they found a parking lot right next to the town docks and marina. They parked their bikes and wandered toward the shops, restaurants and bars.

"Let's have a cocktail at that neat place with the patio that we went by called Cafe Blasé and watch the people go by," Tommy suggested.

As soon as the boys sat down at an outside table under a Coors umbrella, a pretty waiter named Bruce, tippy-toed over to introduce himself and take their orders.

As soon as Bruce returned with a chilled bottle of California wine, Gallo Chardonnay, and started to open it, Joe spoke to him. "This town looks really busy. How many people actually live here?"

"The full-time winter population is only about four to five thousand people, but in the summer, it balloons to at least two hundred thousand. Most of the souvenir, clothing and fast food outlets that are here close during the winter and this place is like a ghost town."

Doc had to ask, "Why is Cape Cod such a large gay community? What's the attraction?"

"It's a place that we all like to come to for the jobs and the weather, besides, we all like to be in the same area for social reasons," a somewhat indignant Bruce answered.

"Well, it sure is a pretty town," Tommy added to take the edge off the discussion. "Would you please bring us another bottle of wine when you get a chance."

"I'd like to go back to Hyannis and take a look around there. Maybe we can get to see the Kennedy Estate," Mike mentioned.

"Sounds great," Joe said, "but I'd like to get back to the hotel so I can have a nap for a couple of hours before we go out for the evening. None of us got much sleep last night."

They all finished their glasses of wine and when they paid the tab, Bruce didn't bother to thank them. It appeared that Doc's silly questions about the gay community offended him. They all sauntered by a number of shops on the way back toward the town docks.

The traffic was much lighter at that time of day and it didn't take them long to get back to Orleans. Just past the inn where they had eaten lunch, they made a left turn where a sign read Chatham and rode into that small town about ten minutes later.

After traveling another half an hour to the southwest out of Chatham, along Nantucket Sound, they passed Nantucket Island and Martha's Vineyard that were located far out in the ocean in the distance to the south. It wasn't long before they pulled into the marina area of downtown Hyannis. The town was on a small inland bay with three large marinas that were filled with hundreds of boats of all kinds and sizes.

The bikers left the Ocean Street docks after looking around and went south on Barnstable Road, past the JFK Memorial, then right on Gosnold to Ocean Avenue, west to Greenwood and on to the Kennedy Compound. It turned out that the estate was so far off the road and so well hidden behind trees that it couldn't be seen. They turned around and went back the way they had come and went north to the Cape Hyannis Hotel.

As they coasted their bikes through the tunnel into the court-yard and parked near their rooms, they all mentally noted that Bryan's motorcycle was missing. As soon as the got off their bikes, Tommy and Mike immediately went to their room for a nap and Doc and Howie poured themselves another drink and turned on the television. Joe poured a cold beer into a plastic cup and stepped back outside. He could hear music filtering down through the lush gardens from the outside patio and bar area of the hotel up near the pool.

"I'm going to walk up to the patio bar to see what's going on, I'll be back shortly," Joe said to the guys in the room as he turned to walk up through the gardens.

Howie yelled, "Wait a minute, I'll go with you."
Doc got comfortable in front of the tube as Howie put his drink into a plastic traveler.

Joe and Howie worked their way through the crowd of late after-noon drinkers who were milling around the pool and got themselves another drink as they passed the patio bar. They then walked over to the wire and aluminum fence that ran along the golf course. A large pond was located about a hundred feet or so into a well-manicured fairway that abutted the pool area patio. The sun which was slowly disappearing in the west, cast long dark shadows over the fairway and pond that was full of cattails and surrounded by pine trees.

"What the hell is that black stuff on the horizon?" Joe said pointing far into the eastern sky where a silent black cloud was moving slowly toward them.

"Christ! I can't tell what it is!" Howie answered. "It looks like a flock of birds!"

As the cloud got closer, it became more visible and they could hear faint *honking* sounds.

"They're too big to be ducks. I think it's thousands of Canada Geese," Joe replied.

They stood in awe and watched about three thousand, or even more, Canada Geese start a landing pattern a few miles away that ended up right in front of them. The scene was right out of a nature movie as the geese landed in slow motion all over the pond and fairway. Joe turned around and saw that at least a hundred people had come out of the hotel and onto the patio to watch the spectacle. He and Howie finished their drinks and walked back down through the gardens.

As they entered the room, Doc said excitedly, "The six o'clock news is just starting."

They sat down and glued their eyes to the television as the newscaster went directly into the story about the plane that had crashed northeast of Albany: "The Commander that crashed in Vermont yesterday afternoon appears to be drug related even though no drugs were found at the crash site. Traces of cocaine were found in the wreckage. The FBI and the DEA recovered twelve duffel bags of American currency in cash and they estimate the seizure to be close to fifty million dollars. The surviving pilot is out of intensive care in the hospital in Albany, but he has been no help to the investigation."

"How pissed will Bryan be when he finds out that he left about fifty million dollars at the crash site," Joe remarked to the boys.

The more I think about it," Doc laughed, "I wouldn't be surprised if he's in Atlantic City right now playing Blackjack with one thousand dollar chips with a broad on each arm."

"My guess is he's already back home and has the money tucked away somewhere safe," Howie suggested.

"I guess we'll find out tomorrow. You just never know with Bryan, he may have gone south," Joe added. "Wake me up at about eight o'clock, I've gotta get some sleep or I won't be able to go out and play with you guys tonight."

CHAPTER TWENTY-FIVE

Pinguino had left St. Kitts the day after he had heard the devastating news about the crash of the Commander. Not only had he lost one of his oldest friends, but he had lost a substantial financial bonus that he would have received had the plane full of money arrived safely back to the island. He was also extremely disappointed that he had to leave the resort because he had met a very horny gal from Chicago who was just starting a two-week vacation. As soon as he got back to Medellin, he went directly to Castrillo's safehouse and played the waiting game with his boss. Bracho's report about the missing money was long overdue.

Before leaving the island, Pinguino had contacted a Medellin Cartel associate in San Juan by telephone and gave the order to have the Puerto Rican airplane mechanic killed for his inept work on the Commander. As the two men sat in the safehouse and waited for news from Beatriz Bracho, the mechanic and one of his younger brothers, who was in the wrong place at the wrong time, lay in pools of blood in a dirty back alley in downtown San Juan. The local police and the DEA thought that the killings were just more random acts of drug related violence that was a plague in the over-populated island city that had become known as the drug center of the Caribbean and had been more recently labeled *Little Miami*. Pinguino knew only too well that when Pablo Rivas or Diego Castrillo gave an order to have something done, that order was to be carried out immediately without any questions asked.

The two men had been in close quarters for hours and things were very quiet. They hardly spoke. They just waited for the next telephone report from Montreal. The cell phone finally rang and

Castrillo picked it up immediately.

"The news just reported that twelve duffel bags of money were found at the crash site. We put *thirteen* bags onboard. The authorities also confirmed that they recovered between forty-five and fifty million dollars. I know that there was at least fifty-five million on that plane!"

"So there's one duffel bag missing that contains somewhere between five and ten million dollars. Has your brother been able to find out anything about the bikers?"

"He found out that there was a motorcycle gang in the area when the plane crashed and there is a possibility that they were at the crash site before anyone else got there. The ambulance driver saw four bikers while he was on his way to the crash site. The gang was traveling southeast, away from the downed plane."

"Where did they go?"

"My men continued in the direction they were heading when they were last seen and a gas station attendant just north of Boston remembered a gang of bikers that stopped for gas late in the day. He remembered that they were on their way to Cape Cod, just south of Boston."

"Where's your brother now?" Castrillo inquired.

"He and another of my men are in the Boston area right now and are on their way to Cape Cod as we speak. The trouble is that the Cape is a busy tourist haven this time of year and there are probably all kinds of bikers in the area. It's a peninsula about fifty miles long so it may take my men some time to locate the bikers we're looking for."

"You know what Pablo gets like when things go wrong. Get some more men down there no matter what it costs. Get our associates in Boston to help. Whatever money was taken by those bikers has to be found and it has to be found fast," Castrillo almost ordered.

"I'll call you as soon as my brother reports any more news." Beatriz hung up the phone.

Castrillo was in a foul mood because he had met with Pablo Rivas right after the news of the plane crash and Rivas had nearly been out of control. He had lost fifty-five million American dollars that the cartel needed badly. Castrillo and Rivas had been friends since childhood, but he now feared for his life. The financial loss was one thing, but the embarrassment of such a fiasco was another. Leaders in the Cali Cartel, his main competition for the world cocaine markets, were laughing at him. Castrillo had the feeling that if he could recoup the millions that had gone missing from the plane wreck that would start to make amends with his boss.

The gorgeous day became a beautiful evening that eventually turned into night. Castrillo and Pinguino fell asleep at about the same time hoping that a new day would bring better news.

The next morning, Pinguino wondered if this was the day that he might be sent to Boston as he was one of the few cartel members that were still virtually unknown to the authorities and could travel internationally. He and Castrillo still hadn't spoken very much. He knew that it was best to only speak to his boss if he was spoken to. They just waited for the next telephone call from Beatriz to learn how the hunt for the missing money was progressing. The cool morning turned into a very humid afternoon. Pinguino sat outside on the small balcony overlooking the city and periodically glanced around at the twelve, armed bodyguards that were stationed around the fully treed and walled property. He hoped that he wouldn't have to travel abroad so he could return to his own home to be with his wife and four little girls. He was starting to miss them. Castrillo was resting on the couch in the living room when his cell phone finally rang.

"What the hell's going on up there? You were supposed to call me this morning!"

"My men got to Cape Cod but they haven't located the bikers yet. They said that half of the motorcycles in North America are at the Cape this time of year. They have been looking for a group of four or five guys with a big heavy-set man with a mustache," she explained.

"Are only two of them searching or did you get some help from our people in Boston?"

"I called our contact in Boston for some help and he's sent a few of his men down to Cape Cod. They are working their way down from Boston to Hyannis and my men are going to work their way out to the end of the peninsula to Provincetown."

Enrique Parejo was the cartel's main-man in the Boston area. He ran the Boston operation just as Beatriz did in Montreal. He had assured her that he would do whatever he could to help her men locate the bikers they were chasing.

"When will they report to you next?"

"My brother is supposed to call me tonight, unless he has some good news before that, so as soon as I hear from him, I'll call you."

Castrillo hung up the phone without another word and began to pace back and forth in the living room. As Pinguino sat quietly in the only shaded spot on the balcony, he struggled to get up enough nerve to ask his boss what the news was from up north.

"Have they found them yet?" He asked quietly.

"No, they haven't found the bastards and I have to call Pablo and tell him. Do you want to call him for me?"

Pinguino didn't bother to answer because he knew that Castrillo didn't mean it. Pablo Rivas only spoke to the top cartel members and not to the rank and file, especially regarding matters of extreme importance. Castrillo reluctantly picked up his cell phone and began to dial.

CHAPTER TWENTY-SIX

D oc opened the door into Joe's room just after eight o'clock and yelled at him to get up, but he didn't move. His head had been spinning with thoughts of Bryan and the money ever since he had gone to bed so he didn't have a very restful nap.

By nine o'clock, Joe was showered and dressed. He was all decked out in his dancing duds and actually felt a lot better than he had when he first woke up. He was wearing a yellow, short-sleeved shirt, a fairly new pair of jeans and his tan boots. Joe opened the door into the other room and immediately noticed that the two loons hadn't moved since he had left them nearly three hours earlier except to get themselves drinks. They were both half in the bag.

"Are you assholes goin' dancin' tonight?" Joe asked as he grabbed himself a cold Bud.

"Soon, we'll be ready to go dancin' soon," Howie replied as a scotch touched his lips.

"Doc, you're still drinking beer, take this one. I think I'll have a scotch and water instead," Joe suggested and Doc took his open beer when it was offered.

Joe poured himself a stiff drink and sat down in one of the chairs near the patio door. "Has there been anymore news about the plane crash?"

"Doc won't change the bloody channel. The Blue Jays are poundin' Atlanta."

"Get your asses in gear! Those little sweethearts are going to be in the bar waiting for us," Joe suggested. "Now that Bryan has left, you guys may be able to get a date!"

Doc said with a laugh, "I don't think that I'll be able to walk tonight let alone dance."

Tommy and Mike burst through the patio door and Mike let out a hell of yell, "What's happening?"

The yell startled the guys in the room. The two of them had just finished eating in the hotel dining room. Mike and Tommy rarely missed dinner.

"What's the crowd like in the lounge?" Howie asked.

"It's starting to fill up," Mike answered. "We walked through the bar on the way back and all those girls from Buffalo are sitting at the same tables."

"Come on Doc, let's get the hell moving." Howie said as he got up and went into the bathroom to get organized.

Joe poured himself another scotch and asked the others, "Are you guys havin' a cocktail?"

"I'll be right back. I've got some vodka and Tia Maria in my room so I think I'll have a Black Russian," Tommy said as he slipped out into the hall.

This was usually some kind of an omen. If Tommy started drinking Black Russians, it was going to be a long night. Mike decided to have a beer.

"Do you think that Bryan made it back home yet?" Mike asked. "We should call his place in Lindsay and see if he's there."

"Screw him! You'd think that he would've let us know what the hell he was doing," Doc answered. "If the asshole wants to talk to us, he knows where we are."

Tommy arrived back in the room with all the mixings for Black Russians and poured himself one in a large plastic glass. He was brave because the glass was full of straight alcohol.

Howie wandered back into the room in his underwear, drying his hair with a towel, and started to get dressed so Doc got up and went into the bathroom and shut the door.

"Black Russians!" Howie laughed when he saw them and poured himself a large one.

He and Tommy were both real treats when they drank them. Joe knew right at that moment that the evening could very easily turn into a *pig show*. With Howie, Doc and Tommy all half-in-the-bag, the girls from Buffalo wouldn't stand a chance.

As soon as Doc was dressed, they all wandered up through the dark gardens toward the bar and the sound of the music. The girls waved as the five bikers made their way toward their end of the room. The women would miss Bryan, the big spender from the night before, but it became apparent fairly quickly that Tommy might take his place. He was on a roll and ordered everyone Black Russians.

The Righteous Brothers began to sing *You've Lost That Lovin' Feelin'* and from across the tables, the pretty brunette that Bryan had danced with the night before motioned Howie toward the dance floor. The rest of the guys talked to the girls as the music played and Doc and Tommy ended up on the dance floor with a couple of the other gals. All the girls were very friendly and ready to party. Mike sprang for another round of Black Russians just as Tommy returned from the dance floor and stopped beside Joe who was standing at the long bar nearby.

"We'll head for Atlantic City first thing in the morning so we should get these gals to bed early tonight," Tommy said with that laugh of his that he can't hold back when he's bombed.

"Great! Willie Nelson said it best, I'm ready to get *On The Road Again*."

As Joe finished the sentence, he felt a light tap on his shoulder and turned. In front of him stood an absolutely stunning woman who he didn't really recognize for a moment.

"Mary! You remembered where we'd be. It's great to see you again!" Joe said surprised to see her and as he looked her up and down, he recalled that she had been quite attractive in her waitress outfit at the Orleans Inn, but there in the lounge, she was gorgeous.

"At least you remembered my name," Mary replied with a broad smile.

Mary and a girlfriend had driven over to the Cape Hyannis from Orleans, which they often did on Thursday nights. She had on a low-cut, cropped-top blouse that left her belly button showing and white hip-huggers that were extremely tight. The girl was absolutely Playmate material.

Joe formally introduced himself and Tommy to the girls and gave them each one of the Black Russians that were already sitting on the bar. Nancy, Mary's friend, and Tommy really hit it off and started talking immediately. Right at that moment, another Righteous Brother's tune, *Unchained Melody*, started to play. Joe was dying to get Mary onto the dance floor and hold her wicked body close to his.

"This is a great song," Joe said to Mary, "would you like to dance?"

They slipped into the middle of the pack on the dance floor. The next song was one of Bob Seger's greatest hits, *Old Time Rock 'n Roll*. The fast dance went well and after the next slow one, they joined the others back at the bar.

Tommy and Nancy were deep in conversation and the bartender dropped off four more drinks that he had ordered while Joe and Mary had been dancing. Doc, Mike and Howie had their hands full taking care of the gals from Buffalo.

"I hope you girls like Black Russians. They really make me horny!" Tommy said with that same drunken laugh that had become his trademark.

Joe and the two girls laughed more at him *laughing* than at what he had said.

"Don't order me anymore," Joe said, "they have the opposite effect on me!"

Mary squeezed his hand and smiled that beautiful smile and said quietly, "You are definitely not allowed anymore of those drinks tonight!"

Joe hoped that the comment was a message. As he took another hit from his last Black Russian another slow song started to play and without even asking, he took Mary by the arm and led her out onto the dance floor once again. They danced very close.

Tommy and Nancy had also danced the same song and they all came off the dance floor at the same time. Joe ordered two more Black

Russians for them, a gin and tonic for Mary and a scotch and water for himself. When the drinks arrived, he commented directly to Mary.

"I hope you noticed that I'm not drinking anymore of those other drinks."

"Don't worry," she said with a cute smile, "I noticed!"

As the evening went on, the lounge became so warm and humid that Joe and Mary decided to go out onto the patio to get some fresh air. They left Tommy and Nancy with the other guys and the girls from Buffalo. They stopped by the fence at the edge of the golf course where Joe and Howie had been standing earlier and moved very close to each other. It was another beautiful, starlit night with a slight breeze and the music from the lounge filtered out into the evening air, across the patio and out onto the golf course. Joe and Mary put their arms around each other and kissed a long and gentle kiss. They kissed again and again and she pressed her firm body against him. Joe decided that it was time to make a move.

"Would you like to see where I'm staying?" Joe asked with a smile. She answered him with a long passionate kiss. They walked very slowly, hand in hand, down through the dark gardens toward the rooms that were still fully lit up at the far end of the rear building. They stopped about twenty-five feet from his room for another kiss. Joe's attention drifted to his wide-open screen door. He knew that he had closed it tight before he had left for the lounge.

As Joe continued to look toward the rooms, he saw a shadow of someone moving around in Doc and Howie's room. He knew that they were in the lounge with the others. Joe quietly motioned for Mary to stay hidden in the darkness of the gardens. He slipped into his own room through the open patio door and moved quietly toward the doorway into the adjoining room. There was a short, stocky man, dressed in dark clothes, leaning into the closet with his back toward Joe ransacking Doc and Howie's belongings. Joe immediately decided that the best thing for him to do was to overpower the thief, before the guy even knew what happened, and hold him down until Mary called the hotel management and the police.

Joe moved silently and quickly through the doorway toward the intruder, but his surprise was ruined. The thief turned slightly and their eyes met for a split second. Joe grabbed the collar of the guy's leather jacket with his left hand and cocked his right fist for what he hoped would be a stunning blow. It wasn't a perfect maneuver because the guy turned quickly to his left, spun around and swung his left arm back. He caught Joe across the left side of his head with a backhand. Joe was knocked off balance and crashed against the wall in the corner near the television, but he dragged the intruder along with him by the collar that Joe had locked in his left hand. As Joe bounced off the wall, he let go with a perfect right to the guy's face. The force of the punch made him reel back. Joe lunged at him, and the momentum of his flying body, propelled them over the corner of Doc's bed and into the small space between the two beds.

As they wrestled to their feet, Joe caught a glimpse of a gun in the guy's right hand that came out from under his jacket. Joe's heart skipped a beat. He grabbed for the gun with his left hand and strained to keep it pointing away from his body. The gun discharged twice, in rapid succession with deafening noise and the two bullets lodged high in the wall above Howie's bed. At the same time, while he held the lapel of the guy's leather coat with his other hand, Joe rolled backwards onto Howie's bed and pulled the guy over him. He lifted his knees and pushed up in such a way that the man was thrown upside down and through the air before he crashed into the table and chairs in the corner near the patio door. The intruder lost his grip on the gun as he was flipped upside down and Joe ended up with it awkwardly in his left hand. As Joe stood up between the beds, the dark-complexioned man scrambled to his feet and immediately crashed through the closed screen door taking it off its runners and outside into the patio area with him.

Joe dashed through the door to the patio and just caught a glimpse of the thief as he disappeared into the darkness through the covered walkway that led out to the main parking area in front of the hotel. He wasn't prepared to follow the guy into the night.

***

It was well over an hour before the night manager and the police officers that had been dispatched to the routine break-in were finished asking questions. During that time, all the other guys had returned from the bar for a nightcap, including Tommy and Nancy. Doc and Howie determined that nothing was missing from their room so they poured a drink and relaxed.

The police took possession of the still partially loaded Browning 38 and remarked that they thought that it had been handled far too much to get any prints from it. Joe had jokingly asked if he could keep it for a souvenir. The police then took the time to explain to him that a lot of simple break-ins end up with some innocent person getting killed for no reason. Joe promised that the next time something like that happened, he would back away and call the cops without getting involved. The police decided that the intruder was probably just a druggy looking for a few fast bucks for a fix and he wouldn't be returning. The gang decided that it was bedtime and everyone disappeared, including Tommy and his new date, Nancy.

The first thing that Joe did when the others left his room was make sure that all the doors were locked. He carefully pulled the curtains in front of the patio door and then lay down on his bed beside where Mary was sitting. She lay down on one elbow and kissed him very tenderly.

"It looks like Nancy has decided that you two are staying the night."

Mary's answer was another kiss.

They cuddled and kissed for a few minutes and Mary went to the washroom to get ready for bed. Joe stripped down to his underwear and put a couple of condoms in a convenient location so they would be available. He went directly into the washroom when she was finished and when he came out, Mary was in bed in the nude waiting for him, so he dropped his shorts and joined her. Joe gently rubbed his hands all over her body as they kissed and he caressed her full, firm breasts. She moaned quietly as he touched them and kissed her body. They were both tired, but they made love and eventually fell asleep in each other's arms.

CHAPTER TWENTY-SEVEN

Enrique Parejo was in bed making love to one of the runners-up in the last Miss Massachusetts Pageant when his private line rang next to his bed. As the *numero uno* of the Boston Cartel with strong ties to Medellin, he hated getting calls at night, especially when he was entertaining. As soon as he heard the voice, he knew that it was one of the men that he had sent to Cape Cod earlier in the day to help his associates from Montreal track down a motorcycle gang that had stolen a substantial amount of money from them.

"This had better be important!" Parejo growled into the phone with an accent that was definitely South American, but tempered by living in New England.

"I think I found the gang of bikers our friends are looking for in a hotel in Hyannis."

"Where the hell are you now?" Parejo asked.

"I'm in Cape Cod. For a few bucks, the night clerk at the Cape Hyannis Hotel told me that there were some guys on motorcycles staying there. It took me some time to find their rooms in the large complex and when I did, the bikers weren't there, but the patio doors were open, so I was able to get into two adjoining rooms and take a good look around."

"Did you find the money or anything to indicate that they were the bikers who stole it?"

"I didn't find any money in the first room I went through, but I did find a couple of newspapers that were folded to articles about that plane crash up in Vermont. I was just starting to search the adjoining room when I was surprised by one of the bikers."

"What the hell happened?"

"The guy jumped me from behind and we ended up rolling around the fuckin' room. I pulled my Browning out during the fight and it went off a couple of times. During the scuffle, he ripped it right out of my hand and I lost it. I got the hell outta there as fast as I could."

"Where are you now?"

"I'm down the street from the hotel but I think I should get outta Hyannis fast and get back to Boston because a couple of police cruisers just pulled into the main entrance of the hotel and the cops might start looking around. The clerk could identify me."

"Yeah, leave right now. We don't need to get too involved in Montreal's problems." Parejo answered and hung up the phone.

He immediately dialed Luis' cell number that was on a small pad of paper near his phone. Luis and Fernando were staying at a motel in nearby Barnstable for the night and Parajo had been given his number earlier in the day by Beatrice Bracho.

Luis and Fernando were watching a porno flick when his cell phone rang.

"Hello," Luis said as he picked it up on the first ring.

"This is Enrique. One of my men just called from somewhere near the Cape Hyannis Hotel and he thinks that he found your bikers."

Parejo explained what had happened at the hotel in Hyannis and as soon as the call was over, Luis passed the information on on to Fernando who was lying on the other bed.

"If there are cops all around the hotel tonight, I don't think that we should go near the place until morning."

"We sure as hell shouldn't! Fernando agreed.

"Parejo said that his man didn't find any money in the rooms but did find newspaper articles about the plane crash. They must be the bikers we've been trying to find. Who else would save newspaper stories about that plane crash in Vermont?"

"Only the guys we've been following!"

"I'll call Beatriz and let her know what's happened and tell her that we'll go over to the Cape Hyannis Hotel first thing in the morning and have a little talk with those bikers."

CHAPTER TWENTY-EIGHT

Joe and Mary started to cuddle in their sleep at about six-thirty in the morning and before they were totally awake, started to make love again. After the lovemaking, they showered together and got dressed. As Mary did her hair in the steamy bathroom, Joe opened the door to the adjoining room to see what the other guys were doing.

"Good morning!" Joe said cheerfully. "Why are you guys up so early?"

"We're almost packed and ready to get the hell outta here," Howie answered as he stuffed the last of his belongings into his saddlebags.

"It's about time you got up," Doc said as he came back into the room from outside.

"I'll be ready in five minutes. Have you guys checked-out yet?"

Howie answered, "Yeah, we checked out earlier when we went to the lobby to get a paper and a couple of coffees and Tommy and Mike have already checked out too.

"I won't be long," Joe said as turned and went back to tell Mary that he had to leave.

"I've got a three-day weekend coming up. I could meet you in Atlantic City. There are buses that run from here to there every weekend," she said in a quiet and sad tone.

"I'm on a motorcycle trip with the guys. I can't just take you along with me. I've got both your phone numbers, so if there's any chance that you can join me for the weekend, I'll call you, but we may only stay there for one night. As far as I know, were going on to Washington."

"I've really enjoyed meeting you, Joe McConnell," she said and kissed him again.

"It's been great meeting you too."

Joe packed his personal things quickly. He put his sleeping bag under his arm, picked up his saddlebags and tank bag and walked through the adjoining room and out the patio door with Mary right behind him. Tommy and Nancy were chatting near his Honda and Mike was tying down the last of his possessions to his bike. It only took Joe a couple of minutes to put his things in place on his Harley and he was ready to leave.

He turned to Mary and gave her one last kiss and then she and Nancy said their good-byes and disappeared through the walkway. Joe headed back to his room through Howie and Doc's open patio door for one last look around. As he came back through the adjoining room, the guys' air conditioner was humming loudly, so Joe pulled the patio door closed behind him out of habit. For some reason, it snapped locked. Howie attempted to take one last look in his room but couldn't get back in through the door, so he didn't bother.

Doc laughed and asked Joe, "Are Mary's tits as big as they look?"

"Bigger! She's got nipples the size of saucers!" Joe answered with a smile as he leaned his Harley off its stand and pushed it toward the walkway through the building. "I'll meet you guys out in front near the main entrance. I still have to check out."

Joe fired up the bike after he got through the walkway and into the parking area and rode slowly down toward the front entrance of the hotel. He didn't bother riding up under the main entrance canopy because there were two vans and three cars loading up with a number of kids running all over the place. He parked his bike at the edge of the parking lot.

As Joe approached the front desk, the only clerk on duty was busy talking to two dark-complexioned men. One was more solidly built then the other. The men wore slacks and sport jackets over casual shirts and the smaller man, who was doing most of the talking, had some sort of an accent. Joe wasn't paying much attention to them and stopped at a stand of tourist brochures nearby to wait until the clerk was free to wait on him.

All of a sudden, the subject matter of the discussion at the front desk caught Joe's attention and his heart began to race. Out of the corner of his eye, he saw the smaller man, who had been doing most of the talking, slide a one hundred dollar bill toward the clerk and try to hide the fact that he had done so. Joe thought that it was odd because the men didn't seem to be checking in or out of the hotel, so he nonchalantly started to pay more attention to what they were talking about as he pretended to read the brochures.

". . . if they have three rooms, how many are there?" The smaller man asked the clerk.

"There are six guys, two in each room."

"How many of them are on motorcycles and when did they arrive here at the hotel?"

"There're all on motorcycles and they've been here for two nights," the clerk went on, "but the men in rooms 118B and 120B checked out earlier this morning."

As Joe fumbled with the brochures, his ears were glued to the conversation that was taking place a few feet from him. All of a sudden, it dawned on him, *The two men are asking questions about the motorcycle gang from Canada!*

"Do ya' know if there's a big man with a mustache with them? Well over six feet and real heavy-set," the small man continued.
"I shouldn't be giving out this information," the clerk whispered quietly and cautiously.

Even though Joe was not looking in their direction, he could tell that the smaller man slid another bill to the clerk. As Joe pretended to show interest in the brochures, he felt a brief and cold stare from the small man as the Colombian turned and looked directly at him.

"There is a big man in the group, kind of loud, and I'm sure that he has a mustache."

"What's the number of the room that hasn't checked out yet?"

"Room 116B. Go down that hallway to the end and turn left," the clerk answered.

Joe stood there almost paralyzed, in a state of shock, as the swarthy-looking men thanked the clerk and headed down the hall to the rear wing of rooms. They were going to Joe and Bryan's room. His heart started to pound as images of the two men raced through his mind; *Did the men have anything to do with the break-in the night before? Are they looking for the money that Bryan stole? Are they the police or drug dealers?*

"Can I help you?" The clerk turned to Joe.

"No thanks," Joe replied, holding up a brochure, "I've got just what I need."

As the men disappeared into the darkness of the long hallway toward the back wing of rooms, Joe turned and hurried toward the reception area. He breathed a sigh of relief as he went through the main door and saw that all the other guys had just brought their bikes to a standstill, right next to where his motorcycle was parked, and their bikes were still running. Joe, still totally shocked, threw his leg over his bike and fired it up.

"Let's get the hell outta here as fast as we can!" He said with a concerned look.

"What the hell's the matter with you?" Howie asked. "You're as white as a ghost!"

"Let's get moving! We have to get out of here now! We'll stop down the road and I'll tell what just happened in the lobby."

They all left immediately with Tommy in the lead and Joe last. They went west on Route 6, onto the four-lane expressway and back over the Sagamore Bridge. Joe was in the lead by that time, pacing the group at a clip well above the speed limit, trying to put some distance between them and the men at the hotel. Twenty minutes later, Joe led the gang onto the ramp to Highway 495 to New Bedford and Providence, and shortly after that, he pulled into the first rest area they came across and the guys followed with anticipation.

Joe described, fully and exactly, what he had witnessed and heard at the front desk of the hotel. The bikers were speechless. None of them knew what to think about the situation.

"Did the two guys look like cops? How were they dressed? They

might have been police, the FBI or the DEA looking for the fuckin'
money that Bryan stole," Doc remarked.

"If they were cops or agents, I don't think they would've paid
that little prick behind the counter for information. He would've
given them what they wanted for free," Joe offered.

"What the hell did the guys look like if they didn't look like
cops?"Tommy asked.

"They both had dark complexions, black hair and some sort of
accents. The smaller man did most of the talking. The big guy
looked like a real tough son-of-a-bitch." Joe went on, "I hate to say
it, but they looked Cuban or South American!"

"For some reason they seemed to have Bryan's description,"
Howie observed. "The news said that one of the pilots survived.
Maybe he saw Bryan take the money."

Mike added, "The news also said that the crash was drug related, so if those guys aren't cops, then they could be drug traffickers!
I don't like the sound of this."

"I don't know what to think either," Doc said, "but we had better try and find Bryan and let him know what the hell happened."

"We'll stop down the road and try to phone him. His note did
say that he was going home," Joe said as he started his Harley. "We
really have to tell him what happened because if those guys are drug
dealers and not cops, it could be bad. They like to kill people!"

Just before eleven, two hours out of Hyannis, they came upon the
New Haven exit and Tommy signaled to the rest of the gang to follow him off the turnpike. The group ended up parked in front of a
funky-looking restaurant and motel just off the expressway called
Captain Fantastic's which was right next to a gas station.

"I'm starving. We all missed breakfast," Tommy said.

"I hate to tell you this, Tommy, but I didn't check out of the
hotel. Those guys at the front desk scared the hell out of me. I think
that my room was in your name," Joe explained.

"They'll put it on my credit card if give them a call and tell them
you've left."

"While you're on the phone, why don't you call Bryan in Lindsay and tell him what happened in Hyannis," Howie said to Tommy.

They wandered into the restaurant and were quite impressed with the place. The front part of the premises served fast food and there was a small steak house and bar at the back that was much fancier. Captain Fantastic, a short, bald Dutchman with a big smile who introduced himself as Peter, directed the guys to the back room where the tables were larger. Doc and Joe went for a leak and Tommy went down a hall to find a payphone. The other guys sat down and looked at the menu. On Joe's way back from the washroom, he passed Tommy at the telephone.

"The girl who answered the phone at the hotel said that it was no problem to put your room on my credit card. The amount is three hundred and twenty bucks."

"Did you call Bryan yet?" Joe asked as he pulled a wad of bills out of his pocket and counted off the correct amount for Tommy.

"Yeah, there was no answer, so I left a message on his machine for him to call us tonight at The Ocean Plaza in Atlantic City."

During breakfast, they discussed the men that had been looking for *the big man with the mustache* and they tried to figure out exactly who they might have been.

"As I said before, cops don't have to pay hotel clerks for information," Joe reiterated.

"I wonder if the prowler last night had anything to do with those two men?" Doc asked.

"I wouldn't be surprised. If those guys are looking for Bryan today, they could have just as easily been there last night," Joe answered, "but neither one of them looked like the man who was going through the rooms."

Tommy added, "If they aren't cops or DEA agents, then they must be the drug traffickers who had something to do with the plane that crashed, and if that's the case, all the money that Bryan has belongs to them."

"If there's any truth to that scenario, Bryan had better find some quick way to return their money to them or make the necessary arrangements to give it to the police because if they're drug dealers, he could be in very serious trouble," Doc said.

"They actually kill people who steal from them," Howie added.

"Bryan will probably call us tonight," Tommy continued.

The food at the restaurant was great. They all had the *Fantastic Breakfast* that was advertised in a sign on the window, three eggs, bacon, sausages, beans, homefries, toast and coffee for five bucks. After a night of very little sleep and a back-hander across the side of his head, the food made Joe feel better. His head even stopped aching, but for good measure, Doc gave him a couple of Tylenols from the arsenal of pills he always carried. They finished well ahead of the lunch hour rush and it wasn't long before they were back outside.

"I want to get some gas before we head for New York City," Joe announced as he threw his leg over his Harley. "I'll see you guys over at the gas station."

Howie turned back into the restaurant, "I've got to make a quick phone call. I'll meet you guys over there in a few minutes."

About fifteen minutes later, they had all topped off their tanks and checked to see if any of their baggage was loose. None of them wanted to risk running out of gas or losing something on one of the expressways that traveled through the *Big Apple*.

CHAPTER TWENTY-NINE

Shortly after Luis and Fernando knocked on the door at 116B without a response, they went outside through the fire door at the end of the hall to see if there were any motorcycles in the courtyard. The only thing they found were boot prints and tire tracks in the sandy soil in the vicinity of the end room. The patio door to 116B was locked and the curtains were drawn so the Colombians couldn't tell if the room was still occupied or not. They peered into Doc and Howie's room through the partially opened curtains but couldn't see very much in the interior darkness. The patio door to that room was locked too. The end room was open and a quick inspection confirmed that it had been vacated.

The two men were reluctant to break into 116B in broad daylight in case they made some noise because there were a couple of maids at the far end of the inside hall and three men working in the gardens near the patio. The broken and bent screen door, lying on the grass near the rooms, reminded them that they couldn't risk drawing attention to themselves because the police had been there the night before. They went back to the front desk to ask more questions.

"Are you sure that the men in Room 116B haven't checked out yet?" Luis asked the clerk. "There are no motorcycles parked in the courtyard."

"Positive, but 118B and 120B did check out earlier this morning."

"What names were the three rooms booked under?" Luis continued.

"I'm sorry, we aren't allowed to give out that information," the clerk answered with a look on his face that indicated that he expected another one hundred dollar bill to be offered.

By this time, Fernando was getting a bit pissed at the little bastard behind the counter.

He leaned forward close to his face and said with a heavy Spanish accent, "You are much to young and good looking to have something bad happen to you. I think the couple of hundred you already got is enough for the information we need."

The clerk's face flushed and he quickly hit the buttons on his computer and said, "The same person booked all three rooms, a Thomas G. Yates of Bobcaygeon, Ontario, Canada."

Fernando leaned over the counter, one more time, and in his heavy accent said, "That wasn't difficult, was it? We thank you for your help."

As the two men walked across the lobby, Luis repeated the name a couple of times. "Thomas G. Yates of Bobcaygeon, Ontario, that's easy to remember. Let's have some breakfast while we wait. Go in and get a table that overlooks Room 116B and I'll call Beatriz."

Luis used his cell phone in the lobby and Fernando found a table along the windows overlooking the gardens. The drapes were still drawn and no motorcycles had returned.

Luis got his sister on the first ring. "I have some good news for you this time."

"Where are you calling from?"

"The Cape Hyannis Hotel in Cape Cod."

She went on, "What's the good news?"

"There are six Canadians riding motorcycles who have been here for the last two nights and the desk clerk says that one of them is definitely a big man with a mustache. They are from Ontario so they probably went right past the crash site. Two of their rooms are empty. Whoever was in them checked out early this morning, but whoever is in the third room is still here."

"Have you gone to the rooms yet?"

"Yeah, two are definitely empty and the third one has the curtains drawn and the doors are locked. There was no answer and no motorcycles so they could be back anytime."

"Why don't you just get yourself inside and see who the hell is there?"

"We have to be careful because one of Parejo's men got caught in the rooms last night and the cops were all over the place. There are also maids and workmen near the rooms."

"What are you going to do now?"

"We're gonna have breakfast here at the hotel and wait. The restaurant overlooks the rooms and the patio where they park their motorcycles. If they don't show up by the time we finish eating, we'll find some other way to get into the room. I'll call you later today."

Luis joined Fernando at the table near the windows that allowed an unobstructed view of Room 116B. They ordered and settled in for a leisurely breakfast that they hoped would be interrupted by the return of the Canadians. As they ate, they glanced out over the gardens in the direction of the rooms and patios.

The men took their time eating and then took turns looking at the sports section of the morning paper. They eventually got tired of waiting and paid for their breakfast and left. It had been an hour and a half since their original inspection of the rooms and there had been absolutely no activity near Room 116B's patio during their surveillance and the drapes had remained closed. They men wandered back down the hall toward B-Wing. By that time, the two maids were in other rooms nearby so Luis decided to pay for some help to get the door opened.

Luis and Fernando knocked on the door one more time, but once again, there was no answer. Luis pulled a ten-dollar bill from his pocket and unraveled it so it could be easily seen and walked over two rooms to where a maid was working.

"Excuse me," he politely said as he stuck his head into Room 112B, "I left my key-card in my room and my roommate has gone for breakfast. Can you open my door for me?"

As he asked, the ten-dollar bill was clearly visible to the maid in his outstretched hand.

"Sure," the smiling maid said as she took the offered gratuity, "What room is yours?"

"Room 116B," Luis replied quickly.

It took the maid only a moment to open the door and she immediately went back to her cleaning duties down the hall. Fernando entered the room first, with his Colt 45 in hand, and Luis was right behind him. They shut the door quickly and started to look around. It took only seconds for them to realize that whoever had been staying there had also checked out.

"Look at this paper," Fernando said, "it's folded to the story about the crash in Vermont."

"Son-of-a-bitch!" Luis cursed aloud as he found another copy of a newspaper.

After the Colombians breezed through the adjoining room, they stormed back to the lobby. The mousy clerk was, luckily, all alone at the front desk as the men arrived. Luis reached across the counter, grabbed the clerk by the tie and jerked him forward close to his face.

"Room 116B is empty! They've checked out! Look at your fuckin' records again!" Luis snarled as he let go of the guy's tie so he could move quickly to his computer.

"I've been here all morning and no one has checked out of that room," he said shaking.

The clerk started to punch buttons and was so nervous that he kept making mistakes. He tried to correct them as quickly as possible so he wouldn't infuriate his new friends any further.

"Christ! They have left! I know that they hadn't when I spoke to you earlier. I've been here the whole time!" He hit the buttons one more time and the screen confirmed that the occupants of Room 116B had in fact checked out. "Let me talk to the girls in the back office where the switchboard is and see if they know what the hell is going on!"

"Do it fast!" Luis snapped.

The clerk went quickly to the doorway at the far end of the reception desk and talked to the unseen workers in the back office and then came back, sheepishly, to the Colombians.

"One of the girls says that Mr. Yates telephoned the hotel, just a few minutes ago, and advised that his friends had forgotten to check out when they left this morning. He had her put the charges for Room 116B on his credit card," the clerk explained in an apologetic voice.

The angry men turned and left the lobby without saying another word to the clerk. They went out the main door and walked to the far side of the canopy-covered reception area and stopped where the shade met the sunshine. The brilliant sun was high in the sky overhead and it was a beautiful day as Luis and Fernando stood there at the edge of the parking lot trying to decide what to do next. At that moment, three motorcycles heading toward Hyannis roared past on the main road in front of the hotel.

Luis just looked at them and shook his head, "The bastards!"

"Damn it! Now we have to start all over again!" Fernando said.

"If they left before we got here this morning, they have more than a two hour head start. They had to either go back north toward Boston or south to New York City. I think that Beatriz should call Parejo again, just in case they are going north. She should also call Briceno in New York City so he can give us a hand locating them if they went south. At least we now have a name and we know that they're Canadians. I think they're probably still heading south because they're only about three or four days out of Ontario on a motorcycle trip and are probably on holidays for at least a week and maybe even two."

As the men walked toward Fernando's car, Luis called his sister on his cell phone and described what had happened at the hotel. She agreed to call her contacts in Boston and New York to help locate the bikers. It wasn't long before the Colombians were traveling on the four-lane expressway over the Sagamore Bridge with Fernando at the wheel of the Lincoln.

"At least we know there are six Canadians on bikes with Ontario plates," Luis was thinking out loud, "and we also have a name, Thomas G. Yates from Bobcaygeon, Ontario."

"What are we gonna do?" Fernando asked.

"We've been following these guys south for the last couple of days so I think that they're still traveling south. We'll continue on to New York City and check out a few service centres, gas stations and restaurants along the way. I'm sure that Briceno's men will locate the bikers on the Connecticut Turnpike into New York City sometime today."

CHAPTER THIRTY

It was another bright, sunny day with wisps of white clouds that streaked across the light blue sky. The next leg of the trip would take the bikers to New York City, two hundred miles south, but they would be able to make good time traveling on expressways. They had traveled through Rhode Island and Connecticut on the Connecticut Turnpike, not far from the shores of the Atlantic Ocean, or more specifically, Rhode Island Sound and Long Island Sound. The scenery and sightseeing had been fantastic with the deep blue ocean on the left, bright green forests to the right and the New York City skyscrapers on the horizon.

As they approached the outskirts of the huge city, the heavy traffic began to bunch up, but it was moving along well at about fifty. The expressways that ran through New York City were terrifying. It was like riding through dry, underground canals as they were most often below street level. There were high concrete walls on both sides of the highways and the bikers often traveled under other expressways and even under buildings or whole city blocks in the downtown core that created long dark tunnels that were almost spooky.

Every so often, there were wrecked vehicles that had been just left on the roadside. Anything of value had been stripped from them and they were left behind in twisted piles of rusting metal. Some of the abandoned cars and trucks looked like they had been there for years because they were totally covered in a heavy coating of dark rust. The idea of stopping or breaking down on one of those expressways in the middle of the city was something the guys just didn't want to think about.

As Joe cruised along, at the same speed as the heavy traffic, he gawked around at all of the unusual sights. The skyline of skyscrapers was magnificent and he caught many different glimpses of the Empire State Building far in the distance through the periodic openings among the other tall buildings. He had never seen it up close before.

As he gazed around at the sights, the traffic suddenly came to a complete stop. He hadn't been paying attention. By the time he hit the breaks it was too late. There was no way that he was going to stop in time to avoid an accident. His brakes locked and his tires started to squeal and smoke. Just before he was about to crash into the rear end of the car in front of him, he let off on his brakes and aimed the motorcycle down the very narrow, paved shoulder to the left of the vehicles on the inside lane. There was barely enough room for his bike between the guardrail and the other cars that had already stopped. It took him about four car lengths to finally stop the motorcycle and he had no idea how he had avoided at least scraping one of the other cars that he had passed by. From that moment on, he kept his eyes glued to the road and the traffic and that was the last time he ever saw the Empire State Building.

All the bikers found the ride through New York City very hectic, but they eventually cruised over the George Washington Bridge and passed a large sign pointing the way to Newark. They had all made it safely through the large city and were, by then, in New Jersey traveling south on the New Jersey Turnpike. The traffic was still fairly heavy and Tommy, Mike and Doc, who were out in the lead took the next exit ramp that read *Garden State Parkway*, which winds its way south through the state, parallel to the ocean, to Atlantic City. Joe and Howie were trailing back in the traffic behind the other guys.

Howie moved his motorcycle over close to Joe's bike and yelled for Joe to follow him. They drove right past the Atlantic City exit, where the other guys had gone, and continued south on the New Jersey Turnpike past another sign that read *Philadelphia*. Joe had no idea what Howie was doing or why he hadn't followed the others so

he pulled up beside him. Howie just looked over at him and started
to laugh that crazy laugh of his.

"Where the hell are we going?" Joe yelled at him over the sounds
of the bikes and traffic.

"I've got a date in Philly!" The loon screamed back and laughed
some more.

Joe had no idea how long it took the other guys to realize that he and
Howie were no longer behind them. It didn't really matter that the
two of them went missing because they were all headed for the
Ocean Plaza Hotel and Casino in Atlantic City anyway and if Joe
and Howie didn't get there that day they would get there the next.
Joe hoped that Tommy, Doc and Mike would contact Bryan about
the men that were looking for him and have those problems resolved
before he and Howie arrive in the gambling mecca. Joe had been
thinking about Bryan all day and had decided that Bryan would
have gone back to Ontario as fast as he could to put the money in a
safe place. Bryan had found the solution to all of his problems.

As Joe and Howie traveled deeper into New Jersey, the expressways became much older and narrower. They were in a much poorer state of repair than the roads in New York State. The northeast
part of the United States that they were now traveling through had
about twice the population of all of Canada and there was a lot of
history in the area. That part of the country had been developed
long before America had even become a nation. They passed a sign
that read *Trenton: 20 Miles*, so they knew that they were going in
the right direction.

As the rush hour traffic started to build up, Joe's legs and ass
were so sore that it was time to stop for a rest. Joe waved at Howie
and pointed to his gas tank and pulled out in front of him. At the
next exit, they found a busy gas station with a variety store and they
pulled into different pumps. As soon as their tanks were filled, they
moved the Harleys over to the store.

"Where the hell are you taking me?" Joe asked as soon as he took
off his helmet.

"I met a broad in Florida the last time I was down there and I told her that I'd buy her dinner in Philadelphia tonight," Howie explained with a big smile that became a laugh.

"When did you talk to her last?"

"I called her from Captain Fantastic's in New Haven this morning and told her that you and I would be in Philly about seven-thirty tonight."

"How the hell did you know that I'd be going with you?"

Howie answered with that laugh of his, "I knew that I could trick ya'!"

"You crazy bastard! How long have you known this gal?"

"For about half an hour. I met her in the airport bar in Ft. Lauderdale on my last trip to Florida. She and some friends were waiting for a flight back to Philadelphia."

"Where are we going to meet her at seven-thirty?" Joe asked shaking his head.

"At a neat restaurant and bar in Philly that is a fifties and sixties dance bar that serves Chinese Food. Its called *Wok'n Roll,*" Howie answered with that crazy laugh again.

The laughing was contagious and Joe could hardly answer him as Howie went into the store to get a couple of beers, "You are nuts!"

Joe had his sleeping bag off the back of his bike when Howie returned.

"What the hell are you doing now?" Howie asked.

As Joe unrolled his sleeping bag that he used for a backrest, he answered him.

"My ass is killing me so I'm going to get my pillow out of the bag so I can sit on it. We've been on these bikes all day. I don't know if I can do this for another two hours. My leather jacket is rolled up in here too and I'm going to put it on."

They drank their beers while Joe put his sleeping bag back in place. He put his leather jacket on and placed the pillow longways along the seat in readiness for the rest of the trip. Joe knew that it wasn't very macho, but at least he was going to be more comfortable. By the time they got back onto the Turnpike, the traffic was heavier and moving at a much slower pace.

The rush hour thinned out as Joe and Howie continued south toward the old stomping grounds of the likes of Ben Franklin and William Penn. They were cruising along at the speed limit when all of a sudden ten motorcycles, traveling in the same direction, joined them. It was a *real motorcycle gang*. They all rode Harleys with high handlebars, full leathers, including vests and chaps, black boots, beards, long hair and tattoos. Automatically, Joe raised his left arm in a very friendly greeting gesture as they went by him. Six of the wild and untamed bikers went by Joe and on past Howie. The seventh rider slowed down as he pulled up beside Joe and looked over at him and laughed. As they traded glances, Joe knew the guy was looking at the pillow that he was sitting on and he knew that he must have been one pretty sight to that tough guy. Joe laughed back, pointed at his pillow and shrugged and thought, *At least he's laughing!*

Joe's new buddy had on the full bikers' regalia; some kind of an army helmet, a full beard that hadn't been trimmed in years, worn black leather from head to toe and three tattoos on the large arm that Joe could see, but his Harley was *pink*. He rode beside Joe for what seemed to be an eternity looking over at him sitting on the pillow, but he was still smiling. He had noticed the Ontario plates and leaned over toward Joe and laughingly yelled above the engine noise.

"Do all Canadian bikers ride on pretty pillows like that one?"

Joe answered him with a laugh to maintain the friendly interaction, "I've been on this fuckin' thing for over ten hours and my ass is killing me!"

The tough guy gave Joe a *thumbs up* sign with another laugh, cranked up his speed and pulled away. The big biker then slowed down next to Howie. The two of them yelled back and forth in some kind of a high-speed conversation, laughed with each other, and then he took off followed by the last few members of his gang. As the last biker went by, Howie increased his speed and pulled right in behind them. Joe did the same.

The Canadians became associate members of a real motorcycle gang for about forty minutes and they covered a lot of miles. The gang drove at speeds much faster than they had been traveling and Joe and Howie were amazed at the way the traffic gave them a wide berth. They didn't even worry about the state police that had been parked on the roadside at two locations. As the gang approached the Norristown exit on the Turnpike, Joe and Howie's new buddy slowed his hog down until he was right along side them once again and yelled.

"We're pullin' off here to have a couple o' beers at one of our regular joints. Why don't you Canadians join us for a beer? I'll even buy!"

Joe, who was right beside him, looked at Howie and the two of them nodded to him. "Great! We'll follow you guys."

Without even slowing down, the motorcycle gang pulled off at the Norristown exit and went toward Pennsylvania. Joe and Howie stayed bunched right up with them as if they really belonged. A mile down the road, the bikers pulled into a seedy looking bar called *Dedo's Roadhouse* and they all parked their motorcycles together, out in front, near fifteen or twenty other bikes already there. Their high-speed buddy introduced himself.

"Howdy, I'm Mickey M." He raised his right arm for the usual biker's handshake.

Joe raised his right arm and locked thumbs with their new friend, "I'm Joe M., the M. stands for McConnell, and this is my buddy Howie. How're ya' doin'?"

Howie completed the ceremonial handshake and said, "You fuckin' guys don't give a shit about the cops. We sure covered a lot of miles since we started to ride with ya'."

"What cops!" Mickey M. laughed. "Ontario Plates! I was in Toronto last summer."

"That's were I live, right downtown," Joe advised. "How did you like our city?"

"Hell, we really liked it. We had one big bash with the Para Dice

Riders up there. We'd go back to Toronto," Mickey M. answered. "Come on in for a beer."

The three of them followed the last couple of wild looking gang members into the bar and they all sat at a few tables that had been pulled together near the jukebox. One of the bikers ordered four pitchers of draft beer and Mikey M. introduced the Canadians to his buddies.

"This is Howie and Joe, they're from Toronto." Mickey M. went on, "That's Steve, Dino and Lou. You can introduce yourselves to the other guys at the far end of the table."

The Canucks acknowledged all the gang members, but they had difficulty remembering all the names. The bikers seemed to be a friendly bunch. A short, Greek guy, named Cooly, who was one of the owners of the establishment, delivered the four pitchers of beer. As the beer made its way from the pitchers to the glasses that were scattered around the tables, Micky M. introduced the owner to the Canadians.

"Cooly, these guys are visiting from Toronto, Canada. Joe and Howie."

"Nice to meet ya', one of these pitchers is on the house for our guests, we don't get many Canadians down here," Cooly said as he turned and went back to the bar.

"Thanks, Cooly," Howie commented as he left.

"Where are you guys from?" Joe asked.

Steve answered, "We're all from Philadelphia. We were in New York for a couple of days partying. Where are you guys headed?"

"We're going to Philadelphia for the night to meet some friends and then we're going on to Atlantic City for two or three days," Howie explained, "and after that, south to Washington."

"Joe, do all the bikers up in Toronto usually ride around sitting on *frilly pillows* like yours?" Dino asked as all the bikers around the table broke up.

"Just the *Bitches*," Joe said with a laugh. "We've been on those fuckin' bikes since eight this morning when we left Cape Cod and my ass is on fire."

"You guys are kinda lucky. We usually don't let bikers who sit on fuckin' fancy pillows ride with us," Lou commented as a few of them laughed again.

"OK, OK! I'll put the damn pillow back in my sleeping bag." Joe answered with a laugh. "The pillow's one thing, but Mickey M. is riding a *pink* fuckin' Harley!"

As soon as the comment was made, all of the bikers immediately quit laughing and looked very serious. They all looked first at Joe, as if they couldn't believe what he had just said, and then they looked directly at Mickey M. as if something bad was about to happen.

"My hog ain't fuckin' pink . . . its *peach*!" Mickey M. said in a very serious tone trying to act like he was really pissed.

All the other bikers started to laugh. They had heard that line many times before.

It didn't take the group long to finish off the first four pitchers of beer. It was starting to get late so it was time for the Canadians to get back on the road to Philly.

Howie said, "I'm afraid that we've gotta get the hell going."

"It was great meeting you guys," Joe said as he reached into his pocket for some money and threw a twenty-dollar bill on the table to cover some of the beer.

"We don't want you guys from Canada paying for beer down here, it's on us." Mickey M. said as he handed Joe back the twenty and he took it to be polite. "Me and Dino are takin' our old ladies to Atlantic City for a few days tomorrow, maybe we'll bump into you guys down there and ya' can buy us a beer."

"Sound great," Howie said.

"Thanks guys. I want you to know I'm gonna get rid of that frilly pillow right now!" They all laughed some more.

Joe and Howie had a leak before they left the bar and then went back to the Norristown exit and pulled out onto the Turnpike. The two Canucks continued south toward Philly and Joe, still sitting on his pillow, pulled over close to Howie and yelled above the highway noise.

"What did Mickey M. say to you when he pulled up beside you on the Turnpike?"

Howie smiled and started to laugh, "I asked him if we could ride along with them."

"What did he say to ya'?"

Howie went on, bouncing up and down, trying to control his laughter, "He said that we could ride with them on one condition."

"And what the hell was that?"

"*As long as the pussy sitting on the pillow stays well out back!*" Howie broke up and couldn't stop laughing.

"Fuck him! I still think his Harley's *pink!*"

CHAPTER THIRTY-ONE

A s Doc, Tommy and Mike continued south, they eventually noticed that Joe and Howie had gone missing. They initially thought that they were just lagging behind in the traffic, but soon realized that they had disappeared. Tommy thought that they had just missed the turn onto the Garden State Parkway and that didn't really matter anyway because they were all going to the Ocean Plaza. They stopped for gas at the Toms River cut-off and the young gas station attendant who filled their tanks fell in love with Doc's Harley. Doc even let him sit on it for a few minutes. After a short break, they continued south toward Atlantic City and the famous Boardwalk.

The Garden State Parkway links the millions of gamblers in New York City and northern New Jersey with the casinos to the south. The beautiful eight-lane highway has four lanes going both north and south, with a wide, treed median, that cuts the view to the vehicles that travel in opposite directions. The Friday traffic was heavy as usual.

The flat, Atlantic City Expressway into the gambling city had been built on reclaimed lands, with thousands of acres of cattails, bulrushes and water on both sides. All the large major casinos that had been built along the Atlantic Ocean dotted the horizon as far as one could see. The only scenery on the way into Atlantic City, except for the swamp, was about a hundred billboards, done with the usual American flare, touting the various games of chance and all the different entertainment that was available at the casinos. Most of the casinos had been built on the famous *Atlantic City Boardwalk*; however, there were two very large and spectacular complexes, a few miles to the north, on the way into the city.

Two major casinos had been built right next to the large, arching rainbow-bridge that was the entrance to the small, island town of Brigantine. Harrah's was to the west of the bridge and the Trump Castle to the east. Both casinos were on Absecon Channel, an access route that linked the ocean and the inland waterway, and they had large marinas that were full of yachts and sailboats. The Trump Castle looked huge in the distance and its parking garage was almost the same size as the hotel and casino. It had been built in the shape of a real castle for *King Donald and his Court.* Harrah's was just as large and quite unique. The rainbow-bridge over the channel sloped up into the blue sky between the two large complexes.

Tommy yelled to Doc, "The Ocean Plaza is down on the Boardwalk. Follow me."

On the way to the ocean, they traveled through a very poor part of the city where many buildings were boarded up or condemned, however, it appeared that people still lived in them. All of a sudden, the terrible, sprawling slums, turned into billions and billions of dollars worth of first class, resort hotels and casinos. The contrast within just a few blocks was shocking.

The main reception area of the Ocean Plaza Hotel and Casino was in, what could be described as a tunnel, underneath the casino and a large tower of rooms. The tall, well-dressed doorman wasn't overly impressed as the group of bikers arrived until he found out that they had reservations for the weekend. He gave them directions as to where to park their motorcycles while they went inside to check in. He also advised them that they would have to park their own bikes in the underground parking garage, as the employees were not allowed to touch them. They walked past the planters and shrubbery, through a huge revolving door, directly into the main lobby of the hotel and on toward the front desk.

The Ocean Plaza, located at the more southerly end of the Boardwalk near Caesars, the Trump Plaza and the Trump Regency, was an opulent structure that stretched forty floors into the skyline. The top five were filled with expensive suites that were reserved for the very wealthy and the highrollers. The hotel boasted five restaurants, a seven-hundred-seat theatre and a health club. The lobby was architecturally crowded, in that there were twelve four-by-four foot pillars of dark mirrors, trimmed with red and gold that towered sixty feet into the air. The reception desk, along the wall to the right, was a hundred feet long with a number of workstations, each with a computer. A single escalator ascended from the lobby to the main casino one floor above. At the end of the reception area, there was a hallway leading to the ocean that passed by a couple of restaurants and a small lounge. The actual location of the famous Atlantic City Boardwalk was just through the revolving doors, past the lounge, on the ocean side of the complex.

On the way to the main desk, Doc spotted a bank of house phones and suggested to the guys that, just for fun, they should call the hotel operator and see if Bryan happened to be there. They all really thought that he had gone home. Doc was shocked when he found that Bryan was in fact registered.

"Hello!" Bryan's voice was loud and clear on the other end of the line.

"What the hell did you take off for you loon?" Doc asked into the phone.

"Because I was tired of all the bullshit. Where the hell are you guys?"

"We're right here in the lobby you crazy bastard!"

"Get the hell up here right now, the party's just starting. I'm in Room 3630!" Bryan said.

Tommy and Mike just shook their heads as they learned that Bryan was actually there.

"Let's go up to his room and see what the hell he's up to before we check in. The motorcycles will be all right where they are for a little while," Doc decided.

They found the elevators just past the escalator, entered one and pushed the button for Bryan's floor. As the three of them walked down the long corridor toward Suite 3630, they could hear Bryan's laughter resonating down the hallway. Doc knocked on the unlatched door of the room, pushed it open and the three guys walked into a very large and beautifully decorated suite. Bryan, in a golf shirt and his underwear, was sitting in the middle of a double bed, just to the left of the entrance, not far from the door, with two *movie stars*, in their underwear, a blonde and a redhead. He had a bar set up on a small table nearby.

"Where the hell have you guys been?" Bryan asked with a laugh. "These two little sweethearts and I have been here for two days waiting for you!"

Bryan and the girls had obviously had plenty to drink.

"Who are your friends?" Tommy asked.

"This is Karen," Bryan said as he pointed to the redhead, "and this is Susan." She was a blonde. "This is Doc, Mike and Tommy," he said pointing toward the newcomers.

Bryan continued, "Why don't you guys pour yourselves a drink? We've really got a head start on you. Where the hell are Joe and Howie?"

"We lost them in traffic just after we got into the northern part of New Jersey. They may have missed the Atlantic City cut-off," Mike explained. "They'll probably be along soon."

"We haven't checked in yet or parked our motorcycles. We just left them in the reception area," Doc said. "I may as well stay with you, who knows when the other guys will get here."

Doc smiled at Bryan and looked at the two girls.

"That's fine with me. There's lots of room," Bryan answered and then turned to Mike and Tommy. "When you guys get settled, come back here for cocktails."

The guys left Bryan with his new friends. They were all shaking their heads as they walked down the hall and decided that Bryan was too drunk to deal with the money issue and besides, the girls were there. They decided to leave the resolution of that problem until morning.

Bryan's suite wasn't the *Royal Suite*, but it wasn't shabby. It had a large master bedroom with a king-size bed, an ensuite bathroom with a separate shower and a double Jacuzzi bathtub. The main room had another double bed, just outside the master suite, that was also used as a sitting area because it had a number of large pillows on it. There was another smaller bathroom nearby, and at the opposite end of the room, there was a living room area with a wet-bar and a large window that overlooked the ocean. The living room had a couch, a couple of end tables with lamps and two easy chairs set up around a coffee table. There was also a writing desk with a reading light and casual chair in one corner.

Mike used his credit card for their room because Tommy had paid in Hyannis. They all parked their motorcycles in a large, corner parking spot with Bryan's bike that they happened to come across. Tommy and Mike's room was Room 2323 and they went directly there to get settled. They told Doc that they would be up to Bryan's room in about an hour.

Doc, carrying all his belongings, knocked on the door of Room 3630 and Bryan opened it and said, "Come on in, let's get this party goin'!"

By the time the other two guys showered and shaved and got back to the suite on the thirty-sixth floor, Bryan, Doc and the two little ladies were all under the influence. The party was well underway and the four loons were in the middle of the bed, all in their underwear, with drinks in their hands.

"Why don't you guys pour a drink and join the party, there's room on the bed for two more fat guys!" Bryan said with a laugh. "Make yourselves at home."

Tommy laughed out loud and said as he pointed to Doc, "I can't even think of having a drink with that thing hanging out!"
All heads turned in Doc's direction and everyone else started to laugh too. His left ball was hanging out of his underwear. After it was tucked back in, the newcomers poured themselves Black Russians and pulled two chairs over to the vicinity of the party. A very jovial Bryan, from his place of authority in the middle of the bed, set out the itinerary for the balance of the evening. He was clearly in charge of the festivities.

"I just ordered a couple of trays of food to nibble on, are you guys hungry?"

"That sounds great, but I still want to have some real food later," Mike said.

Bryan continued, "Let's have a bite to eat here and a few more drinks and then go somewhere and play some Blackjack."

It looked like the girls were along for the haul. Bryan had quietly told Doc that they were both from Philadelphia, where they had real jobs during the week, but they both did a little part-time hooking on weekends. They had taken Friday off work and arrived at the shore on Thursday night. Karen was a salesperson that sold advertising in the city area for a magazine publisher and Susan was a woman's make-up sales representative that covered New Jersey, Pennsylvania and Ohio. Both of them had told Bryan that their day-job incomes didn't keep them in the style that they most enjoyed. They had also told him that they just don't jump into bed with anybody, they have to like the men involved. Bryan and Doc were pretty likeable guys.

Bryan had met the two of them the night before at the Blackjack tables at the Ocean Plaza and had made arrangements to meet them for lunch earlier that day. During lunch, with lots of wine and lots of laughs, Bryan had negotiated their company for the rest of the day for two hundred bucks each and they didn't have to have sex, unless of course, they wanted to at some point. Bryan had promised them that he was expecting five highrollers to meet him later in the day so they must have seen some potential in the arrangement because they were still there.

The young, good-looking bellboy that delivered the food didn't even blink when he walked into the room and saw four people on the bed and two watching from the sidelines, after all, it was Atlantic City where anything goes. Bryan gave the kid a twenty-five dollar chip as a tip and he let himself out. One food tray consisted of mainly rabbit food and two kinds of dip. The other had smoked salmon, capers, onions, and three different kinds of cheeses and assorted crackers. The food was well received by everyone.

Karen, the little redhead, was sitting cross-legged showing very clearly that her hair was natural. Every second time she took a sip of her white wine, she would spill some of it and it would run down the cleavage of her small, firm breasts. Between her giggles and half-heartedly pushing him away, Doc managed to lick up most of what was spilled before it was wasted. The wine spilling and fondling continued and it became obvious that Doc was getting a chubby. He rolled over close to Karen and whispered something in her ear and she laughed and pushed him away. She then leaned forward and whispered something back. Doc shook his head Yes and the two of them rolled off the bed laughing and went into the master bedroom and shut the door.

The party in the other room continued until Doc and Karen rejoined the group. The two of them had drunken smiles on their faces and Doc went right to the bar and got them each another drink. Susan was well on her way by this time and Bryan kept pulling down one side of her bra strap exposing a cute little breast, about a 34B, and she didn't seem to care. Tommy and Mike were still sucking back Black Russians and were starting to feel pretty good too.

Bryan, from the middle of the bed, announced about ten o'clock that it was time to get ready to go to the casinos. He left to have a quick shower.

Susan and Karen immediately got up and looked around the room for their clothes.

Doc took the rest of his stuff into the bedroom and stepped into the shower as Bryan got out. When he finished, the girls took over the ensuite. As Karen passed Doc on her way into the bedroom, she gave his groin area a tender squeeze through the towel that he had wrapped around himself. The girls shut the bathroom door as Doc joined the others in the main part of the room.

"What the hell did you do in the bedroom?" Bryan asked because not knowing the details of what had happened was driving him crazy.

"I gave her a hundred for a blow-job! I would've just lost it gambling anyway."

"Was it worth it?" Mike asked.

Doc replied with a laugh, "I'm gonna give her another hundred later!"

"Bryan, did Doc tell you about the two guys that were looking for you at the front desk of the Cape Hyannis Hotel?" Tommy asked.

"I really didn't have a chance to mention it to him. We were kinda busy."

Tommy went on, "When Joe went to check out of the Cape Hyannis Hotel this morning, there were two, dark-complexioned men at the front desk, questioning the clerk about a bunch of guys on motorcycles, and more specifically, about a big man with a mustache."

Bryan answered, "McConnell's too fuckin' excited about the money. He's probably dreaming or just confused about what happened at the hotel. Every bloody motorcycle gang in the country has a big man with a mustache in it."

"What if it was the police or the drug dealers looking for the money you took and they really do have your description?" Mike asked.

"What a bunch of horse shit!" Bryan answered. "No one saw me pick up the duffel bag of money at the crash site, not even you guys."

Bryan quickly dismissed any such notion that he had been seen taking the money and offered the guys two thousand dollars each from his stash. The duffel bag of money had been placed in a private hotel locker for safekeeping, but he had kept out about fifteen thousand dollars to have some fun with in Atlantic City.

"Joe was serious," Doc added. "We forgot to tell you that someone ransacked our room the night before the men showed up and there's the possibility that both incidents are related."

"Screw him! Neither one of those things mean anything. Here's a couple of grand for the night, we may as well have some fun," Bryan said as he held the money out toward them.

They were all pretty well half in the bag so they kind of shook their heads and took the money that was offered. Nothing more was said about the men that Joe had supposedly seen.

"I need another Black Russian," Tommy said and Mike asked for one too.

Bryan continued to talk to Tommy and Mike, "If you guys decide to spend your money as foolishly as Doc did, find your own dates. I think we're gonna keep these two."

They got the hint as the girls came out of the bedroom all dolled up in pretty, tight-fitting sundresses that were fairly low cut and well above their knees.

The main foyer of the Ocean Plaza was full of people coming and going. There was the constant sound of coins falling into metal trays, bells ringing and people screaming, filtering down from the casino on the floor above. The six partyers took the escalator up from the lobby.

As the group sauntered into the casino, among the rows of tables of chance, Doc decided, "Bryan, let's grab those two empty seats at that twenty-five dollar table."

"Perfect, I'm really in the mood to gamble!" Bryan said as he and Doc took the seats and the two girls cuddled right up to them as if they were going to bring them luck.

"There are seats at the ten dollar tables just over here," Tommy said to Mike.

"Christ! Look at all the attractive women milling around here on their own," Mike, commented. "How many of them are working part-time on weekends?"

Tommy and Mike played Blackjack for about an hour and a half and both of them broke about even so there was no real excitement or reason to continue playing. They were both hungry for a solid meal so they decided to leave and find a place to get something to eat. They told the others that they were heading out and went back to the main floor of the hotel where they found *Ye Olde Steak House* back toward the Boardwalk. They both ordered huge New York Cut Steaks, mushrooms, baked potatoes and salads and as soon as they finished eating, they took a short walk on the Boardwalk and then went back to their room to crash.

Bryan and Doc started out by ordering drinks as soon as they sat down at the Blackjack table and they both got five hundred dollars worth of chips. Things started to go well for Bryan almost immediately. He was on a roll and nothing could stop him. He was up about fourteen hundred bucks and Doc was up about eight hundred and the drinks hadn't stopped flowing since they had arrived. The two fat guys and their dates eventually decided to go to the lounge to enjoy some entertainment while they could still walk and talk.

The lounge was on the casino floor, in the southeast corner, on the ocean and Boardwalk side of the building. They arrived just in time for the last show of the night that advertised a comedian and some kind of a fifties and sixties review. The comedian, who some-one had said was a Canadian and was Rich Little's brother, started the show with *Barnyard Calls* no less. That was all Bryan needed to get into the act. Every time the poor guy did one of his calls, Bryan would answer him with one of the same. There were more barn-yard calls in the audience, than on stage, and Bryan got as many laughs as the comedian. The poor guy finally finished the opening act and both he and Bryan got a standing ovation from a table of real drunks.

The second part of the show was a singing group called *Yesterday's Heroes* that did three acts and were very entertaining. The first set was as Bill Hailey and the Comets and they started out with *Rock Around the Clock*. The second set was with the lead singer dressed as Elvis with the usual white outfit, huge belt and sideburns and he sang a number of Elvis' famous hits. In the third set, the band came onto the stage wearing blonde wigs, white pants and colored tops. They started off the set with *California Girls*. After the show, Bryan, Doc and the girls finished their drinks and went straight back to the Blackjack tables in the main part of the casino.

Around two-thirty in the morning, Doc, who was still up about a hundred, finally complained that he couldn't take it any longer. Bryan had lost all the money he had won earlier and wasn't really ready to leave at that time, but Susan talked him into it. He picked up his chips, with a little help from his friend, and they all staggered toward the elevators. The girls had been staying with friends, but decided to stay at the Ocean Plaza for the night.

Bryan and Susan went directly into the master bedroom. The last thing that Bryan vaguely remembered that night was giving Susan a hundred dollar bill, but in the morning, he couldn't remember if he ever got any value for his expenditure. Doc and Karen crashed in the main room.

CHAPTER THIRTY-TWO

Luis and Fernando had traveled the same route that the Canadians had taken that day from Cape Cod to New York City. They had stopped at about half a dozen service centres, gas stations and restaurants looking for any information that would confirm that the Canadian bikers were actually headed in that direction. It had been a very long day for them as well because they hadn't obtained any positive news about the gang along the way. They had missed Captain Fantastic's Restaurant near the New Haven exit that had been the only place where the bikers had stopped on the first leg of their trip.

It was late in the day when they got to New York City and the traffic had been very heavy, bumper to bumper, and moving slowly. By the time they made their way through the city, they were dead tired and really not in the mood to travel much further, so they pulled into the Holiday Inn near Newark International Airport and decided to crash for the night. Luis hadn't heard from their contact in New York, Roberto Briceno, so there must not have been anything important to report. He decided that he would call him as soon as they got settled in their room.

Luis dialed the number that his sister had given him earlier in the day and after a polite introduction to a man that he had never met before, he asked, "Have you and your men had any luck locating the Canadian bikers that we've been following from Cape Cod?"

"I spoke to Parejo in Boston late this afternoon and he said that there was no sign of them heading north through his city."

"We stopped at a number of places along the Connecticut Turnpike this afternoon and got absolutely no information that indicated that they were still heading south, but I have a gut feeling that they are."

Briceno continued. "My men in north Jersey saw two groups of bikers late this afternoon. The first guys that reported to me saw a motorcycle gang with about eight or ten members heading south on the New Jersey Turnpike toward Philly. My men said that they were a scary looking bunch with Pennsylvania plates."

"What about the other group of bikers they saw?"

"Two more of my men were heading north, back toward the city, when they saw five bikers going south on the opposite side of the expressway. They couldn't get turned around to take a closer look at them."

"Did they happen to see their license plates?"

"They couldn't read them but they said that they were blue and white. What color are the plates you're looking for?"

"That was probably them! Ontario plates are blue and white!" Luis went on, "Did they take the Garden State Parkway south or did they stay on the New Jersey Turnpike?"

"When my men saw them they were north of the Garden State cut-off so they don't really know which way they went, but they had to take one of those highways because they're the only two major expressways that intersect there."

"In the morning, could you have a couple of men try a few gas stations, service centres and restaurants along the New Jersey Turnpike toward Philly to see if there's any possibility that the Canadians went that way and if there is any news, call me on my cell. We'll take the Garden State Parkway down to Atlantic City and see if we can locate them."

"If I have any good news for you, I'll give you a call. Your sister gave me your cell number. Good Luck!"

"Thanks for your help. I'm gonna call my sister right now and perhaps I'll speak to you again tomorrow."

"Fernando, in the morning, we're gonna head for the casinos of Atlantic City. If you'd been lucky enough to find five or ten million dollars, wouldn't you head for the casinos to do some serious gambling and have some fun?"

"That makes sense!"

Luis knew that anyone with the kind of cash that was in one of the duffel bags from the plane could well be on their way to the casinos. He decided that there was no point in going to Atlantic City that night because they might be able to pick up some definite information about the Canadians while they drive down the Garden State Parkway in the morning.

Luis called Beatriz for his last report of the day. The news was not very promising so she decided that there was no reason to call Castrillo that evening. There was no point upsetting him anymore than he already was. She would wait for what she hoped would be better news from Luis the next day.

Luis and Fernando decided to go over to the bar that was next to the Holiday Inn for a few cocktails before going to bed. They would get an early start in the morning.

CHAPTER THIRTY-THREE

Joe and Howie were still on the New Jersey Turnpike after the sun set in the western sky. The traffic got heavier after they left the motorcycle gang and as it got dark, the potholes and cracks in the road were more difficult to see. It was also difficult for the riders to maintain the same rate of speed that they had while they traveled with the real bikers, but they would likely be on time for Howie's date. At just before seven-thirty, they pulled off the expressway and rode into Camden, New Jersey, which was just across the Delaware River from Philadelphia.

They rode toward the river that separated the two cities. A large sign that read the *Ben Franklin Bridge* was just ahead appeared and Howie pulled into a gas station looking for a telephone and Joe followed him. There was a phone and Howie went inside to use it.

Joe sat on his bike and looked at the Philadelphia skyline across the river and wondered what changes had taken place since he had last visited. He had been born there and lived in Drexel Hill, in the west end of the city, until he was fourteen years old. All kinds of old memories flooded into his mind about his family's old house and his childhood friends. Joe had only been back to Philadelphia once since his family had moved to Canada and that had been about twenty years earlier, when he was still a teenager.

Howie, with a couple of beers, said, "The girls are already at the restaurant. We just have to cross the river, go to Broad Street and turn right. It's about ten minutes away."

"Did you talk to your little sweetheart?"

"Yeah, she's at the restaurant with a couple of her girlfriends and she's really looking forward to seeing me," Howie laughed that crazy laugh.

"Do you remember what she looks like?"

"I'm not sure!" Howie laughed again.

"I'll have to give you a tour of my old neighbourhood in Philly before we head back to Canada. I'm looking forward to seeing it again. Where does your new friend live?"

"I think she lives here in Camden, not too far from where we are right now," Howie said throwing his beer can into a nearby trash container.

Joe finished his beer, adjusted his pillow and then followed Howie out into the traffic toward the bridge. The view of the river from the crest of the Ben Franklin Bridge was unbelievable, with Philadelphia to the west and Camden to the east.

Soon after they crossed the river, the guys turned right on Broad Street. There it was, *Wok'n Roll!* Joe wondered, *Who the hell thought of serving Chinese food in a fifties and sixties bar?* They stopped their motorcycles in the parking lot under the brightest light they could find so that the bikes would be safe. Harleys have the tendency to disappear sometimes.

"We should do something with our things," Joe suggested.

"Let's go inside. We can probably throw our stuff in Lynn's trunk," Howie replied.

That was the first time that Joe had ever heard him mention her name. The bikers slowly and painfully stretched their aching muscles and ambled to the main entrance of the restaurant. They were both tired and stiff, but knew that a couple of cocktails would bring them back to life.

The nightclub had been divided into two sections. The Chinese food eating area was to the left of the main entrance. To the right, there was a large dance floor surrounded by tables and chairs, with a long oak bar on the other side of the room. The entertainment was supplied by a disc jockey, from a small booth, in one corner of the room on the far side. It looked like full meals were served in the restaurant area and appetizers and finger foods could be ordered in the nightclub. Howie walked toward a table that had three attrac-tive girls sitting at it.

"How are ya'?" The tall, shorthaired, blonde said to Howie as she got up and gave him a big hug and kisses on both cheeks.

"Lynn Kelly, this is Joe McConnell," Howie said introducing him to his new friend.

"Nice to meet ya'," Lynn said with that American twang. "This is Sharon and Cathy," she went on and pointed to her two friends who were seated at the table.

They were both attractive and well dressed in sexy outfits for a night out on the town. Joe was shocked at how much Cathy's smile reminded him of Trizzi. The ache returned.

Lynn, Howie and Joe went back out to the parking lot. It took only a few minutes to move the saddlebags, tank bags, sleeping bag and of course Joe's pillow into Lynn's trunk so they'd be safe and they were back inside before they were missed.

The first thing that Howie and Joe had to do was get to know their new American friends. The guys each ordered a J&B and water and more wine for the girls. The scotches didn't last long so Howie called for two more and at the same time ordered some appetizers. They chatted, drank and ate for some time in the restaurant area while oldies music played in the background. The DJ didn't start until ten o'clock. Howie and Lynn became enthralled with each other and were so deeply involved in conversation that the rest of the group was totally ignored. Joe didn't think that the situation was all that bad because Sharon and Cathy were very easy to talk to.

Cathy worked for Citibank, in Philadelphia, in the commercial lending department. She was about five-six with medium length, light brown hair that had been streaked with blonde. She looked like she worked out and had a wicked body that she showed well in a tight, blue mini-dress and high heels. Joe often found himself star-ing at her because many of her expressions and movements brought memories of Trizzi flooding back into his mind.

Sharon wasn't quite as tall as Cathy and had shorter auburn hair. She had a much more solid figure than that of her friend, with much larger breasts, but she was in no way overweight. She had on a tight pair of white slacks and a loose fitting blouse. Sharon worked with Lynn at Coopers, Lybrand where she was one of the eastcoast partners' private secretary or assistant. The two of them shared a townhouse fairly close to where Lynn lived in Camden.

They all asked each other all kinds of questions and learned as much as they could during the cocktail hour. They even managed to have a few laughs. Cathy had been with Lynn in Florida when she had first met Howie and she thought that Lynn was acting very strange about this new guy. Lynn usually didn't jump into new relationships very easily or quickly.

"Are you guys going to ignore us all night?" Cathy asked Lynn and Howie.

"I feel like I've known this guy for years instead of hours. I mean minutes!" Lynn laughed.

"It sure does feel a little strange," Howie remarked.

"Joe, do you like my friends?" Lynn asked with a big smile on her face.

"Howie told me that they were both gorgeous, but I didn't believe him. I think I'm fallin' in love!" Joe answered laughing and starting to feel better.

"Lynn giggled and asked, "With which one?"

"Both of them!" Joe answered with another laugh.

The party continued and they ended up ordering more appetizers rather than full course meals and that worked out great for everyone. They all had a lot to eat, a lot to drink and a lot of laughs. Howie told the story about how he and Joe had met a real motorcycle gang on the expressway with Joe sitting on his pillow and they all broke up. They also told the girls the story about the plane crash, but didn't tell them the part about Bryan stealing the money.

The girls noticed that the lounge was starting to fill up so they suggested that the group move to a table in that section nearer to the dance floor. There were a lot of people standing at the long bar and many of the tables had groups of men and women sitting at them. Joe thought, *It's time to Wok'n Roll.* He loved the name of the bar.

A familiar slow song started to play just as they were about to sit down and Cathy grabbed Joe by the arm, "Is your backside to sore to dance?"

Joe immediately led her out onto the dance floor. They danced well together and were comfortable in each other's arms. They rejoined the others back at the table when the song was over and as they arrived, a waitress was delivering another round of drinks.

"I think I'm just starting to come around," Joe said as he unknowingly stirred his new J&B and water with his index finger. "How do you feel Howie?"

"Great! The cocktails really helped," he replied.

A fast song had just finished playing and another slow one started. Just to be fair, Joe grabbed Sharon by the hand and led her out onto the floor. She was also a great dancer and they moved as if they were one. When the song ended, they rejoined the others at the table.

They tried to carry on conversations over the loud music but it was difficult. During the next couple of songs they all finished their drinks at about the same time and Joe ordered another round. Lynn dragged Howie up onto the floor to dance a fast one and Joe suggested to the other girls that they all join them and they did. They danced three fast songs, one after the other, and then Joe decided that he couldn't take it anymore.

"I have to sit down for a rest," he said and they all went back to their table and the new round of drinks, that had been ordered previously, had arrived.

At one time, while Howie and Lynn were dancing, they girls talked about Lynn's small one bedroom apartment and the fact that Joe would have to sleep on the chesterfield in her living room. They thought that it was too bad that he would have to accompany the lovebirds back to Lynn's place because they had never seen her act this way before about a guy.

Lynn and Howie seemed to be in their own little world and Joe continued to talk only to the other girls most of the evening. Joe danced the slow songs with one and then the other and they all danced the fast songs together. Joe took Lynn for a slow dance and when they got back to the table, Howie was alone. The other girls had gone to the powder room.

The slow dances had become slower and closer with both Cathy and Sharon and Joe even managed to kiss a couple of ears and necks without any complaints. If he had to make a choice between them, it would be very difficult, but there was something about Cathy that kept bringing Trizzi back to him. It was the way she smiled, the expressions on her face every once in awhile and the way she moved. He still got that empty feeling whenever she crossed his mind. Joe still thought about Trizzi everyday and often missed her. He tried and tried to stop thinking about her but he couldn't. He truly loved her and there was absolutely nothing he could do about it.

The DJ finally announced last call and last dance. Joe wasn't surprised at the final tune of the evening, *Don't Forget Who's Takin' You Home*, and it started while Cathy was in the washroom. Joe suggested to Sharon that they should dance the first half of the song and he would dance the last half with Cathy when she got back.

The song came to an end and they all sat down with Sharon to finish their drinks. They had a few laughs about the fun evening and Lynn started to talk about the rest of the night.

"The guys can follow us back to your townhouse and I'll drop you two off and then they can follow me to my place. Joe, you get to sleep on my couch," Lynn said.

"That'll be just fine," he replied.

"I think that Joe should stay at our place. We've got two bedrooms and besides, you two love-birds should be alone tonight," Cathy suggested.

Sharon looked at Howie and Lynn and added, "In the morning, you two can come over for brunch before the guys leave for Atlantic City."

"That sounds great to me," Joe interjected quickly, just in case there was some chance that the girls might change their minds.

"Good!" Lynn answered. "So it's settled. Let's get outta here."

Howie paid the bill with his newfound wealth and they all wandered out of the bar and into the parking lot. The motorcycles were safe and right where they had left them.

"I'll get all my things out of your car at Cathy and Sharon's place," Joe said to Lynn.

Joe and Howie really shouldn't have been riding their motorcycles after the evening of partying, but they couldn't leave them in the city because they'd be gone by morning. They followed Lynn's car out into the light traffic for the trip back across the Delaware River.

They traveled back over the Ben Franklin Bridge into Camden and about twenty minutes after they had left the bar, they pulled into a brightly lit parking lot of what appeared to be a townhouse development. The two girls got out of Lynn's car near a couple of parked cars.

Cathy spoke first, "You can park your motorcycle in between these two cars rather than over in the guest parking lot. This is our place right here."

Joe pulled his Harley in between a cream colored Olds and a light blue Firebird and put it on the stand and locked it up for the night. Lynn popped her trunk and Joe went to her car to get his things. Howie was sitting on his bike beside the driver's window talking to Lynn and they were laughing about something. Whatever the conversation, they seemed anxious to leave.

"Joe, do you think that you're gonna be all right tonight or are you gonna need some help?" Howie asked with a laugh.

"I'm not really sure, Howie," Joe laughed, "I'll call ya' if I need ya'."

"See you guys in the morning," Lynn said out of her side window as she turned her car around and headed back out to the street with Howie right behind her.

As they entered the foyer, Cathy announced to Sharon, "We should give our guest the master bedroom," and then she turned to Joe. "Sharon and I can sleep in her room."

"I don't want to be any trouble, just let me sleep on the couch in the livingroom."

"No, you get the master bedroom," Sharon said and led him into the large room.

Joe threw his things onto the bed and put his leather jacket on the back of a chair. The two of them then joined Cathy who was in the kitchen fumbling with the coffeemaker.

"I feel like a coffee," Cathy said. "Does anyone else want a coffee or a cocktail?"

"Coffee keeps me *up* all night!" Joe said with a wicked smile.

Sharon laughed out loud and said, "Its decaf!"

"Oh darn! I'll have one anyway," Joe said. "I hope you don't mind me asking but would you mind if I have a quick shower. I've been on that motorcycle all day long."

"Follow me," Cathy answered, "I'll get you a towel and show you where things are."

Joe followed her back to the master bedroom and she turned on the lights in the bedroom and bathroom and put a clean towel on the sink for him.

"Don't be long, the coffee will only be a few minutes," she said as she left the bedroom.

Joe got what he needed from his saddlebags and went into the bathroom. He had a quick shave, just in case, and jumped into the shower. The process only took him minutes. His eyes looked like the roadmap that he had been reading all day long. He left the bedroom dressed in a pair of shorts and a T-shirt. He was feeling much better and the shower had given him new life.

He could tell that Cathy had been in her bedroom while he was in the shower because the bed was turned down and some of her clothes were on the dresser. As he walked down the dark hall toward the kitchen, he could see that the gals had moved to the living room. The coffee was already made and the whole pot was sitting in a warmer on the coffee table with what looked to be a newly opened bottle of Tia Maria right beside it. As he joined them, he could tell that he had already had way too much to drink. He had watched the girls drink wine all evening and knew that they had to be feeling the booze too.

"Help yourself, there's milk and sugar if you don't want Tia Maria," Sharon said.

It was quite obvious that they had each put a shot of booze into their coffees.

"This'll be great!" He said helping himself to the coffee and a good blast of the dark liqueur. "I feel a lot better now. This is really nice of you gals to put me up for the night."

Cathy was sitting at the other end of the sofa and Sharon was in a nearby chair. Both had their housecoats on and Joe couldn't see any nightgowns under them. They talked about the events of the evening and had a few laughs around Lynn's behavior toward Howie. The girls had known Lynn for years and they had never seen her take to a guy so easily and quickly. She was usually very reserved.

"Are you involved in a relationship back home?" Cathy asked Joe.

"No, my love life has been on hold for the last year or so. I actually met someone last spring that I thought might be the one, but it hasn't worked out," Joe explained as he still saw traces of Trizzi in Cathy when she smiled. "How about you two? Girls as attractive as both of you must have guys pounding on the door all the time."

Cathy answered, "I lived with a guy in this house for a couple of years. We broke up about ten months ago and I haven't been seeing anyone special since then."

"What about you?" Joe asked Sharon.

"I've been dating a guy in the Marines for two years. He's stationed in San Diego so he only gets home every six months, but I go out there to visit him every once in a while. We aren't really engaged or anything, but we have talked a bit about the future when he finishes his hitch sometime next year. Who knows what will happen then."

Joe poured the last of the coffee into the three cups and added more Tia Maria as they continued talking. He got the impression that they were both fairly straight girls who weren't out chasing guys all the time. They both sounded like they were a little lonely. All three were half looped and in silly moods and talked and laughed until the coffee was gone.

"I really don't mind sleeping out here on the couch," Joe said once again.

"Don't be silly, you're sleeping in my room," Cathy said, "but I have to use the bathroom for a few minutes to get ready for bed because all my things are in there."

Cathy went down the hall toward her bathroom and Sharon and Joe put the coffee pot and other things back into the kitchen. Sharon then went directly into the other bathroom to get ready for bed so Joe wandered back to the bedroom and took off his shirt, dropped his shorts and jumped into bed. He heard Sharon finish brushing her teeth and then saw all the lights in the townhouse go out. The only light that he could still see came from under the ensuite bathroom door where Cathy was getting ready for bed. Joe heard a noise in the darkness and felt the covers lift up and Sharon slid into bed beside him totally in the nude. She kissed him deeply.

"We had a vote earlier that you shouldn't have to sleep alone tonight," she said.

"And you're the lucky winner!" Joe laughed.

Sharon answered, "No, we both won!" She leaned over and kissed him again.

Joe wasn't quite sure what she meant.

The light that was peeping through under the bathroom door went out and Joe heard the door open. He felt the covers on his other side lift and another naked women slide over close to him. Cathy's warm, smooth body rubbed against his as she leaned over and kissed him.

She said, "Welcome to New Jersey!"

"How did you guys come up with this great idea?" Joe asked kind of giggling.

Cathy answered, "Neither one of us has ever done anything like this ever before. We both really like you, besides, after months of not dating, we both really need a hug."

"Would you two stop talking!" Sharon said as she kissed Joe like she couldn't get enough. The thought of the three of them having sex together really got her excited.

Joe returned the kiss and then kissed Cathy, as often as he could, alternating kissing one and then the other, caressing, touching and kissing, mouths, breasts, belly buttons, pussies. It was a feeding frenzy! Joe had to lead them into different positions but both of them were drunk enough that they really didn't need much prodding. After awhile, the violent thrashing of bodies ended and the three of them just lay there for a few minutes breathing heavily in a sticky, sweaty pile. They slowly put their heads back on the pillows and cuddled. Joe had one in each arm and no one said anything until the heavy breathing died down.

Sharon was the first to speak, "I can't believe it! I've never done anything like that before and I really enjoyed it!" She laughed out loud.

Cathy added, "The things that people do when they've had too much to drink! But I have to admit, it was fun!"

"I want you both to know that this is the very first time that I have ever been in bed with two women at the same time, at least in New Jersey," Joe said with a laugh, "and it couldn't have happened with two nicer people. Can I move in with you two and stay forever?"

They all laughed, fondled and talked nonsense for a while until all three of them drifted off into a sound sleep.

CHAPTER THIRTY-FOUR

eatriz Bracho really didn't want to call Castrillo in Colombia to report on the progress of the search for the bikers and the missing money because she had no good news, but her call was long overdue. The night before, Luis hadn't provided her with any positive information worth passing on, but she now had to make the call. She knew that he was waiting impatiently.

"After Cape Cod, the Canadian motorcycle gang went south through New York City. They were last seen in the Newark area of New Jersey and have either headed to Atlantic City or Philadelphia," she said into the phone.

Castrillo replied, "*El Doctor* is not in a good frame of mind! I have to find the missing ten million dollars and I have to find it fast!"

"Briceno and his men from the New York area are on their way toward Philadelphia because there were reports of at least two motorcycle gangs on the New Jersey Turnpike yesterday afternoon. My brother and another of my men are on their way down the Garden State Parkway to Atlantic City. They think that whoever took the money will be heading for the casinos. It's only a matter of time before they locate them," Beatriz explained.

Castrillo answered, as he ran his finger down his map of northeastern United States from New York City and found Philadelphia and Atlantic City, "Tell them there's two hundred grand for the men that get my money back from those bikers and tell them to get the hell moving! I have to have some good news for Pablo very soon!"

"I'll call you the minute I have anything further to report," Beatriz said.

She hung up the phone with one finger and immediately dialed the number for Luis' cell phone, rather than call his room at the Holiday Inn in Newark, because she knew that he would be on the road to Atlantic City by that time.

"Hello," Luis said as he answered his cell thinking that it might be a call from Briceno.

"I had to call you back to tell you that Castrillo will pay two hundred thousand dollars to whoever gets his money back. I won't pass this information on to Briceno until we see if you can locate the bikers later today. If we tell him about the reward, he'll have his men all over Atlantic City before we know it. Get the hell moving on this thing now and find those bikers!"

Luis and Fernando had pulled onto the Parkway before eight o'clock in the morning and headed south. It would take them longer than the usual two-hour drive because they would make a few stops along the way. They pulled off the highway at various exits including Long Branch, Ashbury Park and Point Pleasant. At each of those places they spoke to a number of people including gas station attendants and waitresses to see if anyone recalled seeing a group of Canadian bikers riding south the day before. Again, they had no luck.

Further south, as they approached the Toms River exit, they could see one of those tall *Mobile* gas signs protruding up over the trees along the side of the highway. They needed gas anyway so they turned off at what would be their last stop before Atlantic City and drove directly into the gas station. They pulled right up to the pumps, turned off the motor and Luis got out of the car to talk to the kid who approached them.

"Good morning! What can I do for you today?" The young gas station attendant asked.

"Fill'er up," Luis answered. "Did you happen to be working yesterday afternoon?"

"Yeah, I worked right through until seven last night," he replied. "Why?"

"We're meeting some friends from Canada in Atlantic City, about five or six guys on motorcycles from Ontario. They didn't happen to stop here for gas yesterday did they?"

"No, it was kind of a quiet day for bikers. I don't remember a gang with that many motorcycles in it," he answered, "but three Canadian bikers came through here late yesterday afternoon. One of them was riding one of those new Harleys, what a wild looking bike, and the other two were riding Hondas."

"Did the bikes have blue and white Ontario license plates and was one of the men a big guy with a mustache?"

"None of them had a mustache. I don't remember the plates but I do remember them saying that they were from somewhere north of Toronto. Is that near Ontario?"

"Yeah, real close. Did they happen to tell you what hotel they were going to go to?"

"Naw, they didn't mention where they were going to stay. All they said was that they were going to do a little gambling."

"Thanks," Luis said as the tank was filled. He gave the kid thirty bucks for the twenty-four dollar fill-up. "Keep the change."

They went back out onto the Parkway and continued south.

"What do you think?" Fernando asked Luis.

"I don't know why the hell there were only three of them from Ontario, but I have a real gut feeling that we're getting closer to that money. I can almost smell it!"

They continued driving south and turned onto the Atlantic City Expressway in silence.

CHAPTER THIRTY-FIVE

The door to the master bedroom in Suite 3630 at the Ocean Plaza was still closed but there had been all kinds of laughter and noise coming from the occupants. The noises that had been penetrating the door into the main room for some time suggested that they were involved in some sort of a morning exercise program in the sack. The commotion in the room finally died down and Doc assumed that Bryan was spending another hundred.

In the main room, Doc and Karen had been awake for a long time. They had been up early and had opened the drapes of the picture window to let in the brightness of another sunny day. They had even made coffee and sat and enjoyed a cup along with the view from the window that overlooked the ocean and the Boardwalk. The sounds of lovemaking from the other room had made them decide to go back to bed. The morning eye-opener was free because Karen had been feeling guilty about how generous Doc had been the night before.

The lovers soon heard Bryan and Susan's laughter from the shower in the bedroom over the sound of the running water. Doc and Karen were just lying in bed relaxing when the big guy opened the door and stepped out with just a towel wrapped around him.

"How did you two piss-cans sleep?" Doc asked him.

"I didn't sleep at all, Susie wouldn't leave me alone!" Bryan answered with a laugh as he walked over to the large window and looked out at the Boardwalk and the Atlantic.

"How come we could hear you snoring?" Karen laughed.

"I was just resting between jumps!"

"I'm sure! What are we gonna do today?" Doc asked knowing

that the big guy was already thinking about the day's activities.

"It looks like another beautiful day so I think that maybe we should rent a boat and go for a boat ride," Bryan answered picking up the phone book. "We can cruise the intercoastal waterway and maybe even go out onto the ocean if it isn't too rough."

Bryan phoned Atlantic City Charters that was located in Gardner's Basin, in Absecon Inlet, at the north end of the city. Captain Gerry Juby, one of the partners in the business, answered the telephone and he and Bryan had a long chat and, it appeared to Doc and Karen, a lot of laughs. Bryan, who could handle any size of boat, found out that rented boats over thirty-two feet long had to have a captain onboard. They settled on a forty-four foot trawler from one to five o'clock that afternoon and Captain Gerry would come along for the ride. The activities for the afternoon had been arranged. The only things that had to be done were to pick up some booze and mix for the boat and buy the girls bathing suits. Bryan's deal with the girls was that he could pick them out.

Bryan called Tommy and Mike and woke them up. He explained the afternoon's activities and told them to be up to his suite by noon. It sounded fine to them and they immediately went about getting ready for the excursion.

Shortly after twelve o'clock, the four bikers and the two part-time hooks walked into one of the classy ladieswear shops on the main floor of the Ocean Plaza. The saleswomen didn't know what to think of the big man with the mustache that wanted to pick out bikinis for the two young women in the group. Bryan found four suits that he liked. All four were almost identical. They were the thong-type with just a piece of string at the back and very small patches of cloth in front.

"I'm going to treat my nieces to new bathing suits," Bryan said to a friendly saleslady with his usual smile as the girls went into change rooms.

"That's awfully kind of you, Sir," the attractive woman of about fifty replied.

The suits were a hundred and fifty dollars each and there was nothing to them.

"Would you like to come boating this afternoon?" He directed the question back to her.

"Unfortunately, some of us have to work for a living," she responded, "and besides, I really don't think that those bathing suits would do anything for my figure."

"I think that you might look a lot better than both my nieces in one of those suits."

"Flattery will get you everywhere, Sir!"

Just then, Susan stepped out of the dressing room and did a little turn for the boys. The top didn't consist of enough material to blow your nose with and the bottom was a very small triangular patch in front with a thong at the back that was completely hidden by her great buns.

"Boy, have you ever got a great ass!" Bryan commented. "I really like that one."

Karen then arrived on the scene, in full living color, from another dressing room. Her figure was just as cute as Susans and her suit was identical.

"I like this one best," Karen said.

The suits left no part of the girls' anatomies to the imagination. Bryan paid cash for them from a large roll of bills that appeared from one of his pockets.

The two cabs pulled out of the Ocean Plaza, turned right onto Pacific Avenue, and traveled toward the north end of Atlantic City. They turned left on New Hampshire Avenue and drove directly into Gardner's Basin. It was a large marina with at least three hundred boat slips located in Absecon Inlet about halfway between the ocean and the intercoastal waterway and about a mile east of the Trump Castle, Harrah's and the bridge to Brigantine.

The boat that Bryan had rented for the afternoon turned out to be a forty-four foot Grand Banks Trawler with twin diesels. There was a large master cabin down a few steps to the aft of the main salon with a double bed and a four-piece bath. Down a few steps, in front, was a galley that consisted of a fully equipped kitchen with all the amenities. In front there was the V-berth that slept two which had its own sink and a head that could be turned into a shower stall as required. The main salon had an inside navigation station and lounge with a bar and seating area. Outside, there was a flying bridge with a second navigation station, a spacious sunning area above the aft cabin and a large front deck. The boat would sleep six comfortably, two in each cabin and two on a pull-out in the main salon. The kitchen table could also be lowered and made up into another bed. The trawler was made of low maintenance, white fiberglass with all kinds of teak trim and was absolutely spotless.

The bearded Captain Gerry Juby turned out to be a great guy. He was a retired, Canadian bank manager who had bought into the charter business a few years back. He wore a neat, black Captain's hat that looked like it had been made just for him. He had come to Atlantic City for a vacation shortly after he retired back in Canada and met the owner of Atlantic City Charters, Charlie Gorrill, who happened to be looking for someone to share the workload.

As soon as everyone was on board and Tommy and Doc had untied the lines, the large trawler slowly backed out from between its moorings and pulled away from the dock. At Bryan's coaxing, the girls headed into the aft cabin to get changed into their new bathing suits and Captain Gerry, in control of the ship from the flying bridge, headed the boat out of the marina into Absecon Channel and then turned west away from the ocean.

"The ocean is really rolling today so we'll have to stay on the inside," Captain Gerry said. "We can cruise down the channel, past Brigantine, and on to the inland waterway."

"I'd like to stop somewhere for lunch about three o'clock or so," Bryan said to Captain Gerry. "Do you have any suggestions where we can grab a bite to eat?"

"We'll be going right past the Trump Castle and Harrah's and both of those casinos have marinas with nice restaurants."

"That sounds great," Bryan said. "None of us have been to the Trump Castle before."

"Perfect!" Doc agreed.

Bryan and Doc were up on the flying bridge with Captain Gerry. They could see the Trump Castle and Harrah's in the distance, one on either side of the bridge to Brigantine. The Island of Brigantine, located on the north side of Absecon Channel, was a small community completely separate from Atlantic City. Apparently, many of the casino workers lived on the island and commuted to work. As the guys looked back behind the boat, to the east through Absecon Inlet, they could see the white caps on the rolling blue ocean. Down to the south, they could see the large casinos and hotels lined up in a row all along the Boardwalk. Tommy and Mike were still standing on the front deck of the trawler in the breeze.

"Ello, Ello, Ello!" Captain Gerry said, with a phony English accent, as he turned to the rear of the flying bridge and tipped that great hat of his in a welcoming manner.

Doc and Bryan turned around to see Susan and Karen climbing up the ladder from the aft deck in their new bathing suits showing off almost all of their body parts.

"It's not difficult to understand why those bathing suits are against the law in a lot of public places," Doc commented thinking that the gals looked great.

"I think it's time for a drink," Bryan announced and he turned and looked at the Captain. "Are you allowed to drink while you're working?"

"Why the hell do you think they call me the Captain? I can do whatever I want to do aboard this ship. I'll have a gin and soda."

"What a coincidence, that's the same thing I drink!"
As Bryan got up, he turned the Captain's hat around backwards on his head and moved toward the ladder that went down to the aft deck. They all laughed as Gerry fixed his hat.

"Bryan!" The Captain yelled. "Why don't you take over the controls and Doc and I will get drinks for everyone who wants one."

He knew that Bryan could handle the boat because he had heard a few stories about the winters that he and his friends had boated in Florida. Bryan was also paying for the charter so the Captain wanted him to feel special. Captain Gerry and Doc took the rest of the drink orders and went down to the bar. Mike and Tommy joined them in the salon from the front deck.

The drinks continued to flow for the next couple of hours and everyone was getting on quite a glow, especially the girls. Doc talked Karen into taking off her bathing suit top and her cute little boobs bounced around in the breeze and sunshine. After a lot of kidding and coaxing, Susan reluctantly took her top off too. Captain Gerry was having a great time making sure that the girls, and everyone else, had lots to drink. Bryan remained at the helm almost all afternoon and at some point, he even got to wear the Captain's hat. The boat continued west to where the channel meets the intercoastal waterway and then it turned in a large circle and headed back the way it had come, past Harrah's, under the Brigantine bridge and into the marina at Donald Trump's flagship property.

The Trump Castle was a few miles from the main strip of casinos on the Boardwalk and it was in a beautiful setting about a mile inland from the ocean so it had a very safe harbour. It had a more than impressive marina facility that could accommodate hundreds of boats, mostly large cruisers and sailboats. The trawler, even at forty-four feet, looked like a peanut compared to most of the boats that were moored there or visiting for the day.

The gang had lunch and a couple more drinks in the cafe overlooking the marina and the Captain joined them. The girls put their tops back on for the event. After lunch, the boat headed back to Gardner's Basin. Much to the delight of Captain Gerry, the girl's bare breasts reappeared almost immediately. He seemed to really enjoy being around young people, especially girls. After the additional drinks at lunch, there was a lot more groping and kissing going on between the girls and their sugar daddies. Captain Gerry was back in control of the ship, and back in control of his hat, and he got them both back to the berth at the marina safely around five o'clock. Bryan paid for the afternoon rental in cash from his large bankroll and the Captain was more than pleased when he didn't want a receipt. Captain Gerry and his partner, Charlie, had a great working relationship. They shared the cash equally.

"Gerry, come on over to the Ocean Plaza for a cocktail if you're finished work," Doc said. "We'll meet you in the lounge on the Boardwalk side of the hotel, on the casino level, where the entertainment is usually playing."

"Sounds great! I'll be there in about half an hour."

The cab rides back to the Plaza didn't take very long. As the six of them regrouped in the reception area, Mike announced that he was going to go back to his room for a nap. Karen told her date that she wanted to do the same or she wouldn't be able to go out that evening.

Doc replied, "I told the Captain that I'd meet him in the lounge. I'll see you a little later."

Bryan, who had been giggling and carrying on with Susan since they had left the boat said, "We're going back to the room for a *sleep* too."

In his mind, Doc could see another hundred changing hands.

"I'm going with you, Doc," Tommy decided.

The four that were going to bed headed to the elevators and Doc and Tommy continued through the main foyer to the ocean side of the hotel and went up the only other escalator in the complex that also went to the casino floor and the upstairs lounge. The entertainment hadn't started yet so the guys were able to get a good table, front and center, near the small stage that was in one corner of the room. They ordered drinks and settled in to wait for Captain Gerry to arrive and the entertainment to begin.

CHAPTER THIRTY-SIX

Joe had no idea what time it was when he felt the two girls, who had spent the night on each side of him, slide out of bed and quietly leave the bedroom. He heard them puttering around in the kitchen, giggling and talking and making coffee. Then he must have fallen back to sleep. Sometime later, he felt a nude, warm body cuddle up against his back and someone kissed the back of his neck. Whoever it was reached around and fondled his already hard morning muscle. It was in the same state each morning, but sometimes it was real hard-on and other times it was just a pee-on. Joe, half-asleep, wasn't quite sure what it was that morning.

"Good morning! It's time for you to get up for some coffee," Cathy said kissing him one more time on the neck. "You seem to be already up!"

"You know, there's one thing that turns my stomach," Joe advised with a smile.

"And what's that?"

"A couple of warm breasts against my back!" Joe answered as he turned over.

"Very funny. It's about eleven o'clock and Sharon has just gone to the store to get some groceries," Cathy said. "Do you want anything special for breakfast?"

"It's obvious what I'd like for breakfast. Do we have time before Sharon gets back?"

Cathy rolled over on top of him and they hugged and kissed for a few minutes until the condom was in place. She soon got up on her knees and moved back and forth slowly until he slid gently into her. She started to rock up and down and back and forth while he fondled her firm breasts and squeezed her hard nipples. It wasn't long before she slowly lay back down on top of him and didn't miss a movement; faster and faster. She kissed him uncontrollably.

It wasn't long before Cathy was back in the kitchen. She was setting the table for breakfast when Sharon returned from the store and Joe was still in bed thinking about Trizzi. Cathy did it to him every time.

Just as Sharon walked into the kitchen with a couple of bags of groceries, the telephone on the wall beside her rang and she picked it up.

"Hi, are you guys coming over for brunch?" She asked and after a pause continued, "It'll be ready in half an hour . . . See ya' then."

"Why don't you wake our guest so we can get organized," Cathy asked Sharon.

Sharon went back to the bedroom and sat down beside Joe and rubbed his groin area through the blanket and sheet, "You certainly don't seem to be very lively this morning."

"I don't think I'll ever be the same again after last night," Joe commented.

"I must admit, last night ranks right up there with the best nights that I've ever had."

"It's not really like us, but we both had a great time too," Sharon said as she got up and opened the curtains on the window and headed toward the door. "Lynn and Howie are going to be here in half an hour so you had better get up and get moving."

While Joe was under the warm water, he thought about Cathy and how he could tell that she was starting to like him. He seemed to feel more attracted to her than to Sharon for some reason, but he really did like Sharon too, she was one horny lady. He wondered if he was attracted to Cathy because she reminded him so much of Trizzi who still flashed through his mind about half a dozen times a day. He still ached when he thought about her and the fact that Cathy reminded him of her everytime he looked at her didn't help at all.

Howie and Lynn arrived just as Cathy was starting to scramble the eggs. Joe made five Bloody Marys for starters while the eggs cooked. They were all starving and enjoyed breakfast together. They had a few laughs about the evening before and the girls gave Lynn a hard time about taking home a guy that she hardly even knew. Joe made sure that he complained about how uncomfortable the couch in the living room had been to sleep on and Howie gave him one of his little smiles to let Joe know that he was having none of it. They all poured more coffee and laced it with Baileys or Tia Maria and went into the living room to relax after eating.

"What time do you want to head for Atlantic City?" Joe asked Howie.

"I don't think that I'm going to go there today. Lynn has a clambake to go to out at the shore and I'm going to go with her," Howie answered.

"Why don't you all come," Lynn said, "it's at my cousins place and he won't mind."

"I think that I should really go and meet the other guys in Atlantic City although the party sounds like a lot of fun." Joe went on and looked at Cathy and Sharon, "If you girls want to go to the party at the shore, I'll go."

Cathy spoke first. "We have an appointment at three o'clock to be fitted for bridesmaid dresses and I'm sure that will take a couple of hours. We have to do it today."

It was decided that Cathy and Sharon wouldn't be able to go to the clambake because of their prior commitment. Howie and Lynn managed to talk Joe into following them to the party at the shore because it was sort of on the way to Atlantic City. It was at least east. He could stay at the party for a while and then just travel south down the Garden State Parkway. Joe went into the master bedroom to pack his things so he would be ready to leave with Howie and Lynn and Cathy joined him.

"Why don't you stay here for one more night and go and meet the rest of the guys tomorrow? We can all go out for dinner tonight on us."

"I'd like to stay here *forever* but I really should go and find the guys and make some sort of effort to finish the motorcycle trip."

"Are you coming back through Philadelphia on your way to Canada?" She asked.

"I want to spend a few days around here and go back to my old neighbourhood in Drexel Hill to see the house where I grew up and maybe drop in on some old friends."

"When you do, you can stay here with us."

"Sounds great," Joe said. "Why don't you two come down to Atlantic City tomorrow and we'll go out for dinner down there. Maybe go straight to work on Monday morning."

"I'll do that, I don't have any plans tomorrow. I'll talk to Sharon and see if she's game."

"I'll call you tonight from Atlantic City as soon as I find out what's going on with the guys down there, but I'm sure that they're planning to stay for a few days."

All the girls gave Joe their business cards with their home numbers written on them. Howie and Lynn pulled out of the parking lot and into the traffic with Joe right behind them. They traveled directly east toward the Atlantic Ocean.

Lynn's cousin and about twenty of his friends welcomed Joe and Howie. The party went all afternoon and was getting wound up to go on for a long time. About four-thirty, Joe decided to leave and he promised Howie that he would be at the Ocean Plaza if he wanted to get in touch with him. He biked through the small cottage community on the ocean and out onto the Parkway and went south.

As Joe leaned the Harley into the sloping ramp to the Atlantic City Expressway, his muscles still ached and his joints were still stiff. He wasn't sure if all the pain was from riding the motorcycle for so many hours or from his nighttime activities with his new friends. His body felt like he'd just played the seventh game of the Stanley Cup Playoffs. He thought, *The next time I go back to Camden to visit those women, I'm gonna wear my hockey equipment!*

***

It wasn't long before Joe was motoring across the swamp into Atlantic City, past all the billboards, and on toward the tall buildings on the oceanfront. It was five-thirty as he passed the Trump Castle and Harrah's and turned toward the large red letters of the Ocean Plaza. Joe parked his Harley in the reception area and went into the lobby to check in. As he walked, the stiffness left his body and he was feeling better by the time he got to the house phones.

Joe picked up one of the six phones against the wall and got an operator immediately. "Could you please tell me if there is a *Thomas G. Yates* registered?"

Without hesitating, the operator answered, "I'm sorry Sir, there is no Mr. Yates registered at this hotel. This is the second call that I've had for him in the last little while."

"Could you please see if you have a room in the name of Mike . . . never mind! Thanks operator," Joe said into the phone and hung up because he caught a glimpse of Doc walking through the lobby. "Doc! Hey Doc!"

His buddy stopped in his tracks and looked around to see who was calling him. "Joe, how the hell are ya'? Where did you two loons get to?"

"Howie and I ended up in Philadelphia. I think he fell in love because I couldn't get him to leave. It's a long story so I'll tell you all about it later. Where are the guys?"

"I just want to grab some cigars. Tommy's up in the lounge and Bryan and Mike are having a sleep," Doc explained as Joe walked with him through the lobby toward the gift shop.

"What the hell do you mean that Bryan is having a sleep?"

"The lunatic was already here when we arrived. He's in an expensive suite and has latched onto a couple of little sweethearts. He's half in the bag from the boat trip that we took this afternoon and he and his date have gone to the room for a nap or whatever."

"Did anyone tell him about the guys that seemed to be looking for him at the Cape?"

"He just shrugged it off and said that it was all a bunch of bull shit. He said that you're so hyper about the money that you probably misinterpreted what had happened at the front desk of the hotel. He just reiterated once again that no one would be looking for him because no one saw him at the crash site. We really haven't pressed him on the issue since we got here because the girls have always been hanging around."

"Well, I'm afraid that there are going to be some serious problems around that money. We have to come up with some way to make him listen to reason."

"Where the hell is Howie?" Doc asked to change the subject.

Joe told him the story as they walked through the lobby and went up the escalator to the main lounge where Tommy was seated at a table in a middle of the room.

"How are ya' kid?" Joe asked and shook his hand. "Have you loons been having any fun here in Atlantic City? You've obviously had a few cocktails!"

"We've been doing a lot of eating, drinking, gambling and boating," Tommy answered.

"Doc mentioned a boat trip. Where the hell were you boating around here?"

"Bryan rented a forty-four foot Grand Banks and we cruised toward the inland waterway for a few hours and then came back and stopped at the Trump Castle for lunch. We had to take Captain Gerry along with us because of the rules around boat size down here and he's going to join us here for cocktails any minute."

"Has the big guy been flashing lots of money around and attracting lots of attention?"

"Just the usual stuff, he hasn't been too bad. They've all gone for a nap. I guess they just can't keep up the pace," Tommy laughed as he took a sip of his Black Russian.

"I'll bet that Bryan isn't sleeping," Doc explained. "He picked up a couple of weekend hookers who have spent the last couple of days with us. They're actually kinda cute and have been lots of fun. The good news is that they'll do nearly anything for a hundred dollar bill."

Joe continued, "Speaking of money, where is it?"

Doc went on, "Bryan told us that it's in a safe-keeping locker here in the hotel. As far as talking to him about giving it back, he said to forget about the two guys you saw in Hyannis. He doesn't intend to give it back to anyone."

"I've also watched the news since we got here and there hasn't been anymore information about the plane crash," Tommy said.

"I can't believe that Bryan's not listening to you guys. I really think that the shit's going hit the fan around that money," Joe reiterated as his scotch arrived.

Doc and Tommy went on to tell Joe about their trip down from Newark, after they all got separated, and what they had done the night before. Joe explained why he and Howie had separated from them on the New Jersey Turnpike and about the bikers that they had met. He also told them how he had lost Howie to love in Philadelphia.

"I guess I'd better get a room for myself and park my motorcycle. I'll be back in a few minutes," Joe said to the boys as he finished his drink and stood up to leave.

"If Howie's not here, why don't you just stay with us in Bryan's suite, it's huge. There's an extra couch in the living room where I'm sleeping that no one is using," Doc offered.

"If you're sure there's enough room, I'll do that for tonight. Howie and the girls from Camden may show up tomorrow, and if they do, I'll get another room." Joe accepted Doc's offer and then remembered his motorcycle. "I'd better go and check on my stuff at reception."

Joe left the crowded lounge and went down to the main lobby. As he passed the entertainment desk at the very east end of the huge foyer, he noticed a gentleman, probably about sixty, with a captain's hat on walking toward him who fit the description of the *Captain Gerry* in Tommy and Doc's boating story. Joe spoke to him.

"Are you the famous Captain Gerry Juby?"

"I am mate and who the hell are you?" The old guy replied with a twinkle in his eye.

"I'm Joe McConnell, a friend of the guys that you took boating today. Doc and Tommy are upstairs in the lounge waiting for you.

I'll see you up there in a few minutes."

"Doc did say that they were expecting friends today. Nice to make your acquaintance!" He said as they shook hands and continued in the directions that they were both heading.

Joe explained to the doorman that the people whose room he was staying in were asleep and would be getting up soon. He made arrangements to leave his motorcycle where it was because it was off to one side of the reception area and out of the way. Joe gave him ten bucks and asked him to keep an eye on his things.

As Joe joined the guys at their table, a Dolly Parton look-alike dressed in a white, authentic western outfit came out onto the small stage in the corner of the lounge and started to sing. Her backup was an electronic band. The singer was certainly well built and had a cleavage that actually looked better than the real *Dolly's*. There were two scotches in front of Joe's seat when he returned. As the entertainer sang a few great Dolly Parton songs, the guys tried to talk at their table over the sound of the music but it was almost impossible.

Captain Gerry, who Joe found out wouldn't take his hat off for anyone, turned out to be a great guy. He fit right in with the group because he was really young at heart. He was obviously quite a partier and seemed ready to go all night.

The guys stayed in the lounge long after the show was over. It was eight o'clock before Joe remembered that his motorcycle was still in the reception area. It was decided that he would go down and take his bike to the parking garage and the others would meet him in the lobby by the elevators. They would then all go up to Bryan's suite together to see what was going on.

Joe apologized to the doorman for being so long and gave him another ten bucks and followed his directions to the underground parking. He easily found the other guys motorcycles and squeezed his into the same corner parking space. He took his personal things off the bike and rode the elevator from the parking level to the main lobby. As the elevator door opened, the three guys were standing right there waiting for him so they all just stepped in and someone pushed the button for the thirty-sixth floor.

Doc knocked on the door of the suite a couple of times to warn the occupants that company was arriving and then opened it wide for everyone to walk into the room. A sleepy gal wrapped in a bed-sheet looked up from the bed to the left of the door, rolled over, and then pulled the covers over her head in an attempt to go back to sleep. She would have no chance.

"Where are the other loons?" Doc asked the sleepy lady in the double bed.

"They're still asleep," she said groggily.

Doc waved his hand for everyone to follow him and they all had enough to drink that they did. He gave one big bang on the door of the master bedroom and they all walked in to see what the hell was going on. Doc hit the light switch as he led them through the door.

"Christ! They really are asleep," Doc said as he shook the two lifeless bodies.

Bryan looked up in a bit of a daze directly at Joe, "Where have you guys been, you missed all the fun."

"I've been to Philadelphia with Howie and believe me, I didn't miss all the fun at all," Joe answered. "I lost Howie to love. He stayed there with a girl he met."

The gal under the sheet beside Bryan started to move and Bryan yelled, "Susie! Wake up!" He pulled the sheet down a bit exposing a cute little breast. "This is Joe McConnell, my lawyer from Canada. We'll all be safe now!"

"You guys have to get up. Captain Gerry's here for a drink," Doc said.

They all went back out into the living room and Joe piled his belongings in the corner of the room near the writing desk, well out of everyone's way, as Doc started to take drink orders. Everyone found somewhere to sit and the party that had started in the lounge downstairs, continued on in the suite. They heard the shower in the master bedroom and knew that Bryan would soon appear to organize the itinerary for the rest of the evening.

CHAPTER THIRTY-SEVEN

It was noon when Luis and Fernando rolled off the end of the Atlantic City Expressway. The trip from Newark had taken longer than they had anticipated because of the stops that they had made to make inquiries. At their last stop for gas, they had got some good news. They decided to head directly to the Boardwalk and find a place to stay and get settled before they started to search for the bikers. As they went by the Trump Castle and Harrah's to the north, they changed their mind. It was still early afternoon, so they thought that they would check out those two hotels and casino complexes first while they were in that part of the city. They turned left and went toward the bridge to Brigantine and the two large entertainment complexes.

"What if *Yates* didn't register under his own name this time?" Fernando asked Luis. "One of the other's might've signed for the room."

"If he's not registered, we'll drive through the parking garages and look for motorcycles with Ontario plates and if they're not here, we can spend the rest of our time on the Boardwalk."

They stopped at the main entrance to the Trump Castle and Luis left Fernando in the car and walked into the main foyer. He found the house phones, called the switchboard and was soon told that their man was not registered. They then went directly to the parking garage and searched it thoroughly and drove through an outside lot as well. There were a number of motorcycles, but none from Ontario.

They crossed the busy highway to Harrah's, went through the same procedure and got the same results as they had at the Trump

Castle. By the time they finished at both hotels, it was after two o'clock. The Colombians then drove directly to the strip of hotels and casinos on the Boardwalk and pulled into the reception area of Bally's Park Place for no special reason. The location of that hotel was just four complexes north of the Ocean Plaza.

Luis and Fernando had their car valet parked, checked in and went to their room to get settled and decide where to start. It was past lunchtime so they ordered a couple of bottles of Beaujolais Superieur and some sandwiches.

"Let's think," Luis said. "If we had that money, would we stay in a dump? Those guys have to be in one of the dozen or so major hotels and casinos on the Boardwalk."

"Let's phone all of them to see if that guy *Yates* is registered? We might just get lucky and save some time," Fernando suggested.

Luis agreed, "Here's the phone book. You give me the numbers and we'll try them all, one at a time, and see what happens."

"I hope we get lucky because I don't feel like tramping through a dozen or so more parking garages."

The dialing started and there was no *Thomas G. Yates* registered at the first seven hotels. As Luis hung up the phone, there was a knock at the door and room service delivered the food and drinks that had been ordered. Luis poured them each a glass of red wine and took a bite of his sandwich. He then continued dialing all the major hotels on the Boardwalk without success.

After lunch, they decided to search the parking garage of their own hotel first and then walked to Bally's Grand, a sister hotel, at the most southerly end of the strip and work their way back up the Boardwalk and search the parking areas of all the major hotels and casinos.

A while later, they walked out of Bally's Park Place onto the wooden walkway and went south, past Ceasars, the Trump Plaza, the Ocean Plaza, the Regency, TropWorld and the Holiday Inn Diplomat.The Boardwalk was very crowded with people of all nationalities, shapes and sizes. There were young people, old people, joggers and rickshaw runners and there was almost every kind of shop imaginable from T-shirts to palm readers.

It was close to ten o'clock in the evening when they finished trudging through a number of parking garages without finding any Ontario motorcycles. They had worked their way back to the Ocean Plaza. They would start there in the morning. They had done enough for one day and went back to their hotel to get cleaned up for the rest of the evening.

Fernando showered while Luis phoned Beatriz to report on the progress of the search.

"I know that the Canadians are close by, I can feel it," Luis said to her.

"I won't bother calling Castrillo tonight. Be sure to call me by noon tomorrow and maybe you can give me some good news. What are you guys doing tonight?"

"We're gonna get cleaned up, have a bite to eat and do some gambling. We'll get right back on this thing in the morning and I'll call you as soon as I can."

Luis hung up and lay back on his bed. He just relaxed as he waited for Fernando to finish his shower and get out of the bathroom.

They were tired and hungry. They decided to spend a quiet evening in their own casino, Bally's Park Place. They planned to have dinner in one of the restaurants and then play some Blackjack. They wouldn't stay out too late so they could get an early start at the Ocean Plaza parking garage in the morning.

CHAPTER THIRTY-EIGHT

Bryan came out of the master bedroom all decked out in his evening wear; a clean, light blue golf shirt, navy shorts and slip on shoes without socks. He always dressed in the same clothes, only the colors changed. As he passed by Karen, she got up, wrapped in a sheet, and joined Susan in the bedroom to get ready for the evening festivities. Bryan then, just like the Captain, poured himself one of those no-carb drinks, a large gin and soda.

"I feel great but I'm hungry!" Bryan said, "Let's order a couple of those trays that we had last night. We can decide on dinner later."

"That works for me," Doc answered as some of the others nodded agreement.

Bryan took a large sip of his cocktail and then called room service.

"So what happened to Howie?" Bryan directed the question to Joe.

"He had arranged for a dinner date in Philadelphia. I think it was with a gal that he had met at the Ft. Lauderdale airport when you guys were down there last, maybe in the bar while you were waiting for your plane to Toronto?"

"Is she kinda tall, with short blonde hair?" Bryan asked. "I remember her. She was there with some girlfriends and we all had some drinks together."

"I guess that's the one, she is blonde. She seems quite nice," Joe answered.

Bryan went on, "They hardly knew each other. How did the date go?"

"We met with her and a couple of her girlfriends for dinner and

I haven't seen Howie since! I don't think he's going to show up down here at all."

The same bellboy that had delivered the food the night before arrived and put the trays on the coffee table as Bryan signed and gave the kid a twenty. The group snacked while the party continued. The Captain fit right in and appeared to have no trouble keeping up with the others.

Susan and Karen emerged from the bedroom, all dolled up for a night on the town. They both looked great even though they were dressed down.

"I hope that we're not doing anything too fancy tonight," Karen said. "We couldn't wear those same clothes again and we only had casual things left."

Karen had on tight blue jeans, with high heels and a red tube-top that really showed off her cute little boobs. Susan had on fitted white slacks, with heels and a blue blouse that left her belly button showing in the midriff. They looked more like secretaries than hookers.

"Are you girls ready for a glass of wine?" Bryan asked and with the appropriate response, opened a chilled bottle of Rosemount Diamond Chardonnay.

Right after the food was delivered, Mike knocked on the door.

As the newcomer to the group, Joe was properly introduced to the girls. The gang ate and drank and listened to music. While everyone was enthralled in conversation, Joe picked up his gear and went to the bedroom to get freshened up for the evening. Everyone would soon be ready to go out and enjoy the exciting nightlife offered by Saturday night on the Boardwalk.

As Joe left the group, he heard Bryan say, "Captain, I think that we should go for a moonlight cruise later tonight! What do you think?"

"I'll do anything for money!" Captain Gerry replied, not meaning to take a shot at the weekend hooks. "You had better decide soon so I can control my drinking."

"Don't worry about that, I can drive the fuckin' boat better than you can anyway, even when I'm drunk," Bryan laughed.

***

Joe was in the ensuite shaving and thinking about how he was going to deal with the stolen money situation when Bryan came into the bedroom alone and closed the door.

"Did the guys tell you what happened at the Cape Hyannis before we left?"

"Yeah, they told me that you saw a couple of men asking about a motorcycle gang and some big guy with a mustache. Every motorcycle gang in the bloody country has a big guy like that riding with them."

Joe went on, "Bryan, they were looking for a two hundred and fifty pound man with a mustache who was on a motorcycle at our hotel. How many guys with that description do you think were staying there? You can't think that it was a coincidence!"

"No one could possibly be looking for me. You guys didn't even see me pick up the money. You're getting all excited about nothing!"

"Didn't you hear the fuckin' news on the television? The pilot is alive! He survived! What if he saw you take the money? What if the police, or even worse, the drug-traffickers are looking for you? We had a break-in two nights ago at the hotel in Hyannis! Maybe it's related! Bryan, those guys kill people that steal from them!"

"No one knows I have the money; all that other shit is just a coincidence."

"What the hell did you do with the money?"

"It's in a locker where it'll be safe but I kept a bit of money out so we could have some fun while we're here in Atlantic City," he explained. "Do you want some gambling money?"

"You're outta your mind! What did you do with the Beretta?"

"The gun is under the mattress at the foot of the bed on the far side. I meant to get rid of it, but haven't yet," Bryan explained. "I'll throw it into the swamp when we leave town."

"Bryan, those men who were looking for the *big guy with the mustache on the motorcycle* looked like they were Italian or Cuban or Colombian or something. They didn't look like cops. Cops wouldn't have had to pay the hotel clerk for information. What if the guys who are looking for you are the drug-traffickers? What do we do then?"

"You're blowing this whole fuckin' thing out of proportion. Those guys that you saw had nothing to do with me, the money or the plane crash!"

"The pilot could have seen you! What if they are looking for you? If they can find you at the Cape Hyannis in Cape Cod, there's no reason why they can't find you down here!"

"I think that's all bull shit!" Bryan snarled.

"Think about it! If they are drug traffickers and they are looking for you, you're fuckin' dead! You only have two choices! Give them back their money and risk getting killed anyway, or call the police and hope that you don't get thrown in jail!"

"Fuck it! I'll think about what you're saying and make some decisions in the morning. Tonight, let's all go out and have some fun."

Bryan left the room. The financial pressures back home and booze seemed to be taking a serious toll on his ability to think straight. He didn't want to believe that he couldn't keep the money that would solve all of his problems back home. He had no intention of ever giving the money back to anyone. As far as he was concerned, the money was his.

Joe decided that he would try to deal with him in the morning. When he was showered and dressed, he took a minute to call Cathy and Sharon and made arrangements to meet them in the hotel lobby at noon the next day. He had thought about Cathy a few times during the day, but each time he did, Trizzi came flooding back into his mind and her image just wouldn't go away. He still missed her terribly. He also cancelled his reservation for that night and confirmed a room for Sunday night.

While he made the call to Camden, he kept thinking about the Beretta. As he hung up, he bent down and reached in under the mattress for the gun. A quick look confirmed that it was still loaded with the safety on. He put it back, deep under the mattress, out of the reach of the maid who would make the bed in the morning. Joe went back to the living room and joined the rest of the gang to get ready to go out on the town.

They all left the suite and took the elevator down to the main lobby. The gang walked toward the ocean, past the restaurants and out onto the Boardwalk into the pleasant night air. They all had on a bit of a buzz and were laughing and fooling around. There were tourists everywhere. The group meandered up to the Shops-On-Ocean-One that was built on a pier that jutted out into the ocean and then stopped nearby to decide what everyone wanted to do.

"Bryan," Captain Gerry asked, "do you still think that you want to go for a cruise later?"

"Yeah. Let's go in a couple of hours and see the lights of the Boardwalk from the water. The ocean looks really calm," Bryan answered.

Just past Caesars, on the left, they came across an interesting little bar and restaurant called Boardwalk Rogers that was filled with people. A musical instrument, a horn of some kind, was providing the inside entertainment and could be heard playing in the background.

"This looks like a neat spot for lunch. I think that we should plan to come back here tomorrow," Mike said already planning his food intake for the next day.

Bryan answered, "All you think about is food, but it does look like a great spot for lunch. Why don't we meet there at one o'clock tomorrow? I'll even treat!"

They all continued north on the Boardwalk and it wasn't long before they were standing right in front of another major casino, Bally's Park Place.

"Let's go in here and do a little gambling," Bryan suggested, "I feel really lucky tonight!"

Everyone agreed and followed him up the stairs to the second floor casino that was packed with gamblers. The noise of coins klinking and bells ringing and people screaming was almost deafening. Bryan and Doc, and their dates, found a couple of empty seats at a twenty-five dollar table and quickly grabbed them. They ordered a round of drinks immediately and settled in for some serious gambling.

"I'll be back, I'm going to have a drink in the lounge," Joe said to them as they sat down.

Joe weaved through the crowd toward the far side of the casino. Tommy, Mike and Captain Gerry followed him through the throngs of people and up a few more stairs off the casino level. They wandered into a semi-circular bar that didn't seem to have a name in what appeared to be one end of the second floor, main lobby of the hotel. The back of the bar, with built-in coolers and shelving, separated the lobby from the casino.

Bally's Park Place was different than the Ocean Plaza. The main entrance was on the street level, like the Plaza, but guests immediately went up an extra-wide escalator to the main lobby on the second floor, where there was a long reception desk and a number of exclusive shops. The decor was done in golds, greens and blacks and was very rich looking.

The floor of the lounge was slightly raised a couple of steps and was inside an enclosed half-circle divider about four feet high. The divider was filled with green plants that separated the drinking area from the lobby. Customers seated in the lounge could look out into the lobby and shopping area while they were having cocktails. An attractive waitress whose badge read Glenda arrived at the guys' table to take drink orders.

"What's this lounge called?" Joe asked as soon as she got there.

"*Glenda's Lobby Bar*," she replied with a big smile.

Another friendly waitress who was clearing a nearby table put her two cents worth in, "Sometimes we call it *Michelle's Lobby Bar* depending on whose shift it is."

Glenda soon returned with a round of drinks and the guys continued to socialize. Glenda and Michelle were quite friendly and introduced themselves. The guys had a couple of drinks each and Joe decided that he was ready to gamble. The rest opted to stay and have another drink with the pretty waitresses.

Joe found the others right where he had left them and Doc and Bryan seemed to still be on a roll. They were winning again. Another round of drinks arrived at their Blackjack table as Joe joined the small crowd that had gathered nearby and Bryan ordered another round immediately. Things were starting to heat up as the excitement of Bryan's winning streak grew. Joe waited near the table for a few minutes, and soon, a woman got up and left from the opposite end of the table from where Doc and Bryan were playing. He took her seat and sat down next to an African-American man in his late fifties who had the end seat. Joe ordered a scotch and water from the waitress and changed three hundred dollars into twenty-five dollar chips.

After about eight hands, Joe was up about two hundred. The shoe emptied once again and the dealer reshuffled the cards and began dealing. At the far end of the table, Bryan was starting to bet larger amounts of money and he kept on winning. Every time he won, he would let a yell out of him creating a commotion and the crowd of onlookers around the table began to grow. The drinks continued to arrive and Bryan was showing signs that he already had way too much. Doc's luck was running up and down but he was keeping pace with Bryan drink for drink. The girls were a close second.

They continued to play Blackjack and Bryan continued to win. He was getting drunk and loud to the point where it was almost embarrassing. Joe felt the man next to him leave so he moved into the vacated chair because end chairs had always been lucky for him. A tall, dark haired, attractive gal sat down beside him in the chair that he had just left so Joe immediately introduced himself. Laura Healey, a legal secretary from Washington, was traveling with three girlfriends who were spending the night in Atlantic City on their way to New York for some shopping and a few shows. She was quite friendly and got a charge out of Bryan's antics.

As time passed, Joe pointed out his friends, including the girls, and invited Laura and her friends to go boating with them. He also pointed out Captain Gerry, who still had his hat on, standing in the crowd that had gathered around the table because of all the noise and excitement that Bryan had created in that part of the large room. She thought that a boat ride sounded like fun, especially with a real captain along to take care of everyone. She decided that she would talk to her friends, who were at tables nearby, about joining the group.

Joe and Laura played another shoe of cards and when it was ready to be reshuffled again, Joe was still up about two hundred dollars so he decided that it was time to take a break. He asked Laura if she would join him for cocktail at Glenda's Lobby Bar and she did.

"I'll be in the lobby bar when you guys are ready to go," Joe said to Bryan and Doc as he and Laura got up and started to squeeze their way through the large crowd of onlookers.

Doc answered, "We won't be much longer."

Bryan split two aces and doubled up on an already large bet and the first card that turned up was a *Queen*. He let a yell out of him that scared the hell out of everyone within thirty or forty feet and the crowd continued to grow around the table. The next card that came up for him was a *Jack* and it was black. Bryan jumped up from his chair with another loud scream and at the same time, lost his balance. He grabbed the Blackjack table for support and nearly toppled it over along with everyone who was sitting at it. The people in the crowd nearby scattered out of the way and there was a hell of a lot of commotion. The Pit Boss immediately arrived on the scene and told Bryan that if he didn't settle down, he'd have to call it a night. They didn't really want him to leave because he was up about six thousand dollars. They wanted their money back.

Luis and Fernando, a little tired from the long day in the parking garages of a number of hotels on the Boardwalk, had a quiet dinner in their own hotel that night, Bally's Park Place. They had great steaks and a couple of bottles of good French, red wine. After dinner, they decided that they would relax and do a little gambling at the in-house casino before they went back to their room for a good night's sleep.

The two of them were walking through the busy casino when they heard all the yelling and other noise at one of the Blackjack tables nearby that had gathered quite a large crowd around it. Luis was looking toward the commotion as Bryan yelled and stood up and nearly pulled the table over on the other players. As Bryan stood up and fell back and tried to regain his balance, he put himself in full view of the Colombians. Luis and Fernando looked at each other. They didn't have to say anything. They both thought that it was worth checking out the big guy.

Luis worked his way through the crowd that had gathered around the table and was standing directly behind Doc when the man beside him vacated his chair to get as far away from Bryan as he possibly could. The dark-complexioned man immediately grabbed the empty chair and changed a couple of hundred dollars into chips. He looked around the table at the other players and decided that the man he was beside was a friend of the big guy with the mustache.

"Have you had any luck tonight?" Luis asked Doc, with a noticeable accent.

"I'm nearly even, but I may be up a hundred," Doc answered and winked at Karen.

At the end of the next hand Luis continued to be friendly and asked, "You guys look like you're sure havin' lots of fun. Where're ya' from?"

"We're from Canada, just north of Toronto," Doc answered. "You've probably never heard of our small town."

"I might have heard of it. I'm from New York but I've been to Ontario and Quebec."

"The town we live in is called Lindsay. It's in the Kawartha Lakes Tourist Area of southern Ontario about an hour or so northeast of Toronto."

"Don't know it. I have heard of a place called Bobcaygeon. Is it anywhere near there?"

"Yeah, it's only about twenty miles away. A guy traveling with us actually lives there."

Doc didn't notice the obvious sigh of relief that crossed his new friends face.

Another hand of Blackjack was dealt and as the last cards on the table were turned up, Bryan let out another yell. He had won again. He couldn't seem to lose.

"Are you guys down here on a convention or just on holidays?"

"Just a vacation," Doc answered. "There are six of us on a motorcycle trip."

"That sounds like a lot of fun," Luis replied.

"Fun isn't the word for it," Doc said. "It sure has been a strange week!"

Bryan yelled again. He was dealt two aces up once more and split them and doubled his bet. His luck had run out. He lost both hands so he decided to move on.

"Let's get the hell outta here," he said to Doc and the girls as he picked up his piles of twenty-five dollar chips. "Where are the Captain and everyone else?"

Susan answered, "They're all waiting for us in the lobby bar."

Doc also picked up his small pile of chips and the two gamblers and their babes began to leave the table at the same time. As Bryan stood up, it was quite noticeable that he was totally pissed and Doc and the girls weren't much better.

Doc stopped for a moment as he was about to leave and turned to the friendly man from New York and said, "I hope that you have better luck than I did tonight."

Luis had wanted to ask his new friend from Canada a lot more questions about the motorcycle gang and find out where they were staying before he left, but there wasn't much he could do at that moment. All he could do was respond to Doc's comment. "Thanks. I think my luck is already changing!"

CHAPTER THIRTY-NINE

The whole gang ended up in Glenda's Lobby Bar to get organized for the trip to the marina. The girls from Washington had decided to tag along, so the group of twelve left the bar and walked past the exclusive shops and on toward the escalator and the main entrance.

As soon as Bryan, Doc and the girls had left the Blackjack table, Fernando had followed them to the lobby bar and had milled around the lobby inconspicuously, within earshot of the group, while the late night boat ride was discussed. By the time Luis had joined him near the lounge, the partyers were already walking through the lobby.

"Where the hell are they going now?" Luis asked.

"They're going for a midnight boat cruise and it sounds like the boat is located at a marina called Gardner's Basin. They're on their way to get cabs."

"I'll follow them down to the front entrance and keep my ears open. You go and get the car and pick me up there as quickly as you can."

The friendly doorman hailed three cabs with a wave and a short whistle. Captain Gerry reminded Bryan that there was lots of booze onboard from the afternoon cruise and also advised that there was an ice machine at the marina where they could get some ice cubes.

Bryan, Susan, Doc and Karen got into the first cab and it took off toward Pacific Avenue. Joe got into the next cab with Captain Gerry, Laura and one of her friends and Tommy and Mike and the other two girls got into the third. Luis lost himself in the throngs of people that were in the reception area of the hotel and stayed well back from the Canadians and their friends. He heard the marina mentioned once again as a cab driver was given directions. He thought one of the guys looked familiar, *But why? Where have I seen him before?*

As Captain Gerry expertly eased the forty-four-footer out of its berth, no one noticed the lights of the four-door sedan that had pulled into the marina parking lot and stopped quietly in the darkness next to a storage building. The occupants of the vehicle could do nothing but watch as the trawler passed by the end of the pier and slowly disappeared into the night.

"It looks like we missed the bastards," Luis commented. "We have no choice now but to wait until they get back."

"I'm dead tired anyway, why don't we take turns getting some shut-eye. They'll probably be a couple of hours. Wake me in an hour."

"That's all right with me, but there's something bothering me about one of the guys that got into the second cab. I think I've seen him before, but I just don't know where."

"The only places that we got close to them were at the Cape Hyannis and here in Atlantic City. Maybe you saw him somewhere today."

"That's it! I knew I'd seen the son-of-a-bitch before. Remember when we were at the front desk of the Cape Hyannis Hotel? There was a guy standing nearby looking at travel brochures or something . . . that's the same fuckin' guy!"

"You mean they were actually there that morning?"

"They must have been there all the fuckin' time. He must have overheard us talking to the clerk about bikers and their rooms and he got the hell outta there as fast as he could! That's why they didn't check out of that last room!"

Fernando frowned as he laid the back of the driver's seat down and closed his eyes. Luis shook his head in disgust and thought about the close encounter that they had with the bikers back in Hyannis. The two men settled in for a long wait.

***

As the boat cleared the basin, Captain Gerry turned the controls over to Bryan and went down into the salon to see what the girls were doing. Once in awhile, he got lucky. The odd time, a young gal got drunk enough to want to have sex with the old guy. Maybe this would be one of his lucky nights. The sky was full of stars, the water was still and the only noise was the sound of the twin diesels as they purred at idle speed. Bryan turned east through Absecon Inlet and out into the Atlantic and went south toward the maize of hotels and casinos along the famous Boardwalk. The wooden walkway actually started near Gardner's Basin and curled for miles along the shore to a point well south of all the action.

Captain Gerry cranked up the music in the salon and there were even a couple of dancers. Doc and Karen looked like a couple of young lovers. The rest of the group was scattered all over the boat talking and drinking. Joe mixed drinks for he and Laura and the two of them went back up to the flying bridge to see the night scenery. Susan was sitting on Captain Bryan's knee steering the ship. Joe and Laura sat on the cushioned bench-seat on the ocean side of the flying bridge so they would have a panoramic view of the casinos and the spectacular show of lights. They passed the Central Pier that was located where the main part of the strip started in the north and cruised slowly south past Resorts, Bally's Park Place, Caesars, the Shops-On-Ocean-One, the Trump Plaza and the Ocean Plaza. Bryan continued south until they were opposite Bally's Grand, the most southerly major hotel and casino, and then turned the boat around in a large arc toward the shore and headed back north the way they had come.

Joe had put his arm on the back of the seat behind Laura and during the cruise she had snuggled in and got comfortable. Later, as the boat cruised north again, the two of them went down to the salon to get Bryan and Susan drinks and they managed to squeeze in a slow dance before they went back up on top. Laura seemed to like to cuddle and danced very close to Joe. Bryan and Susan were cuddling and fooling around for most of the trip and Joe eventually got around to giving Laura a few kisses that were well received.

By that time, Doc and Karen had disappeared into the aft cabin and Mike, Tommy and the Captain were entertaining the other girls in the salon. They all eventually ended up on the flying bridge as the boat cruised to the north end of the strip and turned west, back into Absecon Inlet, and on toward the inland waterway. They could see the bright lights of Trump Castle, Harrah's and the illuminated arch of the Brigantine Bridge in the distance.

"Can you drop us off at the Trump Castle?" Bryan slurred to the Captain. "I wouldn't mind doin' some more gamblin'."

"Sure, why not!" Captain Gerry answered, with disappointment in his voice because he would have to go back to the marina alone without all those sweet things onboard.

"Why don't you join us by cab after you take the boat back?" Doc asked.

"By that time, I think I'll have had enough. It's been a long day," Captain Gerry answered. "Maybe I'll meet you guys for a drink tomorrow."

The view of Atlantic City from the ocean at night had been quite impressive although the lights didn't nearly have the magnitude or brightness of the Las Vegas strip. It wasn't long before Captain Gerry pulled the trawler up to the main wharf at the Trump Castle Marina and it was met by a dockhand dressed in a white sailor's outfit. Most of the group had drinks in plastic to-go cups, so as soon as the boat docked, they all disembarked. The big guy handed the Captain a roll of bills in payment for the charter.

"Why don't you come into the casino with us for awhile?" Joe asked the Captain.

"It's already going to be really late by the time I get back to the Basin so I'm outta here."

Bryan added, "We're gonna have lunch at Boardwalk Rogers tomorrow at one o'clock. Why don't you join us? I'm buying!"

"Sounds great, I'll be over to the Ocean Plaza around noon. It's my day off so if the trawler is available, tomorrow's charter will be on me."

Captain Gerry had become one of the boys and everyone really enjoyed his company. Joe thought that he also liked hanging around with young people. The guys pushed the boat away from the dock and the Captain, standing behind the wheel on the flying bridge, expertly turned it around in the tight area that was available, and they all waved to him as he slipped silently away and disappeared into the darkness.

The gang went into the casino and Bryan, Doc and their dates sat down at a Blackjack table. Everyone agreed to meet in an hour and take cabs back to the Boardwalk. Joe and Laura found a quiet, little bar and nursed their drinks while they waited. He tried his best to talk her into getting together for a cuddle somewhere, but she couldn't be tricked. She did, however, give Joe her numbers back home just in case the motorcycle trip took them that far south. The four girls were leaving for New York City early in the morning.

Everyone said good-bye to the girls from Washington when they were dropped off at their hotel. By the time the rest of them got back to the Ocean Plaza, it was four in the morning and they all went directly to the elevators. Tommy and Mike got off on the twenty-third floor and the rest of them carried on to the thirty-sixth and Bryan's suite. By that time, Joe had sobered up a bit and was glad that Laura had turned him down. His friends from Camden were scheduled to arrive at noon and he really had to get some sleep.

As Captain Gerry stood on the flying bridge with his left hand on the wheel and his right on the controls, he thought about Sunday. It was going to be a beautiful day and he was looking forward to spending it with his new friends. The wind was still, the water was calm and the sky was clear, except for the millions of stars that reflected in the mirrored water of the marina as the trawler slipped quietly, at idle-speed, into the main opening at Gardner's Basin.

The large boat glided silently and gently in between the pylons at the mouth of its berth and slightly nudged one of them as the nose of the boat got close to the dock. A small burst of power from the twin diesels, in reverse, stopped the boat exactly where it was to be moored for the night. Handling boats that size had become second nature to Captain Gerry. The marina was deserted and any people on their boats were fast asleep. The Captain jumped quietly onto the dock and fastened the lines and then hooked up the shore power for the night. The old fella didn't notice the interior lights of the sedan parked in a dark area of the parking lot flicker.

Luis and Fernando who were already wearing latex surgical gloves, stepped onto the end of the long wooden pier just as Captain Gerry disappeared back inside. He had to throw the electrical breakers to maintain the boat's equipment and charge the batteries overnight. As soon as that was done, he went down the few stairs into the galley and was in the process of putting things into the fridge when he heard a slight noise behind him. The Captain turned his head and looked right into the silver barrel of a Colt 45 that was being pointed directly between his eyes by a young man with a dark-complexion. Another larger, darker man closed the windows and doors of the trawler and drew the curtains in the salon and galley. He also turned the lights down to darken the interior of the cruiser.

"What the hell do you two want?" The feisty, old guy said to Luis as he glanced back and forth at the two men, "I've only got five hundred bucks and you're welcome to it."

"We don't want your money, old man," Luis answered, "where are your passengers?"

"What do you want with them? They're just a bunch of guys out having some fun."

As he finished the sentence, the silver barrel of the Colt smashed him on the right side of his head and the blow opened up a one-inch gash above his right eye and knocked him against the galley seating area. The force of the blow knocked his hat off and it ended up lying in the middle of the table, but Captain Gerry landed on his ass on the floor, below the table, totally dazed. He felt blood streaming down his face into his right eye and he also felt the cold steel of the gun barrel pressed hard against his forehead, just above the bridge of his nose.

Luis continued, "All I want ya' to do is answer my fuckin' questions when I ask them and maybe you'll live to go boating another day. Do you understand?"

Luis lied to him because he knew that the old fella's time had come to an end. He would never be able to go boating again because he had seen their faces.

Captain Gerry nodded his aching head that he did understand.

"Where are your fuckin' passengers?" Luis asked again with his slight accent and in a much more serious tone so the Captain would know that he was finished screwing around.

"I dropped them off at the Trump Castle to do some gambling about an hour ago."

"What hotel are they staying at?"

"I don't know where they're staying. I met them here at the marina when they chartered the boat," Captain Gerry answered as he tried to protect his friends one more time.

The last word was barely out of his mouth when a flash of silver hit him again on the right side of his jaw. Another gash opened and blood splattered on his face, his clothing and the floor. The blow knocked out his partial plate and loosened two of his lower teeth that he'd not yet lost. Blood spurted from a new cut on the side of his chin and poured down onto his chest along with his broken set of false teeth. This time, Luis had to shake him to bring him around.

"You obviously don't want to live much longer," Luis warned as he pressed the silver barrel of the handgun harder against his forehead. "I was playing Blackjack with you and all your friends at Bally's and you were right there with them! What hotel are they staying at?"

Gerry groggily answered, "The Ocean Plaza."

"What's their room number?" Luis asked.

"I honestly don't know," Captain Gerry, gargled, "I was only there once and I was drunk when they took me to their room."

"What the hell is the name of the big man with the mustache?"

"I don't really know his full name . . . his first name is Brian . . . one of the guys called him *Boyle* or something . . ."

Captain Gerry's sentence ended abruptly as the silver steak hit him again on the right temple. He lost consciousness and appeared to stop breathing.

"I can't really tell, but I think that this old guy might have died. Remember, Castrillo told Beatriz that Pablo Rivas wanted someone to die!"

Luis lifted one of the Captain's eyelids with his thumb and then felt for a pulse in the neck area and in one wrist. There was none. Luis reached into Captain Gerry's pockets and found five hundred dollars in one pocket and over seven hundred in the other. The old guy had lied to him. He stood up from his kneeling position and as he looked down at the bleeding old man, he picked up his Captain's hat from the middle of the table. He then turned around and went up the steps into the salon and looked at Fernando.

"I think that we'd better leave a message for those bikers so that the big guy with the mustache knows how fuckin' serious we are about getting our money back!"

Fernando pulled his switchblade from his jacket pocket and a shiny, sharp blade, sprung into view. The loud snapping sound that the knife made as it opened caused a terrifying echo in the quietness of the yacht. This was the big man's specialty.

The two Colombians turned out all the lights as they left the trawler, stepped quickly and quietly down onto the dock and walked slowly back to their car in the parking lot. There was absolutely no breeze in Gardner's Basin that night. The water was so calm; it looked like a mirror that reflected millions of diamonds from the clear night sky.

CHAPTER FORTY

A s soon as they entered the suite, Bryan poured himself something that he really didn't need, a gin and soda, and sat down in one of the chairs in the living room. Susan got a glass of ice water and sat in the chair next to him. Doc and Karen went directly into the master bedroom to have a shower and Joe went into the small bathroom. As Joe stepped back into the room after brushing his teeth, he saw Susan take the drink that Bryan had poured himself, out of his hand, because he had fallen asleep in the chair.

"Will you help me get him into bed?" Susan asked Joe.

"Sure. If we just stand him up and help him, he'll walk on his own."

They both took an arm and led the big guy into the bedroom. As he rolled into the bed, he immediately started snoring. As Joe struggled to roll him over to one side so there would be room for Susan, the shower in the bathroom stopped and giggling could be heard through the closed door. Joe threw a sheet over Bryan and looked at Susan who smiled back at him.

"I hope that he's left you enough room in the bed," Joe said to Susan.

"If he hasn't, I could spend some time with you on the chesterfield in the other room."

"I have to get some rest. I didn't get any sleep last night and friends are arriving from Camden early in the morning," he said as he left the bedroom.

Joe found an extra blanket in the closet and threw it on the couch with his own pillow. He stripped down to his underwear and turned out all the lights in the room except the small one next to Doc and Karen's bed. He fell sleep almost immediately with the likeness of Trizzi flashing through his mind once again. No matter how hard he tried, he couldn't forget her. The back of the couch that he was sleeping on separated him from the other part of the room so Doc and Karen would at least have some privacy.

The next thing that Joe heard, which couldn't have been too much later, was a lot of laughing and giggling that actually woke him out of a dead sleep. He guessed that Doc and Karen had totally forgotten that he was there in the room because they couldn't see him from their side of the suite. They seemed to be totally absorbed in their lovemaking. Joe laughed to himself and wondered how many hundreds Doc and Bryan had spent that day. He couldn't get back to sleep with all the noise in the room so he just lay there with a smile on his face and listened to the final performance of the night.

"Get onto your hands and knees toward the end of the bed," Karen laughed and it sounded like Doc had complied.

"Where are you going now?" Doc asked giggling almost uncontrollably.

"I'm just going to kneel on the floor at the end of the bed behind you."

"Please don't kiss my balls . . . unless you really mean it!" Doc laughed and continued to giggle so much that he was almost in hysterics.

"Just relax and let me have some fun!" She ordered definitely in charge.

Things quieted down for a minute or so and Joe became quite anxious to find out what was happening. He wondered, *What is she doing to him?*

"What the hell are you doing now?" Doc yelled with more giggles and laughter.

Karen gave him an order. "This won't hurt, just relax and stay still!"

"Ohh, I don't think I can," Doc laughed even more.

Joe could hear some kind of blowing sound and then he heard a giggling Doc say, "What the hell are you doing? I'm going to explode!"

Karen ordered again, "Stay still and relax!"

Joe heard the blowing sound again and then a flatulent noise that sounded like a huge fart. Doc was, by then, laughing and giggling out of control and Karen was giving him orders to quit moving. The blowing sound would start again and again and be followed by the farting noise, and this went on four or five times, and the noises were mixed in with hysterical laughter and giggles from both of the participants in whatever was happening. Joe couldn't stand it anymore. He had to find out what was going on.

"Doc, are you gonna be all right?" Joe asked out of the darkness of the room.

Karen, screamed and then yelled, "For Christ's Sake! You scared the hell outta me!"

She then broke into a fit of laughter that filled the room and couldn't stop.

"Joe! You crazy bastard! We forgot all about you!" Doc said still giggling uncontrollably and farting more often and more loudly each time he laughed.

Joe continued, "I couldn't stand it, Doc, I had to find out what the hell was going on over there. It sounds like you two are having a great time."

Joe started to laugh out loud right along with them. It was contagious.

"You won't fuckin' believe this. Karen was blowing air up my ass and my stomach filled up with so much air I thought that I was going to blow up," Doc tried to explain still laughing out of control and letting more air escape as he told the story. "Then she would stop and all the air would rush out of my ass in one huge fart! I could hardly stand it, but it was starting to give me a serious hard-on until you broke my concentration."

He was laughing so hard that Joe could hardly understand a word he was saying and Karen was in convulsions at the end of the bed.

Karen made an attempt to speak but was choking and sputtering, "Quit making me laugh so much, I think I'm going to be sick to my stomach.

"Joe, get the hell over here and let Karen try it on you! It's the wildest thing that ever happened to me!" Doc said still laughing and letting more air escape.

"I think I'll pass Doc," Joe answered out of the darkness, still laughing along with them. "Karen, I have to ask, where the hell did you learn that trick?"

"You won't believe it, but I heard about it on the Howard Stern Radio Show."

"I'm going to go back to sleep now but I may have trouble after that performance. You two enjoy yourselves. I'll put my head under my pillow."

Still laughing, Joe finally fell asleep, but for some reason, he had strange dreams that night. He had a dream about boating with Captain Gerry and the gang and he had taken Laura into the V-berth. He was holding her close, making love to her, and he opened his eyes and Laura was Trizzi. She was looking up at him, smiling at him, kissing him, telling him that she loved him. Some sort of pounding woke him up.

Just before eleven in the morning, there was banging at the door of the suite. It was so loud that the residents of the main room were awakened almost immediately, but Joe wasn't sure if the occupants of the master bedroom had heard the noise or not. Doc got out of bed, pulled on his jockey shorts and answered the door. As it opened, Tommy and Mike, who were quite excited, burst into the room.

"Turn on the eleven o'clock news! You won't believe it! Someone killed Captain Gerry when he took the boat back to the marina last night," Tommy almost yelled.

"What the hell do you mean killed him?" Doc asked still groggy.

Joe sat up on the couch and leaned over the back of it and looked at Tommy and Mike.

Mike answered as he turned on the television, "It was on the morning news! Gerry's body was found by his partner this morning on the boat at the marina!"

The eleven o'clock news introduction had just started and they were all silent as they gathered around the set. The newscaster started with a brief overview of the top stories in the local news picture, one of which was about the body that had been found at Gardner's Basin. He then provided the information that was available: "About nine o'clock this morning, a body was found in a large cruiser at Gardner's Basin Marina in Atlantic City. The body has been identified as Captain Gerry Juby, a partner in a local charter business that operates out of that marina. The deceased, originally from Canada, leaves a son and two daughters who have already been notified. Police speculate that the death occurred during the early morning hours. An unconfirmed source reports that the murder may be drug related because of how the deceased was killed. The execution, and that appears to be what took place, is reported to have taken the form of a *Colombian Necktie*, which is described as slitting the victim's throat vertically and pulling the victim's tongue out through the incision. Such murder tactics are often used by the drug cartels to send strong messages to associates of the deceased. Police are still in the process of investigating the incident and there will be more information available later today."

The whole group was silent after the newscast and Joe turned around and saw that Bryan and his date had joined everyone during the broadcast. Bryan was almost white. Joe wasn't sure if his color was caused by his hangover, or because he had started to seriously think about the men that Joe had seen in Cape Cod.

"It's hard to believe that Captain Gerry was involved in drug trafficking, but I guess the boats could have been used for pick-ups and deliveries," Bryan commented.

"Give me a fuckin' break! That old guy wasn't involved in any of that shit and you know it! He was probably just in the wrong place at the wrong time!" Joe glared at Bryan.

"What the hell do you know about his personal life?" Bryan retorted.

Joe wasn't sure that the Captain's death had anything to do with Bryan and the money but he wanted Bryan to at least think about the possibility. There were too many coincidences.

"I've had enough, Bryan! There have been too many strange

things happening since Vermont. If my friends weren't coming down here from Camden, I'd be gone today. I don't know what you guys are planning, but I'm outta here first thing tomorrow morning."

Everyone was shocked at the news of the murder and although nothing was said in front of the girls, they were all thinking about the same three things that had happened during the last few days. Was there any relationship to the break-in at the Cape Hyannis, the two dark-complexioned men in the lobby and the recent murder of Captain Gerry? Bryan preferred to believe that Captain Gerry was involved in something illegal and was the master of his own misfortune. All the other guys were really starting to think about those things. As the guys talked, the two girls went into the master bedroom to shower and get dressed for the day.

Doc was first to speak when the guys were alone, "Bryan, too many strange things have happened since you picked up that bag of money. I'm starting to get concerned and I think that Joe might be right. Your life could be at risk."

"You guys are all outta your fuckin' minds."

"For Christ's Sake, Bryan!" Joe added. "Too many things have happened that don't make any sense. First, the break-in, then men asking questions about you at the hotel and now, the death of someone who was associated with you and the money!"

Tommy butt in. "There is the possibility that we'll be contacted by the police about Captain Gerry's murder because we may have been the last ones to see him alive."

"Let me think about all these things that you're talking about today and I'll give some thought about what I should do. If we get contacted by the police, obviously, I'll have to deal with the problem at that time," Bryan added.

Doc continued, "There seems to be a consensus that if you don't deal with the money today, we're all going to leave Atlantic City first thing in the morning and you're on your own."

"That sounds fair. Leave it with me for the day," Bryan said as he opened a beer.

Joe didn't really know Captain Gerry very well, so there was always the possibility that his death had nothing to do with Bryan and the money. In any event, there was nothing much that Joe could do at that moment and at least Bryan had started to listen to the guys' growing concerns. Joe had to meet his Camden friends at noon so he talked Karen and Susan into letting him have a quick shower in the ensuite before they had actually finished. After he was dressed, he put his personal things back into the corner of the living room out of everyone's way.

As Joe went out the door, Bryan reminded him about the plans for lunch that had been made the day before. "We'll all be at Boardwalk Rogers around one o'clock."

Joe went to the main lobby and booked his own room for one night pursuant to his changed reservation and by the time he checked in, it was about noon. His room was on the thirty-second floor, four below Bryan's suite, Room 3228, and he had asked for a large room with a king-size bed and a seating area. Joe made his way through the busy lobby to the crowded reception area and found a place to sit on a planter, just outside the doors, to wait for his friends.

It wasn't long before the cream colored Olds arrived with only one person in it. As Joe approached the vehicle, Cathy got out of the driver's door and looked around. Once again, the glimpse of her that Joe got as he walked through all the people reminded him of Trizzi and he got that empty feeling in the pit of his stomach again. No matter how hard he tried, he couldn't stop thinking about her. He couldn't stop missing her.

"Aren't you Joe McConnell?" Cathy asked with a smile.

"It's great to see you again!" He said as he kissed her, "Where's Sharon?"

"Her brother called her yesterday and she had to go to some kind of a family dinner."

"That's too bad, but I certainly don't mind spending some time alone with you."

"I hope you've been behaving yourself down here with your friends," Cathy said.

"I've done nothing but sleep since I got here. Riding that motorcycle is really tiring ya' know," he said and laughed out loud as he thought about the night with the two girls.

Joe picked up the small overnight bag and a hang-up bag that held her clothes that she would need for work the next day and they went inside and walked directly into an open elevator. She had on a white blouse that was tied above her waist showing her flat stomach and belly button and tight white slacks that looked great. She really did remind him of Trizzi.

Joe went on, "I asked for a room with single beds but they didn't have one, so we'll just have to settle for whatever they gave me."

"What a shame!"

Halfway down the hall, the door of Room 3228 opened into a large, well-decorated, bright room, with a living room area, king-size bed and a huge bathroom. The seating area was very similar to Bryan's suite and the large picture window that overlooked the ocean and Boardwalk provided the same view as the more expensive suite.

Cathy moved close to him and said, "I'm glad that you asked me down here today. I missed having you around last night." She kissed him. "I hope that you're not disappointed that Sharon couldn't come?"

"No, I'm not." Joe lied just a little. "I'm glad you're here and we'll have some fun this afternoon because we have to meet all my friends for lunch down on the Boardwalk."

He took her clothes out of the hang-up bag and hung them in the closet while she took her personal things out of her overnight bag and put them into the bathroom.

"Where are we meeting your friends?"

"At a spot called Boardwalk Rogers near Caesars. Don't get excited, it's not that fancy."

"I think I know where it is and I'm sure that it'll be fine.

"Do you want to go down to the Boardwalk right now? We do have a little time before we have to be there!" Joe said as he kissed her again, but she wasn't up for a quickie.

"We're going for lunch!" Cathy said and playfully pushed him toward the door, "We'll have lots of time for a hug later."

They got off the elevator on the second floor and walked slowly through the busy casino and down the stairs and out onto the Boardwalk. They wandered along the wooden walkway in the sunshine and did some people watching and window-shopping.

As they walked, Joe spotted some guys he knew leaning on the rail that separated the Boardwalk from the beach. They were looking out over the sand and rolling, blue water.

"Come and meet the bikers that Howie and I met on the New Jersey Turnpike."

"Do we really have to?" Cathy reluctantly asked because they looked like really wild and tough characters all decked out in their leathers, tattoos and beards.

Joe walked quietly up behind the two tough-looking, gang members who had their backs to him and loudly said, "OK, you guys! You're both under arrest!"

Mickey M. was the first to spin around and he immediately recognized Joe and said in a gruff voice, "You fuckin' asshole! You scared the shit outta me!"

He put his huge arm in the air and Joe and he locked thumbs in what Joe laughingly thought was some kind of biker's secret handshake.

"Where's your frilly pillow?" Dino asked as he turned and raised his hand too.

"Guys, this is Cathy and Cathy, this is Mickey M. and Dino."

"How many of you guys came down here for the weekend?" Joe asked.

"Just the two of us. We brought our old ladies with us but they went to see a fuckin' gypsy to have their fortunes told," Mickey M. answered.

"I'm going to meet my friends at Boardwalk Rogers, a small bar just up the way. If you and your old ladies drop by, I'll buy ya' all a beer. We'll probably be there all afternoon."

"We might just do that if we ever find those bitches again. Thanks for the invite, Joe," Mickey M. said as he and Dino raised their hands for the thumb tug one more time.

"I wonder what their *old ladies* look like?" Cathy asked.

"We may find out a little later if they all come by for a beer. They actually seem like pretty good guys. Here we are, Boardwalk Rogers."

"I've been here before. When you go inside, it's like going back into the twenties."

"That fabulous old building must have been built way back in the era when Atlantic City had it's heyday. They don't make'em like that anymore."

As they approached the restaurant, they could hear the sound of a trumpet reverberating from within, out through the main door and onto the Boardwalk. It sounded like the afternoon entertainment had already begun.

They walked in through the huge wide-open front door on the Boardwalk and it really was like walking into the past. They went by an ancient, oak bar and food area on the right that looked exactly like an old-fashioned soda fountain and then walked by a number of old-style booths that lined the inner walls on both sides of the restaurant. There were a few antique tables and chairs in the middle of an old, worn, wooden floor that had been stained from years of use. Bryan and the gang were squeezed into a booth on the left wall at the rear. They were sitting near another antiquity from another era, an old trumpet player who was later introduced as Walter Jakubowski. He was sitting on a stool with his trumpet in hand and a large tip bucket nearby.

Joe introduced Cathy to everyone and pulled a table and a couple of chairs over and added them to the end of the booth where his friends were seated. Another round of drinks was ordered immediately. The party got underway with another tune from the old trumpet player.

Walter Jakubowski was a good-looking man, about five foot

nine, in his mid-seventies, and he looked like a relic left over from the boom years. His act, *The Boardwalk Blues*, was very famous in Atlantic City and was actually a tourist attraction in its own right. As he finished the next tune, Bryan threw a twenty into the old guy's pail to show him that his style of music from the swing years was really appreciated by the whole gang.

"Where the hell did you learn to blow that horn?" Bryan asked him as a compliment.

"In jail," Walter replied. "I was in the can for nearly thirty-five years and I just got out!"

Tommy added with a laugh, "At least you had lots of time to practice."

The stained, wallpapered walls of the bar had one section that had been dedicated to the trumpet player. It was covered with old newspaper clippings, in cheap picture frames, that praised the man from Cherry Hill, New Jersey. Walter Jakubowski, and his Boardwalk Blues, had been part of the Atlantic City ambiance for over fifty years.

The gang all ordered assorted burgers and sandwiches when the trumpeter took a break and when the food was gone, the drinks continued to flow. Bryan bought lunch as he had promised, but once again, he had stopped at the Ocean Plaza Casino on the way to the restaurant and played a few successful hands of Blackjack. He had won another four hundred dollars in about twenty minutes. Doc ordered a round of Tequila Gold shooters that the group drank in a toast to the trumpet player. The old guy joined them for a shot.

Just as Joe was in the process of ordering another round of shooters, Mickey M., Dino and their two old ladies, came into the restaurant and wandered back toward where Joe and his friends were seated. Joe included them in the next round of Tequila, introduced them to his friends and pulled another old table and four chairs over next to the group.

The girls were scary, but nice. The drinks that arrived disappeared in a toast to new friends and anticipated goodtimes. There were a lot of faces being made and head shaking going on, as the

Tequila shooters were sucked back, even with the use of lime and salt that were supposed to make them smoother. Tommy bought one more round of shooters that also included the real bikers and their dates. Joe and a couple of the other guys threw some more money into Walter's bucket as they were leaving and thanked him for the performances.

Mickey M., Dino and their gals thanked everyone and said their good-byes. After the secret handshake with Joe alone, they headed north. The rest of the group went south.

As they passed the Ocean Plaza, Tommy and Mike decided that they were going to go and have a late afternoon nap and rest up for the evening festivities. Joe and Cathy also thought that some quiet time would be in order if they were all going to go out later. Bryan, Doc and their dates wanted to find another spot for drinks so they decided to turn around and walk north once again. The whole gang agreed that they would meet in Bryan's suite around eight o'clock to make plans for dinner and the rest of the evening. The four that were going for naps went up the back stairs off the Boardwalk, into the Ocean Plaza's second floor casino, and then on through the many gamblers to the elevators and directly up to their rooms.

"Why don't we get into bed and have a cuddle and then we can have some quiet time to rest so we'll feel like doing something later tonight?"

"That sounds like a good idea," Cathy said, as the two of them got undressed.

"I forgot to get my personal things from Bryan's room and bring them down here. I guess there's really nothing I need right now so I'll slip up and get them later."

Joe really liked Cathy even though she was a constant reminder of the woman he truly loved. Every time he thought of Trizzi, he still missed her even though it had been a few months since he had last seen her. He had tried to put her out of his mind, but he just couldn't. He saw Trizzi in Cathy all the time so it was fairly easy for him to get on with the task at hand. They made love for an hour or so before they fell asleep in each other's arms. Cathy had fallen asleep thinking about how much she was starting to care for Joe. He had fallen asleep thinking about how much he really missed Trizzi.

Joe didn't remember another thing until he woke up at about six-thirty. He slipped out of bed quietly so he wouldn't wake up Cathy and got cleaned up and dressed in the bathroom. He had to go up to Bryan's suite to get his belongings.

CHAPTER FORTY-ONE

uis and Fernando were both hyper from the night's activities because they knew that it was just a matter of time before they would have the stolen money and the finder's fee in their hands. The first thing they did at their hotel, was call the Ocean Plaza and ask if a *Brian Boyle* was registered. There was no one with that name, so they tried *Thomas G. Yates* once more and were disappointed again. Luis ordered two bottles of French red wine from room service and by the time they each drank one, they were ready to get some sleep. They crashed just as the sun was starting to peek above the dark-blue horizon on the far eastern edge of the Atlantic.

The Colombians were very confident because they could now recognize the bikers and they knew where they were staying. Luis had been right next to the big man. They knew his first name and at least knew what his surname sounded like. Their relaxed state and the wine put the two men into a deep sleep. They slept too well and much later than they had intended. They didn't wake up until after eleven o'clock.

The phone rang in Montreal at about eleven-thirty and Beatriz answered it immediately because she had been waiting for the call all morning. "Hello!"

"I've got some good news!" Luis said into the phone. "The Canadian motorcycle gang is staying at the Ocean Plaza here in Atlantic City. We actually got close to them in the casino last night. We now know what they look like, especially the big guy. We also know his first name."

"What good is his first name to you?"

"We do know that his last name sounds like *Boyle*, but we haven't been able to find out what rooms they're in yet. We're going over to the Ocean Plaza in a few minutes to see if we can locate them. They'll probably walk through the main lobby and we'll be there waiting," Luis explained. "We should be able to finish this job today."

"At least I can give Castrillo some good news for a change. Call me as soon as anything else happens," Beatriz said as she hung up and immediately dialed Castrillo's cell.

Luis was careful not to tell her how they had obtained the information that they had because she was totally against having unsuspecting members of the public get involved in their business. If she knew that he and Fernando had killed an outsider, she would have been more than pissed. Violence always attracted the authorities.

Just before noon, Luis, carrying a small, white plastic bag, and Fernando, walked out of Bally's onto the wooden walkway and turned south past Boardwalk Rogers and Caesars to the Ocean Plaza. They entered the hotel on the Boardwalk level and went straight down the long hall and into the main lobby. They stopped right at the bottom of the escalator to the second floor casino and looked around at all the people that were coming and going. They could hear the constant whining of slot machines, the ringing of bells and the sound of thousands of coins falling into metal trays. They had no idea that the big man they were looking for had just stopped at a twenty-five dollar Blackjack table on the second floor on his way to lunch.

Just as the two Colombians had entered the main lobby, from the ocean side of the hotel, Joe and Cathy had come inside from the reception area. Fortunately, they had stepped right into an open elevator without waiting and had gone right up to his room. If Luis had seen Joe, he would have recognized him immediately, but they had missed each other by seconds. Joe would have also recognized the two Colombians.

Luis left Fernando in the lobby and went down the stairwell that had a sign above it that read, *Parking Garage*. He decided to take a look for the motorcycles with the Ontario plates. He wandered through the dull, cement cavern for about ten minutes before he found them all parked in the same corner parking spot. Finding the motorcycles confirmed that the old Captain had told them the truth before he died. The next thing that they had to do was to find out what rooms the Canadians were staying in and locate them physically. It was time for a face-to-face meeting with the big guy with the mustache.

Back in the lobby, he told Fernando that he had found the motorcycles and they decided that it was only a matter of time before one of them would show up. Fernando went back to the area of the entertainment desk, near the two restaurants and specialty shops, and hung around there with his eyes trained on all the people. Luis paced the reception area in front of the main desk near the escalator to the casino. He had a full view of the whole lobby. It was right around the time when Bryan and his entourage were leaving the second floor casino for the Boardwalk.

Luis and Fernando stayed in the lobby for the next three hours or so and kept their eyes peeled for the bikers or their friends. During that whole time, no one that even looked familiar appeared. While he was meandering back and forth in the lobby, Luis noticed one of the employees at the main desk. He was a short, good-looking, Asian guy, likely Philippino, about twenty years of age, and he was not enjoying himself. He was working for a tough-looking, bleached-blonde bitch, *the boss from hell,* who was constantly embarrassing him in front of the hotel guests. Luis could tell that she was a total pain in the ass and didn't like the kid.

"Marquez, take your break right now or you're not getting one," the blonde snarled.

"OK, OK, I'm outta here," he answered.

He immediately disappeared through a hidden door to the rear of the reception desk and emerged in the lobby. He walked toward the washrooms that were just down the hall on the way to the Boardwalk near where Fernando was stationed.

The bitch yelled after him across the foyer, "Edgar, you be back here in fifteen minutes!"

Luis entered the washroom just after Marquez and stepped up to a urinal two over from him. Luckily for Luis, they were the only two people in the washroom at that time.

"You work at reception, don't you?" Luis asked.

"Yeah, I do, but not for long," Edgar answered.

"Who's that blonde bitch giving all the orders? I couldn't stand to work with her."

"You're right, man, ain't she somethin' else, but I don't give a shit anymore. This is my last fuckin' day here. The bitch let me go because she doesn't like me for some reason."

Edgar went over to the sinks to wash his hands and prep himself and Luis followed. As the kid was fixing his hair, Luis put five one hundred dollar bills on he sink beside him and the kid looked up at him with his eyes wide open.

"I need some information from the front desk."

He continued to stare at Luis. "What kind of information?"

"There are five Canadian motorcycles in the parking garage with Ontario license plates. One of the guys is named *Thomas G. Yates* and the other is *Brian Boyle* or another name similar to *Boyle*. I want to know what rooms they're staying in," Luis said handing him a piece of paper.

Marquez picked up the money, folded it and put it into his pocket, "These are the names? It'll take a bit o' time 'cause I'll hafta be careful. Where're ya gonna be, man?"

"I'll be around the lobby, you'll see me," Luis said as they left the washroom together.

Edgar got back to work on time so the bitch was happy and Luis went back to watching people in the lobby. He and Fernando continued to look for familiar faces but there were none to be seen that afternoon. It was half an hour before Edgar got Luis' attention and motioned him over to a part of the long front desk that wasn't being used on his shift.

Edgar began, "There's no one registered named *Yates* or *Brian Boyle* but there is a Canadian who is riding a motorcycle named *Bryan Moyle* from R.R.#6, Lindsay, Ontario, Canada. He's in an expensive suite on one of those high-rollers floors, Room 3630."

"There's five hundred more if you can get me a duplicate key-card for that suite."

Edgar's eyes lit up. "I'm finished work in twenty minutes and I'll meet ya' in the washroom. This'll be a bit tricky because they're encoded differently for each new guest."

It wasn't long before Luis saw Edgar walking across the lobby with his jacket on, headed for the washroom, so he followed him. Luis gave him another five hundred in exchange for the newly encoded key-card for Suite 3630. The kid put the money in his pocket with the money he had received earlier and left the washroom and headed down the long hall toward the Boardwalk. Edgar Marquez wasn't working at the Ocean Plaza any longer.

Luis immediately went back to the lobby and found Fernando and said, "We have everything we need to pay our big friend a visit."

He took the plastic bag that Fernando had been holding for him and they went directly to the elevators, and as one opened, stepped inside.

There was no one in the hall when they got to the door that read *3630*. Fernando put his hand inside his jacket on his Colt, as he knocked, and stood off to one side. Luis was the only person who could be seen through the peephole and he decided that if anyone came to the door, he would just ask for *Bryan*, which he thought would at least get the door opened. There was no answer. Luis knocked a second time. After waiting for a minute or so, Luis inserted the key-card that the clerk had given him into the slot and opened the door. The two men quickly and quietly ducked inside and closed the door behind them. Fernando went directly to the master bedroom, with his Colt in his right hand, and Luis looked around the rest of the suite.

"I guess there isn't much to do now but wait for them. Let's take a quick look through this place and see what we can find but don't disturb anything. I'm sure what we're looking for won't be lying around here. It's probably hidden somewhere. I'll take the bedroom and you take the main room," Luis decided.

"We've got the right room, Luis," Fernando said from the living room holding up a couple of old, folded newspapers that described the plane crash in Vermont.

"We may as well get comfortable. There's no telling how long we'll have to wait," Luis said, "they could be out for hours. There's a bar over here so we may as well have a drink and sit down and relax. If we sit in these two chairs, we can duck down behind the couch when we hear them at the door and wait until they're in the room. There's even ice in the bucket! What do you want to drink?"

"I'll have a rum and coke," Fernando answered as he sat in one of the two chairs that were facing the door and right opposite the couch where Joe had slept the night before.

Luis finished mixing the drinks and handed one to Fernando and put his on the coffee table in front of the empty chair that he intended to sit in. He then walked over to the other side of the room near the door. He took Captain Gerry's hat out of the plastic bag and threw it into the middle of Doc and Karen's bed. Luis then went back and sat down with Fernando and they waited and waited. It was just a matter of time.

After lunch, Bryan, Doc and the two girls had walked north on the wooden walkway because most of the action was in that direction. They had stopped at Caesars to gamble and had stayed until they each lost a couple of hundred dollars. Their bad luck made them continue north until they came across a complex that they hadn't visited called Resorts, the Merv Griffin Hotel and Casino, and they stayed there for the rest of the day and into the evening.

They played Blackjack in the casino and drank as many free drinks as the waitress would deliver. By the time they tired of gambling, it was close to six o'clock and Bryan was up about twelve hundred dollars and Doc was up about five hundred. They were still on a roll.

Bryan was in a great mood because he had won again and he decided that they should catch the early show in the Resort's lounge. They found the lounge and sat at an empty table in the middle of the room, toward the rear. There was a group of Canadians seated at the next table and Bryan bought them a round of drinks out of his winnings. The Canucks were so impressed with the size of his wad of money that they invited Bryan and his gang to join them, so the tables were pulled together. The party began once again, and from the state that everyone was in, it appeared that it wasn't going to end anytime soon. The entertainment started and everyone settled in for a while because the show would at least be an hour long.

From the size of Bryan's bankroll, it looked like he had another great day at the tables, or, he had made another trip to the money locker at the Ocean Plaza. He loved to wave his handful of money around. Everyone in the lounge was impressed. They all assumed that he was a highroller and he did nothing to change their opinion. He bought round after round and the party really got happening. Bryan's new Canadian friends hung right in with him.

"Let's have another drink. We don't really have to go back to meet those other guys yet!" Bryan decided.

The party at Resorts Hotel and Casino continued long after the lounge show was over and long after the time had passed when the loons were supposed to have met everyone else back at the Ocean Plaza to make plans for the evening.

CHAPTER FORTY-TWO

Joe was really in a hurry when he got off the elevator on Bryan's floor because all the drinking and eating had finally taken its toll. He had serious stomach cramps and had to find a washroom fast. He literally ran down the hall and quickly slipped his key-card to Bryan's room into the slot and opened the door. It was obvious to him that Bryan, Doc and the girls were not back yet as he slammed the door behind him and rushed to the ensuite in the master bedroom. Joe closed and locked the bathroom door, out of habit, without thinking, and sat right down on the throne. He felt better almost immediately and picked up the Playboy that was on the back of the toilet and started to read it. He never looked at the pictures.

All of a sudden it struck him! A chill went through his body. What the hell was Captain Gerry's hat doing in the middle of Doc's bed? He quickly decided that Bryan or Doc must have found one just like it and bought it for a keepsake. Joe eventually finished reading the jokes on the back of the centerfold and finished his constitutional and washed his hands. He walked out into the bedroom and turned toward the door that went into the main room of the suite.

As he got to the bedroom door, a body stepped in front of him. There was a sudden flash of one of the dark-complexioned men that he had seen in Cape Cod. Joe saw stars almost immediately. The big man's right fist hit him in the middle of his forehead, just above his eyes, as he quickly ducked to avoid the punch. Joe was violently hurled backwards over the end of the bed, head over heels, and crashed into the far corner of the bedroom against the wall. All he could think about was Bryan's gun under the corner of the mattress about three feet from where he had landed. He prayed that it was still there. As Joe bounced off the floor and the wall, he sat up quickly, leaned forward and reached in under the mattress. He put his hand right on the Beretta. As the large, dark man came toward him, with a smaller man close behind, Joe flashed the Beretta into view, cocked it, and pointed it right at the big man's head. The two Colombians stopped dead in their tracks and froze about six or seven feet from him on the opposite side of the bed.

"Don't fuckin' move!" Joe screamed.

He didn't know what the hell to say or do and his heart was pounding inside his shaking body. It worked. They both stopped immediately and half raised their arms in the air. They didn't know what to do either. They were both in a total state of shock at the turn of events. They all just looked at each other. Joe decided right then that they were definitely the two men that he had seen in Cape Cod two days earlier. He slowly got off his knees and rose to his feet without taking his eyes off of them. He kept the gun pointed in their direction as he made sure that the bed was between them and him as if it afforded some sort of additional protection. He tried his best to stop the gun from shaking in his hand because he didn't want them to see that he was really nervous.

Joe, since he seemed to be in control of the situation, was the first one to speak. "This is a Beretta 92F, automatic, that holds fifteen 9mm shells in the clip and one in the chamber and if either one of you bastards moves an inch, I'll empty it into both of you!" He must have sounded like some kind of a nut giving two Colombian drug traffickers gun lessons but he wanted to let them know that he really knew how to handle the weapon. So it was only a semi- automatic! Joe felt each of his racing heartbeats pounding in the lump that was starting to form in the middle of his forehead.

Joe went on, "Put your hands behind your heads and get down on your knees slowly!" He had seen that done in the movies and was almost surprised when they actually did it. "Now, one at a time, you first," he said to the big guy that hit him. "Open up the right side of your jacket with your right hand and then the left side with your left hand and do it very slowly. Before you think of trying anything stupid, I want you to know that I'm a competitive marksman, I can hit five bulls-eyes at ten yards in three point four seconds . . . I can really handle this fuckin' Beretta."

It was a totally dumb thing for Joe to say to them that just involuntarily popped out of his mouth only because he was scared to death, but he really did want them to know that he could and would use the gun if he had to. The Colombians believed him because they did exactly what they were told. The large man opened the right side of his coat. Nothing. He then opened the left side and Joe found exactly what he was looking for.

"OK, with two fingers of your left hand, pull the gun out of its holster and toss it gently, and I mean gently, toward me onto the bed. Very slowly," Joe ordered with an air of confidence and authority and the big guy did it. "Now it's your turn," he said looking at the smaller man who was kneeling just behind and to the left of the big guy.

"I don't carry a gun," he replied knowing that his weapon was in their car.

"Let's do it anyway, first the right, then the left," Joe ordered again.

The smaller man complied with his request immediately. He opened both sides of his coat at the same time, very carefully and slowly. Joe could see that he didn't have anything.

Joe then leaned forward toward the bed and extended his left hand and picked up the gun that he recognized as a Colt 45. He thumbed the safety off and cocked it. He was standing there pointing two guns at two men that he thought were Colombian drug traffickers and maybe even the killers of Captain Gerry Juby. Then he wondered, *What the hell do I do now?*

"All we want is our money back," the smaller man said to Joe with authority in his voice.

"Is that why you killed that old man at the marina last night?" Joe asked, just taking a flyer because of the hat that was out in the other room.

The smaller man continued, "If you and your friends had

returned on the boat last night, that wouldn't have happened. All we want is the money back that was taken from the crash site in Vermont. The old guy died of a heart attack or something, before his throat was cut, and the fancy knife work was only done as a message to whoever took our money."

"If we had come back with him, we'd all probably be dead right now," Joe answered.

"No, we didn't mean to kill the old guy," Luis lied, "he died of a heart attack or something while we were questioning him. All we want is our money back and we're outta here, no innocent people need to get hurt," the smaller guy said again. "It's our information that a big man with a mustache, riding a motorcycle, took eight or ten million dollars from the crash site in Vermont. That would likely be your big friend *Bryan Moyle.*"

Joe couldn't believe his ears. He was in a total state of shock. They even knew Bryan's name. He wondered what else they knew. "There wasn't eight or ten million in the bag," Joe answered before he even realized that he was in the middle of an almost friendly conversation with the smaller man, "only about six million and eight hundred thousand. All I have to do right now is call the police to come and get you guys and no one else will get hurt for sure."

"If you do that, all of you will be in serious trouble both with the police and with us Colombians. If you call the police, the FBI or the DEA, you could all be charged with theft. Even if Bryan stole the money, you have all become a party to the theft because you didn't report it. The fuckin' Yanks will throw away the keys when they put you all in jail. Now, I'm going to tell you something that's much more important and I suggest that you listen very, very carefully. We have the names and addresses of two guys in your group, Bryan Moyle and Thomas G. Yates. We know where you all live back in Ontario so it won't be hard to find out the names of the rest of you guys. If you piss us off much more than you already have, your families won't be safe. They are actually at risk right now! It's only Bryan we want to get our hands on, he's the one that stole the money from us and he's the one that has to pay for his mistake. We don't want anything to do with the rest of you guys who are with him."

There was a short lull in the conversation as Joe thought about the things that the Colombian had said. It did seem to Joe that the rest of the gang had really become unwilling accomplices to Bryan's theft. Some of the loons had even taken some money and spent it. If the whole thing had been handled differently, Captain Gerry would probably still be alive. The more Joe thought about the original theft of the money and fact that it had led directly to the Captain's death, the more he thought that they could all be in serious trouble with the law.

The legal charges and implications became almost unimportant as Joe started to think about the realities of what terrible things could happen to their families back home if they didn't cooperate with the Colombians. The more Joe thought about it, he felt that the Canadian bikers were stuck between a rock and a hard place. He didn't think that they had much of a choice.

"If I can get your money back for you quickly, without anymore problems and no involvement with the authorities, I want a deal that no one else gets hurt, and I mean no one else, not even Bryan. One person has already been killed for no fuckin' reason."

"If you get us all the money back quickly and without anymore trouble, it's a deal. Bryan, thanks to you, is off the hook. The son-of-a-bitch should pay some kind of penalty, but if we get our money back, no one else will get hurt," the smaller man answered.

"Bryan spent ten or fifteen thousand dollars fuckin' around here in Atlantic City."

"That's not a problem."

Joe went on to explain, "I don't know where the money is right now, but I think that it's in a safety deposit box somewhere nearby. How do I know that once you guys get your money back, you'll live up to the deal and absolutely no one else will get hurt?"

"I honestly think Bryan took the money from the crash site without any of you even knowing that he did and you all kind of got caught up in this mess," the smaller guy said. "A deal's a deal, if you get us all our money back, no one else needs to get hurt. If you have any trouble with Bryan, you can tell him that we know that he lives at R.R.#6, Lindsay, Ontario and that Thomas G. Yates is from Bobcaygeon. He had better not fuck us around anymore or a whole lot of innocent people back home could get hurt. No one had better call the police or even talk to them about the death at the marina."

"I'll have no trouble dealing with him," Joe answered as he felt a drip of blood run down between his eyes and along one side of his nose.

"Then, it's a deal," Luis said. "Can we stand up, my knees are killing me."

"I don't think so. You guys are still making me nervous," Joe warned. "When I arrange for Bryan to turn over the money, how do I get it to you?"

"We'll phone this room at midnight to see if you've dealt with your big friend and find out when he'll turn the money over to you, then arrangements for the transfer can be made."

"I'd rather hand it over to you in the morning. I want it to be daylight and I want a lot of people around," Joe said, and asked once more, as if hearing it one more time made it more meaningful. "No one gets hurt, not even Bryan, once you get your money back?"

"That's right, it's over and we all go our separate ways," he answered and went on. "Remember to remind them about their families back in Ontario and believe me, any visits that my associates would make would not be very friendly. Which one are you?"

"You can just call me Joe."

"Well, I guess you can just call me Luis." Then the small man asked again, "OK, Joe, now that we know each other, can we stand up now? I'm really in pain."

"You can both get up, but do it slowly and head for the other room. Don't make any sudden moves because I'd really hate to mess things up now that we have this understanding."

"What about my Colt?" The big man asked with a strong Spanish dialect.

"You won't need it. This whole fuckin' thing is gonna go real smooth and by early tomorrow morning, you guys will be heading out of town with all your money, and the rest of us, including Bryan, will be continuing on our vacation."

The Colombians got up and walked very slowly into the other room and were careful not to do anything to startle Joe. They stopped at the main door of the room with him standing about ten feet away at the door to the bedroom, with Doc's bed between them.

"Joe, I'm gonna let you keep the Captain's hat," Luis said as he got ready to leave, "so you can impress upon Bryan just how deadly serious we are about getting the money back."

"How the hell did you guys get into this room?" Joe asked Luis who gently pulled open his jacket and reached into his shirt pocket with a couple of fingers and pulled out the security card and held it up. "Throw it onto the bed, you won't need it anymore."

He complied. "I didn't have to tell you about this card. I'm giving it to you as a gesture of good faith, but if anyone fucks us around again, all your families will be at risk."

"I'll make sure that you get all your money back in the morning so that this whole mess is over with," Joe said. "There won't be any reason for anyone else to get hurt."

"Joe, I'll call you and your friends in this room at midnight to make arrangements to meet you and the money in the morning. Be sure to be here and you had better have some good news for me," Luis said as the two of them went out the door and closed it behind them.

Joe made sure that the door was tightly shut and the security lock was in place from the inside before he backed his way over and sat down in one of the chairs and stared at the door. He couldn't believe what had just happened. His heart felt like it was going to jump out of his chest. As he looked down at the dull, black Beretta and the shiny Colt that were still firmly gripped in each hand, he felt another trickle of blood run down the side of his nose and realized that he had one hell of a headache. *Now, what the hell am I supposed to do!* He thought.

Joe couldn't help but wonder if the Colombians had made a deal with him that they really intended to keep or if they were waiting in the hall. He thought about the alternatives for a few minutes and then put the two handguns on the coffee table in front of him. He picked up the telephone and dialed his own room code. He hoped that Cathy would be up.

"Cathy, are you dressed?" Joe asked and she confirmed that she was. "Don't ask me any questions and please do exactly what I ask you to do! I'll explain everything to you later."

"What's the matter?" She asked as she noticed the concern in Joe's voice.

"One of my friends is in trouble with some bad men! Just listen to me carefully and do exactly what I ask you to do," Joe said in a very serious tone. "Take the elevator up to the thirty-sixth floor and look down the hall toward Suite 3630. If there are any men in the hallway, any men, don't go down the hall and don't let them know that you have anything to do with that suite. Just get back in the elevator and go back to our room. There's a key-card for our room on the desk. If you have to go back to our room, phone me here at Suite 3630 and describe the men and what they were wearing to me. Are you writing the room number down?"

"Yes, but what's this all about?"

"I promise that I'll tell you the whole story when I see you. If the hallway is empty, and I mean empty, when you get to the thirty-sixth floor, then go to Suite 3630 and knock once, only once, on the door and I'll open it. Just do exactly what I'm telling you to do and be very careful if there are men in the hallway because an extremely dangerous situation has developed, OK?"

"All right, I'll be careful."

"Get going then!" Joe said and listened for her to hang up the phone.

As soon as the line went dead, he got all his belongings from the corner of the room and put them near the door. He put the Colombian's Colt into the top of his tank-bag and zipped it up and kept the Beretta in his right hand.

It wasn't long before there was a distinct, single knock at the door and when Joe opened it, Cathy was standing there alone. Joe leaned out and looked up and down the hallway to be sure that there was no one else around and then looked at Cathy. She appeared totally shocked. Joe had a large, bleeding goose egg in the middle of his forehead with dried blood that had run down between his eyes and onto one side of his nose. He also had the Beretta in his right hand.

"What happened to you? What are you doing with a gun?" She whispered in disbelief with a look of horror on her face.

"I'll explain it all to you downstairs," Joe said quietly as he handed her the rolled up sleeping bag with the pillow inside it. "Just follow me!"

He then picked up the saddlebags and threw them over his left shoulder and picked up the tank bag in his left hand. The Beretta remained in his right hand and tucked in under the front saddlebag that was hanging over his chest as he moved toward the doorway.

"Follow me into the hall and pull the door shut! We'll take the stairs!"

Joe opened the door to the stairwell very carefully and looked in to see if anyone was there before they quickly descended the stairs the four floors to Joe's level and his room. As soon as they were in the room, Cathy closed and locked the door and shook her head in a questioning manner as Joe threw his things onto the bed.

Cathy, very concerned, looked at Joe's forehead again more closely and said, "Jesus Christ! What the hell is going on?"

"Get me a warm, wet cloth and I'll tell you."
Joe poured two glasses of red wine as Cathy went to the bathroom. As she attended to his cut, he tried to decide what to tell her. He didn't want to give her too much information because he didn't really want her involved in Bryan's mess.

"There's a little blood still oozing from a small cut in the middle of the bump. It's starting to bruise already, you'll probably have a couple of black eyes," she said as she finished working on it. "Now, what the hell is going on and what happened?"

Joe decided that she wasn't going to learn the true story for her own safety.

"When I was in Camden with you guys, Bryan, who you met today, lost all of his money at one of the casinos. The silly bastard, who was drunk at the time, was referred to mob money lenders here in Atlantic City who lent him some money until he could get some transferred here from back home. The money that he sent for hasn't arrived yet so Bryan has been avoiding them and they're pissed. When I went up to his room to get my things, two collectors showed up and thought that I was Bryan. They started to kick the shit out of me and I got lucky and ended up with one of their guns during the fight and was able to explain to them who I was and what I was doing there. I convinced them that they had the wrong guy and I promised them that I would make sure that Bryan pays back their boss first thing in the morning. They're gonna call his suite a midnight to confirm the arrangements for the payback or they will be visiting Bryan again tomorrow."

"Why don't you just call the police?" Cathy asked.

"You can't call the police with these guys, they want their money back and they'll get it no matter what. I hate to think what might have happened to me if I hadn't ended up with the gun! They might have killed me thinking that I was Bryan!"

Joe picked up the phone and called Bryan's suite without any answer so he left a message.

"I think I'll have a quick shower. Some cold water on my forehead might help."

During the shower, Joe thought about the Colombians and decided that they had no idea that he had a room of his own. For all they knew, he was staying in the suite. He and Cathy would be safe. When he finished his shower, he tried Bryan's room once more without success. He poured two more glasses of wine and then tried Tommy and Mike's room and there was no answer there either. They had probably got tired of waiting and gone out for dinner.

"We pretty well have to hang around here until Bryan gets back. This situation has to be resolved by midnight or he'll be in serious trouble," Joe said. "If you're hungry, we can order something to eat from room service."

Cathy answered, "I'm not the least bit hungry after what's happened."

Joe and Cathy had a couple more glasses of wine and continued calling the other two rooms periodically without any luck. They talked a bit about Bryan's predicament with the loan sharks and what might happen to him if the money doesn't get paid back immediately. All of a sudden, the phone beside them rang and they both jumped at the same time.

"How are ya'?" A drunken Doc asked. "Where did you get a hat just like the Captain's?"

"I'll tell you when I get up there," Joe answered as he realized that he had left the Captain's hat and the security card on Doc's bed. "Is everyone there including Bryan?"

"Yeah, we're all here. We even bumped into Tommy and Mike down in the lobby. Bring your new friend up for a cocktail," Doc answered.

"Are Susan and Karen still with you guys?"

"Yeah, but they're just getting their things together to go back to Philadelphia."

"I'll be up there in a few minutes!" Joe hung up the phone.

"You can come up with me if you want to, but I really think that it will be safer if you stay here. The loan sharks don't know about this room," Joe explained.

Joe pulled on his blue leather jacket and put the Beretta in the pocket as he walked toward the door of the room. Cathy followed him and kissed him as he left. He climbed the stairs the four floors, rather than ride in an elevator, just in case he saw someone he didn't want to see. Joe still had his key-card for the suite so he let himself into the room. Bryan, who looked totally in the bag, met him just inside the door.

"You missed a great par . . . What the hell happened to you?" Bryan asked as he saw Joe's swollen and cut forehead and the deep reddish purple at the top of his left eye.

"Where are the girls? They don't need to hear what I have to tell you guys," Joe began.

Bryan slurred, "In the bedroom getting ready to leave."
As he finished the sentence, the two half-looped gals came out of the master bedroom carrying their belongings. They gave their dates their business cards for future reference and said their good-byes to everyone. It was the end of a couple of great days for them. Eight hundred dollars each great, plus the new, expensive bathing suits.

As the girls left and the door to the suite closed, Joe picked up the Captain's hat and the key-card off the bed and walked toward the living room where the others were all seated.

"Bryan, you sit down right here in this chair and pay attention to what I'm gonna fuckin' tell you and the rest of you listen too. You're not gonna believe what the hell happened to me!"

"This is Captain Gerry's very own hat! The one that he had on the night he died! The two men who killed him were in this room tonight and here is how they got in!" He held up the duplicate key-card and showed all of them that he still had the one that he had been given. "I don't know how they got this card, but they did!"

He then continued on and told the whole story as it happened, and everyone, including Bryan, just sat there sort of dumbfounded and speechless. There was a lull in the conversation.

"You're lucky that you weren't killed," Mike said.

"Thank God, you left that Beretta under the end of the mattress and you showed me where it was or I would probably be dead right now," Joe, said to Bryan.

"Bryan, go and get the fuckin' money right now before someone else gets hurt," a sobering Doc said in a very serious tone.

Tommy added, "Bryan you've got to give all the money back to them right now before someone else gets killed! They even know where our families live!"

"What makes you think that they won't kill someone else anyway even if I give the money back?" Bryan asked with a slur.

"I've already told you that they recited your full name and

address at R.R.#6, Lindsay and they also know Tommy's full name and that he lives in Bobcaygeon, so if they want to kill someone, they can probably do it with a phone call. I honestly think that I made a deal with them that they intend to keep. They made it clear to me that all they want is their money back without anymore problems and without police involvement," Joe explained again.

"Bryan, for Christ's Sake, they already killed Captain Gerry because you took the fuckin' money! Do you want your kids to be next?" Doc yelled.

Joe went on, "For what it's worth, the Colombians told me that Captain Gerry died of a heart attack while they were questioning him. The fancy knife work was only meant as a message to Bryan that they want their money back and they'll do anything to get it!"

All the guys were staring at Bryan who really didn't seem to be sobering up at all and didn't seem to fathom the seriousness of the situation.

"All right!" Bryan finally said. "I'll give the fuckin' money back to them, but how?"

"We have until midnight to decide how to get it to them so let's give it some thought," Joe suggested. "Bryan, can you get the money from wherever it is tonight?"

"I don't know. I'll have to call the front desk to find out."

"Well, do it right now. I hope you realize how fuckin' serious this mess has become."

Bryan didn't answer Joe.

They freshened up their drinks while Bryan was on the phone. He was told that he couldn't get into the safe-room until eight-thirty in the morning. The guys decided that Joe should deliver the money because he knew the two men. Joe agreed to handle the delivery and they discussed the various possibilities that were available to get the money to them safely.

"Ya' know that bar at Bally's called Glenda's? It's right in the lobby near the casino so there will be lots of people wandering around there in the morning," Joe suggested.

Doc agreed, "That sounds perfect and it's not very far from here.

As soon as the delivery is made, you can get back here fast and we can all get the hell outta town."

The group had no idea where the Colombians were staying, but the more they discussed it, Glenda's Lobby Bar appeared to be the best and safest location to meet them. Everyone agreed with the plan. Bryan, in his drunken stupor, still didn't seem to totally understand the gravity of the situation or fully appreciate all the problems that he had caused. The fact that he had been responsible for the death of Captain Gerry Juby didn't even cross his mind. They were all anxious for midnight to arrive so the matter could be settled with the Colombians.

CHAPTER FORTY-THREE

Luis and Fernando had left Joe in Suite 3630 at the Ocean Plaza feeling quite confident that the stolen money was almost in their grasp. They had gone directly to the elevators, down to the lobby and eventually out onto the Boardwalk. As they walked back to Bally's, Luis thought that even though the tables had been turned and they had ended up looking down the barrels of two handguns, they were a lot closer to getting the money back than they had been all week.

"This new situation will work out for the best because we won't have to get rough with anyone. Violence, as Beatrice always says, usually brings the cops around. I've got a gut feeling that this fella *Joe* wants to return the money to us as soon as he can," Luis suggested.

"What if he decides to call the police and get them involved?" Fernando asked.

"He won't do that and he won't let the rest of them do it either because he seems to understand the predicament they're all in around being a party to the theft in the first place by not reporting it and he also knows that we know where they live back in Ontario. Each time they think about the death of the Captain, they'll be reminded just how serious we are."

"You know, I hit that son-of-a-bitch hard, I should've knocked him out. My hand is still sore. That was one helluva move he pulled on us!"

"It sure the hell was, but like I said, it turned out for the best. If you had knocked him out, then we would've had to wait until the others returned and who knows what might've happened. This way, as soon as we get the money, we can head back to Montreal."

As the two of them entered their room at Bally's, a relaxed Luis announced, "I think that we should celebrate and go out for a nice dinner tonight. I'll even buy!"

"Sounds good to me," Fernando replied as he went into the bathroom. "Since you're buyin', you can pick the restaurant."

"Why don't you have a shower first and I'll call Beatriz and report the new developments to her," Luis said as he picked up the phone.

Beatriz answered on the first ring, and after Luis filled her in on exactly what had happened that afternoon and confirmed the amount of money that the Canadians had taken, she was more than pleased to hear that the hunt for the stolen money was almost over. As soon as Luis mentioned the name Joe to her, memories of her weekend in Toronto flooded back into her mind, and once again, her body ached to be near the man she truly loved.

Beatriz asked, "Who is this guy *Joe* you're dealing with and how the hell did you let him kick your asses like that, are you two slipping?"

"He's just one of the guys on the motorcycle trip. He pulled a classic move on us when he pulled that Beretta out from under the mattress in the bedroom. The only thing that I don't understand is why the Canadians would even have a gun with them?"

"Christ! Did you say it was a Beretta? I had given Jay my Beretta to deliver to Pinquino in St. Kitts because he really liked it when he visited us in Canada. I put it into one of the duffel bags that went onto the plane. Was it a 9mm Beretta 92F?"

"Yeah, it was and I think that he really knew how to use it."

"That's why they had a gun. It was in the bag of money they took from the crash site," Beatriz figured out. "You're damn lucky he didn't shoot the two of you."

"He actually seemed to be pretty cool and under control. I think that he'll be able to deal with the big guy and be ready to deliver the money to us first thing in the morning."

"It sounds like you almost like the guy!"

"I'm impressed with him, especially how he handled the situation."

"Have a good time at dinner and be sure to call me right after the midnight telephone conversation with *Joe*."

As soon as she hung up after the call from Luis, she dialed through to Castrillo's cellular phone. In the safehouse in Medellin, he answered the phone with a snarl. She could tell that he wasn't in a good mood. Beatriz passed on the contents of Luis' report to him and assured him that the money would be back in their hands by noon the next day.

"By the way, Luis found out from one of the bikers he trusts that the duffel bag they took from the crash site contained six million and eight hundred thousand dollars and not the eight or ten million that you originally thought."

"This whole damn thing is taking far too long to get resolved. Pablo is so pissed about losing all that money, a real good plane and two of his best pilots that he wants some blood and I'm afraid it's going to be mine if that money isn't recovered soon. Get back to me as soon as you can tomorrow," Castrillo barked as he hung up.

While Fernando was in the bathroom, Luis had ordered two bottles of Beaujolais Superior, so they could have a glass while they were getting ready for dinner. Fernando signed for it while Luis was in the shower and there was a glass already poured for him when he came out of the bathroom. They were both in great moods and were looking forward to a fun-filled night out. It was the first night that they had been able to relax in quite a few days.

"We deserve a treat tonight! There were a couple of goodlookin' hookers hanging around the Boardwalk entrance to this hotel the other night," Luis suggested.

Fernando replied, "That's a good idea. I liked that little Japanese broad that was there."

About nine-thirty, the two Colombians, dressed in clean shirts but the same slacks and sport jackets that they had been wearing, went down to the main lobby of their hotel and stopped for a drink in the lobby bar to decide where to go for dinner. Strangely enough,

Glenda who was working her last late-shift before going on days served them.

"The restaurant in this hotel wasn't bad the other night," Fernando commented.

"Nah, we're celebrating. Let's go over to the Trump Plaza. The sixth floor of the hotel is called *Restaurant Row* and there are four or five different places to eat. We can have our choice of steak, seafood, French, Chinese or Italian over there."

"The Trump Plaza is right next to where the Canadians are staying. Do you think we should go in that direction on the Boardwalk? What if we run into them?"

"My guess is that Joe and his buddies are dealing with the big guy around the money and they'll all be far too nervous to go out on the town tonight."

The men soon left the lobby bar and strolled through the casino and down the stairs to the Boardwalk. They walked south to the Trump Plaza and as they approached the ocean-side entrance and hallway that goes through to the lobby, they noticed two of the night's finest. A tall blonde in a bright red, leather jacket and mini-skirt and the Japanese hook, that Fernando had seen the night before, in a black mini-dress. The Colombians stopped and talked to them.

"If you ladies aren't busy at about eleven, meet us right here and we'll work out a deal for the night," Luis said.

The little Japanese gal answered, "We'll be here!"

Luis and Fernando continued to the elevators in the main foyer and went up to the sixth floor. The door opened at Restaurant Row and there were four great restaurants to choose from, Ivana's, which specialized in French cuisine, Fortunes, which was oriental, Max's, which boasted the best steak and seafood in town and Roberto's, which offered Italian. It was a tough choice, but it came down to two, Ivana's or Max's. Since they lived in Quebec, they needed a break from French food so they settled on Max's Steak and Seafood.

Max's decor was very opulent, as was all of the Trump Plaza. The interior had a turn of the century ambiance that just expanded the good mood that Luis and Fernando had been in all evening. The waiter led them to an elegantly decorated, corner table where they settled in for a relaxing meal, knowing full well, what they would be having for an after dinner treat.

Fernando asked, "Does your offer to buy dinner include the dessert that will be waiting for us on the Boardwalk?"

"What the hell. Why not! Our share of the two hundred grand U.S. will buy a lot of broads like those two."

They treated themselves to a couple of very expensive bottles of wine, Louis Jadet Meursault, and sipped away at them during the leisurely dinner. They both ended up having Surf and Turf which consisted of a twelve ounce New York Steak and one of the largest lobster tails that they had ever seen that had been flown in fresh from Maine. The whole meal and presentation had been extraordinary and Luis made good on his promise and picked up the tab. They had enjoyed themselves so much that he left a generous tip for the waiter.

As they had promised, the blonde and the Japanese hookers were waiting for them just outside the Boardwalk exit of the Trump Plaza and they joined the Colombians on the walk to Bally's. By the time they got there, Luis had worked out a deal for the night and the girls accompanied them up to their room. It was just past eleven-thirty as the four of them sipped glasses of red wine and started to undress to get ready for the night's entertainment.

Luis had negotiated blowjobs for starters because they had to make a couple of business calls at midnight. They had both undressed and were sitting on their own beds leaning against their headboards and the girls were lying on their stomachs in front of them in the nude. Luis smiled and thought to himself, *Maybe this is why the tops of beds have always been called headboards!* The little, Japanese hook had her head between Fernando's legs taking as much of him as she possibly could into her mouth in one of the most expert fashions that he had ever experienced. Luis was in the same position on his own bed and from the contented expression on his face, he was just as impressed with his hook. They were both still sitting very comfortably in the same positions as midnight approached and without interrupting the performance of his date, Luis picked up the phone and dialed the number for the Ocean Plaza.

"Could I have Suite 3630, please?"

"Hello," Joe said as he picked up the phone on the first ring.

"Hello, Joe," Luis said as he adjusted his seated position as his date continued to work on him while he talked. "Do you have everything arranged?"

"My friend can't get into the safety-deposit box until tomorrow morning so why don't we plan on meeting at ten o'clock."

"What are you proposing?"

"Do you know the lobby bar in the reception area of Bally's Park Place?" Joe asked him.

"Yeah, I do. Isn't that the bar where you guys had drinks before you went for the boat ride last night?" Luis answered without giving an indication that he was staying there.

"Yeah. I'll meet you in that bar at ten o'clock in the morning and I'll have the duffel bag of money with me. I trust that you'll be there?"

"I'll be there!" Luis answered.

"Once you have the money back, this whole fuckin' thing is over and done with and no one else gets hurt?" Joe had to ask so he could hear the answer one more time.

"That's the deal, Joe. If you hand over the duffel bag and all of the money that we talked about is there, that'll be the end of this whole thing. We all go in different directions."

"I'll see you at ten o'clock." Joe hung up the phone.

Luis turned to Fernando and told him that the deal was set for ten in the morning and then he dialed his sister's phone number in Montreal to give her the news. She didn't answer the phone so he left a short message for her. He thought that Beatriz must have been more relaxed too because that night was the first time that she had been away from the phone in a week or so.

The blonde was still hard at work as Luis put the phone down on the bedside table. He was starting to get that tingling sensation in his scrotum area so he reached down and put his hands on each side of her head and helped her finish the job that she had started about fifteen or twenty minutes earlier. At that moment, Luis felt good . . . really good. The time for the meeting was set for the morning and the blonde was there to do anything that pleased him.

CHAPTER FORTY-FOUR

After the midnight phone call from the Colombians, the guys finalized their plans and finished their drinks. Tommy, Mike and Joe decided to go back to their own rooms and to get some sleep because the next day would be hectic. They decided to be packed and ready to leave town as soon as the money was returned. They agreed to check out of the hotel first thing in the morning and meet in Joe's room at nine o'clock, with all their personal belongings, to make the final arrangements. Bryan was to bring the money with him at that time.

Joe picked up Captain Gerry's hat off the coffee table and as he headed toward the door, he gave a bit more advice, "Don't forget to lock your doors tonight, from the inside!"

Joe left the suite and went back down the stairs to his own floor. He was actually feeling more comfortable because it did appear that the money problem would be resolved in the morning and no one else was going to get killed or even hurt. After he got back to his room, he and Cathy sat on the couch for a short time and talked.

"I'm sorry to bring you all the way from Camden to get involved in this mess. We didn't even get to go out for dinner."

"You had no idea that this stuff was going on or you would've probably stayed with us in the city. How's your head?"

"Splitting," Joe said as he got up and walked toward the bathroom. "I think I'll take a couple of Extra Strength Tylenol. Do you want to order something to eat?"

"No, I'm fine," Cathy, answered. "We had better get to bed because I have to get up around six to get on the road to Philly."

As Joe was in the bathroom taking the pills, he brushed his teeth and had a leak. He had showered earlier in the day, but took a warm washcloth and freshened up, just in case Cathy wasn't that tired. Joe's Great Uncle Scott, who was the only gay member of his family, always used to say, *Be sure to wash it every morning, you just never know when someone might want to kiss it!* Uncle Scott's advice had often come in handy over the years.

Cathy did the bathroom thing and came back in the nude and turned out the lights. Joe thought that she felt good as she slipped in beside him but once again, as she cuddled up, a flash of Trizzi went through his mind. Even though his head was full of thoughts of Colombians, Trizzi's face kept appearing. He still missed her everyday. He truly loved her.

Joe broke the silence, "Tommy, Mike and Doc are heading to Washington tomorrow and maybe even further south and Bryan is going to go home. I think I'm going back to your place in Camden. I want to spend a few days in Philadelphia before I leave for home. It's been a long time since I've been to Drexel Hill and my old neighbourhood."

"I'm glad you're going to stay with me."

"Now, where else would I stay? I'll be able to take you out for the dinner we missed tonight. I'll also be able to check on Howie to see if he's all right."

They cuddled and kissed tenderly and Cathy slipped down under the covers for what seemed to be an eternity allowing Joe to just lay there and relax. Later, they made love slowly and quietly before they went to sleep. Once again, Joe had strange dreams about Colombians, Cathy, Sharon and even Trizzi. He knew that he had tossed and turned most of the night and hoped that he hadn't kept Cathy awake.

The alarm went off at six o'clock and Cathy got up immediately and started to get ready for work and the trip to the city. Joe got up and jumped into the shower while she was doing her hair and lingered in the warm water. His head had quit aching but there was some soreness in the middle of his forehead. As he got out of the shower, he looked at his face in the mirror. The lump had gone down a bit but there was some black and blue around one blood-shot eye. By the time he got dressed, Cathy was ready to leave. She looked absolutely beautiful all dressed up for work. It was uncanny how much she reminded him of Trizzi. Joe really liked Cathy, but knew that the relationship couldn't go anywhere while Trizzi was on his mind. He planned to deal with that problem, one way or another, as soon as he got back to Canada. He decided that he would find her in Montreal and tell her that he loved her. There was going to be a future for he and Trizzi or he was going to forget her and get on with his life without her.

"I don't think that I should help you down to the lobby with your bags," Joe said as Cathy gathered her things together, "just in case those loan sharks are around looking for Bryan."

"I can handle the bags myself," Cathy said as she gave him a long, slow, tender kiss. "What time are you going to get to my place?"

"I'll be there around six o'clock," he said as he opened the door for her and they stepped out into the hall. "If I'm going to be late, I'll call you."

"Don't be late," she said as she turned and headed toward the elevators.

Joe packed his belongings into his tank bag and saddlebags, including a keepsake, Captain Gerry's hat. He also rolled up his sleeping bag with the pillow inside and generally got ready to leave town. He left the big man's Colt on the top of his clothes in his tank bag and put the Beretta in the pocket of his leather jacket, as it would not be leaving his side. Joe then decided that there was lots of time to have breakfast and he was starving because he had missed dinner the night before.

The hostess led him to a private table that was secluded behind some greenery and he ordered breakfast as soon as he sat down; corned beef hash, three eggs, wheat toast, coffee and orange juice along with the morning paper.

The waitress brought the juice, coffee and newspaper almost immediately. Joe settled in to do some reading before his food arrived. He slowly read through page one and then turned the page. There it was, right in the middle of page three, *Marina Murder Unsolved*. He folded the paper to the article and soon realized that Luis had told him the truth. The write-up explained in detail that the autopsy of Captain Gerry Juby had revealed that he had in fact died of a heart attack before the fancy knife-work had been performed. There was no doubt in Joe's mind that those bastards had caused his heart attack, but at least Captain Gerry wasn't alive when they gave him the *Colombian Necktie*.

Joe really felt sorry for Gerry, his three kids and the fact that he had been semi-retired, doing something that he loved to do. His partner, Charlie Gorrill, would miss him too because they had shared the same philosophy of life. He was a great, old guy who Joe would have liked to have had the opportunity to get to know better.

Joe read the rest of the paper as he ate his breakfast and when he finished, he went to the front desk and checked out. He then went back to his room to get organized to meet the other guys and get ready for his rendezvous with the Colombians. He got his morning constitutional out of the way and then placed his things in the middle of his bed, all ready to be taken to the parking garage and packed onto his Harley. Joe picked up the phone shortly after nine o'clock and called Suite 3630 to see what was going on. No one had arrived on time.

"What the hell is going on? I thought you were all supposed to be down here for nine?"

"Bryan isn't here," Doc advised. "He said that he was going downstairs to get the money well over half-an-hour ago and he hasn't come back yet."

"I sure hope that the loon hasn't fucked off again and left us *not holding the bag*."

"I'm ready. If he isn't here in the next ten minutes, I'll come down to your room."

Joe pulled the Colt out of his tank bag and looked at it. He put it on the bed beside his belongings and decided that he would get rid of it when he crossed the swamp on the way out of Atlantic City. He then pulled the Beretta out of his jacket pocket and held it in his hands and looked at it. He thought, *This gun probably saved my life!* It was a comfortable gun and felt good in his hand. The dull, black finish made it look awesome. As the time passed, without any word from Bryan, Joe became nervous. He ejected the clip and made sure that it was still fully loaded. He snapped the safety on and put it back into his jacket pocket because it would be going with him to meet the Colombians at Bally's.

There was a knock at the door and Joe opened it with the security chain still in place. It was Tommy and Mike with all their gear. He let them in and told them that Doc and Bryan should be along at any moment. They explained that they were late because there had been quite a line-up at the front desk to check out.

Someone else rapped on the door and Joe opened it the same way. It was Doc with all his belongings and a few cold beers, on ice, in one of the plastic wastebaskets. He explained that Bryan had not yet returned to their room with the duffel bag of money.

"How fuckin' long has he been gone?" Joe asked.

"About forty-five or fifty minutes. The way he's been acting around this money is making me nervous."

Tommy added, "The lobby was extremely busy, but I sure hope that he doesn't do anything stupid like he did in Cape Cod, like take the money and disappear again. I also hope he realizes that the Colombians know my name and address too!"

Just as they were all about to panic, there was another knock at the door. It was opened and in walked Bryan with all his personal things and the duffel bag of money.

"Where the fuck have you been? You were making everyone jumpy," Doc blurted out.

"I had to check out and then I had to wait for the guy who opens the safety deposit room to arrive. He was a little late getting to work this morning," Bryan answered.

Joe explained, "The paper had an article in it about the murder of Captain Gerry and the fact that it is still unsolved. It did confirm that Gerry really did die of a heart attack though and not from having his throat slit. At least he was already dead when that was done to him."

"Not that it matters!" Mike remarked. "Those bastards caused his heart attack!"

Joe picked up the Colt 45 off the bed and wiped it clean with a towel, "I don't know what the hell to do with this. I guess I'll just wipe my finger prints off of it and throw it into the swamp on our way out of town."

"Where's the other handgun?" Bryan asked.

"Its right here," he said patting his jacket pocket. "I think I'll keep it until this whole mess is over with and then I'll throw it into the swamp too."

"Give me the Colt and I'll get rid of it later," Bryan said. "I'll feel more comfortable having it with me until we all leave town."
Joe handed Bryan the handgun still wrapped in the towel.

"Be careful with it! It's fully loaded but the safety is on," Joe said. "I think that we should head for the parking garage and the bikes as soon as I get back from meeting those guys. I have no idea where the Colombians are staying or where they're going after they get the money, but the sooner we get outta here, the better."

Doc interjected, "Its past nine-thirty."

"I'm going south with you guys," Doc said to Tommy and Mike, "I've always wanted to see that part of the country. Are you guys coming with us?" He looked at Bryan and Joe.

"I've had enough of motorcycles to last me a lifetime! I'm heading straight home and the first thing that I'm going to do when I get back there, is sell the fuckin' thing," Bryan answered.

"Joe, where are you headed?" Tommy asked.

"Well, I've only been back to Philadelphia once since my family left when I was a teenager so I think I'll head up there and spend two or three days. I want to go back to my old neighbourhood and look around, besides, someone should check on Howie."

"You've fallen in love with Cathy," Doc remarked, "that's where you're going!

"She's a great gal," Joe smiled and said, "but unfortunately, my heart belongs to another! I may drop by and see her while I'm there."

Mike interrupted, "It's nine forty-five!"

"You guys should stay here until I get back because I'm sure that the Colombians don't know about this room," Joe said once again as he put his right hand into his jacket pocket to be sure that the Beretta was still there and then picked up the duffel bag of money and went toward the door and spoke, "I'll be back here in half-an-hour and we'll all leave town together."

They all wished Joe luck as they closed the door behind him and he headed down the hall toward the elevators. As he got into the elevator, his mind began to race, *What if the transfer doesn't go smoothly? What if the Colombians do want some blood after it's all said and done?* As he carried the duffel bag and the nearly seven million dollars in his left hand, his right hand that was in his jacket pocket holding onto the Beretta began to sweat. He had one finger on the trigger guard and his thumb on the safety.

He walked through the revolving doors and out onto the wooden walkway into another gorgeous day of sunshine and blue sky. The ocean was rolling in a light breeze and there were thousands of seagulls on the sandy beach. There were lots of people out walking or sitting in the sun enjoying the lovely morning. Joe passed the Trump Plaza, Caesars, the Shops-On-Ocean-One, Boardwalk Rogers and continued on toward Bally's Park Place. All Joe could think about was that old Indian in the movies who said, *What a beautiful day to die!* The hand that had become attached to the Beretta continued to perspire.

Sudden, someone nearby yelled and scared the hell out of him and he jumped.

"Hey! You pussy! Where the hell are you off to on such a nice day?"

It was his old buddy Mickey M. He and Dino were having a cigarette and leaning on the railing that separated the Boardwalk from the beach and enjoying the beautiful morning.

As soon as they saw his face, Mickey asked, "What the hell did you run into?"

CHAPTER FORTY-FIVE

Luis and Fernando dumped the hookers by eight in the morning and then ordered coffee and buns from room service. They had a wonderful night and were looking forward to finishing their business with the Canadians. The coffee arrived while Fernando was in the shower. As soon as he was finished, Luis got himself organized and the two of them got dressed for what was going to be their last day in Atlantic City.

By nine-thirty, they were both dressed and having coffee and a few laughs about how the night had gone. Luis had paid the girls a little extra money to put on a performance of their own and they had sat around and enjoyed the show. Immediately after watching the two girls get each other off, the voyeurs had switched partners for a while.

"Now I know why you like Japanese girls," Luis kidded his buddy.

Fernando laughed, "The blonde broad wasn't half bad either. I think *she could suck a golf ball through a hundred feet of garden hose*, but still, I was glad to get the little Jap back."

"I guess it's time for us to head for the lobby bar. Hopefully, this transfer of money will go smoothly and we'll soon be heading for Montreal."

"Do you really think it will?" Fernando asked.

"I think everything will go well, but you'd better go to the car on the way to the bar and get my Ruger. I hope we won't need it, but we'd better be safe than sorry."

"Do you want me to be there with you when this thing goes down?"

"You'd better come with me," Luis said as he placed the *Do Not Disturb* sign on the door. "I think that Joe will be nervous enough that he'll want to see both of us at the meeting."

As soon as the men got to the lobby, they split up. Luis went to check out, but he kept a key-card for the room so they could return there to count the money. Fernando took the luggage directly to the car and picked up Luis' Ruger and put it in the empty holster under his left arm. Just before ten, they got to Glenda's Lobby Bar and sat at a table for four, on the outer edge of the half-circle partition, with their backs to the lobby. Glenda, who was just starting a week of dayshifts, was the only one on duty. The men ordered some orange juice and coffee.

Joe walked up the steps from the Boardwalk into Bally's casino and in among all the early morning gamblers with Mickey M. and Dino a few feet behind him. Many of the gamblers interrupted their games to stare at the rough-looking bikers. Joe had made up some story about the bump on his head and talked the bikers into doing him a favor. They were to merely follow him to the lobby bar and sit well back, out of the way, just for a show of force that would add another comfort level for Joe as he transacted a small business deal. He had told them absolutely nothing about what was going on that morning. The Columbians couldn't see Joe and his two buddies as they crossed the crowded room of gamblers because the back wall and shelves of the bar blocked the view into the casino.

They went up the few stairs onto the main lobby level and as the bar came into view, Joe caught a glimpse of the two men seated at a table on the far side of the lounge. They were looking directly at him. There were no other people in the bar that morning. Joe walked confidently into the lounge enclosure and made sure that he hid the fact that he was nervous. Mickey M. and Dino followed, but sat down at the bar and just stared across the room in the direction of the two Colombians. Joe wanted the Colombians to know that the tough looking bikers were with him. He walked directly toward them with the duffel bag of money in his left hand and the

Beretta in his right hand in his jacket pocket. As he approached them, he thumbed off the safety and carefully left his index finger on the trigger guard.

"Joe, what brings you back here so early today?" Glenda asked, remembering him from his previous visits to the bar, as he walked past her toward her only other customers.

He answered and half smiled, "I just dropped by to meet a couple of friends."

"Can I get you something?" She asked.

"No thanks, I'm not staying long."

"If you need anything, give me a call," she said as she waited on the two bikers and went about her business of getting the bar ready for another busy day.

There were empty chairs between the two men and the isle. Joe walked right up and sat down in a chair at a separate table opposite them. There was about six feet between eye contact. He began to feel more comfortable because his hand on the gun was no longer sweating. He was sure that the men knew exactly what he was holding onto in his pocket.

"Did you have any trouble convincing your friend to return our property?" Luis asked.

"He can be a bit of an asshole sometimes, but here it is," Joe said lifting the bag that was to his left, slightly off the floor.

Luis went on, "As I said before, I have a gut feeling that the big guy took the duffel bag without the rest of you even knowing that he did. If you had all been in on it, you would have each taken one of your own. There were thirteen of them full of cash."

"You're right, but it doesn't really matter at this point. Our agreement is that once you get your money back, no one else gets hurt."

"That's the deal and we'll stand by it if all the money's there," Luis confirmed.

"None of us have opened the duffel bag since Bryan delivered it just before I came over here," Joe stated, "but keep in mind what I told you yesterday. I was there when it was first counted and there was only six million and eight hundred thousand. As I mentioned to you, Bryan may have spent ten or fifteen grand, but that's all that should be missing."

"I believe you, Joe. If the amount is close to that number, we'll be happy," Luis said. "Did you happen to read the paper this morning? Your friend really did die of a heart attack!"

"I read it, but the article didn't say who the hell caused his heart attack!"

"You know as well as I do that Bryan caused all of these problems by stealing our money," Luis answered. "What have you done with my partner's Colt?"

"It's history! You guys won't need it now that you have your money back."

"Where's the Beretta?" Luis asked looking at Joe's right hand in his jacket pocket.

"It's right here," Joe said patting his pocket with his left hand.

"By the way," Luis said with a broad smile, "who the hell are your two buddies over there at the bar and what the fuck's that all about?"

"They're a couple of tough bastards who happen to be friends of mine. Yesterday, when I met you guys, it was two against one. Today the odds are in my favor, it's three against two," Joe said as he stood up and put the duffel bag in the middle of the Colombians' table.

"Joe, that kinda confirms that you don't have a fuckin' clue about our business," Luis said with another broad smile, "motorcycle gangs don't bother Colombians, we shoot those assholes on Sundays just for fun!"

"You're right," Joe smiled back, "I don't know much about what you do or how you do it, but it does make me feel a little more relaxed just bringing them along."

"I guess our business is concluded," Luis stood up and slid the bag toward Fernando.

He then turned toward Joe and extended his right hand to him as if to consummate some sort of real business transaction. Luis wondered if their relationship had progressed to the point where Joe actually trusted him enough to let go of the Beretta.

It had been a long week for everyone and this appeared to be the moment of truth. Joe, thumbed the safety on, let go of the Beretta and slowly pulled his hand out of his jacket pocket and extended it toward Luis. Their hands joined in a firm handshake that Joe hoped would seal the agreement that the ordeal was finally over. The two adversaries smiled at each other with an air of mutual respect.

Joe put his hand back into his pocket and stepped back as Fernando, the big Colombian who had given him the lump in the middle of his forehead and the black eye, stood up with the duffel bag in one hand. He gave them lots of room to leave the lounge. As they walked out of the bar, they smiled at the bikers, and then turned back toward the lobby. As they passed Joe on the other side of the low partition, it was there, in the lounge at Bally's, that Joe had his last contact with the Colombians.

"It's been a pleasure doin' business with ya' Joe," Luis said as he went by and kind of tipped his hand to his forehead in some sort of a parting gesture. "If you ever want to learn all about our business, be sure and look me up."

Joe smiled back, "Thanks, Luis, I'll keep that in mind!"
He watched them walk toward the far end of the lobby until he lost sight of them in the crowd and then he joined his biker buddies at the bar.

"What the hell are you guys drinking, Bloody Marys?"

"Are you sure you don't want something to drink, Joe," Glenda asked again.

"Sure, why not. Give us all a shot of Herradura Anejo, fast, and give me the tab, including whatever these guys had to drink."
Once again, he looked toward the far end of the lobby. The Colombians were nowhere to be seen. Joe clicked glasses with his two buddies, threw the shooter back and shook his head a couple of times and winced as the Tequila burned his throat.

"Did everything go all right with your business deal?" Mickey M. asked.

"It went just great and I want to thank you guys for being there for me. Sometimes a little show of muscle goes a long way. Here's a couple of hundred bucks for you guys to take your old ladies out for lunch or dinner on me," Joe said as he paid the tab and left a generous tip.

"Shit, we don't need that, we're glad to help," Dino responded.

"You have to take it. I won it gambling anyway," Joe insisted. "I have really gotta run now. Thanks for your help and it was nice meeting you guys."

"Nice meetin' you to Joe," Mickey M. replied as they did the thumb-lock thing and Joe did the same with Dino.

"See ya' my next trip to Atlantic City," Joe said to Glenda as he walked quickly out of the bar, back through the casino and out onto the Boardwalk among the throngs of people.

The Beretta had the safety back on and Joe was feeling relieved. As he wound his way through the people on his way back to the Ocean Plaza, he wondered if the handshake with the Colombian actually had any significance, *Was it a sign of trust and are they going to uphold their end of the bargain or is all hell about to break loose?*

As soon as Luis and Fernando got back to their room, they dumped the contents of the duffel bag out onto one of the beds and started to count it. They were much more proficient at counting large amounts of money than the motorcycle gang had been because they did it often in their line of work. Twenty minutes later, they had counted the money and double-checked the count to be sure that they hadn't made a mistake. The second time confirmed that there was only six million dollars in the bag. Eight hundred thousand U.S. was missing! That was well over a million dollars Canadian!

Luis looked at Fernando and said, "That big son-of-a-bitch grabbed eight hundred grand before he turned the money over to Joe! I'm sure that none of the other Canadians know!"

"Are you sure that they're not all trying to fuck us?" Fernando asked.

"Remember yesterday, when we first met Joe? He told us then

that there was only six million and eight hundred thousand and not eight or ten million," Luis recalled, "and this morning, he confirmed that same amount again."

"Yeah, you're right. I'm sure that Joe knew we'd count it before we left town."

"I'd bet my share of the finders fee that Bryan has the eight hundred grand with him right now and the others know nothing about it," Luis said. "Give me my Ruger!"

The Colombians, who had already checked out and taken their luggage to their car, stuffed all of the money back into the duffel bag and rushed to the elevator. Just as the elevator hit the main level, Luis gave Fernando the bag of money.

"You get the car and pick me up at the main entrance of the Ocean Plaza as soon as you can. I'm sure that I can get there faster on foot."

Luis rushed through Bally's lobby and ran down the extra-wide escalator two steps at a time to the main entrance. He ran along Pacific Ave. toward the Plaza, and as he ran, he kept an eye open for the Canadian bikers. As soon as he got there, he rushed through the lobby and took the first elevator that was available up to the thirty-sixth floor.

At that exact moment, the Canadian's were in another elevator that had just stopped at the level of the parking garage where their motorcycles were parked. Luis knew that if he could catch up to them, all he would have to do is confront Bryan in front of the others and they would force him to hand over the money. As soon as the elevator opened on Bryan's floor, Luis ran down the hall to Suite 3630. The door of the room was wide open and a maid's cart was in the hallway in front of it.

"When did the guys that were in this room leave?"

"The room was empty when I got here about twenty minutes ago," she answered.

Luis swore under his breath and ran back to the elevators. It seemed to take forever for a door to open and when one finally did, there were four other people onboard. As luck would have it, two were going to the pool level and two were going to the casino level, and that would mean a couple of extra stops. Luis finally made it to the main floor where he got off. He ran across the lobby, through the door to the lower parking level and down the stairs to where he knew that the bikes had been parked the day before. As he burst out of the stairwell and onto their parking level, all Luis could hear was the muffled roar of motorcycles racing through the underground garage. He caught a glimpse of them going around a row of cars toward the exit.

Luis rushed back up the stairwell that he had run down only moments before and went back through the lobby to the main entrance and found Fernando standing at the rear of his blue Lincoln. As Luis got behind the wheel and Fernando got into the passenger seat, he quickly explained to Fernando what had happened. The blue, four-door Lincoln squealed its tires out onto Pacific Ave. and raced to Indiana, the one-way street that goes to the Atlantic City Expressway. As the Colombians reached the expressway, they caught a glimpse of five motorcycles just ahead of them. By the time the bikers had crossed the swamp in the relatively light traffic, the drug traffickers had pulled the blue Lincoln up close enough behind the gang to be able to tell which rider was the big man with the mustache.

Luis and Fernando watched the big guy closely and could easily see the over-stuffed saddlebags hanging on each side of his Harley. They knew exactly where the missing eight hundred thousand dollars American was and settled in a safe distance behind the bikers to come up with a plan to get the money back.

CHAPTER FORTY-SIX

Joe entered the main floor of the Ocean Plaza and walked past the morning drinkers in the small bar and the breakfast crowd in the restaurant as he headed for the elevators. The main lobby was very busy with people coming and going. He went directly into one of the open elevators and up to his room on the thirty-second floor. All the guys were having a beer while they waited for Joe to return.

Doc handed Joe part of his can of beer, "How'd it go?"

"The Colombians have their money back. They were waiting for me in the lobby bar. I met my biker buddies on the Boardwalk, Mickey M. and Dino, so I took them along with me, just to be nearby and look tough. After some small talk, I turned over the money to them and they left. The smaller guy even shook hands with me after the transfer to confirm that *a deal's a deal*, so I honestly don't think there'll be anymore trouble."

"What did the Colombians say when they saw the two real bikers?" Tommy asked.

"They laughed that I'd even bothered to bring them along and said that back home, they shoot those tough bastards on Sundays just for fun. I don't think bikers scare Colombians!"

Bryan asked nervously, as beads of sweat formed at his temples, "Where did they go when they left? Did they head for their car or go back to their hotel?"

"I don't know where they're staying, but they did head for the main entrance of Bally's. I really didn't hang around long enough to find out," Joe explained.

"Well, let's get the hell outta here," Bryan said anxiously. "I'm ready to hit the road."

He had his gear in his hands before he even finished the sentence and had opened the door of the room and was out in the hall. He seemed very edgy and was certainly hyper.

The rest of the gang sucked back their beers, picked up their things and followed Bryan into the hallway and toward the elevators. He was in one hell of a hurry. By the time he had pushed the button, a couple of the guys hadn't even left the room yet. Everyone seemed a bit anxious, but Bryan was really uptight and was starting to perspire profusely. Beads of sweat formed on his forehead and rolled down his face. Joe thought that perhaps it was just the week of boozing that had finally caught up with him.

As they left the elevator and walked through the garage toward the motorcycles, their eyes searched the rows of cars for the Colombians. Joe still kept his right hand on the Beretta and it started to sweat again, but everything appeared to be quite normal.

It only took a few minutes for them to stow their gear onto the motorcycles and attach the bungy cords to hold everything down. Joe threw his saddlebags over the back of his bike and tied them into place and set his tank bag in the proper spot and firmly attached it. His rolled up sleeping bag, with the pillow inside, was placed in its usual spot at the rear of the seat for the short trip to Camden. Bryan started his Harley first and revved his engine impatiently, a number of times, as he waited, and one by one, the other guys fired up their bikes.

They said their good-byes to each other but they would travel through town together to the intersection of the Atlantic City Expressway and the Garden State Parkway. At that point, they would all head in different directions. For some reason, Bryan had decided that he was going north on the Garden State Parkway toward Newark, and then west past Albany, to Highway #81 and north to Canada, rather than accompany Joe to Philadelphia and go north through Pennsylvania and New York which was a little shorter route. Bryan led the motorcycle gang out of the garage, through the slums and onto the expressway without incident.

As they crossed the acres of swamp, Joe wondered if Bryan had disposed of the Colt 45 even though he wasn't ready to get rid of the Beretta until he put more distance between himself and the Colombians. He felt a little more comfortable as the gang hit the mainland, but had a twinge of concern about having the illegal handgun in his possession. The fact that the Colombians could still be around was enough to make him decide to keep it awhile longer.

The highway signs indicated that the Garden State Parkway intersection was just ahead so, without slowing down, the riders pulled their bikes close to each other and yelled and waved their good-byes. Bryan pulled off first, to the right, on the ramp heading north on the Garden State Parkway. The rest of them could tell from the way his bike was leaning and the sound of his exhaust that he was really cranking it up. Tommy, Mike and Doc took the next cloverleaf that curled around and went south toward Cape May and the Chesapeake. Joe went straight through and continued west on the Atlantic City Expressway toward Philadelphia. He expected to be in Camden in about an hour. No one had noticed the blue, four-door Lincoln that had pulled in behind Bryan as he went north on the Parkway on his way back home to Canada.

Earlier that morning, Bryan had left his suite to get the duffel bag of money from the hotel safe-room and he had serious trouble deciding whether to return the money or just take it and leave town again. The thought of keeping or giving back all that money had played on his mind over and over during the past few days. His mind had been swimming with all of his financial problems and more importantly, the solution to them; the money. He had eventually realized that the Colombians did in fact know his name and where he lived so the money had to be returned. He had also reasoned that there was no possible way that they would know how much money was in the duffel bag because there were a number of bags at the crash site that likely all had different amounts in them. So he came up with a saw-off. He would keep close to eight hundred thousand U.S. and give them back six million. Before he turned the bag over to Joe, he had separated his money from theirs. He had no idea that Joe had already told the Colombians how much money there was in the duffel bag. Joe had only done that to protect Bryan because they had originally thought that eight or ten million dollars was missing. Bryan would have been accused of stealing the amount that wasn't even there.

As Bryan cruised north, well above the speed limit, he glanced up as the sun played hide-and-seek behind a few scattered, white clouds as they moved slowly across the light blue sky. He was anxious to get safely back to Canada and had decided to ride straight through for the eleven or twelve hours the trip would take. There was very little traffic that early in the day so he thought that he would make good time.

One of Bryan's saddlebags was full of dirty clothes and the other was full of cash and the loaded Colt 45. He knew that when he delivered the money to Joe and the other guys that morning, none of them would think any of it would be missing. Taking into account all the serious trouble that Bryan had already caused and the fact that he was indirectly responsible for Captain Gerry's death, no one would have thought for a second that he would put them all at risk again. Bryan was thinking about solving his financial problems with his newfound wealth and hadn't noticed the blue Lincoln that was following him well back in the distance.

Just past the Tuckerton exit, Luis looked in his rearview mirror at the road behind and saw that there was absolutely no traffic in sight. It was also an area of the highway where the median was dense bush with no visibility between the lanes that were running north and south. He stepped on the gas and the blue Lincoln pulled closer and closer to the lone biker. The blue sedan quickly pulled up beside the Harley, in the passing lane, just before an exit to a rest area. As the car and motorcycle approached the exit ramp, Bryan looked to the left to see why the car that had caught up to him at such a high rate of speed had slowed down and was traveling right along beside him, parallel to his motorcycle.

Bryan's startled eyes immediately met Fernando's eyes and his large smiling face. He had never seen the man before, but he immediately knew that he was the man that Joe had described to him. Bryan had no time to react. At that instant, the Lincoln veered to the right, broadsided him and sent his Harley out of control onto the ramp to the rest area at just over eighty miles an hour. Bryan tried to negotiate the right turn, but the motorcycle was going far too fast and it left the pavement, traveled through the gravel shoulder, hit a bump and went airborne and then hit the guardrail that bordered the ramp. The rider was thrown off the bike, up into the air, and on into the dense trees that separated the rest area from the highway. The twisted wreck of the bike careened along the guardrail, rolling over and over, until it lodged itself against a guard-post.

The blue Lincoln had to slam on its brakes after it hit the motorcycle so it could make the quick right turn onto the rest area ramp. The car had been traveling so fast, it nearly missed the exit. Luis made a quick right and bounced and bottomed the car through a shallow, grassy ditch to get off the Parkway and onto the ramp. The Lincoln slid to a stop in the gravel just past the place where the bike had first collided with the guardrail. It stopped halfway between where the rider had been thrown over the fence and where the motorcycle had finally come to rest.

Fernando pulled his switchblade out of his pocket and ran from the car, jumped the guardrail, and found the biker in front of a large Ash tree. Bryan's helmet had been smashed and cracked, but it was still on his head. His eyes were wide open, but there was a large bulge at the back of his neck above his shoulder blades. It was obvious to the Colombian that the biker's neck had been severely broken to the extent that his spine was protruding out of his upper back. Fernando put his knife away as there was no need for any fancy blade work. The big man with the mustache was dead!

Luis ran to the mangled motorcycle that still had the saddlebags attached, reached into his pocket for his knife, cut them loose from the Harley and ran back to the car. He and Fernando arrived back to the Lincoln at the same time, jumped into the vehicle and drove slowly on through the rest area and back out onto the Parkway. The whole encounter with Bryan had taken about a minute and no other traffic had come along the highway. Fortunately, there had been no vehicles parked in the rest area. As Luis drove, Fernando went through Bryan's saddlebags.

"The son-of-a-bitch had my Colt with him and all the money seems to be here in a plastic bag," Fernando said as he pulled a white garbage bag full of money out of the saddlebags and stuffed it into the duffel bag that Joe had given them.

"Is it all there?" Luis asked.

"Yeah, it looks like it. The Colt is still loaded. That's a bit of luck," Fernando said as he put it into his shoulder holster and put Luis' Ruger back into the glove compartment.

"What else is in the saddlebags?"

"Nothing much, just some clothes and personal stuff. I may as well throw the bags out the window, we don't need them anymore."

A police car and an ambulance had arrived on the ramp to the rest area, with their lights flashing, fairly soon after the accident was reported. As soon as the preliminary investigative work was done and the police took their usual pictures of the body and the motor-cycle, the two ambulance attendants loaded the big man into a body bag. They wrestled him onto a stretcher and strained to load him into the back of the emergency vehicle. Eventually the two rear doors were slammed shut with Bryan's body inside. The ambulance then roared through the rest area and out onto the highway with its lights flashing and its siren blaring even though they weren't rushing to a hospital. The passenger was dead.

Later, the police had found Bryan's saddlebags further north on the Parkway just lying on the shoulder with one side empty and one side full of clothes. The officers had thought that it was strange that there had been no witnesses to the accident and that the saddlebags were found a number of miles from the scene. They finally decided that the saddlebags had likely been caught under another vehicle and been dragged up the highway. They also thought that the crash was a routine traffic accident where a biker had gone off the exit ramp too fast and had missed the turn.

The last cop at the scene, State Trooper Dale Kennedy, helped the tow truck operator secure what was left of the Harley into a sling at the rear of the truck and helped tie it down so that it could be transported to the police compound. As the bike was being secured, Kennedy noticed some blue paint on the left side of the bike, in four or five different places, that really stood out against the reddish color of the motorcycle. All of a sudden, he asked the tow truck driver not to leave the area for a few minutes and he began to walk the accident scene.

Kennedy walked all the way out to the main traveled part of the highway just before the exit ramp into the rest area. He found some skid marks that looked very strange. Some appeared to have been caused by the bike and the rest had been caused by some other kind of vehicle. As he followed the route that the bike had taken when it left the highway, he found more tire marks on the road from another vehicle. The fresh skid marks went toward a shallow, grassy ditch, through the grass, tearing up sod, and then back up onto the pavement of the off ramp. A vehicle had tried to stop quickly and had cut across the ditch to the ramp, but Kennedy really had no idea if those events were related. After standing back and looking at all of the skid marks, something really started to bother him about the scene of the accident.

He had no problem finding the exact location where the motorcycle had left the ramp and smashed into the guardrail. The marks where the bike had first hit and each place it hit as it bounced along the guardrail were very clear right up to where it had come to rest. There was no blue paint on the fence or anywhere in the area, just red marks from the motorcycle. The possibility that the motorcycle had been hit by another vehicle haunted Trooper Kennedy. He went back and looked at the motorcycle and scraped some blue paint off of the gas tank into a small envelope. He then allowed the tow truck driver to leave the scene of the accident.

As State Trooper Kennedy walked slowly back to his cruiser, he tried to put all the pieces of the puzzle together. He kept going over and over the physical evidence at the scene of the accident in his mind and it continued to bother him. He thought that it was a long shot, but he got on his police band radio and broadcast a message that was heard throughout northern New Jersey and into New York State by his fellow officers. He signed on with his Trooper's Office code, name and rank and made a report.

"This is Trooper Dale Kennedy from the Tuckerton detachment. Keep a lookout for a light blue car or truck that could be traveling north on the Garden State Parkway with damage to the passenger side of the vehicle. It may have reddish paint scrapes on the damaged area. There is the possibility that such a vehicle was involved in a fatal hit-and-run motorcycle accident in the Tuckerton area within the last hour or so."

Trooper Dale Kennedy had a gut feeling that there was something very strange about the physical evidence at the scene of the motorcycle accident that all of the other policemen had missed.

CHAPTER FORTY-SEVEN

The further Joe traveled from Atlantic City, the more comfortable he felt. He knew that if the Colombians really wanted to find him, they could, by asking questions in Lindsay about the members of the motorcycle gang that took the trip down the east coast of the of the United States. On that morning, the only way that they could find him was if they were following him. Joe had been watching the cars that were behind him since he had separated from the other guys and there were no suspicious vehicles. He honestly felt that Luis was a man of his word and that everyone was safe and sound.

As Joe got closer to Camden, he took the Blackwood exit to get some gas and find a phone to give Howie a call at Lynn's apartment. He thought that she would likely be at work and Howie would be hanging around waiting to hear from someone about whether or not Bryan's predicament was ever resolved.

The phone was picked up on the fifth ring,

"Hello!" Lynn answered trying not to sound too healthy.

"Why aren't you at work?"

"I couldn't stand the thought of leaving Howie all alone so I took a sick day."

"What are you two doing today?"

"I'm really too shy to tell you," Lynn laughed, "but I'll let you talk to Howie."

"Where the hell are you," Howie asked.

"I'm twenty minutes from Camden, near Blackwood." Joe went on, "Bryan has gone home to sell his motorcycle and Tommy, Mike and Doc have continued south to Washington."

"What did Bryan do with the money?"

"It's gone back to the guys who lost it, but it's a long story that gets kind of complicated so I'll have to tell you all about it when I see you."

"You're all alone?"

"Yeah, somebody had to come and see if you're all right."

"Why don't you come to Lynn's place? We don't have any plans for the day and we can't keep doing what we've been doing much longer!" Howie laughed that crazy laugh of his.

"I didn't know whether to bother you or not, but you must be all fucked out by now. Put Lynn on the phone so she can tell me how to get to her place from here."

Howie laughed again and handed the phone to Lynn.

The directions were easy to follow and Joe found himself riding down her street about twenty minutes later. It was an old street, lined with large, Oak trees and evergreens, and on both sides, there were a number of thirty or forty year old fourplexes and sixplexes. Lynn's apartment was on the second floor of one of the fourplexes and Joe pulled his Harley into an empty parking spot right out in front. He then went directly up the inside staircase to her door.

The door sprung open immediately and Lynn handed Joe an already snapped-open Bud Light, "It's good to see ya', Joe," she said as he kissed her on both cheeks. "What the hell happened to your eye and your forehead?"

"The bump on my head is just part of the story and I'll tell you all about it in a few minutes. Are you two still partying?"

"We didn't get back from the shore until after midnight last night," Howie answered. "It was one hell of a clambake!" Howie laughed again. "That's an awful bump on your head."

Lynn went on, "The party went on for two days with all the food and booze you wanted."

"It sounds like you had a lot of fun," Joe said. "I wish I'd stayed with you guys, but if I hadn't met the others, maybe things would have been a lot worse than they turned out."

Joe was settled on the couch so Howie asked, "Now tell us what the hell happened!"

Joe told them the whole story from his arrival in Atlantic City to when all the bikers separated earlier that morning. They were both totally shocked, especially about the murder of Captain Gerry Juby, because they had read all about it. They couldn't imagine what might have happened if Joe hadn't known that the Beretta had been stashed under Bryan's mattress.

Joe reached for his leather jacket and the handgun. He popped the clip and ejected the shell out of the chamber, and handed it to Howie, who was actually a gun collector.

"Before I forget to mention it, Cathy and Sharon don't know anything about Bryan stealing the money or the Colombians. I told Cathy that Bryan had borrowed some gambling money from a loan shark and hadn't paid it back on time and that I had bumped into the collectors who mistook me for Bryan because I was in his room," Joe explained. "The fewer people that know the true story, the better, especially since Captain Gerry died."

"That was a good idea. This is a beautiful handgun; is it ever light," Howie said turning the Beretta over in his hands. "What the hell are you going to do with it?"

"I don't know, I was going to throw it into the swamp on the way here but it probably saved my life. Besides, I was still a bit nervous that the Colombians might still have been following us when we left Atlantic City."

"There are some serious charges for having possession of an unregistered firearm both here in New Jersey and in Pennsylvania," Lynn added. "You should get rid of it!"

Howie handed it back to Joe and he reloaded it, reached for his jacket and answered, "The next time I go over one of the bridges, I'll throw it into the Delaware."

"What do you guys want to do today?" Lynn asked.

"I'm taking Cathy out for dinner because of the mess last night. I assume that Sharon will want to come along. Why don't you two join us? It'll be my treat."

"That sounds fine to me but right now I'm content to just sit around here and do nothing, I'm totally done!" Howie laughed. "I wouldn't mind having a sleep."

They all agreed to have a quiet afternoon. Joe brought his things into the apartment and the three of them just sat around and talked and had a few beers. Just after two o'clock, Howie and Lynn got up and went into the bedroom for a nap. Lynn had said that she would set her alarm for six o'clock. Joe took his boots off and lay down on the couch and used his rolled up sleeping bag as a pillow. He fell asleep immediately with Columbians on his mind.

Joe got hit twice on the side of his head with a silver Colt 45 and blood was running down his face. He was sitting in a chair with his feet tied to the legs and his hands tied behind him. He couldn't move! The big man with the dark complexion was standing over him holding a knife and the blade snapped open. The man asked him, *Have you ever seen a Colombian Necktie?* Joe's heart was racing! He was shaking and sweating and thought the end was near!

Lynn grabbed him by the shoulder and shook him out of a terrible dream.

Joe bolted upright on the couch, totally startled with his heart pounding, and said, "Christ! You just saved me from the Columbians. Thanks for waking me up!"

"Weren't you suppose to be at Cathy's at six o'clock, it's about ten past."

Joe thanked Lynn for the hospitality, and as he gathered up his belongings, she gave him directions to the townhouse. He told her to call them around seven-thirty to make plans for dinner. He grabbed his jacket and other things and went out into the street to his Harley.

It only took him fifteen minutes to get to Cathy's place. Joe pulled his bike in beside Sharon's car and it appeared that Cathy hadn't arrived home yet. Sharon greeted him at the door with a kiss on both cheeks and looked closely at the black and blue bump on his forehead. Cathy had already told her what had happened in

Atlantic City. They threw Joe's belongings into the master bedroom.

"I have a scotch and water ready to be poured for you," she said, "is that all right?"

"That sounds great! I just had a four hour nap and I feel really good," Joe answered.

"Cathy told me all about the problems that you had in Atlantic City. Did your friend ever pay back the money that he borrowed from the loan sharks?" Sharon asked as they walked down the hall toward the living room.

"Yeah, they got their money back and the other guys have continued south on the motorcycle trip, except for Bryan. He decided to go back to Canada."

Sharon grabbed the phone that rang, "Hello . . . Yeah, he just walked in the door and we're sitting in the living room having a drink . . . That's OK . . . I guess we're going out for dinner and Lynn and Howie are going to join us . . . Bye."

"Who was that, Cathy?"

"She has to work a bit late, but she'll be home in about half an hour."

"Why didn't you come down to Atlantic City yesterday? I actually kinda missed ya."

"I went to my brother's for dinner, not that I had to, but because I thought that it was best. On Saturday, Cathy and I had a long talk about what had happened the night before. It was a lot of fun because we had all been drinking and it was spur of the moment. Cathy is starting to like you, so I made an excuse not to go so she could spend some time with you alone."

"I like her too, but I've also enjoyed meeting you. I'm not in a frame of mind to get involved in a relationship right now because I have a problem back home that involves someone else that I have to get sorted out. I've decided to deal with that situation as soon as I get back to Toronto, and if there's nothing there, then I'll be able to get on with my life."

"Have you talked to Cathy about all that?"

"I will before I leave. We didn't have time to discuss anything in Atlantic City. You're coming for dinner with us tonight aren't you?"

"Yeah, I'm looking forward to us all going out together again. It'll be interesting to find out what's been going on with Lynn and Howie."

By the time Cathy opened the door of the townhouse, Joe and Sharon had just finished their second drink and had been having a few laughs at Lynn and Howie's expense.

"Is white wine all right?" Sharon asked, "That's what I'm drinking."

"That'll be fine," Cathy yelled, as she took her suit jacket and other things into her bedroom and then joined the other two in the living room. "Thanks."

Cathy asked about the mess in Atlantic City and Joe confirmed that there had been a happy ending to the story that he had told her. Joe also told her where the other guys had gone and then decided to have a quick shower before they went out for dinner.

Joe went back into the living room and joined the girls after he was cleaned up and ready for the evening. They were still sitting there chatting and drinking wine.

"Did you talk to Lynn and Howie?"

"They're coming over here for drinks before we go out," Cathy answered.

"Have you decided where we're going to eat yet?"

"We'll decide when they get here. There are all kinds of neat places not too far from here. We'll take a cab to wherever we end up going," Sharon said.

It wasn't long before the doorbell rang and Joe got up and answered it. Howie and Lynn arrived for cocktails and they all sat around and discussed the dinner plans. The girls decided that they would all cab it across the river into Philly and go to a busy, little restaurant called Downey's that was located right downtown.

The cab went through Camden, over the Ben Franklin Bridge and through the quaint, old, market area of the city where the original

Rocky movie had been filmed. It continued through the narrow streets and eventually pulled over beside a corner restaurant that had a wooden front, with green and gold trim that was quite obviously Irish.

The interior of the establishment continued the Irish theme with lots of wood, brass and dark green colors. There was a large, wooden, horseshoe-shaped bar that, according to local folklore, had been shipped directly from some famous pub in Ireland. Shiny brass railings and brass footrests had been installed throughout. A small piano player, dressed as a leprechaun, played Irish songs off in one corner.

Dinner turned out to be quite good and they all had plenty to eat and drink. After dinner, the piano player told lots of Irish jokes and led the whole bar into a sing-a-long, so the group from Camden stayed and continued drinking wine until after eleven-thirty. A cab took them all back to the townhouse across the river and Howie and Lynn left for her place immediately.

Everyone was dead tired and ready to get some sleep for a change. Sharon went to her room to get ready for bed and never came back out, but she yelled goodnight as she closed her bedroom door. Joe and Cathy got into her bed, snuggled up and went right to sleep.

CHAPTER FORTY-EIGHT

After Luis and Fernando left the twisted wreck of the Harley and Bryan's battered body in the rest area near Tuckerton, they continued to drive north on the Garden State Parkway. It didn't take Fernando long to find the missing money and his Colt in Bryan's saddlebags. After waiting for another stretch of highway, with no traffic in sight, he threw the bags out of the window of the moving Lincoln. Their job was finally completed and all they had to do was take the money back to Beatriz in Montreal and collect their share of the finder's fee.

As they drove north, Luis had to concentrate on keeping the speed of the Lincoln within the New Jersey speed limit because the cruise control was broken. Back in Canada, especially in Quebec, he was used to driving much faster than the American speed limits allow. They pulled off the expressway at Ashbury Park to have a leak and top up the gas tank and while they were stopped, Fernando grabbed a six-pack of Buds for the trip north. Luis also called his sister for one final report and to tell her that they would be back home in a few hours.

"Hello!" Beatriz said, hoping for good news that could be passed on to Castrillo.

"The job is finished and we have all the money in our possession," Luis said into the cell. "We're just south of Newark and on our way home."

"Is it all there?"

"The biker who we have been dealing with, *Joe*, confirmed the amount that was in the bag when it was taken from the crash site and it's all here, except for about ten thousand that the big guy who stole it spent. We have close to six million and eight hundred thousand."

"Castrillo is really pissed because he thinks that there was more than that in the bag," Beatriz said. "Are you sure that's all the money that was taken?"

Luis went on, "I'm sure that we have all of the money. This guy *Joe* that we met with a couple of times is really quite a guy. He told us the exact amount on two different occasions just to protect his friend. I trust him. I'll tell you the whole story when I get back and you'll realize that I do have all the money that was taken."

"Castrillo wanted the bikers to pay for taking the money, what happened to them?"

"It was only the big man with the mustache that Jay saw at the crash site that took the money and he took it without the other guys even knowing that he had," Luis explained. "You can tell Castrillo that the big guy's history. He had a motorcycle *accident*."

"What about the rest of them?"

"As I said before, the biker named *Joe* helped us get the money back from the big guy and he and the other bikers had nothing to do with taking it from the crash site. They've all just continued on their motorcycle trip, but the big guy has paid for his mistake."

"Get back to Montreal as soon as you can, I want to hear the whole story, especially about this guy Joe who you seem to have developed some sort of relationship with," Beatriz said.

As soon as she hung up, Beatriz took a few moments and thought about her *Joe*, the lawyer from Toronto who she had fallen so deeply in love with a few months before. She still had a terrible emptiness in her body whenever she thought of him or even heard the name, but she knew that their love could never be, unless she changed her life drastically.

Beatriz called Castrillo and reported that the money was finally in her brother's possession. He, once again, expressed concern that there should have been more money recovered and that someone had ripped him off. Castrillo would always think that he had been cheated in some way, but he eventually would have to accept whatever explanation Beatriz gave him. She took one more liberty to settle Castrillo down.

"Before you start to question what kind of job we do for the cartel up here in Canada, I would suggest you think about my relationship with Pablo and the important things that we have handled for you in the past. He may trust me more than he trusts you!"

"Si! Si! I understand. I'm under serious pressure here," Castrillo answered as he got the message. "Our friend is on his way here right now, to my safehouse, because the heat is really on down here. He got a tip from one of his informants that the army and DEA had found out where his other hide-out was and they were about to close in on him."

"When do you expect him to be there?" Beatriz asked.

"Anytime and he'll probably stay for awhile. Things are really getting crazy down here. Seven or eight of my top men have been arrested in the last couple of months, four have been killed and another factory in the Chapare was destroyed two weeks ago."

"I'll call you as soon as my brother gets back to Montreal. He should be home in about six hours," Beatriz said as she hung up the phone.

Luis took a quick look at the road map and decided to catch Highway 87 to Albany and then continue north to Montreal. Fernando snapped open a couple of beers as they headed back to the Parkway and they talked about the week's events. They were both happy to be heading home and were looking forward to getting their hands on their shares of the finder's fee. In retrospect, it had been pretty easy money for less than a week's work and they even got to have a bit of fun in Atlantic City.

They knew that they were getting close to the north end of the Parkway because they had passed the Long Branch exit a few minutes earlier. Luis looked in his rearview mirror and saw his worst nightmare. A police cruiser, with all of its lights flashing, was about a quarter of a mile behind them and closing fast. Luis immediately glanced at his speedometer and knew instantly that he hadn't been paying attention to how fast he was driving. He took his foot off the accelerator and prayed that the cruiser would go right on by. Fernando collected the beer cans together and hid them under the front seat and opened his window to let the smell of alcohol clear from the car.

The police car didn't pass by them. As the cruiser pulled up beside the blue Lincoln, the officer in the passenger seat motioned at Luis to pull over to the side of the road. As Luis came to a slow stop on the gravel shoulder, he left the engine running and put the gear lever into *Park*. The cruiser slowly pulled in behind the Lincoln and came to a stop.

The officer behind the wheel, New Jersey State Trooper Steve O'Leary, got out of the cruiser and approached the driver's side of the blue Lincoln. Trooper Bill McLaren stayed in the cruiser and typed in the Quebec license plate number looking for *wants and warrants*. He got a clean report. McLaren then got out of the passenger side of the police car and walked slowly, and nonchalantly, toward the Lincoln.

By the time O'Leary got there, Luis had rolled his window down on the driver's side.

"I guess I wasn't paying attention and was slightly over the speed limit," he said.

"The speed limit on the Parkway is fifty-five miles an hour and you were going seventy-two," O'Leary said. "Could I please have your driver's license, ownership and insurance?"

Luis handed the officer the three pieces of documentation that he had requested as quickly as he could. He wanted to get the speeding ticket and get out of there.

"I'll be right back," O'Leary said and started to walk back toward the cruiser.

As he passed the back end of the Lincoln, McLaren called him, "Steve, come over here."

"What's up?" O'Leary asked as he joined him at the passenger rear of the car.

"Look at the side of this car. There are a number of small dents and scratches with traces of dark red paint that look fairly recent.

Didn't we get a radio call from Tuckerton earlier about a possible motorcycle hit-and-run accident down there?"

"Yeah, you're right," O'Leary agreed. "Let's call in and see what it was all about."

Fernando had nervously watched the two officers in the rear-view mirror, on his side of the car, as they looked at the damage on the Lincoln and went back to the cruiser. The officers typed in the driver's license data and the second report came back clear. They also called in to reconfirm the information about a possible hit-and-run motorcycle accident that had happened earlier in the day. After they got the up-dated report from Kennedy, the troopers became much more suspicious about the blue Lincoln that they had just stopped for a minor speeding violation.

The Colombians who were still seated in the front seat of their car knew that something was going on. A nervous Fernando had transferred his Colt 45 to his left hand and held it under the front of his jacket as he thumbed the safety off and cocked it.

After the cops looked at the damage on the passenger side again, O'Leary approached the driver's side once more and McLaren walked toward the passenger side of the vehicle. Fernando watched as McLaren came closer to him, and as he walked, he undid his holster and put his hand on the butt of his own gun. Fernando knew that something was up.

"Please turn off your engine and both of you, please get out of the car. As you get out, keep your hands visible and, when you are out, lean against the vehicle and place your hands on the roof and spread your legs," O'Leary said outside the driver's window.

At that exact moment, Fernando panicked. He fired a shot along the right side of the car that hit McLaren in the upper left arm. The force of the bullet made the cop spin around and fall into the loose gravel, and almost at the same time, he started to crawl toward the cruiser. At that moment, Luis quickly pulled the gear lever into drive and tramped the gas peddle to the floor, spinning the tires and throwing loose gravel everywhere. The powerful engine in the Lincoln caused it to fishtail to the right, toward the ditch, and that gave the two policemen a full view of the driver's side of the vehicle.

By that time, O'Leary had his Glock in his hand and he fired five or six quick shots in the direction of the driver and passenger. One of those shots hit Luis behind his left ear. The bullet killed him instantly. The car came to rest sideways, with the front of it partly on the blacktop of the road and the rest of it on the gravel shoulder. The blue Lincoln had come to a dead stop about fifty or sixty feet from the cruiser.

The man on the passenger side of the vehicle tried to push the body of the driver out of the car and onto the road so he could get behind the wheel, but was unsuccessful. At the same time, he fired four more shots in the direction of the policemen. McLaren had managed to get up off the gravel and was stationed behind the passenger door and O'Leary had made it back to the driver's door of the cruiser. At that moment, the passenger fired three more shots at the policemen who were crouched down for their protection, and at the same time, O'Leary and McLaren emptied their Glocks in the direction of the Lincoln. Some of their shots found the front seat of the vehicle, but in the heat of the gun battle, many bullets hit all over the car. One of the bullets that hit the back end, penetrated the gas tank, and the rear of the car burst into flames with a loud explosion that actually lifted the rear end of the car off the ground. Flames shot from the back end of the Lincoln and out of the trunk that had been blown wide-open and black smoke billowed up into the air. The driver's door had partially closed, and except for the sound of fire and flames crackling, everything became very quiet.

"Are you all right?" O'Leary asked McLaren.

"Yeah, he hit me in the upper arm, but it doesn't seem too bad," McLaren replied. "I think one of us must have hit him or the explosion got him. It seems awful quiet."

"Cover me," O'Leary said to McLaren.

He ducked very low and ran behind the cruiser and down into the ditch. He stole very carefully toward the burning Lincoln and kept his eyes on the front seat for any signs of life. From the cruiser, McLaren kept his reloaded Glock trained on the front seat of the blue car and was ready to fire if he saw the slightest movement.

O'Leary, reluctantly, ducked up out of the ditch and moved toward the flaming car and carefully made his way along the passenger side, as he stayed well back and kept his Glock trained on the car. He thought that he could see two bodies lying against each other in the front seat. He quickly pulled open the door with his handgun still pointed at the two men. As O'Leary pulled open the front door, a big man fell partly out of the car and his upper body and head thumped down onto the gravel. O'Leary grabbed him by the arm and pulled him away from the flames. He then went back and leaned into the smoke filled front seat and got a hold of the driver by the jacket and also pulled him out of the burning vehicle. As he reached for him, he noticed flames flashing around a duffel bag in the back seat.

He laid the driver in the gravel, next to the passenger, and went back to the car to recover the two handguns. He also reached back and grabbed the duffel bag just as the flames started to engulf the whole back seat area. By that time, McLaren was standing nearby with his Glock trained on the two men that were lying on the shoulder of the road. The driver was dead. He had died instantly of a head wound. The passenger was still alive, but had been hit once in the chest and once in the neck and was bleeding profusely. He died before the ambulance arrived.

O'Leary and McLaren were shocked when they opened the duffel bag and found nearly seven million dollars in cash! They became local heroes thanks to the intuitiveness of State Trooper Dale Kennedy earlier that day at the scene of what everyone else had thought was just another routine motorcycle accident. The officers believed that they had stumbled on the remnants of a large drug deal that had taken place somewhere in north Jersey.

No one would ever learn the true story of where the money had come from or about the circuitous route it had taken to that spot on the side of the Garden State Parkway. They never did find out that the money had originated on the streets of New York City and had found its way into a duffel bag that had been placed in a plane at a small airfield just north of Albany. They didn't know that the money had been destined for the Caribbean and the coffers of the Medellin Cartel or that it had been part of the large cache of money that had been scattered in a small field in the mountains of Vermont a week earlier. They knew nothing about the Canadian bikers or the big guy with the mustache who had transported the money to Atlantic City. The names and identities of the Canadian motorcycle gang had died with Luis and Fernando.

CHAPTER FORTY-NINE

A s Joe lay in bed the next morning, he heard the girls puttering around in the kitchen and getting ready for the day. By eight o'clock, they were ready to leave for work and Joe was wide-awake so he got up to say goodbye.

"What are you going to do today?" Cathy asked.

"I'm going to call Howie and we'll probably take a ride through downtown Philly and then go out to my old neighbourhood in Drexel Hill. I'm sure that we'll be able to keep busy."

"We'll be home at six, see you then," Sharon said as she went out the door.

Joe gave Cathy a kiss as she was leaving. "I'll see you tonight. Have a great day!"

The house was very quiet as Joe sat there and sipped his coffee. He thought about how lucky they had been to resolve the Colombian problem. He also thought about Trizzi and how she was on his mind constantly. He was in love with her and missed her. He decided that he was going to find her as soon as he got back to Canada and convince her that they were destined to be together.

He also thought about Sanderson, Sturgess and the full partnership opportunity and was sure that he wasn't ready for that kind of a commitment to the law or the firm. He would talk to Jim Sturgess when he got back and negotiate some time off, a sabbatical of one year, maybe two, or he might even leave the firm altogether. It was time to make some major changes in his life.

Joe picked the phone up off the coffee table and dialed Lynn's number. Surely she had gone back to work. He couldn't fathom what was going on with those two. Howie answered the phone and after the usual small talk, Joe told him what he had in mind for the day.

"Sounds great," Howie answered, "I just have to get organized."

"I'm running slow this morning. I still have to shower so why don't you come over here when you're ready."

Joe called the office for the second time all week and everything had gone well without him. No one had even noticed that he was away except Angie, the pretty little receptionist, who asked when he would be coming back home because she missed him. There was only one message from Susan. Joe hoped that there were no problems with the kids.

"Hello," Susan answered.

"Hi, it's Joe, are the kids all right?"

"The kids are fine. Where are you?"

"I'm in Philadelphia," he answered. "I'll be back in Toronto later this week."

"You guys must have split up . . . something terrible has happened to Bryan!"

"He headed home early yesterday morning! What the hell's happened?" Joe asked, as he lost his breath, with visions of drug traffickers running through his mind.

"I got a phone call from Charlie and Cindy Kessler up in Bobcaygeon. They know Pat, Bryan's friend. He was killed in a motorcycle accident yesterday somewhere between Atlantic City and Newark," she explained, "his funeral is on Thursday morning in Lindsay."

A totally shocked Joe asked again, "Does anyone know what the hell happened?"

"The police aren't exactly sure what happened, but it looks like he went into a rest area off the highway too fast and lost control of his motorcycle. His bike hit a fence or something and he died instantly. One strange thing that the police reported was that they found his saddlebags four or five miles from the scene of the accident with dirty clothes in one side and the other side empty."

Joe felt sick to his stomach. He hung up the phone and sat there in a daze. It was hard to believe that Bryan was dead. All kinds of things went through his mind; *Was his death really an accident? Did the Colombians renege on their deal? Did they always intend to kill him?*

Joe couldn't stop thinking about the saddlebags and the fact that they had been found miles from the scene of the accident. All of a sudden, it hit him like a bolt of lightening; *Bryan had kept some of the money!* The two Colombians knew how much money there was because Joe had told them the exact amount when it was first counted!

There was definitely money in the duffel bag that Joe delivered to the lounge at Bally's, but Joe had no way of knowing how much. He didn't count it. Bryan had disappeared for almost an hour to get the money from safekeeping and everyone had been worried. He was also very uneasy after the money had been turned over to the Colombians and wanted to get out of town as quickly as he possibly could. He was sweating bullets on the elevator. He had also cancelled the rest of the trip to rush home. Joe convinced himself that's what had happened. What if the Colombians had decided to kill everyone? He had put them all at risk again.

Joe immediately called Howie and told him the bad news and his only comment was that he was glad that he hadn't gone to Atlantic City. Howie indicated that he was ready to leave for Cathy's townhouse shortly. Joe was quite upset and went directly to the shower and turned on the cold water. His head had started to ache again. He wasn't really in the mood to go sightseeing or to find his old friends any longer.

The traffic was light on the Ben Franklin Bridge and on the river below, so on the crest Joe slowed his motorcycle down and put his hand on the Beretta in his jacket pocket. He sadly said a special goodbye to a handgun that had saved his life and was about to throw it over the rail when he changed his mind. He had grown attached to it. He knew that he was asking for trouble if he kept it in his possession, but he just couldn't throw it into the Delaware.

As Joe took in the panoramic view of Philadelphia from the

bridge, he could see the main thoroughfare over the Delaware River, the Walt Whitman Bridge. He remembered from school as a kid in Drexel Hill that Ben Franklin had been the founder of the first university in North America in 1754, the University of Pennsylvania. He could remember being on the steps of the Philadelphia Art Museum that Sly Stallone ran up in the first Rocky movie. He also remembered, as a giggling kid, standing on the corner of Benjamin Franklin Parkway and 17th Street with friends, looking up at William Penn's *pecker*. Poor Mr. Penn's statue was on the top of a hundred foot pillar and from that corner, a piece of the statue stuck out in such a way, it looked like his *dick* was hanging out. Joe knew that fact was not in any of the tourist brochures.

The two Harleys crossed the Delaware into Pennsylvania and stayed on the freeway. They went through downtown Philly and continued west on Highway 3, over the Schuylkill River and under the expressway of the same name. In Upper Darby, Joe spotted a Denny's and waved at Howie. The two of them pulled in for some breakfast. They talked about Bryan and his *accident* and all of the things that led up to his death and they were both convinced that he had probably tried to keep some of the money. Learning about Bryan's death had put a damper on the day so Joe decided that a ride through the old neighbourhood would do.

After they ate, they traveled along West Chester Pike to the Township Line Road where things started to look familiar to Joe. Before long, they passed his grade school and turned onto the street where he once lived. Joe stopped his Harley in front of 98 Hearst Circle and Howie pulled up beside him. Tim and Brenda Payne, friends of Joe's parents, had bought the family home and still lived there. Joe decided to knock on the door to say hello because he hadn't seen them since he was a teenager, but there was no answer. He left his card.

"Let's go back to New Jersey and take a ride out to the shore for a late lunch. There are some great spots near the ocean that I want to show you," Howie suggested.

"Sounds great, let's do it!" Joe answered.

Back on the expressways, they traveled through the downtown area of Philly once again and went over the Walt Whitman Bridge into New Jersey. About half an hour after leaving Joe's old neighbourhood, they were traveling east on Marlton Pike toward the ocean. They rode for close to an hour at a fairly leisurely pace and eventually ended up at Seaside Heights on the shores of the Atlantic. They pulled their Harleys into the parking lot of a neat restaurant and bar called The Crow's Nest, right on the water, that overlooked a large and busy marina. The bikers sat on the outside deck and watched the cruisers and sailboats coming and going and the large swells on the rolling, blue ocean.

"I'm not going back," Howie said.

"Neither am I," Joe agreed. "Why the hell should we rush all the way back to Lindsay for that loon's funeral after all the shit he put everyone through."

"No," Howie said again with a more serious look on his face, "I mean I'm not going back to Lindsay . . . not ever!"

"What the hell are you talking about?"

"There's nothing for me back there, my marriage isn't working, business stinks and my kid is at an age where he's just about on his own."

"What does Lynn think about this?"

"I haven't told her yet because I just decided today. I really like her a lot and she likes me. I also think that there are some real business opportunities here," Howie went on.

"I can't fuckin' believe it! Bryan's dead. You're not going home. I was the guy that was going to sort out my life on this vacation. I'm in love with a woman who's in some kind of a screwed up relationship in Montreal and I can't see her and after all those years of going to school, I hate my bloody career!"

"Have you decided what you're gonna do when you go back to Toronto?" Howie asked.

"As far as work goes, I'm going to take some extended time off. I'm also going to find Trizzi in Montreal and tell her how I feel about her and see what the hell happens."

Joe and Howie each had a sandwich and a few beers and talked for a couple of hours. They talked about Howie's decision to stay in Camden and what he might find there, where he expected his relationship with Lynn to go, why Joe had been unable to see Trizzi, what her personal problems might be, all their disappointments back home and life in general. It was close to four o'clock when they fired up the Harleys and headed west toward Camden. During the trip inland, Joe decided that he was going to go back to Toronto the next morning. He wasn't sure if he would make it to Bryan's funeral in Lindsay on Thursday morning, but there was that possibility since he wasn't expected back at the office until the following week.

Joe and Howie stopped at a small neighbourhood bar just around the corner from Cathy's townhouse at about ten after five and ordered a couple of beers.

"I've decided that I'm going home in the morning," Joe said. "Have you had a change of heart? Are you coming with me?"

"No, I mean it! I may never go back to Lindsay ever again, except to see my son."

"You are a crazy bastard!"

"If this is your last night here," Howie said, "I'll take you and the girls out for dinner."

"That sounds great, I'm sure that they don't have any plans," Joe answered.

The Harleys left the local bar at six o'clock and Howie went directly to Lynn's. It wasn't long before Joe was in the townhouse parking lot in his usual spot. Cathy and Sharon were home and having a glass of wine in the living room. Joe grabbed a cold beer from the fridge and joined them to tell them about the events of the day and the plans for dinner.

He told them about Bryan's fatal motorcycle accident in northern New Jersey. He didn't mention his suspicions about the accident because the girls didn't know the whole story anyway. He advised them that the funeral was Thursday and that he would have to leave in the morning to get to Toronto Wednesday night. They were both sorry that Joe had to leave, especially Cathy, and her face really showed her disappointment. The only good news was that Howie was going to take everyone out for dinner as a kind of going away party. Joe didn't mention the fact that Howie may stay with Lynn in Camden, forever. There was always the chance that he might change his mind and decide to return home with Joe in the morning. As they were talking, the phone rang.

"It's Howie, he wants to talk to you," Cathy said as she handed the phone to Joe.

"You won't fuckin' believe what I'm reading in tonight's paper. There's a story about a shoot-out between the State Troopers and two drug traffickers that took place yesterday afternoon on the Garden State Parkway just south of Newark. It says that the State Police killed two Colombians and found nearly seven million dollars in their car. Wait until you hear the best part!" Howie went on excitedly.

"What the hell would that be?" Joe asked trying not to sound too excited.

"The cops stopped the car for speeding but it had dents and red paint on the right side of it, so somehow it got tied into a hit-and-run motorcycle accident that had happened further south where a Canadian biker had been killed! Can you fuckin' believe this!"

Joe answered trying to downplay what had just heard. "Well, that fits right into what we were talking about earlier."

"It's all hard to believe!" Howie said. "We'll meet you guys at the Black Angus Steak and Seafood House in Camden at seven-thirty. The girls know where it is."

"What's going on?" Cathy asked a Joe hung up the phone.

"Have you got the Philadelphia Daily News? Howie says there's an article in it that has something to do with Bryan's motorcycle accident and death."

"Yeah, it's in the kitchen. I'll get it for you."

"We're supposed to be at the Black Angus Steak House at about seven-thirty."

"Here's the paper. If we're going out for dinner again, I've got to get ready," Cathy said.

"Me too," Sharon said. "My hair's a mess."

Joe finally found the article about the police shootout with the drug dealers, which wasn't even front-page news, on page eight. He read it quickly and as Howie had said, it did suggest that Bryan's death was a hit-and-run. Joe then knew for sure that Bryan had kept some of the money. He had honestly felt that Luis had intended to live up to his part of the bargain.

The group met at the Black Angus which was only about ten minutes from the townhouse. Howie and Lynn were already seated when they arrived. Joe knew that this wasn't just a send off for him, but was really a special night for them too. As the cocktail hour continued, they all had lots of laughs and when Lynn and Howie told the girls that Howie had decided to stay in Camden forever, they were both in a state of shock. Bryan's death became lost in the wine and booze.

By eleven o'clock, they had eaten a great meal and everyone was feeling no pain. Cathy suggested that someone should throw a pail of water on Lynn and Howie because they were drunk, horny and in love. Everyone was in a good mood except Cathy who felt quite sad that Joe was leaving and she had really sucked back a lot of wine all evening. She was totally pissed by the time they left the restaurant and tears were running down her face. The news that Howie was staying with the woman he loved was just too much for her in her intoxicated state.

The two girls were totally bombed so Joe, who was the most sober, drove Cathy's Olds back to the townhouse. The three of them wandered in arm in arm, the other two making sure that Cathy didn't fall down. She was ready for bed.

Sharon wobbled into her own bedroom to get ready to crash and Joe had to help Cathy get undressed. As soon as she had made some sort of attempt to brush her teeth, Joe helped her to the bed, rolled her in and covered her up. He then got undressed and went into the bathroom. When he came out, he stopped to check on Cathy and to see if she was all right, but she was gone to the world. Passed out.

Sound asleep. He turned out the lights and as he went to close the bedroom door, he could see that Sharon's door was partly open and her light was still on in her room. What else could he do, he was drunk too.

Joe, who was standing there in the buff, pushed the door open the rest of the way and looked at Sharon who was leaning over her bed, in the nude, pulling down the covers.

"Cathy's passed out. She's sound asleep."

She walked over and leaned her nude body against his and kissed him. "I think you should turn out the light and shut the door quietly."

Joe was the last one up again that morning and the two girls were in the kitchen sipping coffee at about quarter to eight when he came around the corner. Sharon was dressed for work and about to leave. Cathy was holding her head in her hands and was still in her bathrobe.

"How's everyone feeling this morning?" Joe asked as he poured himself a cup of coffee.

"I feel great," Sharon smiled. "I have to hit the road. I've got an early appointment."

"I feel like hell," Cathy said. "I'm not going to rush into work today."

"I'm outta here," Sharon said and got up and went to get her briefcase in the hall. "Joe, it was really nice meeting you and I hope that we'll see you again soon."

"Me too," Joe replied on the way to the front door. He kissed her goodbye and said, "I hope that you and Cathy can come to Toronto for a weekend sometime soon."

"I hope we can too. I really enjoyed our time together. Have a safe trip home."

All of a sudden she was gone and Joe went back to the kitchen to finish his coffee. Cathy still looked really rough.

"Are you gonna be all right?" Joe asked with a smile. "You went right to sleep as soon as you hit the bed last night."

"Yeah, I'll be fine in a few minutes. I feel badly that I got so drunk on your last night here. I wanted to make it a night that you would remember."

"I had a great time last night, I'm sure I'll remember it," Joe smiled to himself. "Let's get back in bed for a little while this morning and spend some time together."

After they made love and sat back to relax, they talked about their relationship and where it might go and both of them agreed that they would take things slowly. Joe told Cathy about the other woman in his life and that he was going home to deal with that situation. They decided that they would keep in touch regularly.

They kissed each other a number of times while Joe put on his blue leather jacket and picked up his gear to take it out to his bike. Cathy followed him to the parking lot and carried his rolled up sleeping bag with the pillow inside. She stood there and waited as everything was attached to the motorcycle. He threw his leg over the bike and fired it up. He had decided that he was going home through Buffalo because it was the shortest route but he wasn't looking forward to the ride. It had been another one of those nights of very little sleep.

Joe turned and kissed Cathy once more and as they finished, he noticed that her eyes had filled with tears and they were rolling down her cheeks. He promised her that he would call her as soon as he got back to Toronto, which would probably be around eleven o'clock that night. He kissed her again and as he looked into her eyes, he inadvertently thought of Trizzi once more. He gently wiped away a few tears with one of his thumbs and wondered if he would ever see her again. He put on his helmet and squeezed her hand as the Harley slid into gear. He pulled out of the parking lot and disappeared into the traffic without looking back.

CHAPTER FIFTY

Diego Castrillo had paced around the safehouse for days waiting for news of the recovery of the stolen money. He was nervous because his boss was expected at any time. Since Pablo Rivas' escape from prison, an eight million dollar American bounty had been put on his head and it had become very difficult for him to find safe hide-outs. A reward of that size turned trusted associates into informants and his ability to move freely around Medellin had been curtailed.

Rivas had once supplied eighty percent of all cocaine that reached the noses of North America, but since he had become such a high-priced fugitive, the cocaine centre of Colombia had slowly shifted from Medellin in the north, to Cali in the south. The main reason for that shift in power was the severe pressure that the government was putting on Rivas because he alone had become their primary target in their fight against the drug lords.

Pablo Rivas arrived at Castrillo's safehouse very secretly and quietly slipped into the rear entrance and up the back stairs. He had placed a dozen of his bodyguards at strategic locations all around the heavily treed property, intermingled with Castrillo's men, who were already on watch. As he entered the main room, he saw that Castrillo was sitting comfortably in his large easy chair. There were no friendly greetings. Business had been so bad for the cartel recently that the stolen money was its only potential source of revenue.

"Have you heard from Bracho? Has the stolen money been recovered yet?"

"Beatriz reported that her brother, Luis, has finally got the money back from the bikers in Atlantic City and he's on his way back to Montreal," Diego answered. "She also said that the big guy with the mustache who stole it is dead."

"At least something positive has happened!" Pablo smiled as he thought back to his last meeting with Beatriz when she had visited Colombia. "She's sure one fantastic broad. What a great piece of ass! How much money did they get back?"

"There was close to six million and eight hundred thousand dollars recovered. Beatriz's brother says he's sure that was all of the money that was stolen."

"If she says that's the amount, I'm sure it is. She's never given us any reason to mistrust her. Mind you, she does get well paid for taking care of our interests." Pablo smiled again as he remembered her beautiful body. "There are some real benefits doing business with her."

"She said that she would call again as soon as her brother gets back with the money. She'll want instructions as to what we want her to do with it," Diego advised.

"I'm sick and tired of being on the run all the time. The price on my head is so large that men who have worked for me for years are becoming informants. If I didn't have moles working at army headquarters and in the police departments to warn me when they get new information about me, I would probably be back in prison or even dead by now."

Diego answered, "Maybe we should shut things down and disappear for awhile. We could go to one of our estates in the Chapare and let this shit blow over. We have enough money. If we disappeared, it would give the army and the police time to turn their attention to those bastards in Cali."

"You may be right, we can't keep running like this forever."

As the childhood friends spoke about their many problems, the police, the army and the DEA, which was working with the police and military as advisors only, were closing in all around them. They had pieced together informant's information and some recent data that they had received from their electronic monitoring of the cellular telephone systems in Medellin. The American communications satellite system had pinpointed the location of cellular telephone conversations during the past week. Fortunately, the cartel always used cell phones rather than landlines that can't be monitored by satellite. The authorities had finally got lucky.

The Americans thought that they had located a safehouse that belonged to the high-level cartel boss, Diego Castrillo, who was well known to the authorities because he had escaped from prison with Pablo Rivas. Their satellite had picked up a number of international telephone calls made to and from his cellular phone in Medellin. They had absolutely no idea that Pablo Rivas was there with Castrillo, but their electronic eavesdropping had given them some indication that a few other top level Medellin Cartel members might be. Pinguino had finally gone home to his family a few days earlier. As the men talked in the living room, a cordon of five hundred policemen and soldiers were being put in place around Castrillo's house in a style that was reminiscent of the termination of Butch Cassidy and the Sundance Kid in Bolivia. No one would escape. At that moment, five hundred rifles, machine guns and pistols were pointed directly at the safehouse on all sides. They wanted Pablo Rivas dead or alive, preferably dead.

As Rivas was looking out into the yard to be sure that all the bodyguards were in place, the phone rang and Castrillo answered it immediately. It was Beatriz on the other end of the line and she was extremely upset and crying.

"I just got word that my brother and the man that was with him were killed in a shoot-out with State Troopers just south of Newark, New Jersey. I don't know what the hell happened, but the police recovered nearly seven million dollars that they were bringing back to Montreal."

"Jesus Christ! Is this shit ever going to end?" Castrillo said. "I'm sorry about your brother. Just a minute, there's someone here who will want to hear it directly from you."

Castrillo put his hand over the phone and told Rivas that Beatriz was on the line and what had happened in New Jersey. Pablo cursed and threw a full glass of vino tinto across the room. He took the phone and spoke to his longtime business associate and lover in Spanish.

"I'm sorry to hear about Luis. What the fuck happened?"

"I don't know, but all the money has been recovered by the police and my brother was killed by the State Troopers," Beatriz said in a crying and trembling voice.

Pablo went on, "I can't fuckin' believe it! Things are getting so hot everywhere. The authorities are over us down here and in North America. We were just talking about shutting things down and disappearing into the jungle until all this shit blows over and maybe in a year or so, we'll get reorganized and start shipping product again."

As Pablo Rivas was speaking to Beatriz, gunfire erupted outside the safehouse. He quickly hung up the phone without saying another word to her and the two men ran to the patio door and looked out into the yard. Glass was shattering everywhere and bullets were flying all around the room. Their bodyguards were in a major gun battle with what looked like the whole Colombian army and every cop in Medellin. Soldiers and police were everywhere. The men realized very quickly just how serious the situation was and they rushed around the house to locate their machine pistols as they ducked bullets that were breaking things everywhere.

Castrillo yelled, "The bedroom window goes to the roof-tops, it's our only chance!"

As Rivas and Castrillo jumped from the bedroom window onto the roof of the building next door, bullets ricocheted all around them taking chunks of adobe out of the walls and shattering windows. They both aimed and fired their automatic pistols at the droves of police and soldiers that seemed to be everywhere and they emptied their weapons in their direction as they ducked behind whatever cover they could find. They both banged full clips into their guns and continued to return the fire. The two old friends knew they were in serious trouble.

Pablo Rivas looked at his childhood friend and said, "It's been quite a party my friend, those cocksuckers aren't taking me alive. I'm never going back to prison and they're not going to have the satisfaction of arresting me again or killing me! Goodbye, *amigo*!"

Rivas lifted his automatic pistol and put it against his right temple. He managed to squeeze off three shots before his limp body fell on the rooftop with a thud, right beside Castrillo. At that moment, the infamous Pablo Rivas, the most wanted narco-terrorist in the world, died instantly by his own hand and not at the hands of his enemies. He knew that he had cheated them out of the satisfaction of killing him.

Castrillo was in a total state of shock. He couldn't even comprehend what he had just witnessed. He couldn't believe that Pablo Rivas had just killed himself. He didn't know what the hell to do. He was lost. His life-long mentor was gone. Dead. In a rage, he picked up Pablo's machine pistol in his empty hand and made a dash toward the jungle at the rear of the building with both guns blazing. As he started to run, a hail of bullets that came from all directions smashed his body. He was spun around and thrown backwards on that dirty, tile rooftop on the edge of the mountains on the outskirts of Medellin. He was dead before his bullet-riddled body landed beside the corpse his old friend.

It was the end of an era in Colombia where a street orphan from the slums of Medellin, who had started his criminal career by stealing tombstones from cemeteries and reselling them on the black market, had built an extremely well organized drug cartel into an enterprise with an annual income that rivaled many multi-national corporations and gave him sufficient cash flow to wage an all-out war against a modern nation for many years.

Even after the United States had joined the government of Colombia in the war against Pablo Rivas and the Medellin Cartel, the flow of drugs to North America and Europe had never even missed a heartbeat. The people of Colombia considered Pablo Rivas to be a Robin Hood because he had spent millions of dollars on community projects and had often helped the poor. He would be mourned by the masses as if he were a national hero rather than a bloodthirsty killer and flowers would be placed on his grave daily for years to come.

In the end, it was the satellite surveillance of the cellular telephone calls in Medellin that were made to and from Castrillo's safehouse during the past week or so that had led to the death of one of the world's most wanted men, Pablo Rivas, and one of his top lieutenants, Diego Castrillo. Bryan Moyle, and the rest of the world, would never know that it was his one foolish act of stealing a duffel bag full of money from the site where a drug-plane had crashed in Vermont that had actually brought down one of the world's most murderous and dangerous narco-terrorists and ended the dominance of his organization in the drug markets of the world. His death, however, would do absolutely nothing to seriously affect the daily flow of tons of cocaine from Colombia to the streets of North America and Europe.

CHAPTER FIFTY-ONE

The trip home would take Joe north through the Pocono Mountains of Pennsylvania, through New York State to Buffalo and across the border into Canada at Fort Erie, just west of Niagara Falls. He would then travel the Queen Elizabeth Way for just over an hour directly into downtown Toronto. Joe thought that the whole trip home would take him ten or eleven hours and he was really glad that he still had his pillow with him.

The motorcycle trip down the eastern seaboard hadn't given Joe much time to think about his own future. During the hours of traveling alone that lay ahead of him, he could solidify his thoughts about his vocation and life back in Toronto. He would also have time to decide on a game plan to deal with his future relationship with Trizzi, if there was to be one.

Joe thought about his career. He had gone into the legal profession because of the freedom that seemed to be inherent in practicing law. A lawyer could be his own man, but the exact opposite turned out to be true. Lawyers become slaves to their practices and more often than not, work ten and twelve hour days, often six days a week. After ten years of intense grinding, Joe was burned out. He would negotiate a sabbatical of two years and if his absence for that length of time made no sense to the firm, then he would offer his resignation.

Joe thought about his friends and the people with whom he had come into contact during the last eight or nine days and what life had dealt them. Captain Gerry Juby was a great old guy who just happened to be in the wrong place at the wrong time. It cost him his life. Bryan became a victim of his financial problems, booze or greed or all three combined. The sight of all that cash lying in that field in Vermont was too much for him at that point in his life. It changed him into a totally different person. Howie, had been a successful roofing contractor with a lovely wife and a great son, but he obviously wasn't happy. There was something missing in his life. Time will tell if he ever finds what he's looking for in Camden.

Joe's thoughts continually drifted back to Trizzi, the love-of-his-life, and each time he saw her face in his mind, a knawing feeling returned to his body. She had almost consumed him. There was nothing he wouldn't do to have her back. She had been on his mind daily since their weekend together months before. He had only known her a very short time, but he had fallen head over heels. He knew that he wouldn't be able to get on with his life until he actually found her and made his feelings known to her. He would do that as soon as he got back to Canada.

Bryan's death haunted Joe. All of the facts and circumstances surrounding his death seemed to suggest that Bryan had actually kept some of the money and hadn't returned it all to the Colombians. Joe was convinced that Luis had intended to live up to his end of the bargain if all the money had been returned. Joe was sure that, once again, Bryan had caused the events that had unfolded on the Garden State Parkway.

The motorcycle ride back to Canada was uneventful and the only stops along the way were to get gas, have a leak and adjust the pillow. The old Immigration Officer at the border crossing at Fort Erie had laughed and made a comment about the pillow and the fact that Joe had been the first biker that he had ever seen sitting on one that pretty. They had kibitzed back and forth about how long Joe had been sitting on the motorcycle and had a few laughs. The Beretta had been tucked away under his belt, in the small of his back, under his shirt and covered by his leather jacket. Joe knew that if he happened to be randomly searched at the border, they would only search his bike and belongings and not his person.

Joe got to Toronto around ten-thirty that night and his legs were aching and his ass was sore. In his condo, he threw his belongings onto his bed and went back down to the living room to his favorite chair with the stack of papers that had been piled at his door. He had forgotten to cancel the newspaper delivery. He called Cathy as he had promised, and woke her up, to let her know that he had arrived home safely and then checked all his phone messages. Most were from friends and a couple from relatives, however, there wasn't one from the woman he loved. He picked up the most current paper off the stack.

The third page of the Toronto Star had a full spread about the end of an era in Colombia. It fully documented the death of the infamous Drug Lord, Pablo Rivas. The article described how he had been kept on the run by the government of Colombia and tracked to a safehouse or hide-out and been surrounded by police and government troops and was gunned down just as he was about to escape as he had so many times before. The government took full credit for finding him and killing him. The fact that he had killed himself rather than be taken alive didn't even come out. It went on to say that the safehouse had been located by an American satellite system that electronically monitored cellular telephone calls that were made to and from the house by one of the occupants. The article explained that the calls had related to the crash of what had appeared to be a drug plane in central Vermont, a week earlier, and the millions of dollars that had been found in that wreckage. It went on to say that many of the calls to the hide-out had originated somewhere in eastern Canada, but that the specific source couldn't be located. Joe's head started to spin with thoughts of how Bryan's one greedy act of stealing that duffel bag of money from the plane crash in Vermont had done something that all the might of the United States and Colombia had not been able to do for years. Bryan's solitary act had created a situation that brought down the world's most wanted Drug Czar and changed history.

Joe, of course, was the only member of the motorcycle gang that was able to attend the large funeral that filled St. Mary's Church in Lindsay. Joe helped Bryan one last time. He was one of the pallbearers. He wondered if Tommy, Mike and Doc had even heard about the *accident*. At the reception after the funeral, there was a lot of speculation about the hit-and-run accident that had caused Bryan's death and Joe thought that it was wise not to bother adding any new information to the buzz. After spending some time with Bryan's family, Joe headed for the lake. He spent the rest of the afternoon, evening and night with his parents, grandfather and aunt and uncle at Pleasant Point on Sturgeon Lake and drove back to Toronto the next morning.

Friday morning, Joe dropped by Susan's home to see his boys. He had missed them and they were glad to see him too. He had talked to them three different times while he was away on the trip and knew that they had been doing fine. He made plans to spend some time with them.

At noon, Joe met Jim Sturgess for lunch at Hy's Steak House, on Adelaide Street West, and the hostess led them to a quiet table in the second floor dining room. Their luncheon steak and salad were excellent and Jim even picked up the tab. He had been very supportive of Joe's decision. After a lengthy discussion, it was determined that a sabbatical didn't really make a lot of sense for the firm so it was agreed that Joe would resign at the first of the next week. Jim made it clear to Joe, that if and when his sabbatical was over and he ever decided to come back to the practice of law, there would always be a place for him at Sanderson, Sturgess. Joe agreed to spend the time to transfer his files to other lawyers in the firm in an orderly fashion. After lunch, the two friends shook hands and went their separate ways.

Joe wandered over to a new bar and restaurant hangout on York Street, The Keg, in mid-afternoon to see which of his friends had started the weekend early. There were a number of guys there, checking out the new establishment, who Joe knew, including lawyers, stockbrokers, promoters and investors, so he joined the group. The lengthy business discussions and drinks went on until after seven o'clock that evening when four of the guys decided to go somewhere for dinner. One of Joe's buddies suggested Benihana's of Tokyo in the Royal York Hotel. Each table has its own chef and stove and the food is not only healthy, but also very tasty. The restaurant was halfway home for Joe. Dinner turned out to be a lot of laughs and no one got their American Express Card cut in half by the chef. They drank lots of Sake during dinner and that was an enjoyable change of pace. Joe said goodbye to his friends just after ten and leisurely strolled south the three or four blocks to the waterfront.

As Joe entered his condo, just before ten thirty, the first thing he did was check his phone messages. He was still tired from the long bike trip and the busy couple of days since he had arrived home. He was ready for bed. He pressed the buttons for his messages and Lynn, with Howie in the background, told him how much they had missed him at their Friday night party in Camden, but she hadn't left a number.

The next message was a total shock to Joe. Trizzi had called him for the very first time since they had spent the weekend together months before but she was sobbing and quite upset. She hadn't left a phone number, but the message was that she would call back at ten-thirty. He couldn't believe it. She had finally called him just when he had decided that he was going to find her. His spirits soared just to hear her voice even though she was crying on the other end of the line. He was really concerned and wondered what was the matter. He waited and waited. The seven or eight minutes seemed like an hour. The phone finally rang.

"Hello!" Joe said as he grabbed it.

"Hi, I hope you don't mind me calling you after all this time." Her voice was quiet and she still appeared to be sniffling and crying. "I didn't know who else to call."

"Do I mind if you called? Are you crazy? I've been waiting for you to call me for months!" Joe answered. "What's the matter? You sound like something's happened."

"My brother was killed a few days ago and the funeral was today. I got home tonight, all alone, and didn't know what to do. I had to talk to someone. I haven't been able to get you out of my mind for months. I had to call you," Trizzi explained quite obviously still upset.

"That's awful! What happened?"

"It was an accident . . . a car accident," Trizzi lied.

"I'm so sorry. Do you have any relatives there in Montreal?"

"I'm on my own now," she sobbed, "my brother was my only family."

"I'm really sorry, I wish that there was something that I could say to help. I've been going crazy not knowing where you are and what you're doing. I think of you everyday."

"I think of you all the time too. I've almost called you a hundred times. Tonight, I just had to talk to you," she started to cry again.

"I've missed you so much! I just got back from holidays and I had decided, while I was away, that I was going to find you and tell you how much I love you. Do you want me to come to Montreal tonight? I really think that I should be with you at a time like this."

"I want to be with you too! I have to see you! There's a midnight flight to Toronto. I could be on it," she said still sniffling.

"That sounds great! I'll meet you at the airport," Joe said unable to hide his excitement.

"No, don't pick me up," she laughed, feeling better just talking him, "you sound like you've been drinking and I don't want you driving out to the airport. Besides, the flights are sometimes late. I don't mind taking a limo to your place. I'll be there around two o'clock or shortly after."

"I'll leave a key for you with the concierge. Are you going to be all right?"

"I'll be fine. I've really missed you."

Joe signed Trizzi in and left a key with the concierge. Back upstairs, he whipped through the condo and straightened things up. He picked up any clothes that were lying around and finished unpacking his saddlebags and tank bag from the trip. He thought that the Beretta would be as safe as anywhere just left in the tank bag. He took the bags, along with his still rolled up sleeping bag, and put them on the floor of the empty closet in the guest bedroom. He had a quick shave and shower and got into bed to flick back and forth between Letterman and Leno and wait for the woman he loved.

Joe couldn't believe that she had finally called him and he was ecstatic. He felt terrible that it had taken the death of her brother in a car accident for her to call, but at least she had called him and not someone else. They would soon be together.

It was close to two-thirty in the morning when Trizzi arrived and Joe was sound asleep in his bed, with a light on and the television still on the golf channel broadcasting a replay of some recent tournament. She went directly into the guest bedroom.

Trizzi turned on a small bedside light and threw her small suitcase onto the bed. She took her clothes out of her hang-up bag and hung them in the closet. She looked right at the leather saddlebags, tank bag and rolled up sleeping bag that were on the floor. They didn't even register because she was so tired and spaced-out from dealing with her brother's funeral. She undressed and took her toiletries into Joe's bathroom. She freshened up after the terrible day that she had just been through and turned out the lights. Her naked body slid under the covers and she cuddled up to the man that she had fallen so deeply in love with so many months before. Just seeing him lying there, sleeping, made her feel so much better. She kissed his neck, ears, cheeks and lips until his eyes opened.

"Thank God, you're here! I've missed you so much! I've thought about you everyday!"

"I thought about you everyday too!"

He put his arms around her and they kissed deeply and tenderly. He was afraid to let go of her in case she disappeared again. They didn't talk at all. Not about her brother's death or about the time that had lapsed since they were last together. They just kissed and made love for a long time, slowly and calmly, and then fell asleep in each other arms. They didn't need to talk. They both just needed to hold the one person they truly loved.

CHAPTER FORTY-FOUR

Joe was the first to wake at about nine o'clock in the morning and he just lay there quietly and watched Trizzi sleep. He didn't want to disturb her. Her eyes were puffy from crying, but she was absolutely gorgeous, even more beautiful than he had remembered. As he lay there staring at her, he knew that he loved her more than life itself. He decided right then that he wasn't ever going to lose her again no matter what he had to do to keep her.

Later, Joe carefully slipped out of bed and down to the kitchen to make coffee. He poured two large mugs with a generous shot of Baileys and went back up to the bedroom, and as he got to the door, Trizzi's eyes blinked and she smiled. He put the coffees on a bedside table and opened the curtains to another beautiful sunny day and got back into bed. They sat very close to each other with their backs against the pillows and headboard and sipped their coffees.

"I'm really sorry to hear about your brother's accident. Do you want to talk about it?"

"Not right now, I'll tell you all about it later," she said as her eyes teared up. "There are a lot of personal things that I want to tell you, things I've never told anyone before. We'll talk later. I want to enjoy the morning just being with you."

"I'm so glad you're here," Joe said changing the topic. "You've been on my mind constantly and I've waited and waited for you to call. While I was on holidays, I had decided that I was going to find you, whether you wanted me to or not, and tell you that I love you."

"Believe it or not, I've thought of you too. I've been just sick missing you. I picked up the phone to call you a hundred times but couldn't," Trizzi said.

"Why the hell not? Did you ever resolve your personal problems?"

"The relationship is over. My brother and I had recently decided to take our lives in another direction and now that he's gone, I'm still going to change my life so we can be together, if you want me. We'll have a long talk later and then you'll realize why I didn't call."

She had absolutely no idea how Joe would feel about her after he heard the truth about her past life and the drug business that she and her brother had been involved in over the years, but she was going to tell him everything from the beginning and risk losing him forever.

They finished their coffees and settled back in under the covers in each other's arms. They lay there quietly looking into each other's eyes and they knew that they were in love. They were happy to be together again. The short kisses became longer, the touching became more erotic, and they were soon making love. They didn't want it to ever end.

By eleven-thirty, the lovers were walking along the waterfront looking at all the people. Every nation in the world was represented. They got cappuccinos at Starbucks and continued along the water's edge beside all the charter boats, fishing boats, yachts and sailboats. The harbour was dotted with boats, large and small, and two ferries were passing each other out in the middle going to and from the islands. They could hear the roar of racing cars qualifying for the Toronto Indy that was scheduled for the next day.

Joe kept the conversation light and talked about a few of the things that were going on in the city that evening if Trizzi felt up to it. Her eyes filled with tears every once in awhile and they ran down her face. Joe let her have those private moments to herself to think about her brother's death and the fact that they had finally found each other again. He knew that she had things to tell him but he didn't want to press her.

They walked through the Toronto Musical Gardens near the marina where Joe kept his sailboat. He pointed it out to her as they walked through the beautiful plants and flowers. Joe promised a sail for the next day if the weather co-operated. They turned around at the marina and walked back along Queen's Quay toward the condo. They walked slowly without talking and holding hands, just enjoying being together.

When they got back to Joe's, they jumped into the shower together and wasted a bar of soap rubbing it all over each other. As they finished, Trizzi had another poor spell and as she cried and sobbed for a few minutes, Joe held her close. As her tears dried up, they started to get dressed for the rest of the day. Joe was ready first so he decided to head downstairs and left Trizzi to do all those things that women have to do to get set for the day. She spoke as he was about to leave the bedroom.

"As soon as I'm dressed, I want to sit down with you and tell you my life story and then you'll understand why I haven't been able to call you. There are a number of things that I haven't been completely honest with you about, including the death of my brother, and I want to explain them to you and get them out into the open. You'll find them absolutely awful and may never want to see me again."

"There's no chance of that happening!"

"I have to tell you about these things because I really do love you. I want you to believe that before I bare my soul. In my whole life, I have never felt the way I feel about you toward anyone. It took me months of being sick and depressed over not seeing you that made me realize just how much I care," Trizzi said as she took his face between her hands and kissed him.

"I feel the same way about you."

"I have to tell you some terrible things about my life that could change your feelings for me," Trizzi said, with a serious look on her face. "The kind of life I've led has been far from perfect. I want to change it, change it for you, so we can be together for the rest of our lives."

"Nothing can be that bad," Joe assured her as he kissed her gently, "nothing will ever stop me from loving you. Finish getting dressed and we can talk when you come downstairs."

As Joe went down to the main level, he couldn't even guess what the hell she was talking about. If she wasn't already married, the only other thing that flashed through Joe's mind was that time-honoured profession. He wondered, *Is she a Call Girl?* Joe ended up sitting in his favorite chair, with the morning paper on his lap, but he wasn't reading it. He was thinking about Trizzi and what she was possibly going to tell him; *What could be so bad that I might want to leave her? Why has she not told me the truth about her brother's death?*

As soon as Trizzi finished her hair and make-up in Joe's bathroom, she went back to the guest room to get dressed. She put on her bra and panties and then went directly to the closet to get a pair of pants and a blouse that she had hung up the night before. During this visit to the closet, she was wide-awake. As she opened the door, the motorcycle saddlebags and tank bag on the closet floor, jumped right out at her. She immediately thought, *Joe never mentioned that he had a motorcycle!*

A chill went through her body as she reached for her clothes because bikers had been on her mind a lot lately. As she got dressed, she continued to stare at the bags on the floor of the closet and pictures of her dead brother, Luis, flashed through her mind over and over again. All of a sudden, her body began to shake uncontrollably and tears flooded down her face.

Trizzi's wobbly hands unconsciously reached toward the bags. Almost in a trance, she picked up the tank bag that was on top, and in a sinking motion, sat down on the bed with it on her lap. She trembled as she lifted the bag and gently shook it. It was empty except for something bouncing around inside. Before she knew it, she had unzipped the bag and her right hand was deep inside, searching. Suddenly, she was staring at a handgun right there in her hand. It took a moment before she realized that it was a Beretta . . . her Beretta . . . the one that she had sent south on the plane for Pinguino!

Trizzi's head started to spin and she felt faint. The room was going around and around and the Beretta, inadvertently, fell onto her lap and the bag dropped to the floor. She hung onto the edge of the bed with both hands as she nearly passed out. As the events of the past week and the death of her brother spun through her mind, she started to hyperventilate. All Trizzi could see were crashed planes, wrecked cars, motorcycles, bikers, Luis, Fernando and an unknown biker named Joe! She sat there stunned, in a state of shock, on the end of the bed, with the tank bag between her feet for four or five minutes before she regained her composure.

She picked up the Beretta and just sat there with it in her hands. A vision of her brother, Luis, covered in blood and lying on the side of a highway in New Jersey flashed through her mind. Her hatred for the bikers that had caused his death surged through her body and all that she could think of was that the Joe downstairs was the Joe that had killed her brother!

As she got up from the bed, she kicked the tank bag back into the closet. She cocked the Beretta that was in her trembling right hand and put it behind her back. Unsteady on her feet, she left the bedroom and carefully descended the stairs to the main level. As she caught sight of Joe, her eyes burned holes in him as he sat in his chair on the other side of the room.

Joe looked up and spoke as she came into view, "You look absolutely fabulous with your clothes on. I had forgotten how beautiful you really are!" He immediately noticed a very strange look on her face, she looked really pissed and she had been crying again. "Trizzi, are you all right? Is there anything I can do?"

"You can stay right the hell where you are! I want to talk to you!"

"OK, but what's the matter, you look awful?"

"You never told me that you owned a fuckin' motorcycle!"

"I bought a Harley-Davidson earlier in the spring, a month or two after I met you," Joe answered. "I just got back from a two week motorcycle trip with some friends to . . . "

"Cape Cod and Atlantic City with five other bikers!" Trizzi screamed.

"Yeah, but how the hell did you know that?"

"You're *Joe*, the *Joe* that my brother told me about! You're the fuckin' *Joe* that killed Luis!" She screamed again as the Beretta came into view and was pointed directly at him.

Her eyes filled with tears and the look on her face became so distorted that she looked like she was going to totally lose control. She got light-headed again and had trouble breathing. The room started to spin and her hand shook.

"Your brother?" Joe answered as he sprung to his feet, looking totally dumfounded, and all of a sudden it hit him. "*Luis*! Luis was your brother?"

"Yes, Luis was my brother!" Trizzi screamed waiving the handgun back and forth with tears streaming down her face. "You're one of the fuckin' bikers that stole the money from the crashed plane in Vermont and killed my brother! This Beretta is mine. I put it in one of the duffel bags that went on the plane in New York!"

By that time, Joe was totally in a state of shock. He really started to get concerned because he knew that the Beretta was fully loaded and in Trizzi's state, it could go off at any moment, either by accident or on purpose.

"Yeah, I was at the crash site, but only one of the guys that I was with stole the money! The rest of us had nothing to do with it!"

Trizzi went absolutely ballistic and screamed, "You're one of the guys that caused my brother's death, you and your fuckin' friends. You bastard! You dirty bastard!"

Her whole body was shaking uncontrollably and she couldn't breathe. The Beretta was at the end of her outstretched arms. She was holding it in both hands and trying to keep it steady. It was shaking up and down and back and forth with the contortions of her body. Joe didn't know what to do as he expected the gun to go off at any moment. The woman he loved most in the whole world was pointing a loaded gun at him and she was out of control.

"Trizzi, I didn't kill Luis! He and I almost became friends during the negotiations to return the money," Joe said in a calm voice as he moved toward her.

"Stay away from me! You and your fuckin' friends killed him!"

"Trizzi, you know that I didn't kill Luis, I liked him. You know that it was the big man with the mustache that stole the money and made all of those things happen. I love you more than anything on earth and I wouldn't do anything to hurt you," Joe said, again, calmly and quietly, in an attempt to calm her.

He moved toward her, slowly, as the Beretta shook in her hands and moved back and forth in her extended arms. Trizzi's whole body was shaking.

"I don't know what the hell to think! I've lost my only brother and you and your bloody friends caused his death!" She yelled as tears streamed down her face.

As Joe got close to her, he reached for her trembling hands and the Beretta with his left hand and slowly moved it down and to the side, so that it wasn't pointing at him any longer. She reluctantly let go of the gun and Joe uncocked it with one hand and set it on the coffee table. As he stood right in front of her, he reached for her to pull her toward him and take her in his arms to comfort her, but she was in such a state of anxiety that she would have none of it.

She totally lost it. She tore her hands free and clenched her fists and swung at him a number of times. As she flailed at him out of control, she hit him once on the side of the head and a number of times on his chest and arms. He grabbed her and pulled her close to him and held her very tightly so she couldn't move. She continued to scream at him and tears flowed down her face as she tried to wrestle from his grasp. Joe slowly let her loose and at the same time, he grabbed her very roughly by the upper arms near the shoulders and gave her two or three very hard shakes and screamed back at her.

"For Christ's Sake! Stop it! I'm the one that got the money back from the guy who took it and gave it to your brother and the big man that was with him!"

"My brother would still be alive today if it wasn't for you and your bloody friends," she screamed, still sobbing uncontrollably, with tears streaming down her face.

Joe pulled her close to him again and put his arms around her. He held her tightly so she couldn't move. She slowly stopped fighting and trying to break away. He spoke very calmly, directly into her ear as he held her.

"I had absolutely nothing to do with taking the money! My friend Bryan who is now dead took it without anyone else even knowing that he did! I was the one that dealt with Luis and got the money back and delivered it to him!"

Trizzi's struggling subsided and her body relaxed a bit, but she was still crying and sobbing uncontrollably as Joe continued to hold her close. She sobbed and sobbed against his neck. He kissed the side of her head a couple of times and she put her arms around him and continued to cry. He stood there and held her not knowing what to say or do. It was four or five minutes before she regained her composure enough to speak to him.

"I came to Toronto to tell you that I love you and to tell you all about my life and what I've been doing for a living since I was a teenager. To tell you that I want out, I want to give it up for you. I can't live without you!"

She continued to cry and they held each other tightly. He took her face in his hands and kissed her forehead, her wet cheeks and her lips.

"Christ! Let's think this thing through! I can't fuckin' believe that both of us were involved in that mess. Luis, and the big man that was with him, killed two of my friends during the past couple of weeks and they ended up dying in a shootout with State Troopers in northern New Jersey. I wasn't responsible for the death of your brother!"

"I know! I know! I can't believe all of this! What the hell do we do now?" Trizzi asked still crying and holding on to him tightly.

"We're going to settle down and you're going to start from the beginning and tell me how the hell you got involved in drug trafficking and how all that money ended up in that field in Vermont. When you're finished, I'll tell you all about the motorcycle trip and how Bryan stole the money that got us all caught up in this mess. Believe it or not, your brother and I almost became friends. We actually trusted each other."

"I know," she sobbed, "he mentioned your name to me often and he told me that he trusted you. The strange thing about it all is that every time he told me about the Joe that he was dealing with down in Atlantic City, I would think of you and how much I missed you."

Trizzi eventually regained her composure and told her long and drawn out story about being brought up in Bogota until she was a teenager with a Colombian father and a French Canadian mother. The drug business was rampant throughout the whole country during her teenage years and there was drug money everywhere. Her family, like most of the families in Colombia, was poor and her parents had done what they had to do to survive. The business and drug connections from Bogota and Medellin that her family had developed during those early years had followed them when they moved to Canada about twelve years earlier. Her parents had died a few years ago in a plane crash in the jungles of Colombia.

Before Luis died, he and Trizzi had planned on getting out of the drug business forever and change their lives. The drug deal in northern New York State was going to be their last venture in that business, except for whatever had to be done to dispose of the kilos of cocaine that they still owned, and the money from their last deal was going to be given to charity. Her deceased mother, a nurse, had ties to the Hospital For Sick Children in Toronto when she was alive. She and her brother had already put enough money away in offshore bank accounts to be comfortable for the rest of their lives. She had wanted to leave the business for years, but those feelings were much stronger since she had fallen in love with Joe. Trizzi had decided that as soon as she was able to turn her life around, she was going to find the man she loved, Joe McConnell, and tell him that she loved him and wanted to be with him forever.

Joe told his story from the beginning and about how the drug plane had crashed right in front of them in that field in Vermont. He continued on to the point where the money had been turned over to Luis and the other man in Atlantic City. He told Trizzi about the death of Captain Gerry Juby, at the hands of Luis and Fernando, which she had known nothing about. He described all the events that had led up to the deaths of Bryan, Luis and

Fernando from his interpretation of the information that he had put together from friends and what he had read in the local newspapers in Camden.

"Now that my brother's gone, you're the only person in the world who means anything to me. If we're really going to have a life together, I have to end my association with the Medellin Cartel immediately," Trizzi said. "Now that you know everything about me and the things that I've been involved in for all these years, do you want me to leave and get out of your life?"

"I love you far too much to ever let you go anywhere again without me being with you. We'll just have to work through all of these things together."

"There are things that I'll have to finalize to make a clean break from my past life so I'll have to make careful plans. It will be much easier for me to leave the business now that Pablo Rivas is dead. The Medellin Cartel will be in total confusion and disarray and the top-level members will be in a battle for control of his empire."

"I'll help you do whatever has to be done."

"It'll take me at least a week or so to deal with Luis' personal things, but I really don't think there's too much to do. All of his assets are held in offshore accounts, jointly, with me."

"I probably need a week to deal with my commitments to the law firm here in Toronto."

"During the last couple of months, Luis and I have accumulated four to five million dollars U.S. worth of cocaine that has to be disposed of. I have to do one more deal."

"Five million U.S.! Christ! How many kilos is that?"

"Just over two hundred. Part of it was payment for handling the sale in New York State and protecting the interests of Pablo Rivas and the Medellin Cartel. Our job was basically to make sure that the cocaine was paid for and the money got back on the plane."

"What the hell are you going to do with it?"

"The easiest way to dispose of it, is to offer it to the Hells Angels, the Rock Machine or the West End Gang in Montreal. For the right price, one of those gangs will probably take it all and then I'm out of the business forever," Trizzi explained.

"Have you ever been arrested or put in jail or anything?"

"No, I've always been well insulated from the business, far in the background. The only time that I ever got directly involved in anything was when a large transaction was taking place, like the one near Albany, and the Cartel Montreal was being well paid, and I mean *well paid*, often millions of dollars, to be there to make sure things went well for the people we did business with in Colombia. Luis usually handled all the smaller deals."

"I can't believe all of this!"

"I might be able to make you feel better about my last transaction. Luis and I had decided to leave the business in style. We had planned on giving the proceeds of our last deal to the Hospital For Sick Children because over the years, that hospital has treated a lot of poor Colombian children with all kinds of diseases and deformities," Trizzi explained.

"You and Luis planned on giving the hospital five million U.S.!"

"Yeah, we've made a lot of money over the years and now that Luis is gone, I know that was what he wanted. Our mother would have wanted us to do that too."

"Well, that sounds great . . . I guess." Joe couldn't fathom it all.

The two of them talked for over three hours and the main things that came out of the discussion were that they were deeply in love and they were both ready to change their lives so they could be together. They would have to formulate a game plan to cut her ties with the cartel quickly and cleanly. The things that she told Joe about the drug cartels and the drug business were fascinating. The amounts of money that she mentioned handling over the years were absolutely staggering. She shocked Joe as she alluded to the balances in a number of offshore bank accounts that, since the death of her brother, passed to her by survivorship.

They casually walked up town at about seven o'clock that evening and stopped at a real Irish pub, P. J. O'Briens for a couple of drinks. As usual, Joe, the bartender, delivered a couple of one-liners with the booze. He always loved a good joke. The pub was just a couple of blocks west of La Maquette, an excellent French restaurant, with an outside patio where dinner was served next to a small park that was filled with shrubs and flowers. They had a romantic dinner and enjoyed just being together even though their minds were spinning with all the information that had been exchanged earlier in the day. After they finished eating, they took a cab back to the Westin Harbour Castle Hotel and went up to the revolving restaurant and bar on the roof for after dinner drinks. It took close to an hour for the dull, dark, unlit lounge to make one complete revolution so Trizzi could see the lights of the city at night. They walked back to Joe's condo, through the skyway on the third level that attaches the hotel to the residences.

They got right into bed and cuddled for a long time. They did-n't speak much. They just lay there in each other's arms very happy that they were together. Joe was the first to speak.

"I love you with all my heart and I'll be there for you no matter what."

"I love you too. I've loved you ever since I saw you walk across that crowded room on the first night we met," Trizzi said and kissed him. They made love and fell asleep together, more together and closer than they had ever been before.

Sunday was another beautiful day. They got up early and packed a cooler for a picnic and went directly to the marina. It was Toronto Indy race day at the Canadian National Exhibition grounds and as they walked along Queens Quay, they could hear the racing cars qualifying for the afternoon event. It turned out that Trizzi had sailed before and she loved the water. She even knew what had to be done onboard so she was great help in getting the boat ready to leave the marina. They sailed through the western gap to Ontario Place, around the Toronto islands and then back to the harbour and into one of the many channels among the islands. They found a place to moor the boat by some picnic tables and stopped for lunch.

"What about the Cartel Montreal's last transaction? How soon can you set it up and get it over with? It really makes me nervous that you have to do one more deal."

"I know, but Luis wanted the money to go to the Hospital For Sick Children and there's just too much money involved not to try and do that. I'll contact the buyers and see who'll take all of it at a good price. I have a good working relationship with one of the Hells Angels in Montreal, so I'll talk to him first. I could be out of the business in two weeks."

"What's the best thing for you to do then? Get right out of Montreal and move to my place here in Toronto?"

"Actually, the best thing for me to do would be to totally disappear for awhile and distance myself from Montreal, the drug business and everyone associated with it. Since Pablo Rivas and Diego Castrillo have been killed, the bloody power struggle within the cartel could have far reaching consequences. As soon as the Cali Cartel sees the total collapse in Medellin, they'll take full advantage of the situation and make moves into North American markets that were never theirs before. I don't want to get caught in the middle of all the bloodshed. Montreal could turn into a war-zone among the three competing gangs as soon as the Cali Cartel starts to flex its muscles. No one knows which gang Cali will tie in with in Quebec. You'll be finished work in the next week or so, why don't we take an extended vacation?"

"I had always thought about going on an extended sailing trip for a year or two, what do you think? This sailboat will go anywhere in the world!"

"That sounds perfect. Let's think about exactly what we have to do to be ready to leave in about two weeks. You have to deal with your ex-wife and kids and your law firm. I have to clean up Luis' personal things and complete my last deal."

Later, they motored the sailboat through the numerous canals and channels between the islands to look at the scenery and then went back across the harbor to Joe's marina. They got back to the condo about four o'clock and just cuddled on the couch for a while. They made love again in the living room, on the couch, on the floor, in Joe's favorite chair and they continued to just be together until it was time for Trizzi to get ready to go back to Montreal.

They held hands on the way to the airport, and this time, Joe parked his car and stayed with Trizzi until it was time for her to board the plane. They found a quiet corner in the bar next to her gate and had a drink and talked while they waited.

"I need a week or ten days to clean things up at the office and get the sailboat overhauled and then I'll come to Montreal," Joe explained. "I don't know if I can wait that long to see you."

"I'll miss you too, but I'll be busy. The next time I talk to you, I'll have a plan and a time schedule worked out to do my last deal and go into retirement and we can coordinate your plans around the sailboat being ready in the same time frame."

Joe kissed Trizzi goodbye outside the gate and stood and watched her until she disappeared inside. She turned and waved to him just as he lost sight of her in the crowd.

On his way back into the city, Joe couldn't believe how things had worked out, the plane crash, the stolen money, Trizzi's Beretta, the Colombians and Trizzi's involvement in the whole fiasco. He was concerned about her situation in Montreal, but all they needed was a good plan to put that part of her life behind her. He was concerned about her last drug deal, but four or five million U.S. was a lot of money and the hospital could likely use it. He decided that they would do whatever they had to do to get her out of the drug business forever.

Joe was more than ecstatic about finding the woman of his dreams again. He felt as if his life was just beginning to come together. He didn't care what Trizzi had done in the past or who she was or that she had to commit one more criminal act before she could leave her old life behind. He was blindly in love. He loved her more than life itself.

CHAPTER FIFTY-THREE

On the Civic Holiday weekend at the first of August, the Saturday morning traffic was heavier than usual in the historical part of the city known as Old Montreal. Five burly men in a four year old, dark green, Lincoln Town Car slowly made their way along the busy streets close to the docks on the north shore of the St. Lawrence River. The last of the cocaine that the Cartel Montreal had accumulated in the past few weeks was stashed in the trunk.

A white Cadillac sedan followed closely with a bearded man in sunglasses behind the wheel and an attractive woman dressed in black leather in the passenger seat. The trunk of the Caddy had four large suitcases in it. In the backseat, there was a large empty briefcase in a cardboard shipping box of the same size that had been pre-addressed to a destination in Toronto. Earlier that morning, the bearded man had completely wiped the interior and exterior of the car clean and he and the woman had put on surgical gloves for the trip through the city. They didn't want to leave any fingerprints in the car or in the building where the Cartel Montreal's final sale was scheduled to take place.

The Town Car and the Caddy went east on St. Antoine Street and halfway down the block, turned into a narrow lane between two vacant and run-down warehouses. The cars stopped directly at the rear of the building on the right. One of the men got out of the Lincoln and disappeared into a small, green, battered door. Suddenly, a doublewide trucking door with cracks and peeling, green paint squealed as it rose up along its unused runners and gave access to the cavernous interior. The cars quickly pulled inside and stopped side by side in the center of the large, gloomy and shaded empty space, about sixty feet from the rear of the building. The large rear door was immediately closed.

"Drag that old counter over here! Put it right behind the cars and unload the trunk of the Lincoln," the woman ordered as soon as she stepped out of the Caddy.

Two men carried and dragged the wooden counter that had been leaning against one wall of the empty warehouse into the middle of the floor and placed it directly behind the two cars. Another man opened the trunk of the Lincoln and the contents, which consisted of two hundred and eight kilos of cocaine, almost all in bundles of twenty, was stacked onto the counter top so that it could be easily and quickly counted by the buyers as soon as they arrived.

A deal had been struck with the Hells Angels through one of their top lieutenants, a deadly and violent man named Maurice, who the woman had dealt with in the past. Four motorcycle gang members were expected at ten o'clock and that gave the woman and her men about ten minutes to get ready for them. She wanted this to be the fastest drug deal to ever happen and expected to be out of there within ten to fifteen minutes after the buyers arrived. The five men that the woman had hired for her last deal had worked for Luis on many occasions so she knew that they could be trusted. They had no idea who the bearded guy in the sunglasses and dark blue leather jacket was or why he was even there and they knew better than to ask.

The woman pulled a silver Colt 45 semi-automatic out of her belt and double-checked to see that it was fully loaded just in case something went wrong. She had two extra clips tucked in her pocket. Two of her men lifted sawed-off shotguns out of the Lincoln and cranked shells into the chambers. The other three men grabbed Uzis and an extra clip of shells and made sure that the weapons were ready for action. The bearded guy checked the Beretta that he pulled from his jacket pocket and made sure that he had an extra clip as well. Everyone in the warehouse hoped that the firepower wouldn't be necessary because this was supposed to be a simple sale of two hundred and eight kilos of *white gold* for four million and one hundred and sixty thousand American in cash. The price was discounted to twenty thousand a kilo so the whole inventory could be sold all at once to the one buyer.

The Caddy and Lincoln that were parked on the street-side of the counter faced another doublewide trucking door at the front of the building that opened up directly onto St. Antoine Street. The plan was to enter the building at the rear and leave quickly, when the deal was done, through the large door at the front and disappear into the holiday traffic.

The woman spoke to the man who had opened the rear door.

"Pierre, check to see that the front door is unlocked and ready to open as soon as this deal's done so we can all get out of here in a hurry."

The huge, trucking door at the front of the building was tested and left at the ready.

"Jon, I want you outside. Give me the Uzi and the extra clip. Take my Colt and go across the street with this two-way radio and let me know when the Hells Angels arrive. I want to know how many there are and if they're riding in more than one vehicle. Try and find someplace to look inconspicuous and keep your eyes open even after they're in the building. You never know what might happen!"

"Where do you want these guys while this thing's going down?" The bearded man asked.

"You men with the shotguns stand at each side of the rear trucking door so you can see what's going on from behind them. I don't want any surprises," Beatriz ordered, "and you guys with the Uzis stand against each wall opposite to where the buyers will stop their car when they drive in here. We'll stay behind the counter so we'll have them covered on all sides just in case there's trouble."

"You can feel the excitement in the air," the bearded guy commented.

By ten o'clock, they were all positioned and ready. The six of them in the building waited in the silence for the pre-arranged knock at the rear door. The woman moved over close to the man with the beard and smiled at him.

"I'm really happy that we're together at last," Beatriz smiled. "As they say in Hawaii, *I want you to know that I love you less today than I will tomorrow.*"

"I love you too," Joe said as he smiled back and pulled his handgun out of his pocket and made sure the safety was on and tucked it into his belt under his jacket where he could keep his hand on it. "I sure the hell hope that I won't need this Beretta."

"There's one more thing! As soon as this job is finished, the beard has to go!"

"I don't like it either," he said quietly.

As Joe stood in the quietness and waited, he wondered, *What the hell am I doing here? It wasn't long ago I'd been pissed with Bryan for breaking the law, and here I am, right in the middle of a major drug deal! Love does strange things to people!'*

"*Ils viennant d'arriver,*" the voice on the two-way radio crackled.

"They're here," Beatriz repeated. "How many are there?"

"*Juste une Suburban noir et y a quartre homes dedan,*" the voice reported.

"Four of them in a Suburban! Stay out there and keep your eyes open and if anything, and I mean anything out of the ordinary happens, let me know immediately!" She said into the radio and then turned to her men. "Get ready! They're here!"

The six people in the warehouse waited in quiet anticipation.

"It sounds like a vehicle outside the door," Joe said quietly.

They listened for the three pre-arranged and distinct knocks. Beatriz's man closest to the trucking door opened the small door first and looked out at the only black Chevy Suburban that was there and then looked up and down the laneway to be sure it was clear.

"*Ya juste une auto avec quatre gars dedans a part de ca la ruelle est claire!'*

"OK, open the big door and let them in," Beatriz said with an air of confidence.

The garage door squeaked its way open once again and was immediately closed as the Suburban pulled right up to within six feet of the table full of cocaine. All the doors of the vehicle opened slowly and carefully, so as not to spook anyone in the warehouse, and four of the toughest and meanest looking Hells Angels that Joe had ever seen got out and walked up to the table. The largest one, that got out of the front passenger seat, seemed to be the leader and was carrying a canvas bag that was quite obviously full of money. He had a patch on the right arm of his jacket that had a lightning bolt through the words *Filthy Few* and a 22 below it which bragged to anyone in the know that he had already killed men and had gone to jail for his gang. He was the first to speak.

"Ah, you look fantastique, as usuuaall," he said to Beatriz, with a very strong French accent, as he put the bag of money on the table. "I'm sorree to 'ear about yer brodder."

"Thanks, Maurice," she answered. "Let's get this deal done."

Beatriz reached for the bag of money and pulled the packages out onto the table and started to count it. Joe just stood behind her with his hand inside his jacket on the Beretta. He was getting pretty good at all of this intrigue. His hand wasn't even sweating.

"It look like twenty kilo in each pack," the Hells Angel commented with the Quebecois twang as he counted to see that there were two hundred and eight kilos as agreed.

"Yeah, it is, so it's easy to count."

Maurice took a switchblade from his pocket and the loud snap, as it opened, echoed all through the empty warehouse. He slit small holes in two of the bags and then wet the end of his finger in his mouth and pushed it into the white powder. He sucked his finger after touching each bag and smiled a broad smile.

"*Le stuff est de bonnes qualites!*"

With Beatriz's four armed men behind and at both sides of the Surburban, watching every move of the bikers, one of Maurice's men walked slowly to the back of the vehicle and opened the tailgate so the other two men could stow the cocaine away inside.

"Maurice, this is the final shipment from Pablo Rivas. His days of dealing in cocaine are over," Beatriz said. "It looks like the money's all here."

She stuffed it all back into the bag except for one hundred and sixty thousand American in cash. She turned and handed that amount to Joe and he immediately put it into the trunk of the Lincoln. She then turned and handed Joe the bag of money and he took it directly to the backseat of the Caddy and stuffed it into the briefcase in the box while Beatriz talked to the biker. The money was put into the briefcase in the shipping box and the box was taped shut.

"As always, Maurice, it's been a pleasure doing business with you."

"When all da shit settle down in Colombia and product comes again, you jus' give me a call. Since Pablo Rivas is dead, the Cali Cartel has join wit da Rock Machine and dey're tryin' to take over our market. I tink dere's goin' to be a fuckin' war!" Maurice said as he and his three men turned and walked back toward the Suburban.

As they started to get into it, Beatriz answered him. "I'll be sure to call you, Maurice, if the shipments start to flow again." Beatriz looked toward Joe, with a slight smile, because she knew that she would never be calling him again. "You guys drive outta here going west for at least eight or ten blocks and we'll drive in the other direction."

After a quick look outside through the small door, Pierre started to open the large rear door and right at that moment there was another crackling sound on the two-way radio.

"*Sacre Bleu! Il y a deux autos pleinnes de Rock Machine dans la ruelle, ils vont etre a la porte arriere dans une seconde!*"

"Christ! Maurice! The Rock Machine is here to rip us off!" Beatriz yelled and then turned and screamed to her men, "Pierre, close the bloody door and get ready for the bastards!"

Beatriz barely finished the warning when at the rear of the warehouse, a dark blue Ford station wagon burst through the large trucking door that was almost back down. The door exploded into thousands of pieces. Wood flew in all directions. It was torn off its tracks and hinges and remnants were scattered everywhere. The wagon squealed to a sudden stop as it crashed into the back end of the Suburban about thirty feet inside the building. A maroon Chevrolet that was right behind it also sent pieces of wood flying as it slid to a screeching stop. There were four bikers in each car and as they stopped, the doors of both vehicles sprung open and the rival gang sprung out with guns blazing.

Maurice and his men, who had just got into the Suburban, were a bit shaken up when the rear end of their vehicle was hit by the Ford wagon, but they managed to get their hands on their weapons just in time. The noise of the shotgun blasts and automatic gunfire, from Uzis, machine pistols and semi-automatic handguns was almost deafening as bullets ricocheted all around the empty warehouse.

Joe and Beatriz quickly ducked behind the counter and immediately pulled their weapons and fired in the direction of the intruders. Without even thinking, Joe had his Beretta out of his belt and emptied it in three different directions at the Rock Machine members as wood splinters and chips flew from the counter. Bullets whizzed all around them. He replaced the clip in his handgun so quickly he looked like an expert.

Beatriz had placed her men at very strategic locations so the new gang had pulled right into a crossfire. They didn't have a chance. As they got out of the two cars in the middle of the empty building, firing their weapons in all directions, they were cut to shreds by shotgun blasts and Uzi bursts from all sides. It only took a few moments for them to realize that they had made a terrible mistake. In the short gun battle that took place, five members of the Rock Machine were killed almost immediately and the other three had been badly wounded. As the shooting died down, Joe noticed that one of Beatiz's men and a Hells Angel had also been hit, but not too seriously, and one of Maurice's other men appeared to have been killed.

"Pierre, open the front door fast! Let's get the hell outta here before the cops have time to get here," Beatriz yelled to her men. Pierre ran quickly to open the large, front door and the others ran for the Lincoln. Beatriz rushed for the front passenger side of the Caddy. As Joe reached the driver's door, a few more shots exploded right behind him and he almost had a heart attack. As he ducked quickly beside the car, he looked back and saw Maurice pumping shots, from a pistol, into the heads of the three wounded intruders. If there was going to be a war between the Hells Angels and the Rock Machine, the eight men that had tried to rip them off that day wouldn't be part of it.

***

Joe jumped into the driver's seat, fired up the car and squealed the tires halfway across the cement floor toward the open door at the front. He slowed slightly as he hit the street and turned right. Three blocks later, he made a left turn onto a one-way street. The battleground was by then, far behind them. He continued at a reasonable speed so as not to attract any attention and headed for the bus station that was right in the downtown core. A bus was leaving for Toronto around noon and the box in the back seat would be on it. Someone at the bus depot in Toronto would call the Hospital For Sick Children and have the parcel picked up.

After they left the bus station, they made a few more left and right turns on streets that generally went to the northeast end of the city. Joe soon spotted the expressway that headed out of Montreal and took the ramp onto the eastbound lanes. He stayed well within the speed limit on the way to Joliette. Trizzi kept watch to be sure that they weren't being followed.

They were still shaking and their hearts were racing because neither one of them had ever been in a firefight before. They had been scared to death when the shooting started, but both of them had maintained their composure. They had said very little to each other as they drove through the city. As soon as they were cruising along on the expressway, Joe spoke as he reached for Trizzi's rubber-gloved hand and held it.

"What the hell was that all about? I think that all eight of the bikers that burst into the warehouse are dead and at least one Hells Angel!"

"Christ! As long as I've been in this business, and that's a long time, this is the first time that I ever got caught in a gun battle," Trizzi said. "I think the turf war between the Rock Machine and the Hells Angels has started for control of the Canadian drug markets and it's probably being fueled by the Cali Cartel from the south of Colombia. It's going to be a long hard-fought battle and a lot of bikers will probably die. The Cali Cartel is taking full advantage of the sudden death of Pablo Rivas, and the uncertainty in leadership in Medellin, to gain control of markets that they could never penetrate before. I have no bloody idea how the Rock Machine found out about today's deal unless there's a leak inside the Hells Angels."

"It sure doesn't look like your buddy Maurice is the kind of guy that puts up with any horseshit. Did you see him kill those three bikers that had just been wounded? He shot them right in their faces! The whole thing makes me sick to my stomach."

"Maurice has a deadly reputation. I've never been around people who have been killed before either. Luis and Fernando used to handle anything that got out of hand and they knew that I didn't want anyone hurt or killed, at any time, especially members of the public."

"I can't fuckin' believe that in all that excitement, I actually emptied the Beretta twice at those bikers without even thinking. I sure the hell hope that I didn't hit any of them."

"You probably didn't," Trizzi commented, just so he would stop thinking about the situation, "my men seemed to catch them all by surprise as soon as they got out of their cars."

"Well, thank God it's all over and there doesn't seem to be anyone following us. I wonder how your guys made out after we left?"

"They'll be fine. I saw them come out of the warehouse right after us and you put their money in the trunk of their car. The black Suburban was right behind them."

Joe caught a glimpse of a sign that flashed buy on the side of the highway.

"Look at that, Joliette is only twenty kilometers down the road. In fifteen or twenty minutes, we'll be on the plane and we'll leave this part of your life behind us."

The small airport where they were headed was just on the western outskirts of Joliette and it was one that the Cartel Montreal had never used before. Joe had chartered a small twin-engined Beechcraft and pilot for a one-way trip to the eastcoast of Canada.

The day after Trizzi had arrived home to Montreal, after spending the weekend with Joe after Luis' funeral, two RCMP Inspectors had paid her a visit. Her brother, and the man that had died with him, had been linked to drug trafficking in the Province of Quebec and the

Mounties had wanted to know what she knew about her brother's line of work. After the long interview, she thought that she had convinced them that she knew very little about her brother's business life as she had acted totally shocked to hear that her brother had been involved in the drug underworld. He had always told her that he was in the import-export business. They seemed to be satisfied when they left, but she really wasn't sure. She was afraid that she was probably under suspicion of being connected to her brother's business and thought that she might be under surveillance so she decided to take no chances. If the RCMP really started to dig into the Cartel Montreal, they could probably find some sort of link to her.

Trizzi had decided to abandon her and Luis' apartment as soon as possible and go into hiding until her last deal was completed and she was ready to leave the city. She immediately quit using her telephone and cell, except for the mundane day-to-day things, and made sure that she didn't have any contact with Joe from the apartment. She made her important calls from pay phones. She did what she had to do as quickly as possible and one night, slipped very carefully away from the apartment. She made sure that she wasn't followed and booked into a room downtown, at the Queen Elizabeth Hotel, under an assumed name.

Trizzi had not told the men that worked for the Cartel Montreal that she was going to leave the business for good and even the country. She was simply going to quietly disappear. As Joe and Trizzi had formulated a long-term plan that worked for both of them, they were very careful about contacting each other. They had met only once, at the Ramada Inn at the Kingston waterfront, for one night. Joe hadn't gone near Montreal until all of his personal matters had been taken care of in Toronto. He had eventually met her at the downtown Montreal hotel, two days before the date scheduled for her last drug transaction. They had stayed in the hotel room most of the time, except for one afternoon when Joe had driven Luis' Caddy to Joliette, about an hour northeast of the city, and Trizzi had stayed behind to take care of some last minute matters.

Joe and Trizzi had spent a lot of time formulating their plan because they had different problems to address. Trizzi had to make arrangements to get rid of the last of the cocaine that she had in her possession. She had decided to deal with a buyer that she knew and trusted, someone she had dealt with before, and she gave him a substantial discount if he took all of the cocaine that she had left. She had cleaned up her brother's affairs and had taken care of any matters of her own that needed to be dealt with before leaving. All her money was in offshore bank accounts so it didn't matter where she was in the world, she would always be able to access them when funds were required.

Joe had already been fairly well organized because he had been working toward taking some time off work and disappearing for an extended holiday anyway. Joe's ex-wife, Susan, had been expecting him to go away for some time and was more than happy with the financial arrangements that he had made with her. If he couldn't take the boys every second weekend, she had made him pay a serious financial penalty, which was fine with him, because the kids were well taken care of and happy. He would be able to fly home from wherever he was, on a fairly regular basis, to see them and would be in constant contact by telephone.

The finalization of things at Sanderson, Sturgess had also gone smoothly and he was out of there in just over a week. He had billed the files that he had been working on over the prior months so he would receive monthly payments from the firm that would be deposited directly into his bank account. Joe had sadly sold his Harley-Davidson and his STS because he wouldn't need either one for a long time. He had also contacted his real estate agent, who lived a few floors above him in his condo building, and made the necessary arrangements for his furnished apartment to be rented for up to two years. If it was ever required, the condo could be sold because Jim Sturgess had Joe's Power of Attorney. Although Joe had done extremely well financially over the years, the amount of money that he usually dealt with paled in comparison to the amounts that Trizzi was used to dealing with on a regular basis.

The escape plan that had made the most sense to them was to take Joe's forty-seven foot Jeanneau sloop and leave on an extended sailing trip. He had always thought of doing just that anyway when he got things settled with his law firm. It had taken Joe almost a week to have the boat outfitted for a long cruise and gone over from stem to stern. An inventory of spare parts and the proper tools had been purchased and stored onboard so that any minor repairs could be made if necessary. A new, state-of-the-art, Loran Satellite Navigation System had also been installed so that Joe could pinpoint his position even in the middle of the ocean. He would be able to sail anywhere he wanted to go safely. All of the emergency equipment onboard had been checked and up-dated and the newest and safest life raft available had been purchased that had a search beacon and emergency supplies, suitable for use in international waters.

Joe and Trizzi decided to leave from as close to the east coast as possible because there was no time to motor and sail the boat through the Oswego Canal to the Hudson River and on to New York City and eventually the Atlantic Ocean. It would take far too long. Joe had made the necessary arrangements to have the boat trucked to Halifax, Nova Scotia, so it would arrive there almost overnight. He had then flown down to the east coast and gone to the marina to supervise it being put back into the water and the mast being raised. All of that had gone extremely well and Joe had also made sure that the boat was fully stocked with at least two months' supply of food and drinking water. The freezer was filled with all kinds of meats and the cupboards were stacked with canned goods. There was also lots of beer, wine and champagne onboard. As soon as the boat was ready to sail, he had immediately flown back to Toronto to finalize his personal things there and get ready to meet Trizzi in downtown Montreal.

They pulled Luis' Cadillac into the parking area at Chantel Airport at eleven-thirty that morning. Trizzi left the keys and the ownership in the glove compartment because she had plans for the car. Back in Montreal, she had called Francois, Luis' best friend and one of her most trusted men, and told him that Luis' had wanted him to have the car and where it would be left for him. He had agreed to forget where he had found it if he was ever questioned by anyone.

Joe popped the trunk and lifted the four bags out. He and Trizzi slipped off their surgical gloves and he slid them into one of the suitcase pockets and then Joe closed the trunk lid with his elbow. They picked up their bags and walked toward the charter office to see if the pilot was ready to leave. As they got there, he stuck his head out of the door and told them to take their luggage directly to the Beechcraft that was sitting on the blacktop nearby and that he would join them there momentarily. He advised that the plane had been fueled and was ready to go.

The flight to Halifax International went well, and as agreed, the pilot was paid in cash upon their arrival and he immediately left on the return trip to Quebec without asking any questions of his passengers. Joe and Trizzi took a cab for the thirty kilometer trip southeast of the airport to the Snug Harbour Marina, at Peggy's Cove, where the Jeanneau was moored. As soon as they got there, they put everything on board and got settled in for the long trip that was ahead of them. They unpacked their luggage and stowed everything away. They double-checked their equipment and provisions and soon decided that they were ready to leave port on their new adventure. Joe and Trizzi knew that they would both feel a lot more comfortable once they got out on the open sea.

By that time of the day, the box with the four million dollars American inside was already in Toronto sitting on the hospital administrator's desk at Sick Kids. It would be quite a surprise on Tuesday morning.

The sailboat, *Indecent*, motored out of the harbour of the marina at close to seven o'clock in the evening and as it passed the concrete breakwall and hit the open waters of Pennant Bay on its way to the Atlantic, Trizzi took the wheel to hold the boat steady while Joe hoisted the mainsail first and then the genoa. The winds were strong and constant and generally out of the west so the sails filled immediately. The boat easily sliced through the two to three foot waves at nine or ten knots on a heading set due east that would not change for quite a few days. It wouldn't be long before the speed of the sailboat would be given a boost by the Gulf Stream that curls up from the south and across the north Atlantic from west to east at about seven knots. It would help take them across the pond. All the weather reports had indicated fair weather for the next few weeks so it looked like it was going to be clear sailing. As the view to the east became nothing but dark-blue ocean, Joe set the autopilot. He and Trizzi settled in and cuddled on the bench-seat beside the wheel.

"I can tell that it's going to be a beautiful evening," Trizzi observed. "I'm looking forward to spending it with you all alone on the high seas."

"Well, we're certainly going to have lots of time to relax and get to know each other. It'll be at least three weeks before we see land again," Joe explained as he leaned over close to her and kissed her a long, slow, tender kiss.

"I've been meaning to ask you. Why do you call your boat *Indecent?*"

"It's really a guy thing. *If it's as hard as it can get and as long as it can get and in as far as it can get . . . its Indecent!* "

"That's disgusting!" Trizzi laughed, "But I like it!"

"I'll be right back, I've got a little surprise that I almost forgot about," Joe said.

"I hope it's nothing special because I didn't get you anything."

Joe disappeared down into the cabin and went straight to the head and had a quick shave. A new razor made quick work of the two-week old beard even though the water wasn't that warm. A few minutes later, he was in the galley puttering around and soon returned to the cockpit with a chilled bottle of Dom Perignon, in an ice bucket, with two small champagne glasses. He put the bucket down on the floor and spun the bottle around between his hands in the ice cubes. As the champagne cork exploded into the air and landed in the rolling waters of the Atlantic, Joe filled the two glasses, and as he handed one to Trizzi, he looked right into her eyes and smiled.

"I'm glad that beard's gone. I like it better when your face is really smooth," she smiled.

"From this moment on, neither one of us has to worry about any of the things that we used to worry about," Joe said, "so if you could just pick anywhere in the world that you would like to go, where would that be?"

"I don't want to go anywhere without you. So assuming that you will be coming along with me . . . I want to go to the Mediterranean Sea . . . Spain, Majorca and Monte Carlo."

"It's very strange that you should say that because I just set the autopilot on that exact course," Joe answered as he cuddled up closer to Trizzi on the bench seat and put his arm around her and kissed her. "About two-thirds of the way to Gibraltar, the gateway to the Mediterranean, we'll stop in the Portugese islands called the Azores. We'll spend a few days in Terceira, a pretty town on the Island of Angro do Heroismo, because by that time we'll be ready to spend some time on land. Then we'll continue on to the capital city, the larger town of Ponta Delgado, on the Island of Sao Miquel, where we'll probably stay for a week or so. As soon as we feel like sailing again, we'll head for the Algarve in the south of Portugal and then take our time cruising on to Gibraltar. We'll stop there for a few days and we may even climb The Rock and feed the wild apes that the British keep there to prove Gibraltar is still in British hands. We'll probably walk through the World War II gunnery tunnels while we're up on top. After that, we'll slowly work our way up the Costa del Sol and eventually get to both Majorca and Monte Carlo."

They clinked their glasses in a toast and Trizzi spoke first, "Joe, it all sounds wonderful. Here's to the man I love with all my heart, to the only man I have ever loved, to a new life together wherever it may take us . . . and to the Mediterranean," she laughed.

"And here's to you, Trizzi, the love of my life, and to the Mediterranean, and the Caribbean, and the world, as long as we're together," he answered as they clicked their glasses, had a sip of champagne and then put them down nearby.

They put their arms around each other and kissed gently and intimately, for a long, long time. It was one of those perfect kisses, the kind that would last a lifetime.

EPILOGUE

CHARACTERS

Joe McConnell and Beatriz Bracho
Joe and Trizzi sailed safely across the Atlantic Ocean and began a new life together. They are slowly making their way along the Costa del Sol in southern Spain and plan to tour all of the Mediterranean countries. They may very well show up in another adventure sometime soon.

Bryan Moyle
Fiction is fiction. Bryan is alive and well and is the owner of a hotel in northern Ontario and is still with his long-time partner, Patricia. The bikers did not cavort with wild women on the trip and everyone except Bryan enjoyed the biking experience. He actually flew home from Atlantic City and sent someone to retrieve his motorcycle and it was immediately sold upon its return.

Howard O'Dell
Howie really did end up staying in southern New Jersey with Lynn Kelly and they eventually got married. After nearly twenty years together, Lynn lost a hard-fought battle with cancer and recently passed away. Howie and her many friends, both in Canada and the United States, miss her. Howie has since retired in Florida.

Thomas Yates
Tommy is still an Independent Insurance Adjuster and Real Estate Agent living in central Ontario. He is now married to Nancy, however, not the fictional Nancy referred to in the novel. They are about to embark on an adventure of their own on a thirty-eight foot yacht, from Canada down the Mississippi, to the Caribbean and back north on the Atlantic coast.

Michael Jones
Mike continued his accounting practice in the Kawartha Lakes area of Ontario for a number of years after the motorcycle trip and

continues his profession with the Federal Government. He still makes his home in lake country.

Percy "Doc" Simmer

This character is a figment of the author's imagination and there is no one person that "Doc" was based on. The personality of the character was made up from a mixture of traits from a number of friends who wanted to come on the motorcycle trip but couldn't at the time.

Gerry Juby, Charlie Gorrill, Claire Brown, John Lindsay, Bobby Taylor Phil Nieukirk, Ted Gardner, Paul Dowdall and Greg Hickson

These characters were named for memorable friends of the author, and the other members of the motorcycle gang, that all passed away far too early in life and are still missed by those people whose lives they touched.

Other Characters

Many of the other characters in the novel are named after friends actually using their real names, with their consent, which allowed the author to envision exactly the kind of character he wanted for each specific scene or set of circumstances in the novel.

COMING SOON

OTHER EDGE OF JUSTICE – FALL 2004

Five high schools in the city are devastated by disability and death by a bad shipment of Ecstasy that hits the streets one weekend. Shortly after the funerals of the victims, the local street dealers that preyed upon the students of those schools are murdered, one after the other, and then their suppliers, further up the food chain, start to lose their lives all in the same way. It's not long before the media and the police are calling the unsolved killings, the Oyster Shucking Murders.

To be notified of the Release Date

contact the author

fdouglas@rogers.com